Sons of Steel

ALL THE TIME IN THE WORLD

G. L. Keady

Published in Australia in 2024
by Big Island Publishing

Big Island Publishing
PO Box 3027, Tuross Head, 2537, NSW, Australia.
www.bigislandpublishing.au

ISBN:
E-book: 978-0-9756330-1-4
Print: 978-0-9756330-2-1

Edited by: Canon Doyle
Cover design and art: Brandon Evans-Keady

It's not the stars it's the space in-between…

Gk

This book is dedicated to my two dear friends who, during its writing, passed away.

To Raddo, who never quite deciphered the map to the maze.

And to Powelly, who steadfastly refused to let the negatives get to him, always believing that everything is alright;
it's all a matter of mind.

TABLE OF CONTENTS

Chapter 1: Blood Rain 9

Chapter 2: Artefact 19

Chapter 3: Friday On My Mind....................................28

Chapter 4: Tempus 37

Chapter 5: The Edge..45

Chapter 6: Uso..54

Chapter 7: Bush Telegraph 63

Chapter 8: The Time Being....................................71

Chapter 9: Arachnophobia....................................80

Chapter 10: Stand Down 88

Chapter 11: Tales Of The Texas Rangers....................99

Chapter 12: Dangerous Path 107

Chapter 13: About Time 115

Chapter 14: The Grid....................................124

Chapter 15: The Vault 132

Chapter 16: Skyjacked....................................141

Chapter 17: Courage....................................150

Chapter 18: Probe 159

Chapter 19: Astara....................................167

Chapter 20: The Asking.. 178

Chapter 21: Atrahasis 187

Chapter 22: Kraken 196

Chapter 23: Tis 204

Chapter 24: Stockholm 213

Chapter 25: Candles 222

Chapter 26: Treen 232

Chapter 27: Flight.. 243

Chapter 28: Ambush.. 252

Chapter 29: Storm 261

Chapter 30: Exile 269

Chapter 31: The Key 279

Chapter 32: Snared... 288

Chapter 33: Genesis.. 297

Chapter 34: Devachan 308

Chapter 35: Wake 316

Chapter 36: Retrocognition.. 323

Chapter 37: Payback 333

Chapter 38: Buying Time... 341

Chapter 39: Vale 349

Chapter 40: Coda.. 359

Chapter 41: Bag O' Nails 367

Chapter 42: With That Gun In Your Hand 377

Chapter 43: Harmonic Resonance 384

Epilogue 391

CHAPTER 1
BLOOD RAIN

ALICE STEPPED OUT into the rainy night, a sense of relief flooding over him like a weight lifted from his broad shoulders. The demise of Gorrick marked the end of a battle, yet the understanding remained that the larger struggle would persist.

The rain was easing, granting him a slightly less damp journey back to his apartment. As he traversed the path along Billyard Avenue in Elizabeth Bay, the rhythmic sound of his footsteps on the wet pavement resonated through the night. However, an unsettling feeling began to creep into his consciousness. A thought nagged at him—could killing Gorrick have altered the timeline, as Secta and En-Ki had speculated? A haunting dream from the past surged into his mind. It had placed him in an alternate reality where Secta hadn't injected him with the atom-reducing formula, and he wasn't trapped within a holographic projector. In this alternate version, Secta had merely crafted a holographic duplicate of him, allowing him to continue his life as a rock singer in a metal band. None of the tumultuous events he had experienced would have unfolded—the nuclear disaster averted, no visit to 2087 or the 6th Century BC. No trip to Tokyo in 2047, no battle with En-Lil on Eris, or the venture to 2112—the voyages through time eradicated. The notion swirled in his thoughts—what if it wasn't a mere dream, but a foreboding premonition? Could En-Ki be somewhere, observing? He halted and cast his gaze skyward through the rain, finding only a canopy of low-hanging clouds—no trace of a Watcher in sight.

"Argh!" he growled, dismissing the idea, yet another question immediately commandeered his mind: How had it been so straightforward to eliminate Gorrick? This query sent his thoughts spiralling, akin to a wheel of fortune, pondering which answer it would ultimately land upon—or which timeline.

A notion ignited within him, compelling him to hastily retrieve his cell phone. The familiar digits of Vee's number beckoned. As the screen's glow illuminated his face, he heard the soft approach of a vehicle. His gaze darted across the street to the black SUV that had pulled up. The driver's side window slid open, revealing a hand emerging from the shadows. However, instead of the anticipated gesture, the extended hand lacked a particular finger. Recognition struck Al—this was the very same guy he had sighted through the sniper's rifle's night scope. The man whose finger he had severed with a bullet. Relief washed over him momentarily, affirming that the timeline remained unchanged. Yet, reality descended swiftly as the hand retreated, replaced by the ominous muzzle of a silenced firearm, directed straight at him. Commander Daniel Walker pulled the trigger, and in rapid succession, three shots resounded—thud, thud, thud. Alice crumpled to the ground as the SUV accelerated away.

The heavens opened up, releasing torrents of rain. Alice's life essence mingled with the rainwater, forming a crimson pool around his prone body, its rivulets coursing into the gutter, a silent testament to his extinguished existence.

Vee awoke abruptly to the jarring ring of the phone. The voice on the other end from the hospital bore grave news—Alice was now in critical condition, sustained only by life support and teetering on the precipice of death.

"Where were you when I needed you? I've always been there for you," Al's voice carried a mix of frustration and desperation.

"I was there ... that is why we are conversing now, while your physical form languishes in a coma. The task remains incomplete," En-Ki responded.

"It's a never-ending cycle, En-Ki. Every time I think I'm done, it starts all over again."

"I understand how it may seem that way, but I assure you, that is not the truth. The menace of En-Lil continues to loom."

"No, it doesn't. I ended it. I killed him."

"You killed Gorrick, not En-Lil. I will know when En-Lil's presence is eradicated. Though you have mitigated his influence, your species is on the brink of facing its ultimate trial. Without your abilities, your kind will not endure. The path you have tread has led you to this juncture—the knowledge you have amassed has been your preparation. This is the culmination of your quest, Alice."

"You'll need to give me more than that, mate."

"Your species, through technological advancement, has emerged as a potential threat to other civilizations. Your outreach efforts to contact extra-terrestrial life have inadvertently alerted malevolent beings to your existence. Benevolent species are few and far between, while the attention of a particularly malevolent force has been drawn to your kind. Do you want to live, Alice?"

Alice had made a remarkable recovery from what doctors had diagnosed as fatal wounds. It was the first time he had been without Secta's shape-shifting pills, which had previously saved his life after being shot. After two days in an induced coma, much to the perplexity of the doctors, Alice woke up, got out of bed, and checked himself out of the hospital.

Six months later...

A potentially active stratovolcano, Mount Apo, located on the island of Mindanao in the Philippines, had recently been shaken by a minor earthquake that caused a landslide. The Davao Department of

Volcanology dispatched a drone to survey the site, and a LiDAR scan was requisitioned for the location. The mountain was a favourite among recreational rock climbers and needed to be certified safe after such a significant landslide. Upon studying the LiDAR scans, it became clear that the landslide had uncovered a World War II gun emplacement. Following protocol, the Davao Museum was notified of the discovery. The scans indicated the possibility that this site could be the location of a repository of artefacts that were once believed to be nothing more than legend: the infamous Yamashita treasure. Due to this potential, explorer Henry Vitale and his assistant Ito Santos were commissioned by the Davao Museum to undertake an expedition to Mount Apo and assess the site.

After struggling through dense undergrowth for two days, they finally reached the location.

Henry checked his GPS, which was consistently transmitting their position back to the Museum Expedition Operations centre in Davao. Unbeknownst to them, the GPS signal was also being monitored by another party with designs on acquiring the treasure.

Henry and Ito discovered the machine-gun nest. It contained a rusted old Type 92 heavy machine-gun, a standard issue for the Japanese army during World War II. Knowing that it held no strategic value, they realised there could only be one logical reason for a machine-gun nest to be situated in such a remote location: to safeguard a secret that the Japanese had gone to great lengths to hide.

Henry began scouring the area for signs of excavation. Within a couple of hours, he found the evidence he needed: halfway down the rocky slide, he encountered an abundance of old mining tailings.

Henry and Ito started digging. After an hour's work, they had dug deep enough into the hillside to place several explosive charges to expedite the process. They took cover and detonated the explosives. A powerful explosion sent a wall of dust and debris billowing out of the hole it had created.

The two explorers entered the small cavity, discovering that the explosion had exposed the entrance to a tunnel. After spending a few hours removing rubble, they finally entered the tunnel.

Night had fallen by the time Henry emerged from the tunnel. Covered in dust and standing beneath a vast canopy of stars, he used his CAT S-61 satellite phone to contact the expedition operations centre and provide them with an initial report on their findings. He had just begun outlining a basic inventory when a sudden beam of white light from above engulfed him, accompanied by a powerful whirlwind so intense that it knocked him off his feet and severed the phone connection.

The daunting task of teleporting thousands of Red Wheel sufferers through Kairos and back to the 22nd Century had been an unprecedented success. Consequently, the international governing body, United Nations Time Travel, approved the immediate construction of a second Kairos at the Desertron facility in Waxahachie, Texas. This was a UN-sanctioned joint venture between OTT and the newly formed TTA: Time Travel America, with OTT overseeing the project due to their expertise and experience.

Dr Robert James and his family had relocated to Texas for him to oversee the construction and subsequently take command of the facility once it became operational. General Larry Freeman was appointed director of TTA, which also incorporated US Space Command. The facility's primary purpose was to utilise the process designed by OTT to heal Red Wheel sufferers from each of the countries infected in 2112, starting with the USA.

In keeping with the tradition of Kairos, the Ancient Greek word for a moment in time, the new facility was named Tempus, the Latin equivalent. Dr Christina Phillips had assumed the position at OTT vacated by Robert James.

After the magnitude of the Red Wheel operation, all members of OTT took a brief break to recuperate. Following that, it was back to business as usual. Secta focused on the construction of Tempus in

Texas, while the Professor and Hope worked on modelling a cold fusion energy source using the element Velodium. Karzoff and Viktoria kept a close watch on Zen Corporation, especially since Alice had reported that while he had eliminated Gorrick, the same couldn't be said for En-Lil, whom they suspected had found a new host. They were also attempting to locate Commander Daniel Walker to charge him with the attempted assassination of Alice.

Alice had informed OTT that En-Ki had warned him to be cautious of a threat from a new malevolent alien species. Apart from a sighting of an Unidentified Submerged Object (USO) off the coast of Mexico, nothing else out of the ordinary had been reported since a UFO had appeared over the White House some months back, conveniently disappearing once the UNTT's Temporal Prime Directive was signed by US President Oprah Robinson.

As for Alice, Vee, and Blake, they were at a loss. There was always a sense of comedown following a massive time travel mission, and the last one was no exception. However, that would soon change.

Al was at Café Epiphany, having breakfast with Vee. He grumbled to her, "Nah mate, I don't think it's rubber glove."

Vee cracked a cynical smile. "Well, Al ... from where I'm sitting, you look like a bloke in love."

He brushed a dribble of maple syrup off his chin with a serviette and then pushed the plate he'd wiped clean of French toast to one side. "I just miss her company."

"Yep, tough with her being over eighty years into the future ... like you just can't phone, text, or Zoom her."

They were talking about Toeghan Hitz, with whom Alice had had a brief affair. She had been left with Turk and Morri in 2112.

"Seems every time I meet someone I like, they either live in the future or the past," he groaned, "or they get whacked."

"Yep, so let's do a recount ... it was Zule in the post-apocalyptic future, wasn't it? Oh, and Djard there as well? ... then Sonoko in 2047, that bird ... um, Sabrina in 576 BCE and now Toeghan in 2112?"

"Don't forget Aya in 2,500 BC, and then poor Stain," he rested his elbows on the table, shoved his face in his hands, and grumbled, "I can't win."

"Hey, what about Tippy?" Vee said, as though the thought was divine inspiration.

He almost sang through his hands. "Nar, she's the band's manager."

"Okay ... so, what about Hope? It's pretty obvious she's got the hots for you."

He groaned even louder. "Argh."

"Ah, so that's whom this is really about ... Hope is it?" she said, having a light-bulb moment.

Alice spread his fingers just enough to peek at her through the latticework. "What am I going to do? She's my biological daughter." He lowered his hands and gazed out of the window behind Vee.

"Have you told her it can't happen?"

"Sure," he snarled, "but she reckons she can become transgender or something to fix that."

Vee was blown away. "Transgender? What she's going to become a bloke?"

"No, no, no, it's not that it's ... um ... trans something ... oh, I remember transgenic ... means she can get rid of my genes from her DNA or something like that."

"Wow," she exclaimed, "didn't think that was possible."

"Huh, a few months ago you wouldn't have believed you'd be visiting 2112?"

"Yeah right ... I hear you," she admitted.

"Mate, around this mob, anything is freaking possible," Al emphasised, with raised eyebrows.

"You're not wrong." She reached across the table and took his hand. "I won't mention the L word, but do you have feelings for her ... right?"

"Oh, I guess so ... well, at least I did for the original Hope."

Just then Blake came in and sat down at their table. With a cheeky smile, he said, "Hey guys, hope I'm not intruding."

"Hope being the optimum word ... No mate, it's all good," Al beamed with a return smile. "Sit down, how goes it?"

Blake leaned closer to talk conspiratorially. "I got a call a few minutes ago from my old boss. Word is a treasure has been found in Mindanao in the Philippines, and Jax De Ville has been sent there to check it out."

"Sent by who, the CIA?" Al questioned.

"For sure," Blake confirmed.

"Why would the CIA be interested in a treasure?" Vee asked.

"That's what grabbed my attention," Blake admitted.

Al frowned. "That's if it was the CIA, maybe it's Boston University or someone?"

"No, my boss got word from the States it's a CIA operation all right, apparently, she's got Buddy Holman with her," Blake explained.

"That bloody no-good bum! Yeah well, that confirms it then, doesn't it?" Al said, remembering how he'd belted Holman in the nose for spying on Vee outside her apartment block.

"A CIA mission all right, but why?" Vee questioned.

"That's the burning question." Blake said, then ordered a coffee from the waiter.

Vee added, "Maybe we should check it out then."

"Let's bring it up at this morning's eleven o'clock meeting," Al proposed.

They were all gathered in the OTT boardroom, awaiting the arrival of President Mal Low and Dr Luna Cairn, the director of UNTT. Mal entered the room, took a seat, and greeted them jovially, "Good morning all."

"Where's Luna? I thought she was with you?" Professor De Luz inquired.

"She's on a call to UNTT in New York. We can get started without her," Mal suggested.

Karzoff spoke up. "So, I will begin. Surveillance of Zen confirms that Gorrick Khan departed Sydney for Tokyo before Operation Red Wheel commenced. So, Alice, it was definitely not Gorrick Khan you disposed of ... that supports the theory that En-Lil has jumped into a new host. Viktoria?"

The tall, naturally tanned South African with striking strawberry blonde hair took over. "There was no CCTV footage of the assassination attempt on Alice. Three spent cartridges were found at the crime scene. We lifted a fingerprint off one, and it matched Commander Daniel Walker."

Al sank down in his seat with his legs crossed and grumbled, "There's hardly any point in pursuing it, guys. Their lawyers will only get him off, like they always do."

"True, but we need to go through due process, Al," Mal clarified.

Viktoria continued. "We have detected one new face that seems to be getting the VIP treatment at Zen." She picked up a remote from the table and pressed a button. A video flashed on the sixty-centimetre wall monitor, showing a young attractive black-haired woman in a stylish navy-blue business suit wearing dark glasses like a movie star. She was leaving the Zen building to board a waiting limousine. Viktoria rewound it, froze the video, and then zoomed in on the woman's face. The resolution was incredible. "Our drone has taken a shot of the target every day for the last six months, so she's not just a visitor to Zen. We have nothing on her ... we don't even know her name. She doesn't show up on any FRS database worldwide. What we do know is that Gorrick hasn't been replaced as expected, which could well mean this woman is the replacement President of Zen."

Viktoria shut down the video and took her seat again.

"Secta, how's it going with Tempus?" Mal inquired, changing the subject.

"Another week and it will be online," Secta reported.

Just then, Dr Cairn entered and took a seat. "Sorry, have I missed anything important?"

Mal spoke up. "No, Secta was just telling us that Tempus should be up and running in a week."

Luna was surprised. "My goodness, that was quick."

"Helps when you already have a working model," the Professor declared.

"My office was asking if Turk and Morri could make contact with survivors in the USA to initiate the treatment program, or should Alice go?" Luna questioned.

Secta said, "I think it has to be Alice along with Turk and possibly Morri. They can leave from here; there's no need to wait for Tempus. What say you, Al?"

"It's a whole different ball game, isn't it? The way we found Morri and Turk led us to the problem, but I wouldn't know where to start in another country," Al admitted.

"Didn't you learn that all the big cities in the world were wiped out?" Vee asked.

"Yeah," Al agreed, "I guess that eliminates the capitals ... they'd all be no-go-zones for sure."

"Perhaps you only need to find one group of survivors to lead you to the rest, like you did with Turk," Luna suggested.

Al scratched his head, trying to think it through. "There was already social unrest in the States, and you know them, they're always armed; they shoot first and ask questions later."

Hope had an idea. "If we research where nuclear fallout bunkers are today, it might narrow the field. You'd have to expect they'd come up with the same MO as we did ... you know, fortifying existing bunkers."

Mal liked it. "That's an excellent idea, Hope. Luna, can you access that sort of info through the UN?"

Luna nodded her head. "I could give it a try."

Mal scanned the faces at the table. "Okay, what's next?"

Blake filled them in on the supposed treasure find in the Philippines. They decided to gather more information on it before giving it any serious consideration.

CHAPTER 2
ARTEFACT

VEE REGARDED BLAKE, Hope, and Secta sitting opposite her at Café Epiphany seriously, "I'm worried Al isn't up to a mission like that yet."

"You know your brother, it'd take more than a bullet through his left kidney and another into his left lung to stop him," Secta claimed.

Hope added, "Plus a through-and-through near the sternum that somehow missed everything vital."

"The guy has a charmed life; anyone else would be on a slab," said Blake.

"Well, he does have a guardian angel," Secta added.

"He told me it feels easier for him to risk his life than to live his life without risk," Hope said.

"Hmm, well, a statement like that makes me wonder about his state of mental state health after what he's been through," Blake suggested.

Secta got up, his coffee finished. "I'm going back to the lab; work summons."

"Wait, Secta, can you stay a moment? I've something to discuss with you guys," Blake said, urgently.

Secta resumed his seat to listen. "Go ahead."

"Just after the meeting this morning, I got another call from my old boss in Canberra. He's speaking with Mal right now. It seems there's more to this treasure find in the Philippines than we first thought." He had them intrigued, gifted with the skill of a great storyteller able to captivate an audience with an air of mystery and then have them hanging on his next word… he knew it, paused, and then went on. "When I first started working with archaeologist Jax De Ville, it quickly became apparent her research was mostly concerned with the interpretation of ancient Sumerian texts. She had recently returned from years in the Middle East, where she had been trying to prove some of the claims of Sumerian mythology. Now, I never got to know why, but over time I did learn she was enamoured by Yamashita's treasure because there was some kind of connection with it to Sumerian myth."

"Wasn't Yamashita a General in the Japanese Imperial Navy during World War II?" Secta quizzed.

"Yes. You see, Japan occupied Micronesia before and during the war. It was known there were ancient ruins on the island of Pohnpei at a place called Nan Madol. Now, these weren't just any ruins of an ancient civilization; they were unique. Considered the eighth wonder of the world, the ruin was built from massive granite blocks that could only have been mined from over two thousand miles away … and even then, it would have been virtually impossible for the indigenous population at the time to have transported them over the ocean in the flimsy vessels they had."

"When was this?" Hope inquired.

Blake's face displayed amazement. "Over two thousand years ago."

They were astounded. With his interest piqued, Secta requested eagerly, "Go on."

"During the war, Yamashita had his men excavate the ruin at Nan Madol, and they unearthed three platinum sarcophagi. Now, there are several reasons for this being extraordinary … firstly, platinum isn't found anywhere in the Pacific region; secondly, it comes from meteorites … space, and thirdly, each of the sarcophagi was three and a half metres long and weighed several tons. In addition, they were sealed so well, they couldn't open them, no matter how hard they tried … there was no sign of a seam or a joint; they were like one solid block." Blake paused for impact. The eyes of his colleagues were filled with curiosity. He continued. "Somehow they managed to exhume the three sarcophagi. Two were taken to Japan, and Yamashita took one with him to the Philippines, that he hid with the rest of the treasure trove he'd accumulated over years of plundering."

"One for me, two for the government," Secta said, with a derisively raised eyebrow.

"What's the connection between the sarcophagi and the Sumerians?" Hope queried.

"I have no idea … but Jax De Ville would because my old boss believes that's what has been discovered in Mindanao and what has attracted the attention of the CIA."

"But why?" Vee queried. "Would it be the value? It must be worth millions. What happened to the other two sarcophy-thingy's?"

"Worth millions, that's for sure. I don't know what happened to the other two, but it'd be worth researching. That brings me to another point: my old boss believes the find has attracted the attention of one of the most nefarious black-market racketeers in the world, Handerson Bolt … and believe you me, this bloke is a piece of work. He'd move heaven and Earth to get his claws on something as valuable as a platinum sarcophagus, to then flog it to the highest bidder."

"Where's he from?" Vee asked.

"An American … former CIA, a wicked bastard. I've had a number of run-ins with him over the years. In fact, he was the very reason I was put on Jax De Ville's case in the first place, after he'd ripped off a treasure in Tahiti that had been found by a joint Oceana-American archaeological expedition off Tuamotu Archipelago."

"I still don't get how, as intriguing as it is, OTT should be interested in this," Secta said, getting to his feet ready to leave.

"I suppose because if the sarcophagi are related in some way to the Ancient Sumerian texts, as De Ville seems to believe, then it could well be extra-terrestrial … the Anunnaki, for instance," Blake proposed.

Secta slowly sat back down, the relevance becoming clearer.

Blake locked eyes with him. "And, if it is alien, the question is, who or what is inside of it?"

"Now that would pique the interest of the CIA for sure," said Secta. "Hope, can you do some research on the other two sarcophagi and then any connection between Nan Madol and Ancient Sumerian mythology? The work of Zecharia Sitchin might be a good start. Vee, you work with Hope, find out as much as you can on the subject. Blake, get us a report on the movements of Jax De Ville and the treasure. Get onto the Oceana Consulate in Manila for an update on the find. If they're not onto it already, then fire them up. Put it all together with a nice pink ribbon around it, and we'll take it to Mal to see if we can get involved. I agree with you, Blake; there just might be something in it."

Electra was standing at the reception area window, gazing at Sydney Harbour dazzling in the midday sun. Her PA, Regina Fych, glanced up at her from behind her desk and couldn't help but notice the uncanny similarity between Electra's habits and her former boss Gorrick; he would also stand at the window gazing at the view in the very same manner. Though she regretted Gorrick's death, Regina was delighted that her new boss was a woman. At six-four, young, blessed with the figure, grace, and elegance of a photographic model, Electra was scintillating. However, there was one thing that Regina found odd: Electra's voice sounded exactly like her own. That was because Dr Li, following Gorrick's instructions, had sampled Regina's voice to be programmed into Electra's vocal subroutines, without Regina's knowledge, of course. She had no idea Electra was AI and, possessed by En-Lil.

Electra, in the six months since the death of Gorrick, had slipped into the governing chair of the powerful Oceana Chapter of Zen Corporation, as though it had been custom-made for her. The hive had insisted on sending a replacement for Gorrick, suggesting Gorrick Khan should return to Oceana from Japan, but En-Lil had overruled them, asserting authoritatively that it was time for a change.

Electra's voice cracked like a whip. "Tell Adamski to meet me in the boardroom immediately, Regina."

"Yes, ma'am."

Five minutes later, Professor Adamski entered the spacious boardroom where Electra was waiting, seated at the head of the long board table.

"Sit beside me, Uri," she said, patting the chair.

The short, bespectacled Russian dressed in an obligatory white lab coat obliged.

"Do tell me the status of Aquila?" Electra said smoothly.

Adamski nervously cleared his throat and then said with a thick Russian accent, "The tests using the new organic processor have been impressive, but with Gorrick gone, I am uncertain if we can use the same means of connectivity—"

Electra cut him off matter-of-factly. "I can provide the meditative neural link you require, so that will not be a problem."

Adamski was pleased. He had presumed the unique means of accessing the future through Gorrick's miraculous remote trans-dimensional viewing ability they had developed would have been lost with his untimely passing. He fiddled nervously with his glasses as he enquired, "D … do you intend to be the traveller as well, ma'am?"

"No, we will need to find someone, but for now concentrate on getting Aquila up and running. The priority is to bring Honor home. Give me an update on the RF program?"

"I have grown more processors and delivered them to Dr Li. After you resurrected the program, she is confident you will be impressed by the new cyborg model."

"I hope so. Thank you, Uri."

The scientist left. A few minutes later, the dashing Commander Walker replaced him. He stopped upon entering and stood at attention to militantly state, "Ma'am?"

"Commander, please take a seat," Electra said, affably. "It seems Black Alice has fully recovered." She watched him sit.

"Yes, I've heard," he said sternly, in an old-fashioned British public-school accent.

"He is a tough customer ... foiling our every effort to eliminate him."

Walker shook his head. "I don't know what I can say, ma'am."

"We move on ... An extremely important artefact has been recently discovered that I want destroyed ... and when I say destroyed, I mean to the point that only dust will remain of it, and even then, the dust will need to be cast to the wind. The problem I have is the artefact is so valuable there are a great number of collectors desiring it. I want you to do the job," she explained.

"What is the location of this artefact?"

"Mindanao in the Philippines."

"Do we have a contact there?"

"Yes, a black-market antiquities dealer," she said.

The look on his face suggested he had an aversion to black marketeers. "Hmm, I know the type, merciless ... so, is there a figure on it?"

"No, not as far as I know ... the artefact is still in the jungle."

"How big is it?"

"About three and a half metres in length by two metres wide, weighing over a ton, I believe."

"That's one hell of an artefact..." Walker exclaimed. "I don't know why, but I was thinking it would be smaller?"

Jax De Ville and Buddy Holman stepped out of the Airbus H-145 Eurocopter onto the scorching tarmac of Davao's Francisco Bangoy International Airport. Waiting to greet them, standing beside a late-model red Pajero, was Amaya Alvarez, curator of the Davao Museum of History and Ethnography.

As expected, it was hot and humid. Though acclimated to the heat, Jax still felt a sense of relief when she climbed in behind the driver of the air-conditioned Pajero. The patina of perspiration on her forearms instantly dried, causing her skin to itch.

As they set off, Amaya turned from the front passenger seat to chat with her guests. "I would like to invite you to lunch," she said, in American English, with only a slight Filipino accent. She had obviously been schooled in the USA.

"That would be lovely, Amaya. Thank you. Do you have any news on the find?" Jax asked, the plump forty-year-old.

"No, we are concerned after losing contact with the expedition two days ago, ma'am."

"Just call me Jax."

Holman snarled, "Has any of the treasure been brought out of the jungle?"

Jax considered his brash approach unnecessarily uncouth. It came across as racially prejudiced: an arrogant air of superiority.

Intimidation was reflected in Amaya's answer. "N ... No, sir. The expedition has not returned."

"You get an inventory?" Holman badgered.

Amaya passed him a folder. "We only received a short satellite phone call from them before we lost the signal. All that was mentioned is documented here, sir."

Holman opened it to read for himself. Jax had to lean over to study it.

"Why is there no mention of the goddamn sarcophagus?" Holman spouted, angered by the thought that the arduous trip might be a waste of his precious time.

Amaya reacted defensively, "Because I was ordered by your office in Manila to keep it under wraps, sir."

"Of course," Jax said placatingly, shooting Holman a condemning glare for being presumptuous. She suspected him of gender bias to add to his obvious prejudice.

Holman got the message and shut up for the rest of the ride.

The Pajero pulled up outside RD Crab Shack Restaurant.

"Here we are," Amaya happily announced. "I wasn't sure if you could tolerate traditional Filipino food, so I chose this restaurant because it specialises in crab dishes cooked American Cajun style."

"That's at least one positive thing to come out of our meeting," Holman grumbled while climbing out of the vehicle.

"Sounds fantastic, Amaya." Jax said, leaned close, touched her fingers gently on Amaya's arm, and whispered, "Don't worry about Holman, his bark is worse than his bite."

"It's called time dilation," the Professor told Alice.

"Glad to know it's got a name, but it doesn't explain why everything freezes for thirty seconds or so only at the arrival end of a wormhole."

"It's to do with the polarity at the terminal end, Al. You might note the vortex spins clockwise at the terminal end, whereas at Kairos it spins anticlockwise. This sets up a positive electromagnetic field at the terminal end and a negative field at Kairos. The positive field produces a shockwave, which bends time, slows it down ... a momentary lapse in time. The traveller isn't affected by it because the electromagnetic field of his altered atomic composition is synchronized with the polarity of the vortex. If that makes sense," Vic tried his best to explain in layman's terms.

Secta came in, sat down in the lounge setting in the Professor's office, and joined the conversation. "Is this about synchronized polarity?"

"Alice asked why everything freezes for thirty seconds or so whenever he pops out of a vortex and questioned why the same doesn't occur at the Kairos end on return."

Secta chuckled, "Alice has a predilection for clever conundrums."

"Now I know it's to do with polarity. It's seriously useful ... the big freeze has saved my butt a bunch of times."

Secta changed the subject. "Christina has come up with an algorithm she'd like us to model, Vic."

"She's one smart bird, that one," Al said.

"Yes, too brilliant for the job, in reality ... she's seriously overqualified. But I'm not going to complain," Secta admitted.

"Nor me," Vic seconded. "So, do tell?"

"If it works, it would initiate two quite complicated tasks. Firstly, it would allow metal to pass through Kairos, and secondly, it would allow a signal from a remote to open a micro-wormhole at the traveller's discretion," Secta explained.

"Now I see why you reckon she's overqualified, that's bloody brilliant," Al exclaimed.

"Let's not get too carried away, it's only a bunch of code at this stage, it will need to be tested. You know how much trouble we've had trying to come up with getting anything other than organics through Kairos," Vic complained.

"You're showing your age, Vic. You've transitioned from an optimist to a pessimist. We know Kairos IV in 2047 has it, so we must succeed," Secta said with a crafty grin.

CHAPTER 3
FRIDAY ON MY MIND

BUT VIC WAS serious. "No, my friend, it's not about age. However, your observation could be construed as ageism!" he said with a comical wicked chuckle. "No, after bringing all the Red Wheel sufferers through Kairos and what happened to that lass, Black Friday, I now feel the conviction of a higher sense of obligation to safety."

"Black Friday, from the Queanbeyan settlement with Flash Harry? I didn't hear about that. Why, what happened?" Al asked.

Secta and Vic exchanged a guilty look, and then Secta chose to do the explaining.

"We had put over four thousand folk through Kairos without a hitch, then it came to Queanbeyan. You were still recovering after the shooting, Alice. By then, we had the system down pat, but what we hadn't accounted for was the different atmospheric conditions unique to each location. For instance, Avalon and the other bunkers were free of contamination, but it wasn't so with Queanbeyan.

"Morri, Turk, Dr Luna, and Toeghan Hitz were in the underground remains of the Queanbeyan District Hospital at OR II, organizing the teleportation of the diseased through Kairos. They had them corralled into batches of three hundred, which made it easier to get them through the vortex one at a time."

The vortex was obscured inside a dark-curtained portable enclosure so that each victim thought they were only going to experience something as simple as an X-Ray and wouldn't realise they were actually being transported through time. It was critical to keep the process secret. Once fitted with a Clock Drive, they were led behind the curtain, at the back of which was the open vortex to pass through. They exited Kairos at the other end, received by Secta, the Professor, Hope, or one of the other OTT team members. Then they were led along a curtained-off passageway in through the control room and into the dispatch cubicle. The console and all of the scientific gadgetry being operated by Dr James were hidden behind the curtain. A simple green light signalled Robert to dispatch the person back to 2112. Once out of the vortex into the enclosure they'd originally entered, totally unaware of their journey, Luna or Morri would lead them out of OR II. Full recovery depended on the state of each individual's health, but in general, it only took a matter of hours before they were active again.

It was different for the cases close to dying or those too feeble to even walk. They were helped onto a specially designed organic gurney that was wheeled into the vortex and transported through the wormhole with the victim on it.

Two days it had taken to get the majority of the Queanbeyan colony through. Luna had devised a roster to allow assistants some downtime to rest. Once all the badly infirmed had been treated, only a healthy few, those without Red Wheel, remained, and one of those was Black Friday. As a leader of the Queanbeyan colony under Flash Harry, who was confined to a wheelchair, she was privy to the time travel process and so waited until last to be treated. It would only be precautionary because she was in good health.

An American, Flash Harry was sympathetic to the infirmed and had tirelessly stayed throughout the entire process to watch every one of his people pass safely through Kairos. He was next to go. Friday wheeled him over to the curtain and stopped for him to have a chat with Turk.

"I managed to save a bottle of champagne we found a few years ago," Harry said with a deep chuckle. "Chances are it's in good nick …

interested in cracking it once we're done?"

A mosquito landed on Turk's arm; he slapped at it but missed. "Sold!" Turk said, searching the air for the pesky insect. "Bloody thing, don't get them at Avalon," he muttered to himself.

"They're a damn nuisance here, too much putrid water lying about," Harry explained.

Luna wandered over, looking very tired. "Alice is right, Harry, you're the spitting image of a famous and well-loved actor of our time, Morgan Freeman."

"Happy to know that, Luna. We'll drink to Morgan as well!" He grinned at Friday. "Now, come on, my dear, wheel me into oblivion."

Dressed as the nurse, Friday had originally been trained as such, rather than the chamois bikini-clad warrior she had become. She wheeled Harry through the curtains and then helped him onto the gurney waiting there.

"I don't know what I'd do without you, Friday," he said emotionally, perched on the gurney, tears welling up in his eyes.

"Don't you worry, Harry, I'll be here right when you get back," she said with a warm smile, and then gave him a gentle peck on the cheek.

It was as though they were joined at the hip; they depended on each other. She pushed the gurney into the vortex.

Five minutes later, he and the gurney popped back out.

"What a ride!" Harry exclaimed to Friday, who was waiting for him. "Hope met me on the other side and gave me a note to pass on to her folks. A damned incredible experience, that."

Friday helped him into his wheelchair, and then wheeled him out for Luna to remove the Clock Drive.

Harry handed Turk the note. "Hope sent this for you and Morri."

While Turk was reading it, Luna walked Friday, the last candidate, over to the curtain.

"Friday," Harry called to her, "they know you're last, and they're expecting you to arrive in your bikini," he punctuated with a devious little chuckle.

"Sounds like my namesake Black Alice has been telling stories," she sniggered light-heartedly. "See you in a flash, Harry."

Luna attached the Clock Drive to Friday's neck, and she entered the cubicle alone. As she was stepping into the vortex, the mosquito that had been harassing Turk landed on her forearm for a feed and was subsequently carried by her into the vortex.

"Well, at least that's what we think happened," Secta summarised. "I was waiting with Vic and Hope in the event room for Friday to arrive. Karzoff and Viktoria were there as well, busy taking down the partitioning. Rob was now visible through the control room window that we'd had concealed and announced incoming over the intercom.

"Then, what emerged from Kairos was absolutely horrendous. A hellish abomination of a thing, so frighteningly deformed, so badly mutated it was almost indescribable. Friday's molecular structure had been merged with the molecules of the mosquito, which had produced a half-human, half-insect monstrosity. At first, we didn't know what to make of it. We had no idea an insect could have entered Kairos with her.

"It was a live, breathing bulbous blob of a thing, an entanglement of human limbs, insect mandibles, and two of the most horrific bulging compound eyes, four times the size of a human's, and made up of hundreds of lenses allowing it to see in all directions. They were flicking about madly in a state of manic confusion. The face still had a human shape with a nose and a mouth under the inhuman mandibles. It was the stuff of nightmares, absolutely terrifying.

"It staggered toward me on multiple spiny insectoid legs with a single human arm extended plaintively, a finger pointing at me condemningly. The mouth opened wide as if to speak. I wanted to hear what it had to say, but it just coughed and spluttered, expelling something from its mouth that bounced on the tiled floor: teeth. It repulsed me; I looked back at it. Strings of saliva were hanging from its lips and chin. It groaned and whined mournfully, like an injured dog. When it lunged at me, Hope let out a scream loud enough to wake the dead. That alerted Viktoria and Karzoff, who swivelled around from what they were doing and upon seeing the monstrocity drew their automatics and opened fire.

"It was the best thing, really; it probably wouldn't have lived much longer, and by the terrible groaning sounds it was making, it must have been in fearful agony."

Alice was struck dumbfounded by Secta's graphic description. Eventually, he spoke up. "What happened then?"

Secta was obviously disturbed by his own explanation, and so the Professor answered for him. "We froze the body for further study. Would you like to see it?"

"No way! I've seen enough monsters," Al groaned. "So, who told Flash Harry? He would've been devastated."

"Secta immediately went through Kairos to tell him," Hope said, dolefully.

Secta had his face in his hands. He took them away and peered sorrowfully at Al. "That was one of the toughest things I've ever done. The poor guy was so grief-stricken."

"Yes, she meant everything to him," Al said, reassuringly patting Secta on the back. "I've since built a filter similar to SAGE that detects alternative DNA and prevents it merging with the principal's molecular structure," the Professor explained.

"So, it can't happen again?" Al asked.

"No, it can't," Vic confirmed.

Jax gazed out of the restaurant window at the spectacular view. She was lost in her thoughts, deaf to what Amaya had asked, hearing only the sound of the whistling wind outside. Quite suddenly, she snapped out of her reverie as sound returned to normal.

"Do you have jet lag?" Amaya had asked.

"Oh, no … no … sorry, I was just thinking about what you said before. You mentioned a strange sound in the background of Henry's satellite call. Is there any chance you can sample that sound for me to send to our office? They might be able to determine its nature."

"Yes, of course. I'll arrange that now." She took out her cell phone and typed a text.

While Amaya was working on that, Jax turned to Holman and said, "I don't believe we have any choice but to go to the location and see for ourselves."

"No, I'd rather wait to find out what that noise was."

"Do I detect cold feet, Agent Holman?" Jax muttered, accusingly.

Holman straightened up in his seat and pumped his chest out with bravado. "No such thing ... just being cautious."

Jax pulled a face, spurning his excuse.

"My office will forward the sound sample to your phone, Jax."

"Good, thank you, Amaya. Can a chopper take us to the exact location?"

"I don't see why not," said Amaya.

"Excellent, I'll arrange one," Jax said, determined to move forward.

"When for?" Amaya asked.

Jax pondered for a moment, then said confidently, "First light tomorrow."

This decision resulted in Holman shooting Jax a hard glance, clearly offended she'd chosen a time without consulting him. Jax didn't care. The food arrived.

A debate was underway at a critical meeting of OTT staff and President Low on how to finalize the next step of the Red Wheel treatment program.

Luna was anxious. "Secta, have you figured out how to target a location in the US in 2112 to send a wormhole?"

Secta stood up to explain. "We've researched potential bunkers in cities outside of the capitals you provided, but there's an issue. Those bunkers may no longer exist in 2112 or might be uninhabited ... we don't believe it's worth the risk."

"Then we need an item from a location there for Kairos to lock onto ... just like when you sent Alice into the past. Surely that would work?" Luna argued.

"It's quite different, Luna. We can access items from the past, but you can't access an item from a future that hasn't happened yet," the Professor clarified.

Al spoke up. "There's really only one answer: we use the coordinates of a capital city."

Secta argued, "They'd be candidates for dangerous radiation levels, Alice."

Dr Christina Phillips, new to OTT, cleared her throat and tentatively suggested, "If I might say something ... if my new algorithm works, then the travellers could wear Hazmat suits for protection."

"Yeah, like astronauts," Vee agreed.

The notion had them seriously thinking. Secta glanced at the Professor, who shrugged his shoulders, and then at Hope, who raised her eyebrows—the idea had merit.

"You're both absolutely correct. However, I still worry that high radiation levels could make it a death sentence," Secta concluded.

"I don't know," Hope interjected, "didn't Flash Harry say they believe Canberra was safe enough to enter?"

"He sure did," Al confirmed.

"Then Los Angeles might well be the same," Mal said.

"It's not much different than the trip to Chernobyl ... similar risk ... in fact, roughly about the same amount of time after the explosion ... thirty years, give or take," Al added.

Mal asked, "So, what do you think, Secta? How far have you advanced on Christina's algorithm?"

"I'm still running modelling tests," Hope said, "they'll be done by tomorrow."

Mal summed up. "Good, then are we agreed that should the tests prove successful, a course of action will be determined for an away mission to LA in 2112? The objective will be to assess the Red Wheel epidemic there?"

Secta glanced questioningly at his science staff—they collectively nodded. "Yes," Secta affirmed, and then resumed his seat.

"Would that include me?" Luna asked.

Al answered, "Not until we've completed a recce."

Mal moved the topic forward. "Anything on the treasure in the Philippines, Blake?"

"Yes, sir," Blake said, rising to his feet. "Word has it that the two explorers who discovered it have not emerged from the jungle and are presumed dead. Our consulate reported an hour ago that a helicopter has been chartered for tomorrow morning to make a drop at the location. Intelligence suggests it could be De Ville and Holman. I also think the black marketeer Handerson Bolt would be in the mix after the treasure."

Karzoff leaned forward in his seat, alerted by something, and spoke up. "Did you say Handerson Bolt? Yesterday, I intercepted an email on Honor's phone, which we still have ... it was from this individual Handerson Bolt, asking for three million crypto for something he referred to as 'the sarcophagus'. I've been waiting for another email to clarify the context."

"Was the email cc'd to anyone?" Viktoria asked.

"Yes, Regina Fych."

"That's Gorrick's PA," Viktoria confirmed.

Mal frowned. "What would Zen want with a sarcophagus?"

"Isn't it strange that both Zen and the CIA are so interested in acquiring this?" Vee questioned.

"Déjà vu," Al complained. "First it was the Ark of the Covenant that everyone wanted, then it was the An-Zu bird, and now it's a bloody coffin."

Secta's brow furrowed. "It can't be the antique value attracting them, surely?"

Vee added, "It is made of platinum isn't it?"

"True, but as I mentioned before ... it has to be what's inside of it," Blake proposed.

As Blake took his seat, Hope stood up. "You asked me to research the three platinum sarcophagi taken from Nan Madol on Pohnpei."

"Remind us again where that is, Hope?" Mal requested.

"Micronesia. It's located in the Western Pacific Ocean. I won't delve into the archaeological opinions about the ancient ruins on Nan Madol, but I'll mention that they raise questions. For instance, they shouldn't be there because they were constructed from a type of basalt that isn't native to the area. Moreover, the massive basalt logs used in their construction couldn't have been transported to the islands using the vessels available to the natives two thousand years ago. In addition to that, the platinum sarcophagi, each measuring three metres in length by two metres in width and weighing over a ton, are out of place. Platinum isn't found in the Western Pacific—it's almost most exclusively sourced from meteorites. A couple of other peculiarities: there was undecipherable writing on the outside in bas-relief, and they were sealed. There were no visible seams, and they couldn't be opened. So, if that doesn't ignite your imagination, nothing will."

CHAPTER 4
TEMPUS

HOPE CONTINUED, "**NOW** comes the really weird part. General Yamashita sent two sarcophagi back to Japan and kept one for his personal collection, as legend has it. He buried it in the Philippines along with a cache of treasure he had accumulated over years of plundering. The two sarcophagi arrived at a naval port in Japan, and because they couldn't be opened, they were stored in a nearby naval warehouse beside a racecourse. They would have to wait until after the war to be examined more thoroughly. At 12:02 p.m. on August 9, 1945, that racecourse was the epicentre of the detonation of Fat Man, a uranium atomic bomb. It was the Nagasaki racetrack ... eighty-seven thousand people were killed that day. Most people don't know that it was a much more powerful explosion than the one that levelled Hiroshima. The warehouse and the two sarcophagi were vitrified.

"Now, what makes this even more intriguing is that there were two aircraft assigned to the mission: a B-29 nicknamed Bockscar carrying the bomb and another B-29, The Great Artiste, as an observer to take photos. They had two primary targets, Kokura and Niigata, but both were covered by low clouds, so the bombardier ordered the mission aborted. Both planes had circled the targets for so long, trying to find a break in the cloud cover to make the drop, that they were running out of enough fuel to return to Okinawa. As they were passing over the coast of Japan on their way back, two odd things happened.

Firstly, a strange craft was observed by several members of the flight crew, but it was never formally reported. Secondly, with clouds covering the world below them, a circular gap suddenly opened in the cloud cover, just large enough for the bombardier to drop the bomb through."

"So, what makes that strange, Hope?" Mal inquired.

"Well, from reading the memoirs of the bombardier, who has since passed away, you get the impression that the strange craft they saw had created the circular hole in the cloud for them to deploy the bomb through."

"Why?" Al asked.

Hope paused, then said firmly, "Maybe to ensure that the two sarcophagi were completely destroyed."

Al nodded. "You're suggesting it might have been a Watcher?"

"Only two of the aircrew saw it. Bockscar was at twenty-six thousand feet, and they said the craft was well above them, with sunlight reflecting off it as if it were an aircraft. But it couldn't have been; nothing could fly that high back then. Besides, they said it was stationary," Hope explained.

"All of a sudden, we have a connection. Maybe this is why Zen is interested. En-Lil. Maybe this last sarcophagus wasn't supposed to be found? There must be something important inside the object," Al pondered. "Look, I'll only need Turk and Toeghan with me on this mission, so why not have Blake and Vee check out the sarcophagus in the Philippines? I've got a gut feeling about it—something doesn't add up."

Mal stood up to conclude the discussion. "Good idea, Al. Blake, can you and Vee work with Hope to see if you can find any connections between this sarcophagus and ancient Sumerian texts? I'd like to know what's captured the CIA's attention. It's likely linked to Jax De Ville's research. I'll speak with Colonel Freeman and exert some pressure to see if he can gather any information from his sources."

Dawn broke, and dressed in army fatigues, De Ville and Holman stood at the concierge of the Marco Polo Hotel, waiting for transportation to the airport. The Pajero pulled up right on time.

Inside the car, Jax inquired about the items she had requested Amaya to gather for the expedition. Amaya turned from the front passenger seat and replied, "All the items are in the trunk, ma'am. Did your team find anything from the sound sample?"

"Yes, it was a chopper—a Robinson R-44, to be precise," Jax answered.

"Incredible that they could tell that from the sound," Amaya remarked.

Holman added, "The R-44 is a small chopper, seats three. There's only one in Davao, at the Mindanao Helicopter Charter Service."

"Would you like me to check with them to find out who hired it?" Amaya offered.

Holman smirked, saying, "Done. It was chartered by CONVEC Inc., an oil exploration company, for a flight to Mount Apo. Are you familiar with them?"

"No, I'm not. Did the helicopter return? There are many flights to Mount Apo each day; it's a popular tourist destination," Amaya explained.

"Yes, it did return with its two passengers. So, we're none the wiser," Holman concluded firmly.

It only took twenty minutes for the twelve-kilometre journey to the airport. Ten minutes later, they were airborne.

The Philippine Navy Bell UH-1-H Iroquois chopper was such an old-timer that it had their teeth chattering from the vibration. However, it was the best option they could secure in the limited time. With the side panel open, wind rushed in with gale force, creating such noise inside the cabin that they had to shout to communicate through their headgear.

Holman checked the clip on his handgun; he was determined not to enter unarmed. Amaya had gone to great lengths to provide him with the weapon.

After a ten-minute flight covering the forty kilometres to Mount Apo, they reached their destination. The last signal from Henry's GPS had provided them with the location. They had confirmed it by triangulating the satellite phone signal from his final contact. The target wasn't at the summit of the nearly three-thousand-metre mountain—the highest point in the Philippines—but rather on a ridge at 800 metres. The main climbing access to the three peaks was on the other side of the mountain, while their destination lay in thick tropical jungle.

Jax was an experienced rock climber, unlike Holman. The pilot had cautioned that there was no suitable landing spot, so the plan was to hoist them one at a time onto the ridge, wind permitting.

Approaching the craggy black volcanic ridge surrounded by dense rainforest, Jax requested a flyover to inspect the target. The pilot hovered the chopper over the location, allowing them to observe the freshly excavated area that Henry had worked on. However, there was no sign of life or any bodies, living or dead. Then, a powerful gust of wind hit the chopper, throwing it off course. The weather was deteriorating rapidly. Jax asked the pilot to attempt the drop, but the pilot argued against it due to safety concerns.

Holman noticed the trees below bending under the force of the strong winds. The chopper was being buffeted by high-speed updrafts. While Jax insisted on proceeding, Holman overruled her and ordered the pilot to abort.

"This chopper and its crew are for rescues," Jax reasoned with Holman, "they know what they're doing."

"Yes, but I don't," Holman countered.

The pilot chimed in, trying to offer some reassurance. "Ma'am, no problema. We can make another attempt as soon as the weather clears."

Jax reluctantly agreed, saying, "Copy that. Return to Davao."

At 10 a.m. OTT were back in the boardroom. Each of them with completed research into their respective forthcoming missions. Luna and Mal were there.

"You've got call-centre eyes, Hope," Al said.

She smiled cheekily, "What's that mean?"

"People that work night shifts in call-centres get dark circles under their eyes," Vee explained, with a chuckle. "I know, I worked at a call-centre in Perth for a while."

Hope grinned, "Yeah, I can relate to that … haven't had any sleep … but I did get everything done. The tests on Christina's algorithm were a complete success … I've copied you Secta, Vic."

Mal's PA brought in a tray of coffees. "Here guys, this'll perk you up. You look half asleep," Rita said, light-heartedly.

"Yes Hope, I looked it over with Vic earlier this morning. I think you can go ahead and install it Christina," Secta agreed. "Once it's up and running we can send a drone through to LA to test radiation levels there."

"And film it," the Professor added excitedly, the new innovation adding even more to the sense of adventure.

Mal declared, "Amazing, this algorithm is going to revolutionise the entire time travel process."

"Exactly, I think Christina should be commended," the Professor said.

They applauded her. Christina blushed.

"It opens the door to teleporting anything," Luna said, in awe of the development.

Mal got the meeting back on track, "So, Hope, Vee, Blake … what did your research into the sarcophagus reveal?"

Vee answered. "Hope was pretty tied up testing the algorithm, so she directed us to do the research. By the early hours of this morning she'd finished, so we went over what we'd found and then she did some more on it herself. So, I'll let her fill you in."

Hope rose. "There is the Nephilim theory ... known as the children of the Watchers. Ancient Sumerian texts have them as an early creation of En-Ki before humans, and it is written they were part human, at least looked human. They were meteorologists and once En-Ki had created humankind, the Nephilim warned him a great catastrophic deluge was coming that would wipe out his creation, humanity. The Anunnaki called a meeting at which En-Lil and twelve other gods including En-Ki were made swear a sacred oath that earthlings were not to be spared from the great flood. En-Ki broke his pledge and advised one of his human creations, Ziusudra, how to survive it. Alice's old friend the prophet Ezekiel wrote of the Nephilim as being great warriors.

"There are many stories about the Nephilim some biblical and some regarded myth, mostly the truth is obscured by our cultural lens. In the Judeo-Christian story they are either fallen angels, giants or a race of hybrids spawned by human women who'd had relations with fallen angels. In the Sumerian story, En-Ki created seven demigods to help educate his creation, humans, and called them the Apkallu, not Nephilim. They interbred with humans and after the great flood four of the human-Apkallu hybrids evoked the wrath of En-Lil.

"And then there's the reptilian story ... in that the Nephilim were from the Anunnaki home planet of Nibiru and that its proximity to Earth was the cause of the great flood. The reptilian Nephilim interbred with human survivors of the flood. According to Sumerian mythology when the four Apkallu or Nephilim; Nungalpirriggaldim, Pirriggalnungal, Pirriggalabsu, and Lu-nana, survivors of the flood, died, hundreds of years later after having interbred with humans, each of them were entombed in a sacred sarcophagi. These were taken to a distant place on Earth to be hidden from En-Lil. It was said that one day when needed, they could be revived from their sleep—very Arthurian. There are two possible scenarios and I'm certain there would be more."

"It doesn't matter if there are more, if any of this is true then that's why En-Lil's onto it, he'd want that sarcophagus destroyed wouldn't he?" Al reckoned.

"Sounds like a fairytale to me," Luna said.

"Beware of the black cloak of human ignorance, Luna," Secta warned. "We deal all the time with stories regarded by most as being myth, whereas we're expected to believe and not question stories from organised religion. Within the murky mists of myth, there resides a link to the truth. If there is one iota of truth in these parables, then Alice is right, and this sarcophagus is far more than just a coffin made of precious metal."

"I'm convinced," Al affirmed. "Blake, you okay to go check it out?"

Blake smiled, "Yes. Our consulate reported that Jax and Buddy Holman tried to drop in by chopper to the site on Mount Apo this morning, but the mission was aborted due to high winds, so that's bought us some time. They also got me the exact coordinates of the site. We need to get rolling, we've already given the opposition a head-start."

As Hope sat down, Mal spoke up. "Okay, shall we send them to Davao through Kairos, Secta?"

"Given the circumstances, I'd have to say yes," Secta affirmed.

"Wait, I don't know if this is convincing enough to warrant sanctioning a time travel mission," Luna protested.

"I spoke about this with Colonel Freeman last night. He did some checking and phoned me back. The CIA is convinced of a connection between the sarcophagus and the Watchers. This stems from the research of Jax De Ville and the relativity to all the recent Watcher activity ... so Luna, I think it is definitely warranted," Mal explained, strenuously.

Before Luna could react, the Professor asked, "Al, is there any way to ask En-Ki about the sarcophagus?"

"That's a great idea," Vee concurred.

Al nodded, "I could give it a try."

"All right, I'll approve it," Luna acquiesced.

"Good," Mal said, appreciatively. "So, what about the other mission, Secta?"

"We'll send a drone to LA 2112 this afternoon for photo reconnaissance. Once we extrapolate the information, if it's all clear, we'll send a com-drone to talk with Turk about the mission."

"What if Tempus in the USA is still functioning in 2112. We're building it right now, aren't we?" Christina suggested.

All of them with the exception of her were staggered by how they'd all overlooked such an obvious solution to the problem.

Secta glared at her and then erupted with, "Brilliant idea, Christina … simply brilliant."

CHAPTER 5
THE EDGE

JUST AS THE meeting was drawing to a close and they were all rising from their seats to leave, Al noticed the Professor doodling intensely on a notepad and asked him, "Professor?"

Vic looked up sharply and once realising the meeting had adjourned, said hurriedly, "Wait ... wait everyone, there's something I need to tell you."

They all stopped and then resumed their seats to listen. The eccentric-looking professor held up the notepad he'd been scribbling on. "This is what I call the TL-100, an acronym for time-loop one hundred."

They all peered at the scratchy sketch that had formulas and writing all around it. "It might not be easy to see here, but the time-loop is like a miniature Kairos. As the name implies, it is a loop, which means when it is entered, one only passes through a wormhole for a nanosecond and comes out the other side in virtually the same place and time."

His explanation wasn't really clear enough for them to grasp. "Don't get it Vic, why?" Al asked.

"I get it," Christina said. "It's a portable Kairos expressly for Red Wheel sufferers ... they pass through it for long enough for SAGE to strip them of the disease ... it's brilliant."

"Yes, exactly. I couldn't have put it better myself. It doesn't actually generate a wormhole; it simply allows the Clock Drive to reduce the participant to atoms so to speak, pass them through SAGE, and then restore them in a matter of seconds. I thought we could put them around the world," the professor said, excitedly.

"Yes, we could put them in selected cities all over the world now, before the Cyberwars even happen, protected from harm for us to send away teams through to activate in 2112," Secta said.

Luna was thrilled. "What an incredible concept."

De Luz admitted, "It's only a theory, mind you, but the math seems to work."

"If I may, talking about the TL-100 and Tempus, wouldn't it pay to check Kairos in 2112 to see if can be activated?" Christine asked.

"You mean in Sydney ... here?" Al queried.

"Yes," Christina agreed.

"You would expect that when the nuke takes out Sydney, OTT would remain functional, so you'd expect Kairos to still be here? I remember my first adventure into the future ... Sydney had been destroyed by a nuclear accident, but Secta was still alive on OTT level 7," Al said, "that was before Kairos had been invented of course ... but it means the facility had survived."

The notion had Secta up and pacing the floor. Christina continued, "From what I can gather, Kairos was built to withstand almost any catastrophe. In fact, in reading up on previous missions, had not Dr Secta in 2047 mentioned he was operating Kairos IV? That certainly tells us Kairos was in operation thirty-three years before Sydney was nuked ... so one would have to assume it stayed in operation at least until the bomb hit."

"Yes, and like Kairos is now and Tempus will be, nuclear-powered, so one would expect if it wasn't damaged, to be functional," Secta said.

"If it was, then it would make sending away teams around the globe to fire up TL-100's much easier. It could be the main focus of it," Luna proposed.

"Indeed," Secta agreed. "Probes or drones would first have to be sent to evaluate the safety of each location."

The meeting had achieved a great deal and produced a vast array of critical assignments. The Professor and Hope would get to work generating a computer model of the TL-100 for testing. Secta, Alice, and Christina would send a drone to Tempus in 2112 to assay radiation levels and complete a photographic survey, while Vee and Blake would leave promptly through Kairos for Davao to investigate the sarcophagus. In the meantime, a drone would be sent through Kairos to the Avalon bunker to open dialogue with Turk, Morri, and Toeghan.

But with all that, there was still one thing nagging Alice: he needed to know what En-Ki knew about the sarcophagus. He had a gut feeling about it, and experience had taught him to pay attention to his instincts.

On his way out of the boardroom, Mal stopped Al and said, "She's one hell of an asset, isn't she?"

"Who?" Al asked, a little distant, his mind on En-Ki.

"Christina, what a find."

"Oh, yeah, for sure."

The progression of OTT was ironic because only a few city blocks away, Professor Adamski was proudly unveiling Aquila II, Zen's time travel competitor to Kairos.

Located ten levels below the Zen building, Aquila II promised, with the deployment of the new processor brought back from 2112 by Cronus, to give Zen an advantage over any time travel competitor.

En-Lil, contentedly occupying the AI Electra, convinced that the processor would also provide them the army of cyborgs required to put his program of world domination back on track, was tormented by the sarcophagus having shown up in the Philippines. He needed it destroyed and quickly because it posed an extreme threat to all of his plans. Aware of what it might be capable of, the thought of it falling into the hands of OTT was unimaginable; it would give them back the edge. The complication of the arrival of the sarcophagus, along with the need to get the RF cyborg soldier campaign ramped up after the last fiasco, and the ongoing battle with OTT, meant Electra needed more executives she could trust. Though her experience had been jaded by a number of failures, Honor was still the best candidate but would need to be brought back from 2112. However, with Commander Walker on a mission in the Philippines, Electra was in a quandary as to who could be the next time traveller. She decided to ask Dr Li and went to her laboratory.

"Doctor, with Commander Walker on an assignment, I need a time traveller. Do you have a recommendation?" Electra asked.

Li stared at her boss for a long moment across her desk, making up her mind, then said, "I'm sorry ma'am, but the only alternative to the Commander would be you. A neural link wouldn't be required this time for Aquila because we already have data from sending Voltaris Idram there, so you could change form to make the trip."

It made perfect sense; she was better equipped as Cronus than anyone else.

Electra's full, black-painted lips curved into a devilish smile. "Thank you, Doctor. I will consider your recommendation."

She left the lab and immediately rode the elevator down to Aquila, where she found Professor Adamski flat out on the floor of the room housing the mainframe quantum supercomputer, working on it with two technicians.

"Professor, I'd like a word in private, please."

She startled him. He nervously struggled to his feet and then followed her obediently into his private office annexed to the control room. They took seats.

"We need to send a traveller to 2112, to bring back Honor. With Commander Walker unavailable, I am the best qualified. What say you?"

"With the new adjustments, metal can pass through Aquila, so we would not need to alter you other than for you to revert to the image of say Cronus, perhaps … and we already have the coordinates. So yes, if you are prepared to take the risk," he said, with a shrug of his narrow shoulders.

Her big almond-shaped, unblinking dark eyes drilled him with a cold hard stare. "What risk? Do you have reservations as to the reliability of your invention?"

"No, no … the risks are at the other end, that is all," he affirmed anxiously, the failures of the past telling on him.

"You need to get over your guilt, Professor. It gives the impression of uncertainty."

"Yes ma'am, I will work on that … thank you. When do you want to leave?"

Electra thought it over for a moment. "I think sooner the better. When can you have it ready?"

He sat straight up in his chair with a surprised expression, not expecting it to be so soon. "Um, four hours…"

"Good." She stood up.

Adamski noticed she never really smiled. That hadn't been the case with either of the Gorrick's he'd known; both would smile and even laugh at times … but then he mentally corrected himself, the Gorrick's weren't entirely AI, were they?

After a series of successful tests, Secta was content with the new algorithms that Christina had installed in Kairos. Metal objects could now be teleported without any problem, and reopening a vortex to allow travellers to return at will was operational. The algorithms were set to revolutionise time travel for OTT.

For the surveillance of Tempus in 2112, they had decided on using a disc-shaped drone that the tech team had constructed. With a radius of only forty centimetres, it was equipped with a GC-20 dosimeter and a Geiger counter, along with a miniature digital camera.

Christina brought up the coordinates on the computer and was ready to send the drone they had affectionately named Bill on a journey through time.

"It's quite bizarre that we're going to look at a completed apparatus that we've only just begun building," the Professor mused.

Alice could relate to that and declared, "Is that another one of those scientific time paradoxes? ... we're going to look into a future that hasn't happened yet."

Christina laughed.

"You might find it amusing, Christina, but I come across these paradoxes all the time. They do my head in," Al admitted.

Secta joined them after placing the drone in the dispatch room.

"All set. Are you ready, Vic?" Secta said excitedly, always animated when it came to an experiment, especially one involving a new technical device.

As the designated pilot, Vic held the remote controller for Bill.

Christina activated Kairos, and Bill was on its way. Within seconds, they were receiving data. The pictures were from inside what looked to be the lobby of the Tempus facility.

Christina called out a reading from the GC-20. "Dosimeter reading is six mrem."

"That's equivalent to a chest X-Ray," Secta explained, amazed.

Excitedly, Christina pointed at her monitor. "Look at the radiation, it's under 0.05 micro Sieverts!"

The Professor and Secta exchanged quizzical glances. "That's hard to believe..." Secta said with surprise, "normal radiation levels? Check it again, please Christina. No wait, cross-check it with the Dosimeter's reading under exposure."

She clicked through the menu items, found the exposure data, and then reported, "Two point five eight by ten to the power of four."

Secta pulled a small scientific calculator from his pocket and punched in the numbers. "Corresponding. It's safe. Let's proceed, Vic."

All eyes were glued to the large monitor, which was displaying the live feed from the drone.

Bill was hovering about a metre above the floor. Vic slowly rotated it for a three-hundred-and-sixty-degree pan of the location. There was a long desk with a logo on the wall behind it that read Tempus 6.

Secta was shaking his head in awe, "It's unbelievable. We're watching live pictures from a future that's yet to happen. Hmm, that's a nice logo, version 6 no less. Vic, grab a screenshot of it. I'll send it to Robert to use."

"There you go, Christina, another paradox," said Al. "Secta is getting a logo design from the future to use today."

Christina smiled at him, realising how confusing time travel could be.

"It's dusty, a few things broken ... doesn't look like anyone has been there for a while ... I'm curious," Secta said. "There's a photo on the wall. Can you zoom in on it?"

Vic pushed a toggle, and the camera zoomed in on the photo. The shot was of the staff at the launch of Tempus.

Al chuckled, "Ha! Look at that, we're all there ... even you, Christina."

"I see what you mean about it being mind-boggling, Al," she admitted.

"Vic," Al asked, "can you increase the audio from Bill?"

Al wanted to hear the ambient sound while Bill was hovering in the reception area. He heard something and said sharply, "Shush, something's coming."

The others couldn't hear anything. Al's sense of hearing was far beyond theirs; it was one of the superpowers he'd acquired.

A loud bang from a door being slammed shut, then a burst of machine-gun fire. The signal from Bill was cut.

Secta erupted in surprise, "What just happened?"

Christina pressed a few keys and then announced solemnly, "We've lost Bill, sir."

Al leaned back in his chair, rubbing his forehead with his fingers, and growled, "Seems someone there didn't dig our intrusion."

The Professor put down the control unit. "I think you're right, Al."

Secta got up from his chair with a disappointed look on his face.

"I'll prepare THEP in the departure room. Christina, please set up the coordinates for the Avalon bunker in 2112."

Half an hour later, with their spirits lifted by a new adventure, they were staring at Turk, Toeghan, and Morri on the monitor.

THEP was a communications drone that the tech team had designed for two-way video linking, a conference call of sorts. A camera in the Kairos control room transmitted an audio-visual signal through the wormhole to the drone, which appeared in real time on a small ten-by-ten-centimetre screen on the underside of the drone. Simultaneously, a camera on THEP sent a real-time video feed back to Kairos.

Morri beamed them a broad smile, "Hey, guys! How are you? This is one amazing innovation."

Hope entered the control room and upon seeing the feed from her parents, she immediately took over the camera and waved. "Hey Mum, Dad, Toegs."

Morri beamed a loving smile at her daughter. "Hope, how are you, darling?"

"Great! You guys look fantastic."

"It's a brave new world here without Red Wheel and Zen," Morri reflected.

"Hey guys," Turk greeted. "What's news?"

Al spoke up. "We've got a mission planned and wanted to bring you up to speed."

Alice and then Secta explained the plan to go to Tempus and get it working to bring Red Wheel sufferers through. Vic explained how the TL-100 would function. Turk shared how he had conversed with a former Red Wheel sufferer who had been brought back from the brink of death by Kairos and SAGE. The survivor had been to Sydney but was captured by cyborgs due to having Red Wheel. He was thrown into the death camp but had been restored to health. According to him, Sydney was clear of radiation, suggesting that other places might also be safe. The revelation provided food for thought.

Al asked Toeghan if she had any information about Honor and Dr

Mennis. She told him that scouts had reported they were living together in a house near the ruins of the Zen Building.

They agreed to reconvene in precisely 24 hours to allow time for processing all the new information.

Vic landed the drone on the garage floor of the Avalon bunker to resume from where they left off in the next meeting.

Christina said, "This brings us back to what I suggested earlier in the meeting ... to get Kairos in Sydney in 2112 back online."

"Yes, it'd be good to have it dedicated to advanced scouting in all cities for Red Wheel," Al proposed.

"I agree ... but I think the priority should be getting Tempus up and running," Secta said, then questioned, "Don't you?"

They all acknowledged their agreement.

CHAPTER 6
USO

AT **THAT INSTANT,** Blake couldn't help but draw a comparison between Handerson Bolt's profile picture and a face carved from solid rock. The prominent, bulbous forehead, thick bony ridges over the eyes, nose with a Dantesque quality, thin lips, and a chin projecting like a slab of granite, more akin to a natural formation resembling a chin than something shaped within a human womb. Ugly, massive but strong and easily mistaken as a Russian, there was no panic or fear in his face; it was as steady as his voice. Blake finished watching the short video file on his cellphone and then handed it to Vee, who was seated beside him in the Kairos control room.

"Check it out, granite-head Handerson Bolt ... one serious lowlife."

They were in the midst of waiting for Christina's signal to proceed with their mission to Davao.

Vee played the video. "I see why you call him that. What a hard-looking dude ... with a voice to match. Where did you get the video?"

"My consular contact sent it. They interviewed Bolt two days ago when they got an alert he'd arrived in Manila."

"What was his explanation for being there?"

"The usual cover story, leisure."

"How could he have learned about the discovery so quickly to react in such a timely manner?" Vee inquired.

"An excellent question. He must have connections within the Philippine government. It's a deeply corrupt place, and politicians there can spot a financial opportunity faster than you can say 'Jack Robinson.'"

Vee frowned, "Who's Jack Robinson?"

"Just an old saying my father used. He didn't have 'quicker than a New York second' in his day."

Christina swivelled her chair around from the console and confirmed, "Everything looks good. Are you both wearing Clock Drives?"

"Absolutely," Vee responded with enthusiasm.

They were clad in jungle green camouflage army fatigues and black berets, the standard OTT attire for missions. Now that they could teleport metal through Kairos, they each carried identical weaponry: a Glock 19 pistol holstered at their hips, a combat knife, spare ammunition clips, and a half-dozen WASPs.

Secta and Al entered the room.

"Must be time for you two to split," Al said.

"Yep, just waiting on the signal from CP here," Vee replied.

"So now it's CP … Cool…" Christina quipped as she flicked switches on the console.

"Do you have WASPs?" Secta asked.

Blake answered, "Yep, six each, and I've got two of the new big boppers."

"Big boppers?" Al questioned.

"Yes, a new load for maximum damage, bigger than the fat one's I gave you Al for blowing up rocks," Secta said. "Thought they might come in handy."

Christina humorously chimed in, "Okay, who's on first?"

Secta chuckled, "Ah, one of the classic comedy sketches—Abbott and Costello."

"Indeed, and equally as good," Christina suggested, obviously a comedy buff, "the Danny Kaye glass with the poison sketch … Ai it, it's a killer."

"Ha! This lady has even more refined taste than I presumed," Secta said, clearly impressed.

"Right, I'm up," Vee declared. "Bye, Al." She gave her brother a quick peck on the cheek. "Farewell, Secta. See you later, CP. Stay vigilant; I'm concerned about the lack of a cell phone signal there."

"Use the remote to open the vortex if there's no signal," CP suggested. "And remember to move the micro-dot vortex with you when you leave a location—just press the red button on the remote. I presume you were both briefed on its usage?"

They both gave a thumbs-up in response.

The slender remote they carried was so small that it fit comfortably in the palm of their hands. It featured only four coloured buttons: green for enlarging the vortex, red for shifting its position, blue to signal for emergency help, and yellow—which currently had no designated function.

The brief storm had subsided, leaving the skies over Davao clear and serene. The CIA agents were led to the waiting chopper by the two-man flight crew. Jax was resolute, determined to see the mission through this time.

In just fifteen minutes, the helicopter was hovering over the ridge of Mount Apo—a perfect set of conditions that fulfilled Jax's hopes.

Meanwhile, reports were spreading across news wires about an Unidentified Submerged Object (USO) event off the coast of California, near San Diego. A fishing vessel's crew of ten had encountered a bizarre fate: nine of them were disintegrated by a strange beam emitted from an alien craft that had emerged from beneath the water's surface, adjacent to the trawler during the night. The lone survivor, the ship's captain, recounted the chilling experience. According to him, as they were hauling for squid, their nets became entangled, and suddenly the water around them lit up with an eerie fluorescent green glow. The captain had never witnessed anything like it before. He reported the presence of a massive object lurking beneath the twenty-four-metre trawler. As it surfaced, it revealed its enormous size, resembling a football field. Remarkably, it did so silently, devoid of lights and without causing any displacement of water. The captain described an unsettling unnaturalness about it. While the crew crowded the trawler's side to observe, he remained at the helm, watching through the windscreen. He managed to capture a series of photographs on his cellphone, although the darkness made it challenging to clearly depict the alien craft.

Suddenly, the object elevated itself from the water and hovered ominously. In complete silence, it discharged a single orange beam towards the trawler, striking amidships and instantly obliterating the crew. The captain claimed that the crew had been melted by the beam's impact. He had even captured an image of the beam connecting with the trawler. The USO then swiftly streaked away into the sky, vanishing faster than a speeding bullet, leaving no sound behind. The trawler, its structural integrity compromised, listed, snapped in two, and swiftly sunk. The captain, clinging to a lifebuoy, managed to stay afloat until daylight arrived and he was ultimately rescued.

The photograph of the beam colliding with the ship and crew was nothing short of extraordinary, and had gone viral. This time, the USO event defied explanation from the military or the government. Unlike previous incidents, the truth could not be hidden under layers of disinformation. Ironically named Kirk, the captain of the trawler swiftly became a celebrity, with numerous headlines playing up the connection to "Star Trek."

Mal grinned cynically at Luna. "Seems the temporal prime directive has taken a new twist with Captain Kirk back in the news."

She let out a suspicious chuckle. "And his first name is James to boot."

Mal frowned, "What do you make of it?"

They were seated in the alfresco area of Doyle's Seafood Restaurant in Watson's Bay, having lunch. Luna gazed at the view of Sydney Harbour, its waters glistening like jewels in the noonday sun. "I don't know," she lamented, "the basic tenant of the ancient alien theory is these UAPs or USOs have been visiting us since time immemorial, and it doesn't seem they have ever caused any trouble … until now," she paused looking up into the cloudless blue sky. "Now, it worries me."

"Yes, I can't help but wonder if they're always the same race of aliens," Mal said, following her gaze into the sky and then down to the table beside theirs occupied by his four extremely obvious bodyguards.

"Yes, didn't Alice say En-Ki said there were a number of different species?"

Mal nodded slowly, "He did … but he also warned we have attracted the interest of one of the most malevolent of them."

"Do you think this horrible circumstance off San Diego is what he was referring to?"

"Could be." Mal's expression changed to deadly serious. "It certainly piqued the interest of US President Robinson."

"Is that because the cat is now out of the bag when it comes to UAPs or is it a legitimate fear?"

Mal pulled a tight-lipped grin with a squint. "Both, I'd say."

Luna's cellphone poised on the table rang. She peered at the ID. "I need to take this, its Maralina."

Mal knew for UN Director General Maralina Bostok to call at this hour it must be important.

Luna wandered off along the promenade chatting to Maralina while Mal took a sip from a glass of a rouge pinot noir, while being seduced by the panoramic scenery before him. After a few minutes Luna returned and resumed her seat. Mal could tell by her expression there was trouble.

"What's up?" he asked.

"There have been three more cases of alien attacks … all close to strategic military bases. One off Cadiz in Spain, right next to the US Navy base at Rota ... another close to the Clyde Naval Base near Glasgow, Scotland, and then another near the Russian nuclear submarine base at Severomorsk. Maralina is worried it might be the start of something."

Mal was concerned. "Was is the same MO as San Diego?"

"In two cases worse. A scientific research vessel, an icebreaker, was sunk as it was coming in to dock at Severomorsk. Fifty-five fatalities, three survivors, and then another fishing vessel in the Firth of Clyde, twenty-two lost, six survivors. All the same."

Mal pondered out loud. "Are these things being caught spying on Naval bases and reacting or is it deliberate, I wonder?"

It was decided they had no choice but to go to Tempus in 2112.

"Why not kill two birds with one stone and activate Tempus while we're there?" Al submitted.

Secta wasn't comfortable with the idea. It would mean him going on the mission with them to handle the technicalities.

He queried, "Wouldn't it be wiser to first establish if Red Wheel is actually a problem there? Might not be."

It dawned on Alice he shouldn't be considering risking Secta, and so he changed tack. "You're right. Okay, let's just do a recce. I'll need Turk and Toeghan here; better let 'em know."

"Go get your trappings together, Al. Vic and I will sort Turk out," Secta advised.

Alice left the control room to get kitted up.

A short while later, Turk and Toeghan stepped out of Kairos and were greeted by Secta. He led them to the armoury where they found Alice.

Half an hour after that, the three of them were in the control room geared up, ready for the mission to Tempus.

"I've remotely inputted a new data file to your implant, Alice,"

Secta advised leisurely. "It's an interface with your graphene lenses Vic developed that will provide you a radiation readout. When you switch to infrared vision, there's a small green number bottom right. Try it now."

Al mentally switched. "Yep, I see it … point zero nine."

"Yes, four points higher than normal due to your proximity to Kairos, but anything under two point zero is safe. It is calibrated to blink when the radiation is one point five and getting dangerous."

"Cool. Anything else?"

Secta continued, "Yes, you've got your vortex remote, and you're up to speed on its functionality, yes?"

Al nodded, "Yep,"

The three of them were dressed in disruptive grey pattern camouflage fatigues. Al was wearing a red beret, with Turk and Toeghan wearing black ones.

Hope and the Professor came in.

"All set?" Vic asked.

"Just about to jump," Turk said, with a smile.

Hope gave Turk a big hug, happy to see her dad.

"Bit of a step up for you, Toeghan. Looking forward to a bit of action?" Vic asked.

Toeghan smiled. Her entire demeanour had changed for the better since spending time with Turk and Morri.

"Can't wait, Professor," she said.

While Hope, Turk, and Toeghan chatted about Morri and the goings-on at the Avalon bunker, Vic went over to Christina at the console and asked, "Everything ship-shape?"

She smiled, always in a pleasant mood. "No tap-backs so far … the algorithm is working like a charm."

"Excellent."

She swivelled around and said, "Okay, ready when you are, Al."

Normally, there was a degree of tension prior to the commencement of a mission, but Al and Turk were so keen to work together again that it made for a more positive atmosphere. It could also have had something to do with the chemistry between Toeghan and Al … it was there for all of them to sense.

Turk stepped out of the vortex and was met by Al and Toeghan, covering him. They were in the Tempus control room rather than the lobby where the drone had been destroyed, thought to be safer even with the momentary motion lapse.

Al immediately checked for radiation; it was point zero nine, the same as the Kairos control room. Though there were no lights, it was easy enough to see. The control room looked similar to the one they were familiar with at Kairos. It wasn't dusty or decayed, and Al couldn't see any noticeable damage, so he was feeling confident it could be reactivated. After pressing the red button on the remote for the micro-wormhole to track him, it was time for some exploring.

Al drew his Glock. "Okay, let's cruise. I'll lead; Turk, take up the rear."

He opened the pressure door, went through the decontamination section, and out through another heavy-duty door into a corridor. Al had a scale drawing of the Tempus layout on his organic implant, so he could see the elevator was nearby but figured it unlikely to be functioning even though it was nuclear powered. He decided to give it a try anyway. They navigated the dim corridor to the elevator lobby.

Al pressed the call button and lo and behold, it worked.

"That's a good start. There are twenty-three freaking kilometres of tunnels down here with seventeen access shafts … we could have been in for a helluva hike if the lift hadn't worked."

"You'd have to think down here would have been the safest place in America during the war … how deep are we?" asked Turk.

"Two hundred feet … twenty stories. You're right, mate, this is even more secure than the Avalon bunker."

"Do you think whoever took out the drone lives down here?" Toeghan questioned, looking nervously about, expecting at any moment for someone to leap out of the shadows.

"I dunno, but I guess we'll find out soon enough," Al said.

The elevator arrived. They entered to ride up to the lobby. Inside, Turk looked down at the floor. "Footprints. People use this."

Al checked the rads again—it hadn't changed—still acceptable. It was a fast and silent elevator, with one dim light and large enough for ten passengers.

"My ears just popped," Toeghan muttered with a cackle.

"What's that?" Al asked.

She spoke louder, "I said my ears just popped."

Al joked, "Sorry, can't hear you; my ears just popped."

They laughed. Al was in good spirits with his waggish sense of humour.

The elevator stopped and the door slid open. They weren't expecting to be greeted by what confronted them.

CHAPTER 7
BUSH TELEGRAPH

THE NUMBER OF guns aimed at them was a worry—more than a dozen. Al was thinking to quickly press the down button but figured if they were trigger happy, his finger might not reach it in time. Instead, he chose a big friendly smile, and that seemed to do the trick.

"Hey, now that's no way to greet friends, is it?" he asked warmly, raising his hands chest-high in surrender.

But the look on their faces was more of a freak-out than of fury. As if they'd all simultaneously received a message to look left, then in perfect timing, they looked sharply back at Alice again, wild-eyed.

Al leaned out of the door to peek at what they'd looked at that had freaked them out so. He saw it was a framed photo on the wall commemorating the launch of Tempus. What had rattled them was Alice, dressed as he is now, standing in the centre of the photograph, flanked by Dr Robert James, General Larry Freeman, Secta, the Professor, Christina, and Hope.

"Oh, that! Well yes, that's me all right, I can explain ... I'm Black Alice ... and these guys here are Toeghan and Turk."

The guns slowly lowered, their faces smeared with camouflage paint turning from astonishment to fascination. A young woman dressed in ripped and torn old army fatigues stepped forward with her hand extended to shake.

"Hi Alice, I'm the great-granddaughter of Dr Robert James,

Cheyenne James, and this," she motioned at a young man behind her, "is the great-grandson of General Larry Freeman ... Rip Freeman."

Al stepped out of the elevator and shook their hands. Turk and Toeghan followed.

On the floor near the reception counter was what was left of the crashed drone.

"Oh, that must have been yours, sorry," Cheyenne said.

Al smiled. "It's okay, I understand ... the first reaction would have been defence."

"We thought it belonged to the Rangers," Rip snarled.

"The Rangers? Who are they?" Al questioned.

"We will explain soon enough. For now, we need to leave here, it is too dangerous. Come with us," Cheyenne said, stepping into the elevator.

Al signalled, and they all boarded ... a seriously tight fit: sixteen of them.

"We could get busted for overloading," Al quipped, he and Turk towering above the others.

It was obvious to Al that Cheyenne and Rip were the oldest; the others looked to be teenagers.

Cheyenne pressed the button for the 17th floor.

Alice checked the floor plan on his implant. "The laboratory floor ... is that where you live?"

Cheyenne shook her head, "No, it is where we hold meetings. We live in tunnels on the twentieth."

"Anyone know a good elevator joke?" Toeghan quipped, jammed like in a sardine can.

The door opened, and Cheyenne led them out to a set of double doors that she swung open. Inside was a small lecture auditorium in which fifty or so people were seated waiting. It was well-lit, clean, and modern. The red fabric-covered seats were configured on a steep angle for an unobstructed view of the stage.

The others stayed behind while Cheyenne led Alice, Turk, and Toeghan along an aisle, up four steps onto the stage. Cheyenne took centre stage. The room fell silent.

"Kinfolk," she addressed them, "I present to you … the legendary … Black Alice!"

Alice was taken aback by the standing ovation. He humbly held up a hand. "Please, please … I don't know why there's such admiration, but I appreciate it. I don't suppose I would be telling you anything new when I say that we have travelled in time from the past to visit you. From the location and the names Dr Robert James and Larry Freeman mentioned, I know we're all family. I'm accompanied this day by Turk, chief of the Avalon bunker in Oceana in this year, and Toeghan, who also works with Oceana Time Travel. We recently cured thousands of sufferers of a dreadful disease called Red Wheel that had infected the people of Oceana in this time zone following the seven-year war. The fatal disease was planted by Zen Corporation and was intended to kill off mankind within a generation … and would have done so had it not been for Dr Secta and Professor De Luz back in my time, coming up with a cure. We're here to assess the extent of the disease in America. We chose to come to Tempus because it is our sister time travel facility, and through it, we believe we can treat the infirmed."

An unexpected murmur of discontent rumbled from the audience.

"By your reaction, you must have a story that could have bearing on our plans. I think then before we proceed with anything, you need to fill us in. Thank you."

Cheyenne led them off into a smaller room backstage.

"Take a seat, the leading elder will be here to speak with you in a moment," she said.

Alice noticed all of them had a complexion similar to the pale, ghostlike members of the Queanbeyan community. Sunlight obviously was something they avoided. They weren't robust in any way, quite frail, thin, and undernourished.

A decrepit old man slumped in a wheelchair was pushed into the room and positioned in front of Alice. A few thin strands of white hair left on his head, his face wrinkled by the ravages of time … but in his pale blue old eyes, Alice recognised a person he knew. A shaky, frail, bony hand covered in age spots and pellucid skin, reached out for Alice to grasp.

"Robert," Alice said, smiling, "Dr Robert James."

Turk and Toegs also shook the old man's hand, having met him a number of times in the Kairos control room.

His voice raspy and faltering, Robert said, "Alice, Turk, and Toeghan … ah, memories flood back of Kairos," he spluttered and coughed.

"He's a hundred and eighteen," Cheyenne said proudly.

Robert touched Alice's arm to get his attention, the way old folk do. Al had to lean closer to hear him clearly. "Had we finished Tempus by the time you left?" Robert croaked.

"No."

Robert grinned. "So, you don't know we used Vic's TL-100 to cure our people of Red Wheel then?"

Alice chuckled … it was another of those paradoxes. During the interim from when they'd left, OTT had obviously distributed the TL-100 to cure Red Wheel sufferers worldwide.

"Good to know it worked," Al said, beaming a big grin.

"Oh yes, it worked all right, everywhere in the world, and it allowed me to live longer than expected … But it didn't stop them … no, no … did it?" Robert said, getting quite riled up.

Alice frowned. "Them?"

Cheyenne stepped in to placate the old man. "Calm down, Poppy. Don't get yourself in a pickle. Alice is here to help. You should go rest now … don't worry, I will tell him everything."

After Robert had been wheeled from the room, Cheyenne sat down to tell them the story of Tempus.

They had known the war was coming after being warned by OTT. In fact, as part of the TL-100 installation process, OTT had explained what it was for and why it was necessary, so the countries that had one were very much aware of what to expect. The thing was the TL-100 was for the treatment of Red Wheel, not for the prevention of it.

She further explained, "The military and the government had no idea Tempus would be a strategic target for a nuclear strike. They did, however, anticipate a strike on the missile base at Grand Prairie just fifty-four kilometres from here. As a result, the region took two big nuclear hits on the same day.

"The staff at Tempus had been well-drilled. Robert, over a hundred years old then, had fought to have the entire complement of staff evacuated through Tempus 6 to another time, but the UNTT had overruled that. So, for our safety, we went deep underground into the twenty-three kilometres of subterranean tunnels.

"In the years before the war, Larry and Robert had built a sanctuary in the tunnels to house and feed two hundred people but only enough for one generation. What had not been factored in were the Rangers."

"So, tell us about the Rangers?" Al asked.

"Okay, they're from outside this facility … people who survived the bombs. Many of them are from the Texas Rangers, a local law enforcement guild, and then some from the military base in nearby Waxahachie. They had a bunker, but that didn't prevent them from catching Red Wheel. They knew we had the cure, but instead of asking to use it, they decided to take it by force. We have been fighting them ever since."

"So, they have Red Wheel?" Turk clarified.

"Yes, Robert said that if we saw out a generation in hiding underground, the Rangers would eventually die out. What he failed to foresee was that the Rangers would devolve into feral savages who nowadays are so starved for food that they have become cannibals."

"Why not just give them the TL-100? You don't need it," Toeghan questioned.

"We don't know if we can still catch Red Wheel … besides, they don't have the power or the knowledge to use it."

"Couldn't you teach them?" Turk queried.

"I think you underestimate them, Turk … it is difficult to even consider them human anymore … they're nothing but a pack of wild animals."

"How many are there?" Al asked.

"I have no idea, but more than us."

"This will have happened wherever there was a TL-100, I think," Turk told Al. "It's the nature of humanity … to war and fight … one side seeking to dominate the other. While one group has the cure, the other side will want it and probably kill for it."

Al agreed strongly, "You're not bloody wrong, mate."

"What can we do?" Toegs asked.

"Well, we can't just accept that everyone infected has gone feral like the Rangers. We need to visit other places and see if they have the same problem. Cheyenne, does Tempus still work?"

"Yes, Alice, but no-one knows how to use it."

"Oh, yes they do," Al said.

"Who?" Cheyenne inquired.

"Your great-grandfather. He helped build it."

When Jax De Ville and Buddy Holman cautiously entered the cavity in the ridge Henry Vitale and his associate had mined, they were shocked to find they had been beaten to the punch. With guns drawn, flashlights lighting up their faces, Blake and Vee were there waiting.

"Whoa, down with the armoury … seems we've all been outdone," Blake hollered, flashing his torch at the two CIA agents.

"Well, well, if it isn't Blake Green and who's that? Oh, Alice's little sister," Holman belittled.

Jax shined her torch about the low-ceiling space, searching for the treasure and only came up with two mangled, dead bodies spread-eagle on the floor. "I guess that's Vitale and Santos."

"Yes, and they bear an MO that'd be familiar to you," Blake taunted Jax.

"Handerson Bolt," she grumbled.

Holman let out a groan, "Argh! Here we go again, your Moriarty."

"We can safely assume Bolt bolted with the treasure," Vee added, with humour.

Irritated, Holman shrieked, "How could this guy lift a one-ton sarcophagus and all the rest of the treasure out of this cave in such a short time? Like, I know he's your nemesis, but he ain't no Superman," he snarled cynically.

Blake fired back caustically, "Maybe through a wormhole, who knows?"

"Nah, where would he get that technology?" Jax argued.

"Zen," Vee countered, "he could've done a deal with them?"

"If you look carefully at the floor," Blake said, shining his torch at marks, "you can see where something very heavy has been dragged out. I'd say it was the sarcophagus. Then, it was probably hoisted up and flown out to a secret location by chopper."

Holman barked scathingly, "Huh! Sure! That would take one helluva big chopper … where would he get that?"

Blake snapped, "What's with you, Holman? There are plenty of choppers here that can lift a ton; a K-Max-1200, a Bell 205-A, even an Airbus AS-250. You should know that."

"Now you're what, an aviation expert?" Holman snapped. He didn't like Blake, and the feeling was mutual.

"Shut up, Holman. He knows about choppers, he can fly one. Yes, Blake, and we know it … he'd have access to whatever he needs here," Jax said, drawing her satellite phone and then striding to the entrance while dialling. "Amaya Alvarez, please … Amaya … can you get flight reports for the last 48 hours from Davao Airport, please? … Sorry … of choppers coming and going from Mount Apo … and their final destinations. Yes, the treasure has been stolen. Okay … thanks, call me back."

Bending down to avoid hitting his head on the craggy low ceiling, Blake followed Jax outside where he found her studying more marks on the ground.

"You can see where they picked it up, right here," she said, pointing at the spot.

Blake nodded then scanned the stunning view of rainforest eight hundred metres below.

Jax sidled up to him. "I suppose you arrived through a wormhole and you'll need a lift back to Davao?"

"Could be the case," he said, with a devilish grin.

There was an obvious magnetism between them.

"I've missed you, babe," Jax whispered.

"I bet you have, is that why my phone hasn't stopped ringing?" he said sarcastically.

"I'm sorry … but after Tahiti … I … Oh, I don't know … we just seemed to go our separate ways."

"We sure did."

"I've been meaning to ask," she eyeballed him, "have you always known I was with the firm?"

"Uh-ha," Blake confirmed. "Did you know I was a field operative for Oceana?"

"Yes."

"So that makes us even," he said, with a cavalier smirk.

"Are you having a scene with her?"

"Of course."

Her phone rang. "Hello, yes Amaya … good, thank you. Bye." She eyeballed Blake, "An Airbus AS-250, at first light this morning."

Blake acknowledged, "Makes sense, he moves quick."

"How did he find out about it?"

"He knows who to bribe. As soon as the original LiDAR scan came in someone would've told someone else until an official heard of it on the bush telegraph, smelt a buck, and called Bolt. So, where is he?" Blake asked.

"Why should I tell you?"

"Because you and Bozo Holman would have Buckley's of handling him on your own, that's why."

"It's Buddy, not Bozo," she corrected.

"No, it ain't. It's definitely Bozo."

CHAPTER 8
THE TIME BEING

ALICE HAD WAITED for Robert to wake from his afternoon nap. Cheyenne took him to the old man's quarters. It was a large room with three smaller rooms. Al sat on the living room lounge and studied the decor while Cheyenne fetched her great grandfather from the bedroom.

One wall decorated with photographs attracted Al's attention. He got up for a closer look. Robert being a methodical academic had laid out the photo prints in chronological order beginning with the launch of Kairos. Then shots of moments from each OTT mission, from the perspective of the control room at Kairos. A few selfies and shots of Robert with Mal and of course Robert with his family, then, the launch of Tempus ... many of his kids and his wife, then one of her funeral service. As Al walked along the cavalcade of memories, there were more of Rob with Larry, and celebrations of variants of Tempus, I, II, III, IV, V. He stopped at a picture of the launch of Tempus VI, with Rob and staff members in the Tempus control room, however the photo had been torn, missing was the person who'd been standing beside Rob.

"Funny how in all those years on that wall one torn photo would grab your curiosity above all others, Alice," said a raspy old voice.

Al turned to face Robert in his wheelchair. Cheyenne wheeled him over to the lounge setting. Al sat down opposite him.

"Cheyenne, go make us some tea, would you? Sorry, we don't have coffee Alice. I remember how we used to drink gallons of the stuff at Kairos, especially when President Ri was there. Didn't he love exotic coffee? And what about that programmable wallpaper in his office Secta invented? Could sure do with some of that here."

"Coffee?"

"No, the wallpaper. These four walls have been slowly closing in on me for years … eventually they'll compress me until nothing remains but ooze," he said, with a sinister chuckle.

"Some great memories there Rob, even better than programmable wall paper, I reckon."

"I suppose so, but it does get a bit tiring reliving old memories."

"Yes mate, but they sometimes get you through."

"Sounds like the lyric of one of your songs, Alice. You still compose them?"

"Yep … so mate, who was so blatantly edited out of that photo?"

"There's that inquiring nature of yours again. I always thought of you as a rock 'n roll time tripping detective Alice. The sort of hardboiled private eye my grandfather liked so much reading like in Raymond Chandler and Carter Brown pulps. The person edited out as you put it, was Captain Cyrus F. Gordon, a Texas Ranger."

"He was at the launch of Tempus VI? When was that?"

"Huh, an easy date to remember that one, April, Fools Day, 2080 … the day war broke out, I'd turned eighty-six only the week before."

"Why edit him?"

"We had a run in."

"Can you expand on that, mate?" Al asked.

"A private matter," Rob said, dismissively.

Al eyeballed him. "Robert, you are still the director of Tempus, which is under the auspices of OTT. You are obligated to answer my questions."

"Ah, so is this an inquisition?"

"It is," Al confirmed.

He asked facetiously, "Pulling rank on me Al?"

"Sure am."

"Okay, okay," he said, irritably, knowing Alice was right—in effect he was outranked. "He wanted to know the whereabouts of the TL-100, and I wasn't prepared to part with that information. Furthermore, he claimed that because Tempus is a joint venture with Time Travel America, he figured he was entitled to have access to it," he explained, "well, that was just incorrect … UNTT delegated that responsibility to us holus-bolus."

"Let me get this straight, by the tense you're using this is ongoing … did you prevent outsiders from using the TL-100?"

"No, they just needed to apply through the correct channels. But then quite suddenly all the TL-100's went off-line."

"What do you mean off-line?"

"As you well know they were put in capital cities around the world."

"No, I didn't know that … it hasn't happened yet back in my time," Al admitted.

"Right, well they were, and each linked to a UN satellite for operation. Well, when that satellite went down during the war, so too did all the TL-100's."

"Are you saying only some people were cured of Red Wheel?"

"Yes, well it's not prevention … it's a cure … by the time people discovered they had it, the TL-100's were already down."

"So, what happened here?" Al asked.

"We of course had advance knowledge from you actually. So within hours of the nuclear strike, I put everybody here, the staff … one hundred and ten of us, through the TL-100."

"What happened to Captain Gordon and his staff?"

Robert fell silent with a guilty look. He averted his tired old powdery blue eyes from Alice's.

Al insisted. "Robert, what happened?"

Disgruntled, he snapped his answer. "We locked them out."

"Was that before or after the TL-100 went off line?"

"Before."

"Aha, so now I get it. Is that why these people Cheyenne calls the

Rangers still have a bone to pick with you?"

"Yes."

"And are they cannibals like she said?"

"We think so. We captured one a long time ago and he admitted it."

Al badgered him, "Interrogated?"

"Yes, interrogated." The old man said, sorrily.

"You really don't know do you? He might have said anything under stress possibly, torture."

"Yes, possibly," Robert reluctantly admitted.

Al sat back in his chair. He'd gotten to the bottom of the problem and it wasn't looking pretty. Captain Gordon had every right to be upset with Robert. His people and everyone else on the surface were going to be exposed to Red Wheel, and Robert had withheld the cure. There was nothing Al could do for now other than continue with the mission. Reprimanding Robert wouldn't alter anything.

"Okay, here's what's going to happen … we're going to move the TL-100 into a room on the ground floor and your people are going to organise all the sufferers of Red Wheel to pass through it."

"You haven't been listening Alice, it's off-line."

"I will have the Professor find a way around that. As well, I want you to fire up Tempus. I want to check out other TL-100 sites around the country."

Robert snapped. "Can't be done."

"Why not?"

"In 2047 after you left Japan, the UNTT implemented a boot-up code mandatory for every quantum supercomputer running a time travel facility around the globe. By then there were many … it was the only way to control time travel. Whenever the computer driving the operation was booted up, an algorithm logged on to UNTT for a unique start-up code, which provided authentication for the mission. If the authentication hadn't been approved, there would be no start-up code issued and the computer simply wouldn't boot. It was infallible—the perfect solution to stop Zen's Aquila from sending unauthorized missions. However, it also relied on the same satellite as the TL-100 network. Once that satellite went down, along with it went everything dependent on it."

The revelation gave Al cause for concern. Thinking it through, he needed to get the UN satellite back on-line. With his mind made up, he said, "Right, new plan. This is what we're going to do..."

An hour later, Alice met with Turk and Toeghan to fill them in on the situation. It was imperative to contact the Rangers. Ultimately, they would need the UN satellite reactivated, but the quicker fix for now would be to determine a way around the UNTT encryption for mobilization of both the TL-100 and Tempus, and only the Professor could provide that.

Alice used the remote to open the vortex back to Kairos and sent a handwritten message through.

Christina was leaving for the day when Kairos activated and a piece of paper materialised in the event room. She immediately phoned Secta, and within minutes, he, the Professor, and Hope had responded to her call and joined her in the control room.

Christina handed Secta the note. He read it and passed it over to the Professor.

"Well, we hadn't counted on that!" Vic acknowledged. "We haven't even designed encryption like that to know what it is."

"What if they send the TL-100 back to us?" Christina suggested.

"Good idea. I keep forgetting we have the capacity to do that now," said Secta. "Quick, let's get a note back to Al."

When Al received the message from Secta, he realised it made total sense and confronted Cheyenne. "Can you take us to the TL-100?"

Several hours later, the TL-100 unit materialised through Kairos. The Professor had hands on standby to manoeuvre it onto a trolley. It was then wheeled to the Professor's lab for the waiting team to reverse engineer.

The Professor's own handiwork impressed Vic; the TL-100 was almost a scaled-down replica of Kairos. The hoop was two metres tall with a radius of a metre. There were two steps up to it on one side and two down on the other. This was because it was mounted on a platform that held the processing components. The hoop was made of black carbon fibre, as was the platform. Simple in appearance, it performed a very complicated function.

The Professor had his assistants lay the unit on its side so he could access the cover plate on the underside of the platform. Down on hands and knees, he used an Allen or hex key to open the panel. Once removed, Vic marvelled at the innards. "Look at this Hope, what an incredible piece of ingenuity."

"It's not like you to gloat, Vic," she joked.

He glanced up at her. "It's still only an idea, and here I am looking at it. One can't help but marvel."

It took only six hours for Vic to solve the problem and build the component required to fix it. A change to the CPU on the motherboard bypassed the log-on encryption key, and it was ready to go.

Al was in the canteen with Toeghan and Turk having lunch when a vortex opened wide enough for a note to pass. He grabbed it and read it out. "Vic said it's done. He'll now duplicate the fix so it can easily be fitted to other TL-100s ... Brilliant. He'll send it through in twenty minutes ... Okay, let's go to the reception area to receive it."

The problem of getting Tempus back on-line wasn't going to be as easy. The OTT brains trust of the Professor, Secta, Hope, and Christina would now burn the midnight oil trying to come up with a solution.

Electra had chosen to travel to 2112 as Daniel Walker. He was shocked by his surroundings when he stepped out of the vortex in Angel City. Standing amidst the rubble of a destroyed high-rise building and accessing the memory of Gorrick, he quickly determined that the building had been Zen HQ, the designated target. To locate Dr Mennis, he accessed the metadata on Gorrick's OSCI to set up a ping that would rebound off the doctor's implant and lead him to her.

Navigating through the debris, stumbling over rubble and twisted scaffolding, he finally cleared the obstructions and made his way toward a cluster of low-rise houses several blocks away.

Honor was alerted to the sound of footsteps outside and went to the door. Armed with a pistol, she took aim and then wrenched it open.

"Honor."

"Commander Walker?" Honor questioned, stupefied by his presence and slowly lowering the weapon.

"May I come in?" he asked, courteously.

"Are you alone?" she asked, distrustfully, trying to glimpse past him.

"Yes, I am."

"Come in," she said, and ushered him inside, quickly closing the door behind him.

As they walked, following her to the kitchen, he commented, "You seem on edge."

"We are a target ... they blame us for their miserable existence," she complained.

"I see. Where is Dr Mennis?"

Honor sat at the kitchen table, and Walker took a seat opposite her. He wasn't used to seeing her dressed in rough clothing: jeans and a T-shirt.

"She is out foraging for food. Did you come through Aquila?"

"Yes."

"To take me back ... I hope?"

"Yes."

Her thin lips struggled to vaguely curve into a smile.

"What food is she searching for?" he asked.

Her eyes searched him in a silence that lengthened past light-hearted banter. "Mostly rats. There's not much else to eat in this godforsaken world."

"That doesn't sound very appetising."

"Beggars can't be choosers," she snapped.

The front door opened, and a man entered. It took a few seconds for Walker to realise it was actually Dr Mennis dressed as a man. She was carrying two dead rats by the tails in one hand and a shotgun in the other. She stopped abruptly upon seeing Walker.

"Who is this?" she asked, impertinently, flopping the dead rats onto the kitchen table.

"This is Commander Daniel Walker. He has come to take me back to my time," Honor said, curtly.

"No, it is not," Ursula said, propping the shotgun against the table. She took a seat. "Are you?" she added, scrutinising him.

"You tell me," Walker returned serve smugly.

"You, are Cronus. I should know … I created you."

Honor flinched when Walker suddenly morphed into Electra, but without hair—bald.

"This is my form in the past," she said, her voice changed to feminine. "I am Electra. I replaced Gorrick, who is dead, and I host En-Lil. Hello, mother."

Her referring to Ursula as 'mother' shocked Honor. There was a pause while the three of them took stock of the situation.

Then Electra said, "You will both return with me." She morphed back into Walker. Her voice changed to male. "Shall we go?"

"Absolutely," Mennis said, proudly.

Honor glimpsed at the two dead rats on the table and grumbled, "Let's get out of here. I never want to see another of those ugly things again."

A Philippine Navy chopper landed in the vacant car park of a disused single-storey ex-military warehouse on the outskirts of Davao City. It had flown over the area once to reconnoitre. The pilot had spotted a semi-trailer with a shipping container loaded, parked at the rear of the building. They assumed Handerson Bolt was inside, perhaps preparing to load the sarcophagus and the treasure if it hadn't been moved already.

Jax had immediately called Amaya for backup, and help was on the way. However, as the chopper descended, the pilot spotted movement—one of the large sliding doors to the warehouse was opening. Fearing that Bolt had detected the chopper and was about to escape, they had no choice but to land and confront the situation.

CHAPTER 9
ARACHNOPHOBIA

WHILE ALICE WAS speaking to Cheyenne, he was suddenly interrupted by a voice in his head, a voice he instantly recognised as En-Ki.

"Another distraction, Alice. Do you know how difficult it is to locate you when you alter your temporal continuum?"

Cheyenne was wondering why Alice was standing dazed as if in a daydream after he'd asked whether they had any vehicles. She was about to answer when she noticed his eyes glaze over, and even though he was looking at her, he was actually staring at a point past her, at nothing.

"Alice? Alice? Are you alright?" she tentatively asked.

"What do you want, En-Ki?" Al asked mentally.

"The sarcophagus must not be destroyed by En-Lil. It is elemental to the quest."

"Why don't you just transport the thing then?" Al said psychically.

"Alice!" Cheyenne shouted, beginning to worry.

"That's not feasible, Alice," En-Ki claimed.

"Why is it important, and who's inside it?" Al questioned.

"Alice!" Cheyenne insisted and was about to walk away when he snapped out of it. En-Ki had gone.

"Oh, sorry Cheyenne. I have an implant that sometimes interrupts me."

"I'm glad ... that was freaky," she said, relieved, hands on hips.

"They say before the war everyone was fitted with a neural implant."

"Yep, that's true," Al said, vaguely, still mentally trying to process En-Ki's warning.

Cheyenne had been rattled by the sudden change in his attitude. "You asked about vehicles. No, we don't have any other than Great Grandad's collection."

The statement revitalised Alice somewhat. "What's he got?"

"Come, I'll show you."

On the way to the elevator, Al stopped at the door to his lodgings and knocked. "I'll get the others."

Turk and Toegs came out of the room and joined them.

During the elevator ride up to the first floor, Alice was still noticeably introspective.

"You alright, mate?" Turk asked.

"Uh? ... Oh, yeah, sorry, just mulling over some stuff. Got a weird message. I'll tell you 'bout it later," Al said.

The elevator doors opened on level one. Cheyenne led them out into a dark corridor.

"Geez, I'm beginning to hate dark corridors and tunnels," Al complained, "they're everywhere I bloody go."

They reached a red-painted door that Cheyenne pushed through. On the other side was a subterranean car park with around twenty objects underneath tarpaulins.

"Looks like no-one comes in here much," Turk said.

"You're right, it used to be totally off-limits, but now that Grandad's so old, he doesn't enforce his rules as much. Under each tarp is a vehicle of some kind, mostly old gas-guzzling jalopies from a bygone era, antiques, but over here..." She walked past the first row of cars and stopped. "Are my favourites."

There were four tarp-covered objects, only a quarter the size of the others. Alice was still looking distracted, so Turk uncovered one of them. It was a Harley Davidson, in pristine condition. Turk was impressed and checked it over, a true enthusiast.

"A Livewire VI ... nuclear pellet driven. They only made a few of them before the war, the previous models were electric, but this model had heaps more grunt."

"Take a look at the next one," Cheyenne said, with a grin of anticipation, expecting if Turk had been impressed by the Livewire VI, then he'd be knocked out by what was next.

Turk pulled back the cover and reacted exactly how Cheyenne had anticipated.

"I'll be damned!" he exclaimed. "A genuine Harley prototype custom pellet-driven 1250 chopper. It must be the only one in existence."

"No, they made two of them. This one in white livery and under the next tarp, one in black."

"I'll be—!" Turk exclaimed in awe.

"Do you think they'll work?" Toegs questioned.

"Knowing Morri's Wilson J-Car, which is also pellet-driven, there'd be no question of it," Turk explained.

Al uncovered the black one. "All right! This one's got my name on it."

"Can you ride, Toegs?" Cheyenne asked.

"Grew up riding trail bikes on me dad's farm, second nature," she said with an excited grin. The Livewire would suit me just fine."

"Okay, now we have the means to pay the Rangers a visit," Al said.

"Are you serious? Is that what this is about?" Cheyenne roared, angrily.

Al shot her a cold stare, "Yes, Cheyenne. The reason we brought the TL-100 up to the lobby is for you people to commence a healing program for others, beginning with the Rangers."

"There's no way, they'll kill you … they'll kill us. You have no idea what you're dealing with … they are monsters," she barked, dismissing the idea.

"Do you know that from first-hand knowledge?" Turk asked.

"Well, no. But—" she stopped.

The door behind them opened, and Rip came over.

"Stories … that's all … and the one you captured who said the

Rangers were cannibals, I'd say was tortured into saying that," Al growled.

"What are you talking about? You've got no idea," Rip barked indignantly.

"So, you've experienced the Rangers personally, have you, Rip?" Al demanded of the younger man.

"No, but unlike you, I've no reason to doubt what we've been told," he argued.

"What if it's not true?" Al countered. "What if you've all been living a lie?"

"I don't think it's a wise move for you to just turn up here and rock the status quo. After the fall, everything changed," Rip snarled.

Al could tell Rip was getting riled up and figured there was more to his anger than it seemed, so he delved a little deeper.

"What's the fall?" Al asked.

Rip's eyes narrowed, "The great collapse of capitalist nations ... after the war."

"You guys weren't even born ... there were no schools, no libraries; the only window on the world that existed after the war for you was word of mouth. Well, what if that wasn't so accurate, or that you were taught certain things for a reason?" Turk questioned.

Rip snapped back spitefully, "And what would that reason be?"

"What if someone had an agenda and wanted to protect what they had at the expense of everyone else?" Al suggested.

Rip wasn't having any of it. "What a load of crap!" he shouted, turned on his heels, and stormed out of the room.

"Why the hell's he got a rat up his butt?" Al questioned Cheyenne, baffled by his excessive reaction.

"His great-grandfather, Larry Freeman, was killed by Cyrus Gordon, captain of the Rangers," she explained.

"Right, now it makes sense. Would he still be alive?" Al asked.

"Who, Gordon? I don't know ... maybe, he was in his late twenties in 2080 I think ... so he'd be what?" she pondered.

Being the same age, it was easy for Turk to reckon. "Sixty this year."

Al raised an eyebrow at Turk; he didn't think of him as being sixty.

There was nothing he could do to placate Rip, so Al decided to leave it for later. For now, gnawing at him, was what En-Ki had gone out of his way to tell him. Blake and Vee in the Philippines, looking for the platinum sarcophagus, had now become more significant. It was that old gut feeling he'd had that was right once again.

Cheyenne pointed to a ramp that led up to the ground floor and then handed Al a remote to operate the sliding metal exit doors.

As they were walking back to the bikes, Cheyenne admitted, "There's another reason we don't go to the surface ... the Trapdoors."

"The what?" Al asked.

"Spiders the size of a cow. Well, that's what they say anyway ... I've never seen one, but then again, I've never been to the surface either. It all started the year after the fall—"

"Spiders, the size of cows? ... I hate bloody spiders," Al groaned.

"And when was that exactly?" Turk asked.

"When the nukes struck, so 2085. Gordon's Rangers mowed down General Freeman and three others in an ambush when they were on their way to a meeting with him. In retaliation, Granddad sent six more men, but only three returned ... Trapdoors got the others."

"How do you know Gordon's men ambushed Freeman?" Al asked.

"Granddad told us. We know the Trapdoors killed the others because three of them came back to tell the story, and then Granddad went out with a posse to find the three missing."

"Trapdoor spiders might have killed Freeman's team, not Gordon?" Al proposed.

"That would be more likely," Turk agreed.

"Right, well before we go, I need another word with Robert to confirm these stories. Take me to him," Al ordered.

"He'd be taking his nap," Cheyenne countered defensively.

"Not today he ain't." Alice led them towards the elevators.

In the quarters, Al waited for Cheyenne to leave him alone with

Rob. The old guy was grumpy for being awakened prematurely.

"Sorry to disturb your rest, mate, but I don't have time to burn. I need to return soon; something's come up. But before I do, I aim to have the TL-100 operational here, healing Red Wheel sufferers."

Rob grumbled, "I told you before … you'll never get it working; it's—"

Al cut him off, "Listen, you can drop the grumpy old man act with me, alright! I'm older than you…" he paused a moment to let that sink in. "We sent the TL-100 back through Kairos, and the Professor fixed it, so it works fine … now, I need some answers, and I want the truth."

Rob realised Alice had his number and muttered begrudgingly, "Go on then."

"How did Larry Freeman die?"

"The Rangers—"

"Consider what I just said to you, Rob … the bloody truth."

"Alright, alright … I don't know, no-one does. Does that make you feel better?" he snapped.

"No, it doesn't, mate. You've had these people living a lie for an entire generation." Al was angry. He moved closer to Rob, who straightened up in his wheelchair under the threat. Al spoke sternly, "I'm going to have Rip come in here, and you're going to tell him that, you got that?"

"Why upset the apple cart, Alice? We've lived in peace here until you showed up."

"Because you've been living a lie, mate, and that's come at the cost of innocent lives. This cannibal nonsense isn't true either, is it?"

The old man nodded slowly.

"What about the Trapdoor spiders?" Al pressed.

"No, no, no," he pleaded in a panic. "That is true, I swear. I saw one myself … a horrible big black thing. When three out of the party of six that went out to scout for Larry didn't return, and the survivors were so terror-stricken, I took a few more guys and one of the survivors with me to see if we could help the three who had allegedly been taken. We were collecting the remains of one of them; the other two had been pulled down into the ground. That's when one of those cursed things shot out of a hole like a bolt of lightning, snatched one of the boys, and was hauling him back to its nest. The cursed thing was the size of a small car, as dark as night, hairy like an enormous tarantula, with long spindly legs and massive mandibles they call pedipalps.

"Regular-sized Trapdoors are native to Texas and relatively harmless. We've all seen plenty of them before. They dwell in small tunnels capped off with a door. But these were no ordinary Trapdoor spiders. They had been affected by radiation or something and had grown to an immense size."

"Anyhow, we shot and killed it. The boy survived. That's why I can testify to the existence of the damn things. I believe when the shockwave from the bomb hit the military chemical plant at Irving Air Base just forty-five minutes from here, some chemicals were released that mixed with the radiation, causing the mutation. But hey," he coughed and spluttered, "it worked for us ... the spiders have kept the Rangers away. But I suppose at the same time, it prevented us from going anywhere as well. If you're thinking about visiting the Rangers, I'd think again. I know you've faced plenty of monsters in your time, Al, but there could be thousands of those creatures out there by now, and they'd be pretty damn hungry ... there wouldn't be much left to eat out there."

"Yeah, it's not like anything I do doesn't come with a challenge like that. I can handle most anything, but spiders ... nah, I've got arachnophobia ... can't stand the damn things. We're taking your bikes for the trip."

"My pride and joy. Well, if anything can get you past the trapdoors, it'd be them. You know, aside from those bikes, the most enjoyable days of my long life were the early days of Kairos. The excitement of bringing my theory to fruition ... the adventures you went on ... into the great unknown, and how in the early days, we hung on the edge of our seats waiting for you to pop back through that big old hoop, naked to the world," he chuckled, then spluttered, coughing desperately trying to regain his breath.

Alice patted his old mate on the back.

Once his coughing fit was over, he eyeballed Alice and added, "You know, Al, I even know some of your exploits you haven't even been on yet. Ha! Isn't that one of those things Secta used to call a time paradox?"

"Yep, and he still does."

Rob was right; he'd lived through time that Alice hadn't yet encountered, and because he was in the OTT management loop as director of Tempus, he knew the outcomes. It was a weird thought.

"Well, for the sake of the prime directive, don't tell me what I'm going to get up to," Al said, with a friendly sarcastic snigger.

"You're a unique bloke, Al. I'm privileged to have known you, let alone to call you a friend."

"Mate, when I was a kid, they used to laugh at me because I was different, while at the same time, I was laughing at them for all being the same."

That brought a chuckle from Rob followed by another coughing fit.

Spiders or no spiders, it was time to ship out. Al, Turk, and Toegs mounted their bikes and cranked them up. The Livewire was so quiet that Toegs wasn't even sure it was running. But the same couldn't be said of the other two; they thundered like true Harleys, their sounds causing a ripple of anxiety deep in Turk's gut. It reminded him of the choppers belonging to the Rebels that, so long ago, had inflicted so much pain on him and his sister. However, as they roared out into the daylight and the warm wind hit their faces, any anxiety shifted with the gears to maximum satisfaction.

CHAPTER 10
STAND DOWN

BLAKE WAS LEADING the assault. Gun up, with Vee and Jax trailing him, he moved through the searing heat of the day, commando-style, along the side of the warehouse, back-hugging the wall. With the least amount of action experience, Holman lagged behind.

The sound of a door opening behind them stopped Blake. He swivelled around and saw Handerson Bolt had ambushed them from a side door. He had Holman held with an arm around his neck from behind and a .45-calibre pistol up to his head.

Safely in the doorway, Bolt glared at Jax and shouted, "Stop right there and drop your gun, De Ville ... you too, Green ... and your friend there. Now!"

Bolt towered over Holman, who had a look on his face like he'd soiled his underpants.

"Do it!" Holman squealed.

"Stay calm, everyone," Blake shouted, with one hand up in a stop motion, while he slowly bent down to place his automatic at his feet. Vee copied, as did Jax.

"Right, now let's sort this out," Bolt said, with a gravelly voice. "I have something you all badly want. What's it worth to you? Do I hear the first bid?" he said, with a snide, sick snigger.

"How much have you been offered?" Jax questioned.

Weak in the knees, Holman was breaking out in a sweat.

"As if I'm going to tell you that ... but I'll say this much, it's substantial," Bolt boasted, gruffly.

As he finished speaking, a big sliding door ahead of him slid open, and four Filipinos stepped out with assault rifles aimed at them. They were now outgunned.

Jax spoke up quickly to keep it civil. "You know who I work for and what they can afford. Name your price, Bolt. You're not unfamiliar with this sort of extortion."

"Watch your mouth, De Ville. It's called bargaining, and you know me well enough to pull the trigger if I get offended," Bolt sneered.

He was right; she knew exactly what he was capable of. This wasn't their first encounter, but she needed to buy some time.

"Why don't you just let Holman go before he has a heart attack, then we can negotiate this like adults," Blake suggested.

"Both of you are trying to buy time ... you've got the cavalry coming. Get on your phone and stop them now, De Ville, or you can say goodbye to buddy-boy here."

"You overestimate my influence here in Davao..." Jax snapped.

"Do it! ... Stop them, Jax... yes, yes, she's got backup coming," Holman squealed like a wounded pig.

"I'll count to six," Bolt said grimly. "One..."

Jax stood her ground.

"Two."

Blake and Vee were beginning to wonder why she was testing him. "Three."

"Damn it, Jax, make the call!" Holman shouted, hysterically.

"Four."

Jax pulled her phone and dialled. "Amaya, yes ... stand down, I repeat, stand down. I'll call you back," she glared at Bolt. "There, it's done."

"Smash the phone on the ground ... now!" Bolt growled. Then, to emphasise it, he pushed the pistol hard into Holman's right temple.

Jax irreverently hurled the phone against the wall, and it smashed into bits.

"You too, Blake ... and your friend," Bolt snarled.

Blake and Vee produced their cellphones and followed suit.

Bang! A spray of blood painted the warehouse wall. The shot killed Holman instantly. Bolt let him drop to the ground and then said disinterestedly, "That's one less I have to worry about ... now, inside."

He signalled his men to cover the three of them to enter the warehouse through the big sliding door. Bolt slipped inside through the smaller door he'd come out of, dragged Holman's body inside, and then locked the door behind him. His men would dump the body later in a place it would never be found.

The sarcophagus had been loaded onto a forklift ready for the shipping container on the truck outside. There were no signs of the rest of the treasure.

Keeping his pistol trained on them, Bolt growled with a pointed finger, "Go sit at the table there."

The old Naval warehouse built during the 1940s had been deserted for at least half a century. The floor was thick with dust and grime; most of the windows were smashed, the shattered shards scattered about the floor. Other than the old rectangular wooden table with six folding aluminium chairs and the forklift, the rest of the vast space was empty.

They sat at the table as ordered. Bolt took a seat at the head, and the four Filipinos remained standing, fingers on triggers.

"I have no idea what all the fuss is about. You can't even open the damn thing, but I'll tell you what, it's damn heavy. Lucky, I had Henry and Ito do all the heavy lifting getting it out of the cave," Bolt scoffed.

"Then you killed them," Blake said.

"They would've died anyway; both had broken legs."

"That you'd broken after they'd done all the hard work," Blake snarled.

Bolt gave him a cold, hard stare. "It happens ... you know that."

The guy was a real piece of work, merciless. Vee couldn't take her eyes off the man. Blake's description of his granite head was spot-on; it was as though it'd been carved out of solid rock.

"Cut to the chase, Bolt. What do you want for it? I'm over the theatrics," Jax grated.

"Two mil, you know the drill."

"Difficult to arrange without my cellphone," she said, smugly.

Using his free hand, he reached into the pocket of his dungarees and pulled out two cellphones.

Vee couldn't get over the size of the man's biceps and chest. They were emphasised by him wearing only a blue singlet with jungle camouflage dungarees and black army boots. He reminded her of Chip Hazard from the animated Disney film, Small Soldiers.

"Always carry an untraceable spare," he said, smugly, and then slid a cellphone across the table to Jax. "Call, arrange it. I'll give you the account code. When the cash registers, I'll be texted an alert. Remember, I used to work for the firm. I know all the tricks."

Blake pointed out, "Trouble is, how do we know you'll keep your end of the deal? You don't have much of a reputation."

Bolt put his pistol down on the table, dug around in a pocket, and pulled out a metal container. He opened the lid, took out a Cohiba Robusto cigar, and rolled it between his fingers, listening and studying it like it was an artefact worth millions. Once satisfied, he drew a match from the container, struck it on the leather sole of his boot, and lit the cigar; cool, calm, and collected. He took a big toke and then blew a stream of smoke at Blake.

The atmosphere was stifling enough for Vee with the heat and humidity, and now the stench of cigar smoke.

"Isn't this a non-smoking area?" Vee snarled, facetiously.

"Yeah, funny … I love a sassy dame," Bolt squeezed out through the cigar clenched between his teeth.

"You've been watching too many old gangster movies, Bolt," Vee returned the service with interest.

Jax was staring at the phone on the table, contemplating her next move.

Bolt wrenched the cigar out of his mouth and pointed it at her, held between two fingers. "I'm running out of patience here, De Ville."

Vee figured his New Jersey accent had become more pronounced since he lit the cigar and wondered why.

"I don't know, Bolt. I agree with Blake … you have the propensity for not keeping your word," Jax said, smoothly.

Blake was admiring her savoir-faire when Bolt picked up the pistol, aimed it at him, and cocked the trigger.

"Make a move, De Ville, or another one bites the dust," Bolt sang the line of the Queen song past the cigar clenched between his teeth.

Jax knew he'd do it. She hung on a pregnant pause for as long as she could, then picked up the phone. A sly glance at Blake that Bolt missed, and she hurled the phone at him. At the same time, Blake brought up his hands underneath the table and flipped it on top of Bolt. The phone whacked him on the right eye … the gun went off, missing everyone. Vee jumped up and hurled her chair wildly at the four Filipinos.

Blake was on top of Bolt in a flash. He reefed the gun out of his grasp, shoved it hard up under his chin, cocked the trigger, and growled loudly, "Call 'em off. Now!"

Bolt knew he was done. "Okay, okay, don't lose your rag. Lower your guns!" he barked, angrily. They obeyed and then raised their hands in surrender.

Right then, the sliding doors opened, and Amaya rushed in with four military police.

Jax shook her head and satirically said, "Took you long enough."

Amaya told the cops in Cebuano to apprehend the four Filipinos and then smiled at Jax. "Traffic."

Fortunately, Jax and Amaya had previously agreed that the phrase 'stand down' for the sake of the mission would have the exact opposite meaning.

Interstate forty-five was somewhat reminiscent of what Turk had experienced near Avalon, in that it was strewn with burnt-out derelict vehicles. However, that's where the comparison ended. Unlike the forested surroundings at home, this stretch was barren and dry. What had once been prime cattle grazing country had been transformed by climate change, worsened by nuclear fallout, into a desolate, arid wasteland. The heat was blistering. Conditions were so harsh that they had to pause to cover their mouths and noses with masks to filter out the dust and protect their skin from the scorching wind. The fear of encountering giant Trapdoor spiders was enough to prevent them from lingering, and they quickly resumed their journey.

Maintaining an average speed of a hundred and fifty kilometres an hour, they soon reached the outskirts of Waxahachie. They got as close as they deemed safe and parked the bikes under the shade of a tree to formulate a plan. They had been informed that the Rangers' headquarters was on North Grand Avenue in downtown Waxahachie, and it was believed to have an underground bunker where survivors might be living.

As Al surveyed the devastation of Waxahachie, memories of his previous visits came flooding back. In his time, it was a vibrant town, but now it resembled the aftermath of a colossal stomping. The shockwave from the nuclear blast had literally levelled the town. He checked the radiation levels, finding them at eleven, which was acceptable. Al turned to Turk, who had taken a seat to rest in the shade of one of the few remaining trees.

Al sought Turk's opinion. "You're more experienced with this kind of thing than me, mate. How should we make contact?"

"It's gonna to be quite different here, Al. Back home, we're known, but here, we're outsiders. I think we need to employ a strategy similar to what we did in Queanbeyan with the Skulls. We should just walk right in and go with the classic 'take me to your leader' approach."

Toegs chimed in with a different perspective. She had been listening while scanning the town's remnants for signs of life. She interjected, "I see someone over there."

Turk sprang to his feet and joined her and Al to investigate.

Indeed, there was a figure limping toward the ruins. Al chased after him, shouting, "Hey! Hey there! Hello!"

The man, crouched over with the help of a walking stick, halted when he heard Al and waited for him.

Navigating through the debris like an obstacle course, Al finally reached the man without incident. Puffing out of breath, he introduced himself, "Hey there, hope I didn't startle you. The name's Al. Do you live here?"

The old man examined him, squinting in the sunlight. With his straggly white hair trailing down to his waist and ragged clothes, and his posture bent by arthritis, he embodied the image of Father Time.

"You'll need to speak up, young fella. I'm hard of hearing," he croaked, raising his volume.

Al moved a step closer and raised his voice. "I'm Al ... do you live here?"

The man nodded and responded with a Texan drawl, "Hmm, sure do. Lived here all-ma life. See what's left of that building over there yonder?" He pointed with a withered finger.

Al examined the tangle of bricks and twisted metal.

"That was my house. I built it ... they destroyed it. Bastards!" With one eye squinting and the other wide glaring at Al, he snapped, "You one of 'em?"

"No, I've come to aid the afflicted."

"Yer must be talking 'bout Halo. Yeah, goddamn thing wiped most of us out. There are a few left down below ... that's where I call home these days."

"Is there a man named Cyrus Gordon down there?" Al asked.

Again, with one eye squinted, the old man glanced at Turk and then at Toegs, who were making their way toward them. "Well, would you look at that ... a young woman! Haven't seen one of them since before the war. We can't reproduce, yer know?"

"Yes, I know. They're with me ... Cyrus, you were about to tell me about Cyrus Gordon."

"Funny accent you got there, boy. Gordon, yeah, ole Captain

Gordon ... he's still here. He's got Halo, only came down with it a couple of weeks ago. Y'all know 'im?"

"No, but we'd like to meet him. Can you take us to him?"

"What is that weird accent of y'all? Can hardly understand yer."

"We're from Oceana," Al said.

"Aussies, geez ... bin a while since I've heard one of them."

A single powdery blue eye flashed at Al from behind long strands of hair. "I s'pose so, y'all better leave any weapons here, they're forbidden at the Rangers ... that's where we live you know, the Rangers bunker ... I was a Ranger myself in me younger days ... come from a long line of 'em," he explained, forlornly.

As his friends joined him Al made introductions, "This is Toegs and Turk ... and you're?"

"Clay Morgan ... but folks call me Cowpoke."

Al grinned. "Okay Cowpoke, show us a safe place to dump our weapons. Lead on."

Cowpoke led them at a slow pace along a track between the vestiges of buildings mumbling inaudibly along the way, then stopped at what were the remains of a jailhouse.

"This here was the offices of the Texas Rangers. Follow me, watch your step." He led them into the shell of what was quite a large three-storey red brick building and then stopped again, this time at a door in the end wall.

"See that metal chest over yonder?" he pointed his cane. "Put your weapons inside of it. They'll be safe. No-one will want to take 'em ... we're a peaceful bunch round here."

They loaded their weapons into the chest, then closed it. Once done Cowpoke punched a code into a small mechanism beside the door, it clicked and when he pulled it open, a small landing and an elevator door were revealed. He pressed the call button and a servo sounded.

While waiting Turk asked, "Is there much food to find in town?"

"We took everything and brought it down into the bunker after the fall. We also combed the area for survivors and food. A good thing too, coz none of us could go scavenging any more, we're all too old now ... couldn't breed you know? ... Did I already say that?"

"Yes, you did," Al affirmed.

"Sorry, I sometimes repeat myself ... I say, sometimes I repeat myself. Ha! Ha!" he joked.

"Yeah, old age, huh?" Turk suggested.

"Yep son, you get hair growing in places you've got no need for," he chortled as his own joke.

The elevator arrived. "You must have a reactor down there?" Turk said, as the followed Cowpoke into the space only fit to take four or five.

"Yep, down below is linked by tunnels to the former Texas National Guard building with its nuke reactor. Funny how the very thing that's killing us is also keepin' us alive."

"Yeah well. the same can be said of the sun," Toegs said.

"You'r dang right, lassie," he said, playfully nudging Turk in the ribs. "One smart chickadee you is."

The floor indicator had ticked over to twenty-five as the elevator slowed.

"Here we are," Cowpoke announced.

"A long way down," Turk observed.

"Needed to be, that dang bomb exploded not too far from here ... scorched the crap outa everything and everyone ... that's why only a few of us survived ... just the folk privy to this place."

Twenty people all in wheelchairs were assembled to greet them when the elevator door opened. Cowpoke led his new friends out and then addressed the gathering that was mumbling contentiously in unison. "This is Al, shush! I said, this is Al and then there's Toegs and Turk, they've come here to help us." Another murmur of discontent erupted from the congregation. But Cowpoke put up a hand to stop it and then stressed forcefully, "Okay, okay, cut the dang, grumbling. This is the first time anyone has come to give us a hand and they claim they can cure Halo ... so it would be best to treat them with a little respect rather than contempt."

A regal-looking old guy wearing the obligatory Texan cowboy hat, who looked to Alice like pictures he had seen of the American wild-west legend William Cody, otherwise known as Buffalo Bill, complete with a long droopy white moustache and a goatee beard, long grey locks to his shoulders, a strong face with burning intellect in sapphire blue eyes, wheeled ahead of the rest and held out a hand.

"Captain Cyrus Gordon at your service, sir," he purred in a gravelly full-on Texan accent.

"G'day mate," Al said, taking his hand and giving it a firm shake.

Cyrus barked, "What's that accent, son? You English?"

Al shook his head, "No, we're from Oceana."

"Aussies! Well, I'll be damned! I met a few Aussies years ago that worked at Desertron."

"You mean Dr Robert James and some of his staff?" Al quizzed.

Another murmur of uneasiness broke out at the mention of the Doctor.

"Yeah, I trust you're a better stamp of dude than he," Cyrus said in a deprecating tone.

Cowpoke caught the tone and jumped in. "You boys look like you could do with a beer. Aussies are famous for their love of it, ain't they?"

"Especially if it's icy cold, Cowpoke," Turk said, cheerfully.

"Well, that I can promise. Come on, follow me. Come along, Cyrus," he said, leading them in though the gap in the ranks the wheelchair-bound man made for them. A short walk along a well-lit corridor brought them to a bar. It was decorated like you'd expect in Texas: cowboy and rock 'n roll memorabilia on the walls, cowhide stools at round tables. Cowpoke slipped in behind the bar while Cyrus and the others settled around a table. All of the others in wheelchairs had left them to it.

Turk asked, "How many of you down here, Cyrus?"

"Well now, there are two hundred, but there were two thousand … they all died from Halo."

"Yeah, Red Wheel took about the same of our folk," Turk sympathised.

"Red Wheel? What's that?"

"What you call Halo, we call Red Wheel," Al explained. "It's the shape of the rash that comes up when you contract it."

Cyrus showed the underside of his wrist, "Yer talkin' bout this, son?"

It was a nasty Red Wheel.

"Yes mate, that's it," Turk said.

"No matter what yer call it, the dang thing has the same effect … a slow miserable death."

"Well, that's what we're here to cure," Al professed.

"How's that?" Cyrus barked.

"We have a device called a TL-100…"

Cyrus cut him off. "We know all about that dang thing! James has it at Tempus but hogs it so no-one else can use it," he shouted, getting all riled up.

Cowpoke arrived with bottles of Corona. "Now, now, settle down, Cyrus, hear the man out, he's on our side remember."

"That was a mistake of the doctor's … a terrible one. He blamed you for the death of Larry Freeman," Al said.

"Ha! You hear that, Cowpoke? James blames me for the death of Larry!"

Cowpoke handed out the beers then raised his bottle in toast, "To fixin' Red Wheel!"

"You bet," Al said, and then took a long swig. "Ah, that's fantastic. Why don't you tell us your side of the story, Cyrus?"

Cyrus took a big swig, glared at Cowpoke and then nodded, "All right, I'll tell yer."

CHAPTER 11
TALES OF THE TEXAS RANGERS

"**L**ARRY AND I** had arranged to meet on neutral ground at the remains of a Gas Station on Interstate forty-five. I say neutral ground because there was an impasse in negotiation between Dr Robert and myself that Larry wanted to mend. He had told us about the TL-100 and what it could do, but Dr Robert was denying it could be used, said it weren't working. We figured he just didn't wanna help us. At that stage, none of us knew whether we were infected or not. It had only been Larry who'd told me in confidence that the disease would lay dormant and strike us in old age … when the immune system ain't at its best. We all felt fine, so we didn't worry too much. Some that were closer to ground zero had been more affected by radiation, but most of us had had enough warning to get to the shelters and so didn't feel any bad effects.

"But Larry kept insisting we needed to pass as many people through the TL-100 as possible, to kill the dormant virus. And then Dr Robert was insisting the TL-100 was out of commission. I don't know, maybe it was and maybe Larry thought it would come back on-line sooner or later … but there seemed to be discord between the two of them over something. Never did find out what…

"Anyways, I'm drifting off track … I was with two of my officers waiting for Larry at the old gas station … it was sundown … we saw his vehicle coming our way. Then, everything went strange … weird … silent. You know that feeling you get in your guts when something bad's about to happen? Well, Larry's vehicle pulled up and he got out ... there were two guys with him. There was a bit of cover in the remains of the gas station, so we'd set up a table and had enough beers to go round for a powwow. But just as Larry and his buddies were walking over to us, from out of nowhere, came this goddamned gigantic Trapdoor spider, I swear it was the size of a family car ... it came outa nowhere and as quick as a flash, it snatched Larry. The dang thing literally lifted him up with its jowls standing on its hind legs and then carted him off screaming and a yellin ... we was thunderstruck! We'd drawn our guns but hell we would've hit Larry if we fired. Then, it just disappeared backwards down a hole, taking Larry with it. Damned if we could find that hole! Once we heard that eerie noise of the dang trapdoor slam shut it just looked like any other chunk of desert.

"We was looking for it when another six of them things came out of the ground and came after us. They got one of my men and the two with Larry ... we stood there firing at 'em and killed two but we couldn't save the men. When we saw more coming out of the ground, we sprinted to our vehicle like there was no tomorrow and hightailed it the hell out of Dodge as fast as we could go, and we've never been back since."

He paused. The story was terrifying. Al finally spoke up. "Well, that explains a lot. Robert sent out a search party for Larry, and only one of them made it back ... so he took more men and went out to check the guy's story of the giant spiders for himself and was attacked. They killed one spider but made it back ... that's why they've never ventured out of Tempus again. I think over time, an urban myth developed suggesting you murdered Larry, and I think that story suited Robert because between that and the thought of giant spiders, no-one was ever going to brave it out of the base. As for the TL-100, he was telling the truth ... the satellite that operated it had gone down during the war, rendering it inoperative ... but we've managed to get it back on-line."

It was resolved that given the condition of the inflicted, it would be wiser to bring the TL-100 to the Rangers rather than take the ailing Rangers to Tempus. To arrange that they would need to return to Tempus, but before leaving Al went to the bathroom where he opened a vortex through which he sent Kairos the coordinates of the Rangers' bunker. That way, if they were unable to get Tempus back on-line, they could send the TL-100 to Kairos and have them send it on to the Rangers' Bunker.

They promised Cowpoke and Cyrus to return as soon as possible, knowing that every hour counted for the poor folk infected with Red Wheel.

Cowpoke took them back to the surface to collect their weapons.

It was growing dark. Cowpoke said, gravely, "It's near sundown … that'll put you in danger of encountering them giant spiders on the way to Tempus. You're gonna need back-up."

"What you got in mind?" Al asked.

"Follow me."

He walked off with more vigour and determination than they'd seen in him before; it was as though the challenge had lifted his spirits and rejuvenated the man. He stopped at one of the most intact buildings in the area and said, "Your bikes are just over there, see?"

Al could see them nearby. "Good-O, what's in here?"

"A one-seater vehicle I use for emergencies. It's armoured with a few handy weapons. I'll tail you to Tempus for protection."

"You sure?" Turk asked, worried for the old guy doing it alone.

"You bet I am, pity I'm the last man standing to watch yer back but I'm a Texas Ranger, don't y'all forget that," he said, proudly. "Go on … git!"

They headed for the bikes. Once mounted up they drove to highway forty-five and stopped. After a few minutes, a Tankette about the size of a family car, on wheels not tracks, painted in desert camouflage and bearing the famous red, white and blue lone star shield of the Texas Rangers, pulled onto the road. When it got close, Cowpoke's head popped out of the turret and he yelled, "Ain't she a bewdy?"

His obvious excitement caused Al and Turk to exchange an appreciative smile. They knew how invigorating it could feel to be depended on. Al signalled and they headed off in convoy in the direction of the setting sun. Once they reached the open road, the three bikes stayed abreast followed closely by the APC; that way, they all had eyes front, ready for anything. When they came to an obstruction on the road, Al would lead them round it in single file.

The sun was dipping fast on the horizon, leaving the afterglow the only light. The ruin of the Gas Station Cyrus had spoken of was on the side of the highway on an off ramp only two hundred metres ahead. The Tempus building was still fifteen minutes away. Now they were on edge; this was where Larry Freeman and his comrades had been attacked and killed, and it was almost the same time of day. Al's first thought was to hit the throttle and rip past the place, but there was no knowing where the spiders might be. He decided it was best to remain calm and vigilant.

No sooner had that thought left his mind, he saw giant hairy legs emerging from beside the road ahead. Then, across the road, another massive spider loomed out of a burrow. Al hit the brakes, as did Turk and Toegs. They skidded to a halt. Cowpoke pulled up behind them.

"There's another two!" Toegs screamed.

Two more had surfaced behind the others.

"Calm down, kid," Al said.

But then Toegs swivelled in her seat and yelped at two gigantic spiders that had emerged behind them coming their way. They were moving quickly. They drew their automatics and opened fire.

A clunking sound came from behind. Al swung around to look. A panel in the side of the Tankette had slid open, and out from it stepped Cowpoke encased in a fully articulated exoskeleton.

Turk had seen one before. "A Spartan combat exo-suit, saw them during the war ... awesome. The armoured power hands can crush steel, armoured leg braces can move it at a hundred clicks."

Cowpoke let out a battle cry, "Yee-haw!" and then attacked the two spiders coming from behind. The barrage of bullets had killed one of the spiders but they just kept coming. Al looked over his shoulder at Cowpoke while he was firing. The Texas Ranger had a spider in a clinch and was dismembering it. When he caught sight of Alice watching him, Cowpoke yelled out, "Get on that bike and hightail it outa here! I'm alright."

"Not on your life!" Al yelled back, opening fire at the other spider coming at Cowpoke.

Cowpoke bellowed, "A lot of folk are depending on you, son, now get outa here!" He was right. Turk had taken out another spider. There were only two left in front that presented a threat.

"How many of them are there? Al shouted at Turk.

"Wanna make a break for it?" Turk replied hurriedly while firing.

"Let's knock over these last two first," Al said.

Toegs ran out of ammo and was going for a new clip when a trapdoor opened in the ground right behind her.

Alice and Turk mowed down another spider, blowing bits of its legs off spraying blue blood everywhere. A loud scream came from behind them. Al swung around in time to see a massive spider dragging Toegs down into a hole.

Al yelled, taking aim. "Turk, quick!"

"Don't shoot, mate, you'll hit her," Turk warned.

Alice was getting jumpy. It was pulling her, screaming and fighting, into its lair. He couldn't take any more and ran at it.

Turk kept shooting at the remaining spider coming at him, so he couldn't help. He yelled, "Al, no!"

Al got to the spider and tried to attract its attention by waving his arms about. The spider's eight dark red eyes on stalks were glaring at him. It had massive pincers and whip-like antennae. He aimed, but he couldn't get a clear shot at it. Backing into its hole, it would soon drag Toegs down inside and shut the trapdoor. If that happened, she'd be gone.

Just as Alice was going for a pill to morph into the Star Lord, Cowpoke came out of the blue and grabbed the spider before it could disappear into its lair. They fought manically, and he managed to free

Toegs. Hysterical, she crawled on hands and knees across the ground and into Alice's waiting arms. They both watched on powerlessly as the spider dragged Cowpoke into its hole. The horrific sound of the trapdoor slamming shut behind them, the sound Cyrus had told them about, shattered the silence.

Turk had killed the last spider. Spattered in blue spider blood, he went over to Alice and Toegs. They were looking forlornly at the spot in the ground Cowpoke had disappeared into.

"Goddam it, I just couldn't get a shot at the thing!" Al growled, angry they'd lost a friend.

Toegs was sobbing.

"Come on, we better get going before more of them show up," Turk rasped.

They turned away, and with his arm around Toegs trying to calm her, went to the bikes.

A noise came from behind. Fearing more spiders, Al and Turk stopped in their tracks and swivelled with their automatics, taking aim. The earth rumbled … They exchanged looks of horror, expecting another massive spider. A trapdoor lid flew off a hole in the ground, and a huge billow of dust erupted from within. As the dust cleared, Cowpoke emerged from it, grime and blue blood plastered all over him and his exo-suit.

"Yee-Har!" he bellowed loudly, the leg of the spider he'd ripped to pieces held aloft: a well-earned trophy. "It was crazy down there fighting that dang thing!" he hollered excitedly.

Al raced over to him, thrilled to see him alive. "Mate, we thought you were a goner."

"It'd take more than that damned arachnid to defeat this Texas Ranger. I'm fine, now get on yer bikes and get the hell outa Dodge before more of them critters turn up."

"You okay to get back?" Al asked.

"Sure thing, never felt better in my life," he said, with a massive grin. "This'll make one heck of a story when I get back. By the time I tell it, there will have been hundreds of them, ha!"

Al beamed him a big friendly smile, then rushed back to Toegs, who was still shaking like a leaf. "Will you be all right? Not hurt?" he asked her warmly.

"Stirred and shaken maybe," she joked, through chattering teeth, climbing onto the Livewire.

Al mounted up, set to go, shot Cowpoke a wave, and yelled, "Chaa!"

They thundered up the highway towards Tempus.

Walker, Honor, and Dr Mennis stepped out of Aquila, greeted by Professor Adamski and Dr Li.

After Walker had introduced Mennis, Li fitted the wig on Walker, and he morphed into Electra.

"Extraordinary," Honor exclaimed.

"I expect you to work with Dr Mennis," Electra told Adamski and Li. "She will be staying with us now. She will contribute immensely to our bio-engineering programs."

"We are extremely fortunate to have a molecular geneticist with such genius as a colleague," Adamski said, totally bewitched by her.

Lizzy Li wasn't displaying the same enthusiasm, and Honor noticed it, sensing Li was jealous of her new teammate.

A few city blocks away, Luna was in Secta's office when she received a phone call from New York. She left the room to talk in private.

The Professor submitted emphatically to Hope, Christina, and Secta, "There's no way we can get Tempus back online. The TL-100 will need to come back here for us to dispatch it to the coordinates of the Rangers' Bunker Al gave us."

"That shouldn't be a problem," Christina said. "The concern is where else did this same problem occur?"

"I know, I know," Secta admitted, worriedly.

Luna returned and sat down, her face grave.

"What's up Luna, lose your credit rating?" Hope asked, jokingly. There was no love lost between them. Hope figured Luna had sided far too often with the opposition for her liking.

Luna's eyes narrowed. "There have been two unauthorised time travel events in the last twenty-four hours, both from Zen in Sydney."

Hope shrugged her shoulders, "So, what would you expect?"

"They're back up and running, and that presents a serious problem," Secta snarled.

Christina threw out there, "Why is that more of a worry than usual?"

The Professor had the answer, and he didn't like it, "Because they have the new processor."

Unsettled by the news, Hope glared at Luna, "In other words, Luna, they now have far more computing power than us."

"Where was the target? Don't say the Philippines ... please," Secta queried.

"No, ironically, it was Angel City in 2112."

Hope erupted with scepticism, "You've got to be kidding me? What the hell are they up to?"

Thinking laterally, the Professor offered, "I'd say it was to retrieve Honor ... as a matter of fact, you could put your house on it."

"It never rains, it pours," Luna groaned, dejectedly.

"Well, you won't have to worry for the time being. You'll be off to meet the Texas Rangers soon," the Professor said, trying to lift the mood with a chuckle.

It would be Luna's job, as it had been on the last operation, to co-ordinate the processing of the infirmed. However, this time the TL-100 would make the job a whole lot easier.

CHAPTER 12
DANGEROUS PATH

"**W**HY DO YOU** think that despite the millions killed there were more people on Earth at the end of the Second World War than when it started?" Electra posed, calculatedly.

"Mankind has the propensity to procreate even under the most diabolical conditions? At least that problem was solved in my time," Ursula Mennis submitted, being equally callous.

"Exactly," Electra agreed.

Honor wasn't interested in the topic; she'd heard it all before from Gorrick … a claim of overpopulation seemed to be a Zen mantra. She simply put it down in this case to Electra flagging it while hosting En-Lil, who was the one really doing the thinking. Honor was more interested in taking in the decorative changes Electra had made to the vast arena of Gorrick's old office—the makeover had totally personalised it. The island conference area where they were seated had been maintained with the creek and the bridge over it, though it had been transformed from white to matte black paint, so it almost blended into the dim background.

The huge eucalyptus tree was still there, towering over them; however, it was the lighting and the foliage that had been transformed the most. The skylights were mostly covered over, gone were the splashes of colour from floor spot lighting, and all the flowering plants along the meandering creek. They had been replaced by dark sinister exotic plants that gave the entire space a distinct air of malevolence—evil, which quite tickled Honor's macabre taste. Even the lounge setting had been recovered in ink black.

Electra paused and unblinkingly gazed at Honor, "You don't seem to be with us today, Honor. Do you need some time to recover from your ordeal?"

Honor snapped out of it, "No ... I was just admiring your alterations."

"Oh, yes, I had the urge to epitomise my personality in the décor and so forth. I'm pleased you like it."

"It is adorable," Ursula said, responsively. "Tell me boss, I am anxious to get to work, what are our objectives?" Always brimming with enthusiasm, Ursula was the consummate team member.

"The objective remains the same as it was in your time, Ursula," Electra said, and then her voice transitioned into the male voice of En-Lil, which spoke with fanaticism. "Zen will become the ultimate power on Earth to complete the task behest by the lords of space and time."

It was the first time Honor had observed a display of emotion from Electra.

Malcolm Low was in his presidential office at Oceana HQ, meeting with Dr Luna Cairn.

"This is proof that violations of the prime directive are not limited to missions into the past. Here we have technical alterations being made to a TL-100 unit from 2112 that will directly affect us now. In fact, the TL-100 is still only a blueprint. A working model has yet to be produced. You are reverse-engineering a working model from the future, and that, Mr President, totally contravenes the directive," Luna argued, vehemently.

Mal nonchalantly sipped his coffee, reclined in his lounge chair, and then said coolly, "I don't know what you're getting all riled up about, Luna. You've got Zen up the road in complete defiance of

UNTT's authorization rules, and here you are lodging a complaint with me to do with one of Secta's time travel paradoxes. I really don't see the relevance."

"Maybe so. I suppose I should get my priorities right ... but you must appreciate it's incredibly difficult to deal with Zen ... Frustrating would be a more appropriate description."

"So, you take it out on poor old me," Mal said, shooting her sad puppy dog eyes.

She reached across and touched his knee with respectful empathy. "I know, I know, I'm sorry, Mal."

"Look, you've got a job to do with the Texas Rangers; let's concentrate on that for now, shall we? In the meantime, allow us to get on with doing what we do best ... sorting out these horrific situations ... From all accounts, it seems Alice has uncovered a different conundrum that has the potential for more far-reaching effects: the failure of the TL-100 program because of UNTT's encryption encoding, demonstrated by what happened at Tempus."

"Yes, well, there's that paradox again ... Do we prevent that from happening by not encrypting the TL-100? Do we get hold of Dr Robert James now and tell him what Al discovered in 2112, to change his thinking? If we do these things, how will it affect 2112? In my book, that's walking a very dangerous path, Mal."

Mal nodded slowly, reflectively. "Hmm, I see what you mean. We can't take advice on it because there is no precedent. I think we need to come up with a directive that expressly deals with how to handle this sort of problem using Dr Robert James and Tempus as the model ... In saying that, I believe he must never be told."

"In that, we are in total agreement, Mal," she said, rising to her feet, ready to leave. "Time to get ready for my mission."

Mal looked her over. A very attractive middle-aged woman dressed immaculately and groomed to perfection. He got up and gave her a friendly peck on the cheek. "Be careful, Luna. You are vital to our time; you do realise that, don't you?" he said, reassuringly.

"Stop it, Mal, you're inflating my ego," she joked.

Rita popped her head in the door and said, "Sir, I have Blake's former boss Rod McCloud on the line."

"Okay, I'll take it."

As Luna left, Mal pressed the speaker on the hands-free system, flopped into his chair, and said cheerfully, "G'day Rod, how're you doing, mate?"

A gruff voice said, "Mal, I thought to call you right away. I've just heard from the Navy … we've got a ship in the Gulf of Davao that picked up not one but two UAPs there … Isn't Blake on a mission in that neck of the woods?"

"Sure is. Where exactly are they?"

"Directly over Davao City, stationary at about twelve thousand feet. Neither shows on radar, the report is purely visual, and they're both quite different."

"Is that right? How so?" Mal asked.

"One is what everyone has been calling a Watcher … you know, a Tic-Tac-shaped light, but the other is a definite spaceship … like you'd see in sci-fi movies."

"Really, are they close together? What I mean is, do they seem to be working in tandem?"

"That's what's weird Mal … no, they don't seem to be at all. I'm sending through video files of each of them now … can you have your science boffins take a look at them for us?"

"Sure thing, Rod."

"It might also be wise to let Blake know. It's ironic that while he's there checking on this alien sarcophagus thingy, these bloody UAPs conveniently turn up."

"You might be right, Rod. Thanks for letting me know, mate. I'll get Dr Secta on it right away and then get back to you."

Mal terminated the call and then checked his laptop for the footage. After watching it, he decided it was urgent enough to personally visit OTT for their opinion.

Mal found them all in the Kairos control room and greeted them cheerfully, "Hey team, what's up?"

Secta swivelled around from the console and said, "We got a message from Al, and we're waiting for the TL-100 to arrive."

"Again? Didn't he already send it for you to fix?" Mal questioned.

"Yes, he did, and we did fix it, but we can't get Tempus working for him to send it to the Rangers, so we need to do it from here," Secta explained.

"Christina?" Mal said, "Can you please bring up the OTT network on your computer? There's a video I want you all to see."

While Christina attended to the request, the Professor asked, "It's not too often you've got vision for us, Mal."

"I was asked by the director of Oceana Secret Service to get your opinion of it..."

"Sir," Christina said, "video is ready."

After they had watched the two videos of the separate sightings of both UAPs, Secta said, "Can you zoom and enhance the spaceship, please, Christina?"

"Yes," Christina said, and then froze the best frame of it. Then she used enhancement software to sharpen the pixels to a clearer image. The result was amazing.

"Wow, will you look at that thing!" Mal exclaimed.

It was big, gunmetal grey and showing signs of age from a lot of interplanetary action. Triangular in shape with wings and a definite beak, its skin had acute angles to avoid radar detection.

"If I didn't know this was real, I'd say it was a Klingon Bird of Prey from Star Trek," Christina said with a snigger.

"I've never seen Star Trek, but it looks a lot like a much bigger version of the An-Zu bird Al dealt with before," Secta said.

"You're right," the Professor agreed. "Thought it looked familiar."

"As for the other one, it's the same Watcher that has been observed all over the place. Tell us more about what we're looking at, Mal?" Secta requested.

"It is footage of two UAPs in the air at the same time at twelve thousand feet directly above Davao in the Philippines. It was taken by an officer on one of our Naval ships in the Sulu Sea."

"Are you saying these two UAPs are where Blake and Vee are looking for the sarcophagus?" Secta questioned, vigorously.

"Sure am. Can't be a coincidence, can it?" Mal submitted.

"Could that be one of the UAPs reported to have destroyed those ships the other day?" Hope inquired.

"Incoming," Christina alerted them.

Kairos had fired up. Thirty seconds later, the TL-100 materialised, and a team of four technicians rushed into the event room to drag it across the floor into the control room, ready to dispatch it to the Rangers. It was a rush because a couple of minutes later, Kairos energized a second time and, to their surprise, Al, Turk, and Toegs stepped out.

Secta greeted them. "We didn't expect all of you to return, only Al."

"When I tell you what lives between Tempus and the Rangers, you'll understand, mate," Al said, and then put his arm around Toegs, who was still unnerved from the spider attack.

They went into the control room. Hope was noticeably jealous of the affection Alice was affording Toegs, until Alice described the Trapdoor spider incident.

"What on Earth could have caused that degree of mutation in such a short period of time?" the Professor questioned.

"Rob reckoned there was a chemical plant at Waxahachie that took a big hit of radiation from the bomb blast. He figured some of the chemicals from there fused with radiation and caused it. Trapdoor spiders are apparently native to the area."

"That's true ... it wouldn't surprise me at all ... I know the place: West Fertilizer Plant ... forty minutes north of Waxahachie ... probably had biological experimentation contracts with the military," the Professor surmised.

"That could have done it," Secta agreed.

Christina asked, "How are you feeling, Toegs? You still look shaken."

"It was only an hour or so ago, so yeah, I'm still rattled," she admitted.

"How about taking her to the canteen for a feed, Hope? They can't head back to the Rangers bunker until Luna is ready. You too, Turk, you must be starving," Secta said.

"Don't leave me out of a good nosh," Al added eagerly.

As they were leaving the control room, Secta stopped Al and said confidentially, "Before you go, a quiet word, mate."

"Yeah, Secta, I'm all ears."

"Mal showed us video of two UAPs stationed over Davao. One is definitely a Watcher, but the other one looks like a much bigger version of an An-Zu bird. There have been three attacks on ships in different parts of the world over the past few days by UAPs or USOs and an increase in abduction reports … each time the description fits the An-Zu bird, only bigger. The question is: could this be the hostile alien attack En-Ki warned you about? Right now, we're concerned for Blake and Vee in Davao."

Al's mood became serious. "I better get there. En-Ki contacted me at Tempus, don't ask me how … he said he had to go to a lot of trouble to find me."

"Must have been important."

"Reckon, he said the sarcophagus must not be destroyed by En-Lil because it is elemental to the quest. I asked why he doesn't just beam the bloody thing up, and he said it wasn't feasible. When I asked what's inside of it, he didn't answer. It's like a bloody one-way conversation with him sometimes … he dumps on me then just pisses off, leaving me hanging in the air," Al complained.

Secta had cupped his chin, deep in thought. "En-Lil wants it destroyed. That means Zen must be in Davao as well. I think Zen has been playing the CIA and us against each other as a distraction for them to get their filthy claws on it … but why? Why would they want it destroyed? What's in it that makes it a threat?" Secta drifted off, deep in thought.

"Secta … Secta, stay with me, bring me up to speed. They got the sarcophagus, right?" Al questioned.

He snapped out of it, "Yes, yes, sorry, Alice. Ah, what we last heard from Blake was this rogue black marketeer Handerson Bolt had killed the two explorers that found the treasure and then took it to a warehouse in Davao by chopper, ready to ship somewhere. Blake and Vee teleported to the site and found Jax De Ville there with Buddy Holman and the dead explorers. The four of them went after Bolt and got to the warehouse before he could escape with the sarcophagus. There was a gunfight, and Holman was killed. De Ville had called in support and they arrived just as Blake and Vee overpowered Bolt and his men."

"Do we have the sarcophagus?"

"No, the CIA does. The support De Ville had called took it to the Davao Museum of History and Ethnography and put it in a vault for safekeeping. Mal has been on the phone to the US President trying to work out a deal to get it … but it's not looking good. There must be a damn special reason En-Ki wants us to have it, I mean aside from stopping Zen from destroying it."

"Why do the Yanks want it?"

"I have no idea, Al."

"You'd have to think that whoever is in the An-Zu bird wants it as well. Maybe the show of force by blowing up ships was a warning not to mess with them," Al suggested.

"Good shout, you might be right."

"Listen, pack Luna and Turk off to the Ranger Bunker to organise the TL-100. Leave Toegs here; she's too upset … too much too soon for her. I'll have a bite, then send me to Davao."

"That's a good plan, Al. We can use the open wormhole to Blake to send you right to him."

With that resolved, they left the control room and headed for the canteen. Al asked along the way, "How can you keep a wormhole open to Blake while we've been using Kairos at the same time?"

"Good question. We didn't think it was possible until guess who came up with the solution?" Secta said.

"Christina?"

"You got it in one. It works like a conference call with several parties having a digital open line to a hub or a router…"

CHAPTER 13
ABOUT TIME

ALL THE MEMBERS of OTT, with the exception of Vee, Blake, Karzoff, and Viktoria, were seated around a couple of tables they'd pulled together in the canteen. Al was busy tucking into a burger. Luna had joined them, geared up for the trip to the Rangers' Bunker in 2112.

She stood to address them. "While I've got you all here, everyone is privy to the events that have taken place with Tempus, the TL-100, and with the Texas Rangers in 2112. In due course, you will all be required to sign a non-disclosure agreement concerning those events. This is to ensure Dr Robert James doesn't learn about certain events that would directly change the outcome of history.

"Your President has agreed to this measure as we have learned from this experience how a mission to a future date can have detrimental effects on the present. Previously, we thought only missions to the past could have such consequences ... So, in the spirit of the prime directive, it has been decided in this instance to keep the events concerning Tempus in 2112 top secret. Any questions?"

Christina spoke up, "I'm afraid it has already been violated. We sent Dr James the photograph of the Tempus logo taken by the recon-drone in 2112. Apparently, he's already had a graphic artist render it for the new Tempus."

Luna stared glumly at Christina for a moment and then said, "Okay ... then any more details about that mission will be kept from

Dr James. Any problems, let me know."

"Um, I'd just like to add," Al began. "Dr James in 2112 is 115 years old, so he has witnessed missions through Tempus and Kairos that haven't yet happened. Think about that for a moment ... He knows the intricate ourcomes of those missions ... he even has the documentation, reports et cetera." Al let the thought hang in the air. The enormity of it showed on Luna's face.

Even so, they all agreed with Luna's request, though inwardly— with the exception of Luna—they figured the idea was absurd and totally unmanageable. But they let it ride, knowing full well it would be next to impossible to police. Besides, there were more important issues to deal with as far as they were concerned.

Handerson Bolt sat within the confines of Davao City District Jail, perched on the edge of his bunk, elbows on knees, face in hands. Squalid conditions—the tiny cell was filthy, and the ward overcrowded—his only consolation: he had a cell on his own. That luxury had cost him a bribe of three hundred US dollars.

It was 9 p.m. and the lights went out, leaving only the dull red glow from an emergency bulb high up on the corridor wall outside his cell. Bolt wasn't a novice at being behind bars but, as tough as it was, he preferred to be in a Filipino prison than any other. Notoriously corrupt meant the guards were for sale, with pretty much anything available for a price, with the exception of freedom ... but depending on the individual and the amount, even that was negotiable ... however, he didn't have the cash.

He'd just curled up on a bunk that was far too short for his length when the beam from a torch flashed on his face. Shielding his eyes, he sat up squinting.

A guard spoke in broken English. "Okay ra ... Bolt ... you get up ... you're gonna leave now."

The cell door creaked opened. Bolt stood up and then looked

down at his bare feet bathed in a sea of urine and worse.

"I'll need my boots," he growled, gagging on the smell of ammonia.

"Okay, okay, come on … silencio!" the guard snapped hurriedly, in a thick whisper, trying to keep a lid on the covert operation.

Bolt left the cell and walked along the wet floor of the stinking corridor followed by the guard and a shadowy figure that remained silent.

His boots were waiting for him at the guard post. The guard shut the connecting door and turned on the dim light. Now, Bolt could see the shadowy figure was a solidly built westerner.

"Who are you?" Bolt asked, impudently.

"The bloke who just paid 5,000 US to bust you out," he replied, in a thick British accent.

"Cheap," he sniggered, "thought I'd be worth much more than that."

"You overestimate yourself Bolt," the tall man snarled callously.

The guard led them out of the jail and they climbed into a waiting taxi.

"You could do with a change of clothes, you stink. Tell him to take us to your Hotel."

"Driver," Bolt ordered, "Seda Abreeza, salamat."

"What's that?"

"My Hotel like you asked. So, who are you and why'd you spend the skins to bail me out?"

"Name is Dan Walker … now that you owe me one, I expect you to assist me in obtaining the sarcophagus."

"Ah, so that's what this is about. That relic is worth a lot more than five thousand bucks, Dan Walker. How do I know you're not CIA, MI6, Oceana, or whatever?"

"I'm with Zen Corporation. You contacted us about the sarcophagus."

"Yeah, I did … got no reply. How much will this Zen Corporation kick the bin for me to help you get it?" Bolt purred, the thought of easy money infinitely appealing to him.

"How much did you ask the CIA?"

"Two mil," Bolt said.

"Lead me to it and I'll pay you 250 grand, cash ... less expenses."

"Worth considering ... How'd you know where I was?"

"Money talks ... and Bolt ... either you commit now or I stop the cab here and you walk away. Choice is yours."

Bolt looked him over. Walker didn't look the type to tolerate crap, so he eased up on the loftiness.

Blake and Vee occupied the café within the Davao Marco Polo Hotel. Vee's demeanour was far from content. "I don't like it. She still fancies you. I can tell ... woman's intuition," she grumbled.

"Come on, Vee. I just need to talk to her privately. It's the only way I can persuade her. Otherwise, the mission is done and dusted ... with the thing flown out to the States."

"I just don't get why it has to be in private," she challenged.

"Believe me, Vee, I know how to handle her. I'll be back within an hour, alright?" He rose from his seat, and despite her indifferent expression, gave her a peck on her cheek before heading for the elevator.

While he waited for it he thought to himself, "It's just Vee being jealous, comes with being teenager, she'll be cool."

Jax had just finished showering when the doorbell chimed. Wrapped in a white towelling robe, her hair still wet, she opened the door.

"Oh, Blake, I didn't expect you ... come in."

"We need to talk, Jax," urgency lacing his words.

"Alright."

In the expanse of the luxury suite, she guided him to a three-seater lounge upholstered in white leather. "Take a seat. Fancy a beer?"

"That'd be great, ta."

Entering the kitchenette, she retrieved two bottles of San Miguel Super Dry from the bar fridge.

"How did the Firm react to the loss of Holman?" Blake called from the living room.

Jax popped the bottle tops. "Not well. I'll arrange for his body to be flown out with the sarcophagus tomorrow."

Sauntering back to the lounge, she handed him a beer, sat and propped her bare feet onto the glass coffee table.

"Thanks ... You leaving as well?" Blake asked.

"No, I'm staying a few days to go over the remainder of the artefacts with Amaya."

"Cheers, big ears," Blake jested, clinking his bottle against hers in a toast.

Arching an ironic eyebrow, Jax retorted, "It's unlike you to let the prize slip away, Blake. What prompted this spontaneous visit?"

"Now you mention it. Surely before it disappears into the vast annals of the CIA, you have just as much interest to find out what's inside of it as I do?"

She shot him a wry tight-lipped smile.

"But they claim it's impenetrable," she said.

Though the conversation had veered into innuendo, Blake understood the need to stay focused if he was to obtain what he sought. "True, platinum can't be penetrated by rays—Alpha, Beta, Gamma, or X-rays. However, the Davao Doctors Hospital houses an MRI machine that could be used to scan it."

"You'll have to convince me—" Her words froze mid-sentence, her body rigid, as if suspended in time.

Blake wondered what the hell had happened. "Jax? Jax? ... You all right?"

Alice stepped out of the vortex.

"Al!" Blake said, surprised.

Al cruised over and looked at Jax. "Hmm, sorry about the coitus interruptus."

"It's not what you think, Al," Blake stuttered.

"She'll be back any second now," Alice smirked. "Five, four, three, two, one."

Right on cue, Jax unfroze, saw Blake with Alice and shouted, "Al ... Alice!"

"That's me alright ... sorry to bust up your research mission, but the doorbell wasn't working," he quipped. "Now, before you leap to any conclusions, Jax, I'm here to take possession of the sarcophagus. So, let's go pay it a visit to work out the logistics."

Jax didn't argue. Having previously witnessed Alice in action, she knew he wasn't to be messed with. She had no ambition of putting that to the test and simply got up and stormed red-faced into the bedroom to change.

Al called after her forcefully, "No calling in the cavalry, Jax, you hear? Otherwise, there will be consequences."

"Copy that," she responded, bitterly.

Blake sauntered up to Alice and muttered in a harsh whisper, "Mate, I was getting her to commit to having the sarcophagus MRI scanned."

Al eyeballed him. "If that's how you get a commitment, then become a politician. Listen to me, Blake, stay out of my sister's pants. You hear me? I'm not going to deal with her broken heart because of you. Are we clear on that?" The fierce look in Alice's eyes said enough. Blake nodded and gulped ... he wasn't about to argue the point with Alice either.

Al went out onto the balcony for some fresh air while waiting for Jax. It was a large balcony. He walked to the end that faced the bay, grasped the handrail and looked up at the sky. It didn't take him long to find the Watcher in the firmament.

"Is that you up there, En-Ki?" he mumbled to himself. He got a jolt when an unexpected answer came inside his mind.

"At last you have arrived, Alice ... about time, pardon the pun. It was looking as though I would have to do the job on my own."

"Ha! If you could've done that, you would have by now, En-Ki ...

tell me I'm wrong?" Al thought.

"No, Alice. You have a question for me?"

"A fistful of them … what's in the thing?"

"The sarcophagus, nothing. In fact, it is not a sarcophagus at all."

"No, then what is it? And why is it so important that En-Lil wants it destroyed? Does it do something?"

"All I can say for now is you need to hide it … put it away somewhere very safe. Trust me, at this stage you do not need to know any more."

"Okay, okay … another one of your cryptic puzzles, got that. Then who is in the other spaceship up there?… The one parked beside you?"

"They are whom I warned you about, Alice. Remember?"

"What do they want?"

"The sarcophagus of course."

"Well, why don't they just take the damn thing? You know, beam it up or something?" Al complained, in his jocular manner.

"I have no idea," En-Ki admitted.

"Are they on En-Lil's side?"

"No, but they are somewhat related. They both have an interest, you might say."

"Why don't they just fire a death ray and destroy it? Surely they've got the technology."

"One thing you can be certain of, Alice, is they will personally come after it, especially now that you have arrived."

"And how am I supposed to deal with them? Like, as if I haven't got enough on my freaking plate already."

"I will watch over you."

"One last question … how does it open?"

"Remember touching the Orb?"

En-Ki was gone.

"Right, thanks, more of your cryptic trials," Al said out loud, sarcastically.

Blake overheard him and wandered out onto the balcony. "What's that, Al?"

"Uh, oh, nothing. Where's this thing stashed?"

"The sarcophagus? It's in the vault at the Davao Museum. A plane arrives tomorrow to ferry it to the States along with Holman's body."

"Jax as well?"

"No, I'm staying on for a few days," she said, standing in the doorway behind Blake, dressed in a khaki shirt and shorts.

Al looked back up at the bright light in the sky, knowing it was En-Ki's craft, and cursed under his breath, "What have you got me into this time, mate?"

"The CIA has it stored at the Davao Museum. I heard them mention it'll be shipped out to the States in the morning," Bolt told Walker on their way down in the hotel elevator.

At that time of night, there was little activity in the lobby. Bolt handed his key to the night porter at reception, and then he and Walker went to the forecourt to catch a cab. There were no cabs at the rank. The main road was nearby, so they walked there and waited to hail one.

"We'll need explosives," Walker said, circumspect.

"Explosives? What for?" Bolt questioned.

"To destroy it."

"What?" Bolt erupted. "You've gotta be kidding me. That thing is solid platinum, worth a King's ransom. You're paying me two fifty grand for it, and you want to blow it to smithereens? Why? You nuts or something?"

"You can have the remains once it's destroyed. It'll still be platinum, only in a blob if the job is done right."

"What a waste. You better make it worth my while. I didn't go to all the trouble of getting it down from Mount Apo just to blow it up," Bolt whined.

"You lost it, remember? Don't fret. You'll get your money. Now, where can we get explosives?"

"Well, due to the lack of a local friendly explosives store, I'll need to make a few calls," he said, facetiously, "but those CIA bastards took my cellphone, so…?"

"Here," Walker handed his over. "Use mine."

After a few minutes of negotiation with his local gangland contacts, Bolt had the basis of a deal. Keeping his contact on the line, he asked Walker, "They want two K US cash to blow the Davao Museum to kingdom come."

"No, only the sarcophagus, you idiot. Otherwise, we'll have the entire population of Davao on us, and we'll need to be certain it's done. You know as well as I that it's platinum and that it won't be easy to destroy."

"Right. It'll take an incendiary," he told his contact, then put his hand over the phone and told Walker, "These dudes are ex-military. They'll know what to use."

"Agreed then, two thousand cash, a grand down and the rest on completion. We'll be there to ensure it's done. Remote detonation only. No mess-ups," Walker said, coldly.

Walker had a card up his sleeve. He would bail out through a wormhole home as soon as the job was done, leaving Bolt to clean up the mess. He didn't like the guy, figured him untrustworthy.

Bolt finished the negotiations then handed the phone back to Walker. "Done. We'll meet them at The Grid Bar downtown in an hour."

"Good. I need to find an ATM," Walker said.

CHAPTER 14
THE GRID

TURK WAS TAKING a break from aiding people through the TL-100. He'd been diligently at it for hours without any respite. Recognising his weary appearance, Luna had suggested a well-earned pause.

He settled into a comfortable chair, engrossed in a National Geographic magazine from 2079, the year before the Cyberwars. It was a rarity to come across a physical magazine that had endured from a time when almost all media had transitioned from hardcopy to digital formats. He speculated that the spectre of war might have intervened, making it one of the final issues, if not the last.

Flipping through the glossy pages, he relished the stunning photography from an era before the world underwent its transformation. Suddenly, he encountered a story that piqued his interest. Titled "Yamashita's Treasure and the UAP Flap," it recounted the discovery of a platinum sarcophagus in Davao, Philippines.

Turk sat up with heightened excitement as he read that the platinum sarcophagus was believed to have been unearthed by an archaeological consortium led by Professor Jax De Ville. The name struck a chord—it had come up frequently in conversations with Alice, particularly concerning the An-Zu craft he'd encountered in Tahiti.

Continuing to read, Turk discovered that Professor De Ville, in collaboration with Dr Amaya Alvarez, the curator of the Davao Museum of History and Ethnography, was thought to have located the treasure cache in a cave on Mount Apo, Mindanao. Simultaneously, two UAPs, witnessed by thousands, had materialised in the sky over Davao City. The article speculated about a connection between the unearthed artefacts and the UAPs, suggesting that the largest item, a platinum sarcophagus weighing over a ton and believed to contain the remains of an alien King, had vanished under suspicious circumstances from the Museum, with the UAPs taking the blame.

While studying photographs of the museum team standing beside the massive sarcophagus, Turk noticed Vee and Blake. His initial thought was, "I wonder where Alice is?" Unbeknownst to him, Alice hadn't arrived yet at that point.

The story went on to propose that the relic might have been snatched by one of the UAPs. This theory gained credibility from the fact that the sarcophagus was the only item stolen from the vast collection of valuable relics uncovered by the archaeological team. The hypothesis was further supported when both UAPs vanished simultaneously, right after the sarcophagus disappeared from the vault of the Davao Museum. Given its weight of over a ton, there seemed to be no other explanation for its abrupt disappearance.

The daylight photographs of the two UAPs intrigued Turk. One resembled a glowing Tic-Tac, while the other took on the form of a dark, ominous bird-shaped craft. Yet, it was the next photo on the page that triggered recognition within him. The snapshot depicted the scene outside the Davao Museum after the sarcophagus had vanished—a crowd of onlookers had gathered, and conspicuously present was Daniel Walker, the Zen agent he had clashed with inside the An-Zu cave in Tahiti.

Determined, Turk opted to send the magazine back through Kairos.

Christina was wondering what had materialised when Kairos unexpectedly activated and then shutdown just as quickly. She hurried into the event room collected the magazine from the floor and then immediately summoned Secta.

Opening the magazine to a dog-eared page, Secta read the story with keen interest. Then, he sent the magazine through Kairos to Alice in Davao.

Alice was with Vee, Blake, and Jax in the hotel café, having a coffee when Jax froze mid-way through a sentence. The café fell silent.

Alice knew immediately what had occurred. "Oops, we must have incoming." A small object popped out of the thirty-centimetre vortex and landed on the floor. The vortex shut, sound returned to normal, and the café carried on as if nothing had happened. Jax snapped out of it and continued her sentence when she noticed Alice reading a magazine, with Vee and Blake peering intently at it over his shoulder.

"National Geographic Magazine, huh?" Jax said, astonished. "Where did that come from?"

Vee glanced at her and said nonchalantly, "Out of a vortex."

Jax looked puzzled and mumbled, "Oh."

Al showed Jax the article, pointing at the photo of them outside the Museum.

"So, that was taken earlier today," Jax said, a little confused.

"The magazine is from 2079, Jax," Vee said informatively.

Jax was gobsmacked.

"The story tells how the sarcophagus disappeared from the museum overnight, tonight, and look here," he showed her another picture. "That guy in the crowd, head and shoulders above the rest, is none other than Zen agent, Commander Daniel Walker."

"What does that tell us?" Jax enquired.

"Two things," Blake said, "first, the sarcophagus vanishes, and second, Zen is here."

Al sat back in his chair, nodding his head slightly. "I'd bet on Walker being in cahoots with your buddy Handerson Bolt and them conspiring to steal the sarcophagus tonight."

"But Bolt's in jail?" Jax challenged.

"This is the Philippines, Jax," Blake reminded her, "money talks and Bolt walks, it's that simple."

With a furrowed brow, Jax questioned, "Do you think they'll try and take the sarcophagus tonight?"

"Zen has been playing us against each other, Jax, all to buy them time to take the thing. This article says someone takes it … now that could be us, Bolt, Walker, or the UAP," Al declared.

"What UAP?" Jax exclaimed, as if the story had just shifted into science fiction, which of course it had.

"Where have you been, Jax? There are two of them in the sky right over our heads now," Vee exclaimed, frustrated by Jax playing dumb, and intuition telling her that something had transpired between her and Blake earlier … something she suspected Al knew all about.

Motivated, Al switched into action mode. "Right, let's get going. We need to get to the thing first. Jax, do we need anything special to get into the Museum at this hour?"

Jax was taken aback. "Are you expecting to get into the vault?"

"Are you half asleep or something?" Vee badgered, sarcastically.

Jax acted indignant. "No, I know what you're thinking of doing, but there are a couple of logistical problems. Firstly, the vault would be locked, and secondly, the sarcophagus is very heavy. I don't care who gets there first, they won't be able to just break in and run off with it!"

"Unless you have superior alien technology," Al pointed out.

"Beam me up, Scotty?" Blake suggested, jokingly.

Al agreed, "Precisely."

"Okay," Jax said, picking up her cellphone from the table. "I'll phone the Museum curator."

While Jax was speaking to Amaya, the others discussed the strategy. Since Blake and Vee had witnessed the handling of the sarcophagus by the museum staff, they had a fair idea of how to move the heavy object.

"Shouldn't we check out what's inside it, in case the aliens nab it? Otherwise, we'll never know," Blake asked Al.

"There's nothing in it. In fact, it's not what you think it is."

"Isn't it a coffin?" Vee questioned, surprised.

Al confirmed, "Apparently not."

Blake was perplexed. "What is it then?"

Al widened his eyes, "I don't know, mate … all I know is it's not what it seems."

Jax finished the call. "Did I hear you say it's not a sarcophagus?"

"Yeah," Al affirmed.

"But that doesn't make any sense at all," Jax disagreed. "I've seen plenty of sarcophagi before … it sure looks like one to me."

"There are inscriptions on the top, right?" Al asked.

Jax quickly flipped through photos on her phone and then showed Alice. "There, see here? Yeah, I can't decipher them."

Al took the phone and skimmed through a dozen or so photos taken from various angles.

Vee checked over his shoulder. "Looks like gobbledegook to me. You're an archaeologist, you'd at least know what language it is."

Jax confessed, "Well, it's not Sumerian or any other language you would expect."

Al was still staring at the screen. He zoomed in on the hieroglyphs. "Wait a minute, there's something familiar about it … I saw markings like these on the An-Zu bird."

"You're right, so did I," Blake agreed.

"Maybe that's the connection with the UAP?" Jax surmised, thinking aloud.

The cab pulled up on Polo Street outside The Grid. The few surly-looking clubs lined both sides of the street, making Polo Street the epicentre of Davao's nightlife.

Walker paid the cab driver, and the old jalopy trundled off, leaving a fog of belched exhaust fumes in its wake for them to cough their way through. A pounding disco bass from inside the club replaced the rumble of the taxi's clapped-out motor.

"What is this place?" Walker asked Bolt, a look of revulsion on his face.

"My contact's joint … a watering hole."

They approached a big Polynesian bruiser standing like a colossus at the front door. "Hey, Rangi, what's up?" Bolt blurted.

They exchanged a low five, and then the big Samoan stepped aside to permit them entry.

"Normal admission is a hundred Pesos, but nothing for us," Bolt bragged.

"Wow, you just saved me two dollars. You never cease to impress," Walker grumbled facetiously.

The place had the typical nightclub subdued lighting. There was a small dance floor with a pair of scantily clad young girls dancing together. Along the right wall was a long bar, at which about twenty punters were seated and tended to by a dozen girls. The music was way too loud for Walker; it made him feel uncomfortable.

"Follow me," Bolt said and led the way to the rear of the bar, through a door, and into a dark corridor. It was then that Walker realised the bar actually occupied a couple of the front rooms of an old house.

They passed through another door, which opened out into a dingily lit office. The gaze of half a dozen men seated, drinking beers and smoking, was immediately cast in their direction. All conversation abruptly ceased.

Walker felt conscious of being stared at as though he was the next listed item in an auction. Tall white guys were not a common sight in town.

A broad grin cracked on the face of one of the men, obviously the leader. He jumped up and slapped Bolt on the back like he was his old friend.

"Hey, Bolt ... some of my friends inside got word you paid them a visit," he laughed, and the others laughed with him.

"You must have half your family inside, Carlos ... why didn't you get me out?" Bolt growled.

Carlos Arroyo was a scrawny short guy with a rat-like face, large brown eyes, and sunken cheeks. A strong accent and a cheeky attitude, a villain was written all over him.

"You gotta pay the bucks, baby," Carlos sniggered. "Hey, speaking of bucks?"

Walker took a step forward and growled intensely, "What explosive will you use?"

Carlos grinned, two gold teeth on show, "C-4, enough to blow a Sherman tank. Good enough for you, Charlie?"

Walker's expression changed, hardening. He resented being called Charlie and took exception to Carlos's cavalier attitude. He shot the little arrogant man an icy, cold stare.

Carlos could sense from Walker's intense vibe that he meant business and was experienced, probably ex-military. In sharp contrast, he knew Bolt was up for sale to the highest bidder. Walker, on the other hand, he figured, wasn't the sort of individual to be messed with.

Calm, cool, and collected, Walker spoke in a hard, thick tone, matched with a steely stare. "I am not called Charlie ... by anyone. For the purposes of this job, you will address me as sir. That goes for all of you," he scanned them scornfully. "Is that clear?" he questioned, assuming a commanding demeanour.

They received the message loud and clear and acknowledged.

"Hey, no problema ... sir," Carlos said, yielding to Walker's dominance.

Walker withdrew a thousand US dollars from his pocket and handed it to Carlos. "A grand now ... a grand upon completion. The target must be completely destroyed, or you won't get the second grand. What is the composition of the C-4?"

"Bolt told me the target is metal. We use magnesium with white phosphorus in the C-4 mix ... remote detonation."

"Here's an extra thousand," he said, handing over another wad of notes to Carlos. "I want a crash camera on the target, feeding to my phone."

"No problema, sir. Anything else?"

"Bolt, you said it's in the Museum. Where exactly?"

"I overheard them mention the vault," Bolt said.

Walker pondered for a moment then said, "We'll need a floor plan and the means to break into the vault."

"Not necessary. Another five hundred will buy off the security guard," Carlos advised.

Walker inquired, "Will he know the combination of the safe?"

"It's a museum, not a bank, sir. Boboy here worked as security there. Tell him."

Boboy was dark-skinned, short, round-faced, and overweight, in his forties. He was bald with broad cheekbones, a flat nose underlined by a pencil-thin black moustache. His voice was deeper than his appearance suggested. "No combination, just a time lock controlled by security. Easy-peasy. Five hundred will do the trick."

All the Filipinos chuckled. Boboy was obviously the jester.

"Fine. What vehicles do you have?" said Walker.

"One Pajero for us," Carlos said.

"Then we'll need another one and a driver, because we're coming with you," Walker ordered. "I suppose that will be another five hundred?"

They all sniggered.

"Yes, but you get a free beer?" Boboy joked.

They all laughed, even Walker managed a curt smile. He fished into his pocket, withdrew more money, counted it out, and handed it over to Carlos. Then his smile broadened. He had anticipated the negotiation. If it hadn't unfolded this way, he would have been suspicious of their competence. The mood had lightened.

"Now, where's that free beer?" Walker said, raising one eyebrow.

Al was deliberating on the best approach to handle the sarcophagus. Two options lay before him: transporting it through Kairos or enlisting the Oceana Naval vessel stationed in the Gulf of Davao to carry it back home. However, he surmised that the more time-consuming and perilous of the choices would involve getting the sarcophagus to the docks and onto a ship. He was confident he could tackle whatever challenges Walker presented, but the alien craft—well, that was an uncharted entity.

CHAPTER 15
THE VAULT

LUNA AND TURK had finished treating the population of the Rangers' Bunker with the TL-100. The process had taken eight hours, and now, relieved that it was completed, they were taking a well-earned rest.

"Something needs to be done about those trapdoor spiders, believe me, they're bad news," Turk told Luna.

Cowpoke entered the room. "They told me y'all were done. Great job. How long before they'll be feeling better?"

A smile broke on Luna's tired face. "Give them a week, Cowpoke. Their immune system isn't busy fighting the virus anymore, so it'll focus on restoring their health. They'll just need some nutritious food."

Cowpoke took a seat and surveyed the commissary. "Ain't much nutrition left here since it was left up to me to do all the raiding for vittles, why the cupboard is almost bare ... and with them spiders ... well."

"We were just discussing them," Turk said. "We managed to defeat them the other day, proving it can be done. Once your people are back to good health, maybe you could join forces with the folks at Tempus to hunt them all down."

"Makes you wonder what else might have mutated into monsters," Luna said.

"Dang! Never thought of that," Cowpoke said, scratching his

beard. "What y'all gonna do now that you're done?"

"You got enough food to last for a week or two?" Turk asked.

"Hmm, doubt that."

Luna had an idea. "Hey, why don't we send you some emergency rations to help you get through this tough period?"

"Well, that'd be mighty neighbourly of y'all."

Turk asked, "What do we do with the TL-100?"

Luna stood up. "I'll write a note to Secta along with an order for a month's supply of rations."

Upon receiving the note, Secta initiated the process of arranging for Army rations to be delivered to OTT for transportation through Kairos. Simultaneously, he summoned OTT members to a meeting to discuss the fate of the TL-100. Recognising the time-saving potential of bringing back a TL-100 from the future for reverse engineering instead of building one from scratch, the group agreed on this approach. Although Secta anticipated Luna's disapproval, he believed that the urgency of distributing TL-100s worldwide outweighed adhering strictly to the prime directive in this instance.

Once the concerns had been addressed, as they were about to leave the boardroom, Hope spoke up.

"If I could have a moment, please."

They resumed their seats to listen.

"I've conducted further research on Sumerian mythology ... Allow me to share some of my findings. In the epic poem from Ancient Mesopotamia, the Epic of Gilgamesh, dated around 1800 BCE, which describes an even earlier period, it's mentioned that Gilgamesh and his companion En-Kidu were two-thirds god and one-third human. I believe they were direct descendants of En-Ki, possibly his sons.

"Gilgamesh is devastated when En-Lil, with intentions to exterminate humanity, afflicts En-Kidu with an illness that proves fatal ... Gilgamesh embarks on a quest to resurrect him, and this involves seeking out Utnapishtim, another creation of En-Ki. Utnapishtim possesses knowledge of eternal life.

"After a long journey, Utnapishtim leads Gilgamesh through a tunnel to a twin-peaked mountain named Mashu. Now, here's where things take an intriguing turn … Think about Alice's journey to Tahiti and the An-Zu cave … They encounter a cave guarded by two scorpion monsters, which they manage to bypass, and emerge into a beautiful garden by the sea. There, they meet Siduri, a young woman. Gilgamesh shares his quest for immortality, and she directs him to Urshanabi, who instructs him to take Utnapishtim and En-Kidu across the sea in a boat to the edge of the world … to a space in-between on an island. The term 'space in-between' might be significant.

"Let's hypothesise that Tahiti was their destination since we know the scorpion monsters were there. They sail across the sea to the island of Pohnpei in Micronesia and arrive at Nan Madol. The name Nan Madol translates to 'space in-between' in English—could this refer to a space between En-Ki and En-Lil? What if the trio weren't biological sons in the conventional sense, but were instead En-Ki's original creations, not yet fully human? As the epic states, they were three parts god and one part human. Could this have been the reason En-Lil wanted them eliminated? My question is: were the three platinum sarcophagi discovered on Nan Madol the final resting places of Gilgamesh, Utnapishtim, and En-Kidu? Could they have been hidden there to protect them from En-Lil's reach? Is the alien spacecraft over Davao connected to this, given their influence over the Nagasaki bombing to destroy the other two sarcophagi?"

Hope paused, letting the weight of her words hang in the air, before adding, "My conclusion is that the remaining sarcophagus in Davao could potentially hold the body of either Gilgamesh, Utnapishtim, or En-Kidu."

The room was filled with an air of astonishment. Secta began pacing, while the Professor stared into the distance, contemplating the implications. Christina sat with her hands folded, visibly affected. Karzoff doodled absentmindedly, and Viktoria observed the reactions of the others closely.

Secta stopped pacing and turned to them sharply. "I think you've hit the nail on the head, Hope."

"Should we tell Alice?" Christina suggested.

Secta thought for a moment, then said, "No, I think he has enough on his plate for now."

It was 1 a.m., and a tranquil silence enveloped the surroundings, broken only by the faint hum of two black Pajeros driving in convoy along Agusan Circle, en route to the Davao Museum.

Walker occupied the back seat of the second Pajero, accompanied by Sancho. Bolt sat in the front beside the driver, Carlos. The convoy came to a halt as they watched the lead vehicle pull into the car park by the side entrance of the white museum building. The complex consisted of two structures: the main public museum and an adjoining warehouse. The museum was a single-storey stucco building with an office area at the back. The connected warehouse stood taller—a former military storehouse dating back to the 1940s.

A security guard emerged from a recessed area and approached the Pajero, clearly anticipating its arrival. Boboy, having extricated himself from the Pajero, engaged in a conversation with the guard.

Carlos informed the foreigners, "Boboy is making sure the vault is open and de alarms closed."

"Closed?" Walker queried.

"He means turned off—'open' means the alarms are on, 'closed' means they're off," Bolt clarified, familiar with the local jargon.

Carlos reached down and retrieved a silenced automatic pistol from beneath his seat.

Boboy handed an envelope containing a bribe to the guard, who swiftly pocketed it before heading towards Carlos's vehicle, evidently on his way out.

Boboy re-entered the lead vehicle, and it proceeded to the rear of the museum building. However, Carlos didn't follow suit. Instead, he waited for the guard to approach, rolled down the window, called him over, and when he was within proximity, raised his pistol and shot him in the head.

"Sancho, get de money... dump the body," he instructed, calmly. "Meet us at de warehouse."

Sancho disembarked from the vehicle, retrieved the envelope from the dead guard, and handed it back through the window to Carlos. The car drove away, leaving Sancho to address the grim task.

Walker was unimpressed by the needless killing and expressed his disapproval. "Why did you kill him?"

"He recognise us ... he'd blackmail us for more money once he find out what we did here. Collateral damage, you Americans say."

"I'm not American," Walker retorted indignantly.

"Sorry," Carlos conceded, parking beside the other Pajero.

Meanwhile, Boboy and three members of the gang had managed to open the sliding door leading to the loading bay of the warehouse. Guided by the beam of their flashlights, Carlos led Walker and Bolt inside.

It was dark, no moon with only one dim light on the side of the warehouse.

The warehouse interior stretched out as a largely vacant expanse. Stacks of pallets lined one wall, and a yellow and black Toyota 7 series forklift, fuelled by LPG, was parked nearby. The men had already entered the main building, leaving the warehouse area deserted.

Amaya pulled her red Pajero up out front of the Museum. Blake, Vee and Jax were in the back with Al, the front passenger.

Al swivelled in his seat to address the others, "I've a gut feeling someone else is here. Now listen up. If I yell jump ... without hesitation ... I want you, Vee, to open the vortex for you and Blake to go through. No questions asked. Is that clear?"

"Yes," they agreed in unison.

Al continued his instructions. "Amaya, you and Jax stay in the car. If you get out, you do so at your own risk. I can't be responsible for your safety ... understand?"

"Over my dead body, Alice, I'm invested in this as much as you. I'm coming too," Jax argued.

Al knew he was beat—no point arguing over semantics. "Okay, but not Amaya," he reached into his pocket and withdrew a Clock Drive. "Slap this on Jax," he told Vee, handing it to her. "When Vee opens the vortex, you follow her through—"

"But—" Jax started.

Al cut her off, "No 'buts', Jax. Either do it my way, or Amaya takes you back to the hotel now. What'll it be?"

"Alright, alright," she grumbled, reluctantly.

"Amaya, please stay put. There is no need for you to risk your life," Al said.

All the talk of jumping into a vortex had her totally bewildered, she confirmed with a nod. "But first, I will let you inside. The vault is at the rear of the building. I will need to disengage the alarm and the lock. The guard should be here."

Al agreed. They went to the front door. She stopped and told Alice, "The guard should be on duty."

"There's someone else here for sure," Al said.

Amaya tentatively opened up and went directly to the alarm and safe locking system module just inside the door. As soon as she saw it had been disengaged, she turned to Alice and whispered, "The alarms and safe lock have been disabled. You are right, there is someone here," she stammered nervously. "Follow the corridor; the vault is at the end, just before the warehouse. Good luck," she said nervously, and then scurried off for the safety of her vehicle.

It took four men to wheel the sarcophagus atop a four-wheel heavy-duty dolly out of the large vault along a short hallway in through the double doors into the warehouse. Walker, Bolt and Carlos were there to meet it. In the meantime, Boboy had been preparing explosives.

They positioned the three-metre-long sarcophagus in the middle of the warehouse floor. A metre off the floor, there was plenty of space underneath the dolly to pack the incendiaries.

"This is what all the hooha is about?" Walker said, studying the majestic artefact. "It's a shame to destroy it, really."

"Ridiculous, if you ask me ... the thing's worth millions," Bolt whined.

"Shut up. If that maniac Carlos finds out what it's worth, we'll be dead meat," Walker snapped in a harsh whisper.

Carlos was busy helping Boboy stack the explosives up tight under the sarcophagus, so didn't hear them. He straightened up and asked of Bolt, "Hey, is this thing made of silver?"

From what Walker had said, he gave a reserved answer, "Yeah, plated, I think."

"No, no, not plated ... you can tell by all the fancy stuff carved on it. It must be solid silver. This is worth plenty. What's inside? Maybe full of jewels?"

Walker whispered to Bolt, "I don't like this."

Boboy stood back up from fixing the explosives. "We saw gold in de vault."

Carlos ambled over to Bolt and Walker, eyeballed Bolt and said, "Think we need to renegotiate."

"I'll tell you what. After you blow this thing, we'll come back and take the gold," Bolt said.

Carlos sneered at Bolt. "When we blow this thing amigo, everyone in Davao will know. They will be shaken out of their beds, diba? No, no, no ... we need to load the loot right now."

The tension was palpable.

Walker fronted Carlos and gave him the evil eye. "I'll tell you how this will go down. That silver coffin is too heavy to get out of here, right? So, while you finish setting up the explosives with Boboy here, your other four men can grab as much as they can from the vault. That will give them about five minutes. Deal?"

With his eyes locked on Walker's in a cold hard stare, there was a pregnant pause, then a smug grin cracked on his skeletal face. "Okay lang, deal."

He turned and issued orders to his men who immediately darted off to plunder the vault.

Alice, followed in single file by Vee, Jax and Blake, made his way stealthily along the dark corridor. Only Blake and Vee were armed, guns up. Halfway along, Alice gave a sharp hand signal to stop. He turned to Vee and whispered, "Hear that? Voices up ahead."

"That's the vault, they must be inside it," Vee figured.

Al was shocked when he noticed Jax had an automatic. He whispered to her sarcastically, "Is that standard issue for archaeologists?"

Boboy had finished packing the explosives. He looked up from his crouching position at Walker, who was watching intently. "Enough?" Boboy asked.

Walker confirmed with a slow nod, so Boboy fixed the detonator. Once done, he signalled to Carlos it was set.

Carlos handed the remote for the detonation to Walker. "Here, you have de glory."

He then sounded a hoot like an owl for his men in the vault. He waited a second for a response, got it, then said, "Okay, let's go … others will follow."

Alice arrived at a junction. He knew which way to go because of the voices and laughter.

"The safe door is immediately around the corner," Vee whispered.

"Right, wait here." He took a breath and moved quickly around it. After half a dozen skulking steps along the unlit corridor, he could make out four men inside the vault, smoking, laughing and hurriedly loading antiquities into sacks. Al sized it up, then pounced, slamming the huge metal door shut, locking them inside. Muffled complaints erupted from them.

He whipped back to the others and whispered, "Okay, that's taken care of four of them, but there was no sign of the sarcophagus."

"They must have moved it," Jax said.

"It was on a dolly," Blake explained.

A signal from Al and he led them along the corridor. He stopped when he heard footsteps and talking.

"The warehouse is through those doors," Jax said, hastily.

Al silently pushed through the two big swinging doors.

As they were passing through the big sliding warehouse door, Walker ordered, "Leave the door open to let the smoke out Carlos, I'll come back in to check the job is done."

CHAPTER 16
SKYJACKED

T HE **OTHERS FOLLOWED** Alice through into the warehouse. He stopped at the sarcophagus and sharply signalled them. "Stop, the thing's packed with explosives under it."

A loud rushing noise and a powerful bright light poured in through the doorjambs and windows, virtually blasting through every crack in the structure. It was so blinding they were forced to shield their eyes. Along with the light came an electromagnetic maelstrom whirling about so fiercely, the four of them struggled to maintain their footing. It was like being caught in a mini-tornado. The whirlwind whipped up sand, dust, and debris into a swirling, blinding dust devil, so thick it was difficult to see or breathe. Alice whipped off his jacket and wrapped it around his face for protection, and then he yelled out at the top of his voice to rise above the chaotic racket, "Jump ... Vee ... jump!"

Vee quickly accessed the remote Al had given her and pressed to open the vortex.

"Go! Go now! Send back a vortex for me," Al roared.

The three of them did as ordered and rushed through the fury to the opening vortex.

Outside the warehouse, Walker, Bolt, Carlos, and Boboy were engulfed by a powerful light beaming down on the warehouse from above. Gazing up through spread fingers at the light source, they were rocked by a wild electromagnetic whirlwind.

All too supernatural for Carlos and Boboy, they panicked and took off post haste for the car.

Still shielding his eyes, Walker could see three distorted images materialise inside the light up high and descending. He could also make out that the light was coming from a craft hovering about a hundred metres overhead: a spacecraft.

Carlos stopped at the car, puffing out of breath, not from running but from hysteria. He turned sharply to check if the others were following and then freaked out when he saw three bipedal creatures touching down on the ground within the light.

Fighting the mayhem of the electromagnetic storm, shielding his eyes, Alice reached the sarcophagus and bent down to check the explosives packed underneath it. Satisfied there was enough to blow it and everything else in the vicinity to hell, he straightened up, and while resting his hands on the metal coffin to think, noticed the intricate hieroglyphic carvings on the top. Then, he recognised the orb shape En-Ki had mentioned embossed at the centre. At that moment, he realised what he needed to do.

Carlos raised his pistol and opened fire at the strange trans-dimensional beings in the light. They were armour-clad. To Carlos, they looked like medieval knights. One of them raised a weapon and returned fire. A bright orange laser beam shot from the handheld weapon and struck Carlos. He threw his hands in the air and looked down at his body in horror as it began to glow bright orange, and then in a matter of seconds, he melted into a bubbling blob of amorphous slime on the bitumen. Terrified by Carlos's grisly fate, Boboy opened fire at the alien creatures, but he had no sooner pulled the trigger when he was also vaporised into sludge.

After seeing what had happened to them, Bolt lost his nerve and took off for the Pajero, determined to escape.

With his eyes fixed on the alien creatures striding towards him, Walker could now clearly see they were armoured from head to toe like robots. But they weren't moving like robots; they were far too nimble. He quickly assessed the situation like any experienced soldier would and estimated it would be a fight he had no chance of winning, so he pressed the detonator. The resulting explosion was massive, but to Walker's surprise, it stopped just seconds after erupting. Everything had frozen due to the vortex Vee had opened inside the warehouse. Everything, except for Walker and the three aliens, had frozen. Walker had no idea why this was happening, figuring it had to do with the aliens. With no desire to suffer the same fate as Carlos and Boboy, he took off after Bolt. Just as he reached the Pajero with Bolt sitting behind the steering wheel, eyes wide in a frozen stare, the powerful light from the spacecraft overhead shut off and, with it, the mayhem ceased. Then, something unexpected happened: the sarcophagus rolled out through the big sliding doors as though it had been given a massive push by some strange force and stopped.

Inside the warehouse, the vortex closed, and the thunderous roar of the explosion resumed. A massive fireball shot out through the open door. A deafening boom followed as the shockwave hit the warehouse roof, sending a huge fireball and a plume of smoke coiling into the air. Seconds later, flaming pieces of roof began raining down from the sky like molten lava bombs.

Bolt snapped out of the freeze, looked sharply at Walker beside him in the passenger seat, then at the erupting warehouse, started up the Pajero, and floored it.

With tyres squealing in a burnout, it then sped towards the main road, barely beating the shockwave and the flaming debris.

The red flickering glow from the explosion reflected on the belly of the huge dark alien craft hovering above the flaming wreck of the warehouse. A narrow beam shot down from it, immersing the sarcophagus in a bright silvery light. The tractor beam lifted the sarcophagus off the dolly. A hatch slid open in the craft's belly, with a luminous green glow inside. The sarcophagus disappeared inside, and the hatch slid shut. Three beams fired from the craft, immersing each of the armoured alien creatures. They dematerialised into atoms. The lights retracted, and in the blink of an eye, the craft vanished.

Vee, Blake, and Jax had used the existing nano-wormhole stream back to Kairos, so a new wormhole needed to be resent to the Davao coordinates for Alice to return through. Christina had sent the wormhole, and they were now waiting for Alice to materialise.

The Professor was removing the Clock Drive from Jax when Vee stink-eyed Jax and growled at Secta. "I don't like this; he shouldn't have stayed behind."

Secta was equally concerned and slowly nodded his head in quasi-agreement. They were all periodically glancing through the control room window at Kairos, expecting any minute for it to activate.

The phone on the console desktop rang, and Secta dived for it, figuring it had to be important. A look of alarm smeared across his face. He put the phone down and said, "That was Mal ... he just heard from the Navy that the two UAPs they were monitoring over Davao have vanished."

"What the hell does that mean?" Vee growled hotly.

"One of them had moved directly over the Davao Museum, and it wasn't the Watcher," Secta added.

The atmosphere was tense, Vee, Secta, Blake, Christina, the Professor, Jax, Hope, all feeling the strain.

"Listen, calm down everyone. There's no need for panic; this isn't the first time something like this has happened. We all know Alice does things in his own peculiar way," Secta qualified, in an effort to prevent the emotions from boiling over.

"But he was caught in the explosion!" Vee barked.

"She's right, Secta," Blake insisted. "There was enough explosives under that thing to blow it to hell and back."

"I need to go back. Even if the sarcophagus has gone," Jax blurted out.

"Why?" Vee snapped, folding her arms in front of her defensively.

"To examine the rest of the treasure," Jax answered, with urgency.

"Fair enough, I get that," Secta agreed. "But not until morning.

The museum will be crawling with cops ... you'll have a thirty-second freeze window once you arrive to move so they don't think you just materialised out of nowhere," Secta explained.

"I'll go with her," Blake said.

Vee didn't like that and made it known dogmatically. "What for? There's no need for you to see the treasure."

"I agree, he should go, Vee," Secta said sternly. "We need to be certain the sarcophagus has gone and if Alice is there or not ... He could be injured."

Vee barked assertively, "Then I'm going too."

"No, that won't be necessary," Blake said. Before Vee could mount an argument, Kairos activated, and Christina announced, "We've got incoming." Almost instantly, the mood in the room lightened up, optimistic that it was Alice.

The Professor whispered covertly to Secta, "I don't think it's Alice."

When Turk and Luna stepped out of Kairos, Vee's mood descended back into gloom. She burst into tears and stormed out of the control room.

"What the hell's eating her?" Secta inquired of Blake.

"She's not in a happy place right now ... I should have a talk with her," Blake suggested.

"I think that'd be wise, Blake. We can't have anyone acting capricious ... we all have a job to do," Secta said sternly before heading to the event room to greet Luna and Turk.

"Come on, Jax," Hope said, in an effort to lift spirits, "how about I take you to the commissary for a snack?"

Jax smiled wanly. "Thanks, Hope. That's just what the doctor ordered."

Baffled, Christina took the time to check how Turk and Luna could have arrived from 2112 when there was already a wormhole open to Davao for Alice. She found the incoming wormhole had somehow overridden the outgoing wormhole, and that presented something of a conundrum for her.

The Professor was reading a document on his notepad, waiting for

Secta to bring Turk and Luna in from the event room, when he looked up at Christina and said, "I suppose you're wondering how the Davao wormhole could have been overridden?"

Christina swivelled her chair round to face him. "Yes, it certainly did that ... did you know that was possible?"

"The positively charged incoming wormhole is slightly stronger than the outgoing negatively charged wormhole. In fact, though the protons remain the same, the number of electrons is greater in the positive wormhole, which I believe to be the reason incoming has precedence over outgoing."

Slowly nodding her head, Christina acknowledged, "Yes, yes, that makes sense."

Secta led Luna and Turk into the control room.

A throng of spectators had gathered outside the Museum behind the crime scene cordon, gawking at the devastation and the police activity. In the crowd, head and shoulders above the rest, stood Walker. He had come to check what remained of the sarcophagus.

Smoke was still rising from the ruined warehouse. The roof was charred and mostly gone, but the sidewalls had survived, still standing—just. Chunks of debris, mostly roofing, were scattered about, and positioned by the big sliding door stood the heavy-duty six-wheeled dolly that had once held the sarcophagus. Further to the side, at the car park, forensic police were busy dusting a black Pajero for prints left by the gang.

The press was in a huddle on the other side of the police cordon, taking photographs, and a CNN reporter was setting up for an interview with the senior investigating officer. Walker moved closer to listen to the interview, expecting it to be in English. It was, and he quickly learned they considered it an attempted robbery as opposed to a terrorist act, and that the suspects had been arrested. When asked how the police had managed to catch them so quickly, the inspector explained that the accused had been locked inside the museum vault that contained the treasure they had been attempting to steal. When asked how that could have happened, he speculated that it must have been accidental.

"Why would the explosion have been detonated while the robbers were still inside the vault?" the young female CNN reporter questioned with a strong American accent.

By the expression on the middle-aged inspector's face, he was confused himself by the incident. "We are thinking the robbers had explosives to blow the safe, and that these explosives were somehow accidentally detonated. The resulting explosion probably forced the vault to slam shut, locking them inside. We think the person who detonated the massive explosion was caught up in it; nothing of him has been found."

The reporter asked, "I understand they were trying to steal the recently discovered Yamashita treasure. Was any of it taken?"

"Museum curator Dr Amaya Alvarez reported that a platinum sarcophagus is missing. All that remains is the trolley it was on. We are investigating whether accomplices to the others escaped with it. If they did, they won't get far; it weighs over a ton."

Walker had learned enough to conclude that the aliens must have taken the sarcophagus because the dolly had survived the blast and left empty. Though he hadn't succeeded with his mission, he figured the target, now with an alien entity, was as good as if it had been destroyed. Strolling from the crime scene, he phoned Electra. He was surprised when Miss Fych redirected his call to Honor.

"Honor, glad to know you're back. You all right?" he said courteously.

"Yes, I suppose you're wondering why I have taken your call?" she responded.

"I admit I wasn't expecting it ... I—"

"Electra put me back in charge of security," she said curtly. "So, you can give me an update on your mission?"

Walker may have been surprised that he'd been usurped by

Honor in his absence, but he easily shrugged it off. An ex-soldier, he was accustomed to sudden changes in command and so assumed she was up to speed on his mission brief. Aware it wasn't a secure line, he chose his words carefully. "I will need to brief you upon my return, but in short, the target is no longer on Earth."

"Are you ready to return?" she inquired.

"The sooner the better."

"Okay, I will let Adamski know immediately. Find a secure place and text me the GPS coordinates."

"No problem."

He had decided not to pay Bolt the full fee he'd promised because the mission had failed. Instead, he used his phone to deposit a sum large enough to cover his out-of-pocket expenses in Bolt's bank account. Undoubtedly, Bolt would be angry at being short-changed, but he knew with Honor back in charge of security and the division's purse strings, she would take pleasure in resolving the matter with the criminal personally.

With that done, he was set to go. He walked along Filipinas Street until he found an obscure location at the rear of an old factory. He dialled up the GPS coordinates and sent the text to Honor.

A few minutes later, Walker arrived in the Aquila II event room and then made his way to join Honor and Adamski in the control room.

Honor confronted him and asked tersely, "Can you explain what you meant by the target no longer being on Earth?"

"Yes, I presume it was skyjacked by an alien craft just as we set off the explosion to destroy it. I think they beamed it on board."

"How can you be sure?" Honor challenged.

"There is no other explanation. I saw the craft overhead ... I saw three alien creatures descend from it, and then the explosion. The police found nothing but the trolley it had been on, still in one piece. The explosion hadn't touched it."

Walker, of course, had no idea Alice was involved and assumed what had caused the men to be trapped inside the vault was exactly as the inspector had speculated. He also presumed that somehow the force of the explosion had pushed the sarcophagus on the dolly out of the warehouse, though it didn't make complete sense because the explosives were packed underneath the trolley. He decided to let it go.

"Who are these aliens?" Adamski questioned.

Dr Mennis entered the room.

"Commander Walker, this is Dr Ursula Mennis," Honor said curtly. "She returned with me from 2112. Dr Mennis created Cronus and is now working with Dr Li."

"Which will progress the RF project significantly," Adamski said, gloating with admiration for his new colleague.

Honor jumped in before too much praise was dumped on Mennis and snapped, "Our sources in the Philippines reported there were two UAPs over Davao."

"Yes, one of them seemed to be a Watcher, while the other one appeared to be some kind of alien battleship," Walker explained.

Honor's eyes narrowed, "Which of them took the sarcophagus?"

"I don't think it was the Watcher. It must have been the battleship … but I admit it was difficult to see in the blinding light coming from it. I will detail it in a full report."

Ursula chipped in, "Electra won't be pleased; she wanted the relic destroyed."

"Well, at least we know it is not in the hands of Oceana or any of our other terrestrial adversaries," Adamski pointed out.

CHAPTER 17
COURAGE

THE SARCOPHAGUS HAD been positioned in the centre of a dimly-lit circular room. There was nothing else in the room except for its cylindrical metal wall and a small oyster light glowing orange, recessed in the ceiling. There was no sound; it was deathly silent, only the occasional creak of metal under temperature stress.

Alice had been laid out like a mummy inside the sarcophagus for so long that he had fallen asleep. He woke with a start and immediately felt the effects of claustrophobia. The bile of panic rose in his throat ... he reached for the cellphone in his hip pocket, retrieved it, and then used the screen light to see, but the solace was only a temporary calm. The orb button—he said to himself, recalling that the orb button located on the canopy was repeated on the underside of the lid. Hoping it would open it, he reached out a finger and pressed. A click sounded, indicating, much to his relief, that it had worked.

The lid of the sarcophagus creaked open, and Alice rose from within like a vampire emerging from its soil-lined coffin. Before stepping out, he rummaged in his pocket and found a marker the size of a dime. It would emit a signal for a radius of two hundred metres that his implant was tuned to, allowing him to locate it.

He stepped out ... there was atmosphere and gravity. No sense of motion. He scanned the room for a way out but couldn't find any. With an ear against the metal wall, he listened for engine noise, vibration, or any sound of movement, but detected nothing. He noticed a small device countersunk into the ceiling and figured it might be a camera. Presuming he was under observation, he lingered in anticipation of a visit, but when no-one appeared after an hour, he sat on the floor with his back to the wall to wait it out and nodded off.

A sharp sound awakened him. He had no idea how long he had been asleep. As his vision cleared, he realised the sound had come from a panel that had opened like the iris of a camera aperture in the wall. He got to his feet, stepped out of the room into a dimly lit corridor, and had only taken a few steps when a hologram materialised, halting his progress. It was difficult for him to know whether he could walk through the image or not, so he decided to try and communicate with the bipedal figure in the metallic flying suit, blocking his way. Its face was obscured by a darkened wrap-around visor.

"Hello. I'm Alice."

"Step on the light," the feminine voice ordered in monotone.

He looked down at a tiny blinking red light recessed into the floor and complied. He could see by the glow beneath his boot that the light had changed to green under the pressure of his foot. He figured it had scanned him for weapons.

"Follow," the hologram ordered. The voice seemed to come from everywhere.

Al's implant identified the language spoken as Sumerian. That's interesting, he thought. As he followed the opaque image along the curving corridor, he asked in Sumerian, "Where am I?" As he posed the question, he felt a presence at his back and quickly checked over his shoulder. Following two metres behind was a duplicate hologram; he was sandwiched between them.

"No interaction," both holograms said simultaneously.

He mumbled to himself, "Great, a pair of holograms as dumb as a box of spanners."

They led him down a drastically sloping raceway into the dark, oxidized bowels of what he figured was a spacecraft. The walls were wet with a black, mossy slime. The atmosphere, uncomfortably humid, was made worse by an unpleasant, pungent, mouldy smell and an irritatingly loud mid-range hum. But it wasn't until they reached the bottom level that Alice realised the smell was coming from humanity. There were people imprisoned in cages there ... their groans and pleas now audible, and he could see they were in a terrible condition, incarcerated inhumanely like smuggled animals. Thirty small cages in all, each containing a single person. The first cage they came to held a guy in his twenties who, upon seeing Alice, crawled on hands and knees as close as he could to the holographic grid imprisoning him and yelled at Al in English with a parched voice, "They're going to kill us ... we're cattle ... they're monsters. Don't touch the holograms, man, you'll die, they're poisonous."

Al could tell from his accent that he was Afro-American.

"Are we on a craft? How did you get here?" Al said, hurriedly.

"No interaction," the holograms warned in unison, exactly as before. Al figured it was an automated response.

"It's an alien ship; we're abductees. Don't get them pissed or they'll punish you," the prisoner groaned hoarsely. "Wait till they've gone."

The leading hologram waved its hand through the holographic bars enclosing a vacant cage, and the bars deactivated.

"Enter," they ordered.

Al needed to stoop to enter the small cage. The hologram waved its hand again, and the bars reactivated. With Alice confined, both holograms simply dissolved.

It looked to Alice like the majority of prisoners were either asleep or dead. There were an equal number of men and women, and from what he could estimate, all of them aged from their late teens to around forty or so—none older.

Al called out to the man he'd been speaking to, "How long have you been here?"

"Four days by my count, no food, and the only water is what comes off the walls, man. Plenty of the others are dead. I've been eating that black moss crap off-a the walls. It grows back every ten hours. Weird stuff, tastes like hell."

"Are we in flight?"

"No way of telling, man."

"Where were you abducted from?" Al asked.

"Apache Junction in Arizona. You?"

"I was in Davao in the Philippines."

"Everyone here is from a different place around the world. These aliens must go on hunting parties or something because I was the first taken."

"What's your name, man?" Al asked.

"Roy ... Roy White ... and you?"

"Black Alice."

"Ha! My name's White, and I'm black, and yours is Black, and you're white," Roy chuckled.

"Glad you still have a sense of humour, Roy," Al said.

"Black ... Alice ... is that the real Black Alice?" a weak female voice asked.

"That you, Sara honey?" Roy asked.

"Yes, Roy. I thought I heard someone say Black Alice ... is he a new one?" Sara asked.

"Hey, Sara. Yes, I'm new, and the last time I looked, I was the real Black Alice."

"The heavy metal singer?" she asked.

"None other," Al affirmed.

"Wow, a Rockstar ... I'm a fan ... Sara Douglass from Perth ... well, Adelaide, but they took me from Perth," she said, now with a little excitement in her tone.

"When, Sara?" Al asked.

"Three days ago. Some of the others here are from Scotland, Russia, and Spain."

After an hour, Alice had gleaned as much as Sara and Roy had to offer considering there was no apparent rhyme or reason as to why they'd been abducted or by whom. They hadn't seen any aliens other than the same holograms Al had encountered.

Al was pretty confident it was the same UFO responsible for the attacks on ships in Russia, Spain, and Glasgow that Secta had told him about just before the mission to Tempus. He'd drawn the conclusion because some of the abductees were from those places, and that had to be more than just coincidence.

Without warning, the entire craft lurched sharply to the left, as if an aircraft hit turbulence. It rocked the inmates about and woke some who had been sleeping. Then, the omnipresent background whirring sound that Al presumed was from the energy source driving the ship wound down, and a bright, almost blinding white light lit up the entire prison area. The light was obviously designed to awaken the prisoners, and it did the job. After a couple of minutes of intensity, the light dimmed, a servo sounded, and a door spiralled open in the wall between the rows of cells. At the same time, the holographic vertical cell bars deactivated, and the floor of each cell lit up with a dull green, illuminated from beneath. Al wondered what it all meant when the green floor he was sitting on suddenly became live. The electric shock forced him out of the cell into the aisle, which wasn't live. Now Al could see how many prisoners were alive, as the deceased remained in their cells. Roughly half of them made it to the aisle. There was murmuring and groaning.

Roy was close to Al, and then Sara emerged from her cell and stretched.

"Argh! That was terrible. Hi, Al, it's me, Sara," she said, sounding more cheerful than Al had expected.

In her late teens, she wore her blonde hair cropped short, her eyes were dark. She was dressed in a black T-shirt monogrammed with the official classic Queen crest, blue denim short shorts, and bare feet. Athletic and trim, she had a cheeky disposition.

Roy stood at six feet, lanky, with cropped hair, and dressed in the shaggy remains of a grey business suit.

"Hey, Roy, aren't you a bit overdressed for economy class?" Al joked.

"I was on my way home from work. Got my necktie in my pocket.

Y'all never know if we're gonna meet the boss-man," he replied, light-heartedly.

All of them, except Alice, were stretching, glad to straighten up after confinement.

"Wonder what killed those poor dudes?" Al said, referring to those left motionless in their cages.

"Most of them were injured during the abduction. They were nearly dead when they were put in the cells," Roy explained.

The floor beneath their feet lit up green, just like their cells had. Thinking they were about to be shocked again, they quickly moved out through the open door.

Once outside the craft, everything became clear. It was sunny ... the sky was an unearthly yellow colour that graduated to emerald green higher up. The sun was enormous in the sky, much larger than what they were used to, and orange in colour, casting an otherworldly hue over everything. Three moons hung above, two small and one perhaps twice the size of Earth's. Al thought one of the moons was larger because it was closer. Not far away, there was a deep blue ocean.

Al gazed up at the ship overhead. It was massive, twice the size of an Airbus A-380, dark grey and marked with black scores from meteorites it had deflected. It looked like a larger version of an An-Zu bird to him. The outer skin wasn't smooth; it was angular and corrugated, presumably to deflect radar. There were no livery, numerous communication aerials, and as he scanned all around, he could see no signs of any alien beings ... just them, and no signs of life or habitat. Notably, there was no vegetation. The terrain resembled a desert, not with the red or yellow sand of Earth, but orange, stretching all the way to the sea. In the distance, a jagged mountain range of dark red loomed majestically. It reminded Alice of the Taurus Mountains on Earth, where he and Ninurta had dealt with the An-Zu pilot.

The craft stood on skis atop a massive circular metal disk countersunk into the desert floor. It reminded Al of the elevator at the Avalon bunker, only this was much larger. The air was fresh, clean, and fine to breathe. The atmosphere was humid but pleasant enough, with a temperature of around twenty-five degrees Celsius, yet the gravity was less than on Earth. It made Al feel light-headed, as if he could jump much higher than back home.

Further afield, on the ocean horizon of the cloudless sky, ominous thunderheads were rolling and crackling internally with fierce, bright red lightning—an alien storm.

"Where the heck are we? Another planet?" Roy said, awestruck.

But before Al could answer, he was distracted by the sound of a six-metre iris spiralling open in the circular plate they were standing on.

A voice growled in a broad Scottish accent, "Not for me, I'm outta here."

The big, burly, tattooed Scott bolted across the plate, but when he reached the edge of it, he struck an invisible force field. He froze as if electrocuted, and then, to their horror, vaporised into a melted blob of smouldering flesh. The women screamed.

Electra sat motionless in her office, deeply engrossed in meditation. Suddenly, she snapped out of it and spoke, "I am not satisfied that the Astara is still in existence ... it poses a serious threat," she communicated mentally as En-Lil to the hive. "More so, I believe the Nephilim took it."

"For what reason?" the multiple voices of the hive asked within her mind.

"They desire to generate a living being. We're aware that they have been abducting humans from Earth for years, attempting to breed a hybrid. Our knowledge indicates that this was impossible without using the Astara, which is why I suspect they took it."

"What is the basis for your evidence?"

"The report from my agent, Commander Walker. There were two crafts over Davao—one was a Watcher, and I am certain the other was an An-Zu bird."

"Are you absolutely certain this isn't just paranoia, En-Lil? The Nephilim have been your adversaries since En-Ki created them."

"The question is irrelevant ... the Nephilim must not be allowed to succeed," En-Lil emphasised.

Down the hallway from the Kairos control room, in a lab, the Professor and Hope were busy reverse engineering the TL-100 teleported from 2112.

Jax and Blake had been sent back through Kairos to Davao. Blake on a fact-finding mission, whilst Jax would study the treasure before the Philippines Government could impound it, which was inevitable.

Still unhappy, Vee was sitting in the control room with a dour expression on her face, listening to Turk telling Secta and Christina about the mission to the Rangers' bunker. Though she could see Turk's lips moving she was so spaced-out she couldn't hear what they were saying. Alice missing had shrouded her in a veil of anguish, and being unable to do anything about it only increased her frustration.

For Secta, even though he'd experienced Alice missing a number of times previously, he couldn't ignore the nagging suspicion that this time he may have met his match. Alice had after all once professed to him: 'one thing is inevitable, just like a prize-fighter, sooner or later you're going to come up against someone better than you.'

Rising from her seat to leave, Vee said, "I don't know that I have enough emotional bandwidth to handle this."

"Vee," Turk called after her.

She stopped at the door and looked back forlornly.

"It's all part of what we do, mate," Turk said, compassionately. "Come here, sit back down let me tell you something."

Vee respected Turk and complied, dawdling back and taking her seat.

He paused then said, "You know, I've been through some sticky times with Alice … any one of them would have stopped the heart of the average bloke. So, I want to tell you about courage. When Al occupied me, I had been sentenced to fight to the death in the arena like a gladiator. It was a walled arena, unarmed, we were forced to fight the hardest, most brutal bastards I'd ever come across … and I tell you, I've come across plenty. The thing-of-it is, I couldn't help him, my implant had been shut down by Gorrick's wicked offsider Dr Mennis … you met her … so, there was Al, alone in the arena, armed only with his mind and fists, up against impossible odds—two brutes on motorbikes armed with spears. The game was appropriately called Deathball. Like basketball a ball had to be thrown into a hoop … but there was only one hoop and it was positioned three metres up the wall of the arena. Three hoops for the prisoner would gain him freedom … and you know what? Nothing was going to stop Alice from winning … nothing. I know of no-one more noble, more courageous or tougher than that bloke."

"Coming from you Turk … there could be no greater accolade," Secta said, respectfully.

Vee had teared up. She knew Turk was right … on the few occasions she'd seen her brother in action, no-one could equal him … except maybe Turk.

The big feller gave her a bear-hug, then held her at arms-length and said, "Be as brave as your brother girl, because that's what he would demand of you … am I right?"

Nodding her head, she wiped away the tears. Turk's passionate narrative had grown her mentally taller in confidence. "I hear you Turk, thank you. Did he win?"

He grinned, "I'm here, that pretty-much says it all."

CHAPTER 18
PROBE

THEY WERE STRUCK frozen by what they had witnessed. It was then the gruesome reality of their dire situation impacted fully. They knew now that with such merciless captors, any attempt to escape would be an exercise in futility.

They were all startled when an eerie rumbling sound faded up from deep within the circular open cavity at their feet, forewarning something was coming their way. In fearful anticipation, they huddled together like frightened animals.

Alice knew he needed to take control. He was the fittest, he was the most experienced, and above all, he wasn't intimidated.

"Now listen, for those that don't know me, I'm Alice ... stay calm, don't panic, you can see what happens by the Scot if you panic. We'll get through this ... trust me."

Even though the ominous sound of whatever was coming out of that dark hole was increasing in volume, Al could feel his appeal for calm working.

A strange dark green globular-shaped vehicle rose out of the void. It hovered to wait for the aperture to iris shut and then it settled down on the closed disc. A hatch opened in its nose, and a ramp extended, which fluoresced green and blinked inviting them to board.

"Okay, let's go on board ... I'll lead the way," Al said, taking the initiative. He presumed that just like the An-Zu bird he'd experienced before, everything to do with this alien species would be automated.

He stepped onto the ramp to enter the craft, not expecting anything threatening. As he progressed up the sloping ramp, he noticed lights countersunk in it, blinking from green to blue when he stepped over them. Upon reaching the doorway, he stopped and turned back to watch the others coming up the ramp. He let several of them pass him and told them to wait just inside the door. A few of them weren't in the best shape and had to be helped up the incline by others. When the first of the injured captives tried to step over the ramp light, it changed to red. She was instantly paralysed, unable to move. The ramp lit up red, and a line of green lights illuminated back down the ramp along the disc back inside the spacecraft from whence they'd come.

It dawned on Alice that it was a sensor that had detected imperfection and was rejecting the person commanding her by way of the strip-lights to return to the ship.

Al called to her, "Miss, you'll need to return to the ship."

"No, no … I can't," she said, in a panic still unable to move but capable of speech.

Al made his way to her and told her compassionately, "Look, I reckon this is a fitness test. If you go back to the ship, I think they'll return you home. I don't believe they mean you any harm. If they wanted to hurt you, they would have done so by now."

"But, but I, I'm afraid, Alice," the woman in her late thirties stuttered worriedly.

"Come on love, I'll help you." He took her by the arm, the light intuitively changed to green, and she was released from the paralysis. It allowed Alice to help her back down the ramp towards the ship. A total of four abductees were rejected, and Al helped each of them back.

From inside, the seven remaining captives watched the ramp slide back, and the door glide closed. The interior of the globular transport was featureless. Just one round window like a ship's portal and a big empty space like in a bus with straps suspended from an overhead gantry for them to hold while standing.

"Feel like an animal at an abattoir headed for the big chop," Roy whispered to Al.

"I don't know mate, I get the impression they want us for some special purpose. I don't reckon they aim to kill us."

Sara was eavesdropping and added, "We'll find that out soon enough, won't we?"

The craft travelled at about three hundred clicks at around five hundred metres above ground with uncanny silence. Al was intrigued by the propulsion system—he couldn't fathom it. When after about fifteen minutes he felt the sensation of the craft slowing, he checked out of the small window. They were passing over a rocky, volcanic island with a coastline of dark blue waters. There was no sign of habitation.

"What do you see bro?" Roy asked.

"I think we're about to land at an island resort," Al joked.

He was right about landing, wrong about the resort.

The craft entered an aperture that spiralled open in a mountain on the island.

Hopeful he would finally get to meet his captors, Al waited at the shuttle door for it to open. He was disappointed when exiting was only a repeat of the boarding procedure. Despite this, Al remained confident they would soon make first contact.

The floor lights guided them inside a massive grotto hewn from mountain bedrock. It looked to Alice like an extinct volcano, and that made him wonder why they would be residing underground—could it be that the surface was too hazardous?

A line of green squares illuminated, directing them to cross a vast floor. The squares stopped at a large set of metal doors recessed into the craggy cavern wall. It was obvious after the terrible demise of the Scotsman that stepping off the path could be fatal, so they were exacting with their footfall.

A sensor detected they had assembled at the metal doors, and the doors slid open. Beyond them, they could see a massive cavern containing a city. They were transfixed by the engineering skills it must have taken to construct it.

There was one gleaming white high-rise globular-shaped building that reached more than halfway up to a gargantuan skylight that enclosed the cavern at least two hundred metres above the ground. Around it were smaller globular buildings like houses. All the buildings were connected by two pipes of clear tubing that snaked throughout the city, through which they could see globular vehicles shuttling back and forth.

"This is incredible," Al mumbled. Then, a storm suddenly struck with fury outside, pounding the skylight with torrential rain and lighting up the cavern with reflected dramatic radiant red lighting. Thunder reverberated like the drums of hell. It all became clear to Alice why the inhabitants were subterranean dwellers; little could survive the brutal force of the tempest outside. He figured it had to be the storm he'd noticed when he'd first set foot on the disc from the craft.

"Whoa, glad we're in here, that thing is sic," Roy said.

"You're not wrong, mate," Al agreed. "They must get whacked by storms a lot, explains why they're underground."

The entire cavern vibrated with each cacophonous clap of thunder.

In the midst of all the mayhem, a white rectangular pillar-box rose out of the path in front of them. A door opened in it, and squares leading to it fluoresced green. Al led everyone inside, where they found a ramp of illuminated green squares sloping down.

After a five-minute descending walk, they reached a platform inside the huge clear Perspex-like tube that connected the buildings.

Sara shuffled up beside Alice and told him, "This is like a magical mystery tour."

"Nothing to fear so far, Sara. Let's hope it stays that way," Al cautioned. That old gut feeling of his had materialised a warning of imminent trouble.

After three globular shuttles had passed at speed, one pulled up, but the bubble had no door.

"How do we get in the damn thing?" Al wondered out loud.

Then it just opened. Al was amazed, "Weird," he said, and stepped inside.

The bubble-pod was floating within the tube without touching the walls, using some sort of electromagnetic force field.

Once they were all on board, it sealed shut and then moved off slowly at first, then gradually speeding up. It had a seven-foot ceiling and twelve seats, spacious. The only discomfort was the lack of aircon—the air was thick and difficult to breathe.

Within seconds, the shuttle popped out of the tunnel it was in and moved through the city. Still, Al hadn't seen any signs of life or vegetation.

"What do these people eat?" he asked Sara.

"Yeah, I was thinking the same … no supermarkets … no shops."

"Nowhere to grow anything," Al said.

"One thing is for sure, they must be big. These seats are meant for giants," Sara observed.

Al realised she was right. He hadn't noticed that the interior of the shuttle was designed to take bulky creatures; he was only taking up half the seat.

"We know they're an advanced civilization by their spacecraft … they could be millions of years ahead of us," Al proposed.

Sara managed a giggle. "At least we know they'll have two legs and two arms like us."

Al frowned, "What makes you think that?"

"I caught a glimpse of one when I was abducted. It had skin like a lizard."

"Seriously?" Al said.

"I think so."

The shuttle plunged below the city ground level and stopped at a platform. The aperture opened in the pod and strip-lights on the floor showed the way to a corridor. There was no other way off the platform. It had the clinical appearance of a penal facility, hospital, or a laboratory. Al's gut feeling of trepidation had just increased—he'd seen similar set-ups plenty of times before, even his own base at OTT.

They arrived at a corridor with doors on either side. The doors were eight feet high and wide, a further indication of the size of the inhabitants.

On approach, the first door opened. Al, Roy, and Sara went through, and it closed behind them, permitting only them to enter.

Al figured the room was either a laboratory or an operating theatre because it was filled with a curious array of chrome gadgetry. He wasn't impressed by the operating room table centrally located, which had a large surgical light over it. Then, the unexpected ... the green glowing floor tile under their feet changed to red, incapacitating them.

"What the?" Al questioned.

A whirring sound came from several metal articulated arms around the operating table that moved locking into preparatory positions. The surgical light came on, bathing the table in a white spot.

Green strip lights then extended from the floor tile Sara was standing on to the operating table and blinked.

She knew exactly what that meant and panicked. "No, no ... I don't want to do it ... I don't like this at all."

"If you don't, you'll be electrocuted, babe," Roy said, through gritted teeth, the paralysing effect making it difficult for him to speak clearly.

A sensor somehow detected Sara's compliance and released her from paralysis to mount the table. Whimpering, she lay on it and closed her eyes. Immediately the mechanical arms went to work. Her ankles were secured by automated clamps, and then her wrists were clamped to the table. Though she struggled against the bonds, there was no real choice other than to acquiesce.

The automated arms went to work utilising a number of different implements to examine and probe her body.

With tears trickling down her cheeks, Sara turned her head to Alice, who could do nothing more than offer her a look of sympathy.

It was the kind of invasive probing that had been reported by abductees returning to Earth over the years. Alice thought that somewhere in another part of the building, the procedure was being monitored by someone. Hoping the audio was being monitored as well as the vision, he called out, "Why don't you show yourselves? You're an intelligent species, why the hostility?" When nothing happened, he shouted angrily. "Why? Hear me? Damn it!"

"What's that jive you're talking, man?" Roy asked.

"Sumerian, I guess," Al said, angered by the lack of response.

Roy shot back a bewildered glance with eye movement only. "What if they don't speak Sumerian?"

Al wasn't prepared to try other languages.

When one of the articulated arms produced a spike and inserted it into Sara's navel, she let out a shriek with the pain and then passed out. It was a blessing in a way; at least she didn't have to endure the physical pain of what was to come.

After an hour of what Al figured was torture, the mechanical arms retracted, locked into place, and a door slid open at the far end of the theatre. Al couldn't turn his head to look at the door; he just heard it open. Perhaps he was finally going to meet the host and wasn't disappointed when after a minute or two, a giant bipedal armoured creature strode into the room, up to the gurney, and glared down at Sara.

Al gave it the once-over. At first, it reminded him of one of Zen's RF-20 cyborgs, but massive … at least eight feet tall. When it turned side-on, it reminded Alice of the An-Zu pilot he'd fought in 2,500 BCE; Ninurta had killed.

"Hey you, we need to talk," Al tried in English.

While leaning over Sara, it snapped its head sharply to glare at Al. It was garbed in a dull grey coverall that appeared to be a metallic skin. Though a visor was obscuring its face, its hands were bare, and he could see it had five human-like digits on each hand only with pale, scaly reptilian skin similar to the description Sara had given of the alien that had abducted her.

With a voice as muscular as its body, it spoke in monotone, as if through a small speaker and not a mouth, "I have nothing to say to you, human."

Alice thought, at least I've got it talking. It had answered in Sumerian.

Al thought to try a long shot. "My name is Black Alice ... I am an envoy of En-Ki," he emphasised the name. It resulted in a pregnant pause, with the Alien continuing to eyeball him. Al figured it was either thinking or covertly communicating with its comrades. It straightened up and looked towards the door it had entered through. Another Alien, a replica, appeared there, entered, and grabbed Al by the arm. The lights instantly changed to green at Al's feet, releasing him from the paralysis, and then led him out.

"Hey, what about me?" Roy cried out through clenched teeth in protest.

CHAPTER 19
ASTARA

IT DIDN'T LOOK to Al, by the décor, that it was going to be a take-me-to-your-leader scenario. They were descending a steep ramp deeper into the bowels of the building, with the giant pushing Alice along. Alice figured he could hear ocean waves breaking against rocks outside. The fury of the storm had long since abated, allowing other sounds to be clearer, more obvious. The wind was howling like a thousand wolves outside, adding to the grimness of the circumstances.

Al asked over his shoulder timidly, "Where are you taking me?"

"You were not taken … you came within Astara," the alien answered in an offended tone.

At first, Alice thought it had misunderstood the question, then realised it hadn't but sought to qualify. "If Astara is the sarcophagus, then yes," Al said apologetically but happy to have continued dialogue.

"You are a threat," it snapped and then prodded him to continue.

It was a long dimly lit craggy natural rock ramp that snaked as it descended, slippery underfoot due to its mossy dampness. But that didn't seem to bother the big alien, who strode on confidently, each huge stride of his big metal boot loudly pulverising the loose gravel underfoot.

Al stopped and questioned, "Why?"

The alien looked down at Alice in the eerie twilight as though thinking and then said, "Are you aware of the power of the Astara?"

"No, I have no idea."

Again, there was a pregnant pause. "Then ask that question of your god En-Ki," he said, with a forceful tone. "It was he who created it." He gave Alice a firm shove to move him along. Al got the impression that by the short lapses in dialogue, he wasn't talking to a single entity but many. The thought struck him that the alien might be AI, one of many in a hive like the Gorricks.

"Look, I'm here in peace," Al said in a conciliatory tone. "I got inside the Astara to avoid being killed by an explosion … nothing sinister about that."

"There is a secret to opening it."

He had him there, and so countered, "You wanted the Astara; well, I delivered it … stopped it from being blown to bits … the least you can do is be thankful and return me to my planet … Where am I anyway?" Al asked.

He got no response. They arrived at a holding bay enclosed by a laser grid, the same as on the ship. Inside it, in a space larger than the cells on the ship, were two men asleep on the floor.

Al contemplated popping a pill and thumping the alien but changed his mind. First, he needed to find out where he was and how to get himself and the sarcophagus out of there.

The alien waved his hand to deactivate the laser grid. Unwilling to continue the conversation, he aggressively pushed Al inside the cell then reactivated the grid.

"Wait, that's no way to treat—"

The alien cut him off, "Your destiny will be decided on." He turned and strode off.

"Damn!" Al growled, exasperated.

From behind him, a measured voice in a minatory tone caught him by surprise. "It has no feelings, no emotions, it does not care."

Al spun around sharply to face the voice, speaking Sumerian. One of the prisoners had sat up and was knuckling his eyes. The other one remained motionless.

Al looked the young feller over, and his immediate impression was that he was a wild man. His skin dark-tanned, shoulder-length unkempt black hair, beard of a few days' growth, of average height, athletic, dressed like an Iron Age barbarian. His eyes darting about packed with irrepressible curiosity. But there was something odd about the eyes that Alice couldn't quite put a finger on.

"Who are you?" Al asked.

"Vale Tarz ... Who are you?" He questioned in an arrogant, self-confident tone.

"Black Alice," Al said sternly, extending his hand to shake. Vale took it but shook it like it was an unfamiliar action to him. His mood lightened.

"Who's that?" Al asked, referring to the guy prostrated on the floor that hadn't moved.

"That was Ixon, he died a while ago from his wounds."

"Died? Why didn't you tell the guard?"

"Bah!" he barked, shaking his head. "It would have no care."

It was then Alice noticed what was different about Vale's eyes. The whites were really white, but the pupils were black and elongated like those of a cat, and the iris was a gold colour. Quite captivating.

Al scratched his head. "So, where are we Vale?"

"We are on Atlan, the island of the Nephilim."

"What planet ... or what world is this?" Al corrected.

The question surprised Vale. "This is Kor, of course. Why would you ask such a question? Are you not of Kor?"

Al chose not to answer until he'd learned more. "You called the guard it, why?"

"Because Nephilim are other ... they do not die like us. But they can be killed."

"Are they artificial intelligence, whereas you are human?"

Vale shot Al a look of simian cunning. "Hu-man?" he quizzed. "No, we are Korman."

"Korman, huh? Hmm, where are your people?" Al asked, realising he was still speaking Sumerian.

"Our castes live on floats."

"Floats? Like in the ocean?"

"Yes."

"How did you and Ixon get captured and why?"

"Our fishing boat was blown off course by a storm. It washed up here; we were taken. Once taken, there is no return. I think they use us for body parts."

"What do you mean body parts?"

"The Nephilim must replace body parts when they fail. They cannot reproduce."

Al immediately had flashes of being on an operating table twice with Zen planning to transform him into one of their diabolical cyborg monsters.

"Oh right, I get it … they're cyborgs." It was then he noticed his implant menu indicated he was actually speaking Ancient Hebrew. He recalled the language from when he visited Jerusalem in 587 BC. "Do you know their language?" Al asked.

"No. But they speak ours."

Vale slipped his arms under Ixon to lift him. "Come, help me."

"Why, what are you doing?"

"Trying something I could not manage on my own," Vale said, through tight lips.

They stood the dead body up as best they could, still gripping him. It was then Al realised the nature of the dead young man's wounds. His innards were hanging out of a cavernous cut in his abdomen, with foul-smelling gunk dripping onto the floor.

"Argh, that's gross," Al complained.

"Drag him to the grid," Vale grunted, under the strain. Ixon was heavy but still flexible because rigor mortis hadn't yet set in.

"On the count of three, throw him at the bars, get set to jump through if it makes a gap," Vale said.

Al froze. "Whoa, wait right there … then what? Huh?"

"I know the way they brought me in … I think we can escape."

"To what?"

"If you wish to stay, that is your choice. Just give me a hand with

Ixon."

Al paused to think, then said, "Alright, I'll help you, but then you'll be on your own."

"Fine, if you want to end up a ... what did you call them? A cyborg?"

Al helped drag Ixon close to the laser banding. Then, on a count of three from Vale, they heaved the corpse at the banding. There was a massive surge of energy that caused the dead body to writhe and smoke. It did exactly as Vale had predicted: the banding turned red and blocked enough of the laser bands to open a gap, which he immediately stepped through. A loud irritating pulsing alarm sounded.

While the body of Ixon smoked and fried in the grid, Vale stood on the other side, hands on hips. "Last chance, Black Alice. The Nephilim will be here soon."

Al rolled his eyes and cursed, "Damn!" above the dreadful din of the alarm, and he jumped through.

Vale led Al on the run along a dark narrow corridor that descended toward an even lower level in the opposite direction from where Al had originally arrived. The alarm was fading behind them, replaced by the loud crashing of waves against rocks.

Al saw a light at the end of the tunnel. Vale had been right, there was an exit. The young man climbed through a small gap in the rocks the light was streaming through, with Al hot on his tail. When he emerged on the other side, Al found he was standing on the narrowest of ledges of a sheer craggy cliff, eighty feet above waves violently crashing on the rocks below. There was nowhere to go but down.

"Now what?" Al barked, hands on hips, puffing out of breath, being ravaged by a strong sea breeze.

"Down there, on the rocks ... my boat."

Al peered at the jagged black volcanic rocks below, white water waves breaking over them. "You call that thing a boat?" he growled. The blast of an updraft blew his hair about wildly. The boat was nothing more than a canoe made of animal hides.

"How are you going to get to it, jump?" Al barked facetiously.

"It is a good boat," Vale said, as if offended, and then without hesitation, jumped off the cliff.

A jump into waves pounding against sharp volcanic rocks wasn't exactly what Al had in mind. The crunching sound of large feet on a pebbly surface came from behind him. It was ample motivation, so he let out a sigh of surrender, "To hell with it!" and stepped off the edge. He plunged feet first into the frothing blue water.

By the time he popped to the surface, Vale had fetched the canoe and paddled out through the breakers to collect him.

Al struggled on board. Spluttering, he said, "That was invigorating." The water was a slightly different texture than what he'd expected ... thicker and not saltwater, but greater buoyancy than on Earth, making it easy to swim in. He sat in the flimsy craft tapping water out of his left ear and asked, "Anything down there?"

"Where in the sea? Sure ... some things with ravenous appetites."

"Great, now you tell me," Al whined.

"If I told you before, would you still have jumped?"

"Hmm, maybe not." He looked up sharply at the cliff edge they'd jumped from and was astounded he'd done it. The setting sun reflected off the armour of two guards standing at the precipice. He'd made the right decision but wasn't too thrilled about floating in a flimsy canoe on a sea brimming with starving monsters. He did, however, take solace from Vale's obvious sailing skills.

After a few hours, they were consumed by an inky darkness. Vale spotted something. "There, in the distance, a light ... must be a float."

Al was relieved to see the speck of light on the horizon, though in sitting up, he noticed a huge swirl of blue phosphorescence in the water. There were big things moving about below the boat.

"What the heck is that in the water?" he squawked.

"Heck? Oh, creatures. They sense we are here. Keep your hands away from the edge; they will be hungry," Vale said with a cheeky smirk.

Al immediately drew his knees up and clasped his fingers around them. "You've got to be kidding, mate."

It took another gruelling hour of Al watching the light on the horizon growing larger before they were finally near enough to make out the silhouette of a float. According to Vale, they were lucky the sea had been smooth. Al dreaded what it would've been like if it was rough. As smooth as Vale reckoned it was, it still made him nauseous.

The float was man-made, about the size of a football field, and on stilts. A large sea gate blocked the entrance. Al looked up at the massive gate, wondering whether it was built to keep something big out or something in. He could make out huts on the float platform above and a lighthouse that stood out like a sore thumb. It had been the source of the light Alice had been anxiously watching grow larger while on the frightening dark sea.

Vale paddled the canoe up to the gate. It looked to Al to be made from something other than timber. Gripping its craggy surface to prevent the canoe from drifting away, Vale struggled to his feet and called out, "Hello, London! I am Vale Tarz, son of Odin Tarz, chief of Stockholm. I request safe harbour!"

Al realised that among his caste, Vale was more than just a fisherman. Seems he was the son of a chieftain. He was also intrigued by the names London and Stockholm.

After a couple of minutes, the gate was opened by someone on the other side using a system of ropes and pulleys from the gantry spanning it. Vale paddled the canoe in through the small opening into a tranquil lagoon.

Blake, Jax, and two museum staff members were loading treasure out of the vault onto a dolly. It was late morning, and they'd been at it for a few hours when Amaya brought out a tray of drinks for morning tea.

The warehouse had been left a burnt-out shell—the walls were charred, and the roof mostly blown away. Due to the roof's condition, they decided to move the treasure inside the museum in case it rained; storms had been predicted for later that day.

Amaya set the tray down on a bench and then handed out mugs of coffee. They looked as though they'd been through a bushfire, with their faces streaked with soot and clothes soiled.

"What do you think its value, Jax?" Amaya asked.

Resting against the bench, Jax wiped away a wayward strand of hair that had stuck to her sweaty forehead and said, "Some of it is extremely valuable, but not as treasure as much as its intrinsic value for collectors and museums. I think most of it should stay here in Davao, so that after it has been cleaned up, you can display it."

"Yes, it would be a drawcard for us, that's for sure," Amaya agreed chirpily, the thought of such a good revenue spinner exciting her.

Blake had a small ornate-looking wooden box in one hand and a mug of coffee in the other. "I think the contents of this box would be worth a king's ransom," he muttered, perched on the bench next to Jax. He put down his coffee and opened the box to show them. It was filled with fine jewellery: rings, necklaces, and pendants. Blake took out a ring to show them. "It's an emerald, at least ten carats. Probably be worth around a quarter of a million dollars, I'd say."

"Where would it be from?" Amaya asked.

Holding it up to the light to admire its beauty, he said, "China, I'd say. Yamashita plundered Northern China and Manchuria."

"Ha," Amaya scoffed, "if the Filipino Government gets its grubby claws on that, it will end up on the finger of a politician's wife."

"Of that, you can be sure," Blake agreed. "Check this out … a ruby necklace with diamonds, worth a fortune." He held it up.

"I'll take that," a familiar gruff voice rang out from Handerson Bolt, standing with a silenced automatic aimed at them.

"Well, if it isn't the mastermind of the failed sarcophagus heist!" the last two words from Blake, a full-throated roar.

Jax sharply straightened up from the bench, pulled a pistol from her hip pocket, but before she could fire a shot at Bolt, he fired. At the same time, Blake jumped in front of Jax, took the bullet just below the rib cage, and sank to the floor on his knees, holding his chest. He poised there momentarily, glanced up at Jax with blood pumping through his fingers, and then he collapsed.

Amaya and her two Filipino staff members nervously raised their hands in surrender.

Bolt strode angrily toward them with his arm extended and the pistol aimed at them.

Jax felt her hand go limp. The pistol slipped from her fingers and bounced in slow motion onto the floor. The bullet had passed through Blake into her chest. Her eyes rolled back in her head, her knees gave way, and she collapsed on the floor beside Blake. Panting in short breaths, she crawled her fingers along the ground, trying to reach Blake's hand, but stopped just short.

Bolt turned his gun on Amaya. She sized up the menacing figure before her, fully aware that her time was running out. He had no intention of leaving her alive—this man was a murderer, and he wouldn't tolerate witnesses.

A macabre smirk twisted Bolt's chiselled features, and he opened fire. Three shots rang out in rapid succession, silencing Amaya and her two staff members forever.

With his objective achieved, Bolt retrieved the box of jewellery from the floor beside Blake's body. He carefully gathered the scattered items, arranged them inside the box, closed the lid, and then nonchalantly walked out of the warehouse as though nothing had happened. He didn't bother taking more of the treasure; the box of jewellery would suffice and would be relatively easy for him to smuggle out of the Philippines. All that remained was to dispose of the murder weapon and catch his pre-booked flight to Manila. From there, a connecting flight would take him to Hong Kong—his plan seemed foolproof. After having the jewellery appraised by his black-market contacts in nearby Macao, he planned to sell the collection for a quarter of its value in cash, a haul that would still amount to a considerable sum.

Upon receiving news from Zen's New York office that the suspected UAP over Davao had now moved to the sky above New York, causing panic, Electra swiftly summoned her team to a meeting.

Standing at the head of the board table, Electra addressed her team, "This situation gives us a unique chance to finally eliminate the Astara. We need to find a way to infiltrate the UFO positioned over New York. Dr Li, do we have a suitable cyborg for this mission?"

Li shot Ursula a furtive glance, then looked back at Electra, nervously cleared her throat, and then after a slight cough admitted awkwardly, "Ma'am right now we do not have a unit capable of autonomous instruction, we can only feed instructional code and that would be rendered impossible if the target was to leave into space. We would lose contact."

Ursula tried to support the doctor. "There have been setbacks in developing this because of technological limitations this time presents us."

Displaying a glare of dissatisfaction, Electra briskly snapped, "All right, all right, but we cannot afford to forgo this opportunity. We will need to teleport an agent on board the craft so, Honor, give me your recommendation," she requested sternly.

"Only Commander Walker ma'am. He's the only agent with the necessary skill set. But how can we be certain a human will survive in the UFO?"

"Uri can you ascertain that?" Electra asked the small Russian scientist.

Adamski sat forward in his seat and steepled his fingers in front of his face. "Um, the coordinates … I will require the exact coordinates of the craft in order to send a probe on board to evaluate—"

Electra cut him off handing him her cellphone. "Here, will this suffice."

Adamski copied the information from the phone to his device and then stood up abruptly. "I will do it immediately," he said, excitedly, up for the challenge.

Electra watched him leave and then told Honor, "Place Walker on standby."

"I have already given him notice," Honor said, putting her phone down on the board table. It buzzed. She collected it again and peered at the screen. "Walker asked for an assistant."

Electra thought about it, then said, "I agree. He would be unlikely to succeed alone. We cannot afford another failure. Ask what he has in mind?"

Honor could tell En-Lil was doing the talking, because he was far less tolerant than Electra's programming. Her phone buzzed. "No, he doesn't … we have serious limitations when it comes to agents trained with time travel skills."

"Then I will accompany him," Electra said, resolutely.

Ursula erupted, "Ma'am, would that be wise? Perhaps I should go or Honor?"

Electra/En-Lil said emphatically, "This is a critical mission. The Astara must be destroyed."

CHAPTER 20
THE ASKING

PRESIDENT **MAL LOW** concluded his hands-free phone conversation after an extensive talk with US President Oprah Robinson. She had reached out because a UFO hovering over New York City carried the same signature as the one previously seen over Davao. Additionally, she had inquired about any communication from Blake Green, as her office had not received updates from Jax De Ville, who was a day overdue in submitting her daily report. This had sparked concerns. Mal hadn't received any word from Blake, so he promised to investigate and provide her with updates. He promptly summoned OTT executives and Luna to his office to discuss the situation.

"If we place a probe on that ship, we could search for Alice's marker," the Professor suggested.

"Using the newly developed mini-probe by the technicians?" Hope questioned.

"Why bother? I'll go," Vee urged.

"Me too," Turk chimed in.

"Although we admire your courage, that's not a viable option," Mal stated firmly.

"I need to make a call to check on Blake in Davao," Karzoff mentioned, getting up and hastily leaving the room.

"Is the new probe ready?" Mal inquired.

"Given the circumstances, I believe so. It's our only opportunity, so it must be ready," Secta explained.

"Very well, then proceed, Secta. Luna, what updates do we have from the UN?"

As Secta, the Professor, Hope, and Christina departed to prepare the probe, Luna leaned forward in her chair, showing a frustrated expression. "Mal, I'll need your support to shut down Aquila. I received a report earlier this morning about more unauthorised missions. The latest occurred within the last 24 hours, from Davao back to Sydney."

"That would involve their field agent or agents returning. It's highly likely they were involved in the Davao Museum explosion," Mal responded angrily.

"There was only one traveller, but an earlier event to 2112 involved three others. This needs to stop, Mal, and it's becoming a frequent occurrence within your jurisdiction," she urged.

Mal reclined in his chair, arms folded defiantly. "I could argue that Zen broke the UNTT rules, Luna, but work with Viktoria and resolve this with Karzoff. Whatever you decide, I'll support it."

Viktoria nodded, "Sir," and led Luna out.

Rita Vallins peeked into the doorway and inquired, "Coffee, sir?"

"Yes, please, Rita. Also, connect me with President Robinson, I need to update her on our actions regarding the UFO."

"Yes, sir. Oh, Dr James called from Texas. He wanted to inform you that Tempus will be operational in two days."

"Good news. Let OTT know," Mal instructed.

Karzoff entered the office with urgency, passing by Rita. "Sir, apologies for the interruption. I have spoken with the Consulate in Manila. Blake has been shot and is in the hospital on life support. Dr Jax De Ville is also severely wounded. The Davao Museum's curator and two staff members are dead. The police suspect a robbery but do not know the specifics as yet."

Mal swiftly rose from his seat, expressing concern. "Holy mackerel! Have our navy ship off Davao send a chopper to transport the ship's doctor for Blake and De Ville's care. Then get them out of there. I'll speak with the Americans."

Remaining seated beside Turk, Vee was devastated and exclaimed, "Oh, my god!"

Turk added, "Sounds like a professional hit ... likely Handerson Bolt."

"Unless it was the Zen agent, who then escaped through Aquila," Vee proposed.

Rita stood at the door, awaiting Mal's instructions. "Rita, ask Luna for the timeframe when Aquila was used. It might help us determine if they were involved."

"Yes, sir," she replied before heading back to her desk.

Over the next hour, they gathered more information about the hit. The Zen agent's estimated arrival in Sydney was before the attack, indicating that Zen was not responsible. This pointed at Handerson Bolt as the likely assassin. Karzoff contacted the Oceana Consulate in Manila, instructing them to prevent Bolt from leaving the Philippines.

For now, all they could do was monitor the situation. Vee felt the stress intensely due to her emotional attachment to Blake, a relationship that had recently been strained and worsened by unresolved differences.

"I should have been there," Vee expressed bitterly.

Mal sensed her frustration was rooted in not being allowed to accompany Blake and Jax back to Davao.

"Vee, no-one is to blame for this tragic incident except the person responsible. If you had gone, you might have been harmed. Our focus now is on resolving the situation. We need to get Blake to safety, apprehend Bolt, and concentrate on supporting Alice."

Turk placed a comforting arm around Vee. "You know Mal's right, Vee."

She nodded, took a deep breath, and with a slight teary glint, agreed with a determined nod. "Yes, you're right, Mal. If the probe on the UFO detects Alice, then promise me I can go after him."

"Agreed. What about you, Turk?"

"Absolutely."

The phone rang. "This will be the US President," Mal stated.

Coracles and canoes were moored in the lagoon. Vale quickly ascended the wharf and offered a hand to Al, helping him out of the unstable canoe and onto the platform.

Torches burning along the lagoon's perimeter illuminated the float effectively. A crowd gathered at the wharf's edge to greet the visitors. Alice felt the stares directed at him, likely due to his unfamiliar attire and perhaps his skin tone, which contrasted starkly with theirs, making him resemble an albino.

A robust man garbed in blood-red robes from neck to ankle made his way through the crowd to the front. "Vale Tarz!" he announced with a booming voice, "I am Doevan Gish, Mayor of London. Welcome."

Vale acknowledged his companion. "This is Black Alice. We managed to escape capture in Atlan."

A wave of disbelief rippled through the crowd. Escaping the clutches of the Nephilim was an exceedingly rare occurrence. The people of London understood that being captured equated to a death sentence.

Mayor Gish, adorned with heavily tattooed facial markings, raised a hand, heavily inked as well, to signal his subjects. "Let him speak."

Alice assessed the mayor. Shorter and more robust than him, Doevan's tattooed face bore signs of adolescent acne scars. His complexion was darker than Vale's but lighter than his robe. His eyes had large, dark irises that seemed to dominate his gaze, giving them a bird-like appearance. Above his eyes were thick black, short, straight brows. His chin boasted a neatly trimmed goatee. His head, shaped like a pearl, was cleanly shaved, with shadowy stubble forming a precise wreath. Alice was intrigued by the tattoos, somewhat similar to his own.

"We were fortunate," Vale responded. "My canoe ended up on the rocks, so we leaped from a high cliff to reach it."

A man in the crowd exclaimed, "He'is not from here!"

"Could he be one of them?" a woman screamed.

Al raised his hands and smiled, "Hey, hey, settle down. I understand I look different compared to you, but I assure you I'm human ... I come from another place. Just like Vale, I was captured. His bravery and cunning allowed us to escape."

Murmurs echoed as the word "human" circulated.

"All we seek is a safe haven until the morrow," Vale asserted for all to hear. "After that, we'll continue on to Stockholm."

The proposal met their approval. The crowd dispersed, and individuals made their way back to their homes.

Mayor Gish offered them a warm, pearly smile. "People here can be anxious. My apologies. Join me in my hub; we will drink there, and you can stay until the morrow."

"Cool," Alice replied amiably. The scene felt as though he'd stepped into a medieval village.

Doevan's brow furrowed. "I see. My hub will indeed be warmer for you," he interpreted, misunderstanding Alice's choice of words.

Al realised the miscommunication and swiftly added, "Nice ink, Doevan."

As he led them towards the most prominent and intricately designed hut on the promenade—a manse—Doevan responded, "Thank you. Do I refer to you as Black or Alice?"

"Al will be fine."

"My body is adorned with tattoos, as you mentioned, depicting the history of our float. I am like walking history," he said with a hint of humour.

Al was intrigued. "Do those markings pass down through generations?"

"Yes. And what of your tattoos, Al?"

"They're ancient symbols representing good fortune."

Doevan seemed to enjoy the conversation with Al. It was evident he relished discussing his people and himself. Al recognised an opportunity to learn more about their origins. He wondered if they were descendants of Earth abductees who had managed to escape the Nephilim. He sensed that understanding this was crucially linked to his quest. Somehow, it all revolved around the sarcophagus, referred to by the Nephilim as the Astara. He needed more information about it.

Doevan halted them at the entrance to the manse.

Al looked up, marvelling at the sight of three moons rising on the horizon in the night sky. These moons differed significantly from Earth's, but they were equally breathtaking.

"I should warn you; tonight is the ritual of the Fire Circle. Do you celebrate it in Stockholm, Vale?"

"Yes, of course. It lasts for three days, and today is the last day," Vale replied.

Al quickly accessed Fire Circle on his implant, the result floated in front of him as a heads-up display only he could see—Secta's latest update—it read: Fire Circle — A free spirit gathering in which the attendees dance around a fire. It was a Pagan festival celebrated on Earth — another tie. These folk were into a form of paganism. He didn't consider that being a bad thing because most Pagan rituals related specifically to seasonal changes. He quickly read more information: The ritual as with all Pagan rituals celebrates human life passages: the beginning of life, fertility enhancements, conception aids, pregnancy blessing and the passage to adulthood. At the end of life, there are Pagan crossing-over rituals, wakes, funerals, burials or the scattering of remains.

"Which specific Fire Circle ritual is this?" Al inquired.

"I see you're familiar with our Sabbat, excellent. This is the ritual of the Asking. Come, let's enter," Doevan said, guiding them through a curtain.

Al hadn't anticipated such a spacious circular room. Illuminated by two roaring fires, a pentagram was marked on the floor. At its centre stood a dais of red stone, as tall as a person. Around the fires, about forty figures were dressed in black hooded robes, swaying and moving.

Their movements paused when the visitors entered.

Doevan gestured, and the dancers resumed their weaving and writhing. Surprisingly, there was no accompanying music, which struck Al as unusual. The ritual unfolded in an odd silence, with the sound of their body movements creating the only rhythm.

One of the dancers leaped onto the dais—a middle-aged woman with a stout build, dark glistening skin covered in sweat, and a broad face. Her ecstatic eyes fixed on Al, her prominent features moving eccentrically as her open mouth revealed her protruding tongue. Her curly black hair sprayed droplets of sweat as she moved her head. She danced with her body gleaming in the firelight. Her actions triggered a response from the other coven members—men and women, young and old—who gathered around her, dancing in unison.

Impressed by the spectacle, Al raised an approving eyebrow at Vale.

Doevan nodded, indicating for Vale and Al to follow him through the room and exit to a smaller annexed room at the rear.

It was clear that they had entered Doevan's personal chamber. He offered them seats in the room, illuminated by candlelight and adorned with magical artefacts. The arms of his chair were made from stacked skulls of creature unfamiliar to Al.

As Doevan settled into the distinctive chair, he appeared more like a sorcerer than Al had initially thought.

"Are you in need of food or drink?" Doevan inquired, motioning for them to sit.

"That would be appreciated," Vale responded, adhering to a sense of ritualistic etiquette.

Doevan clapped his hands, and within moments, a young nubile girl entered. "Bring food and beer," he ordered.

The girl had long wavy black hair cascading down her back, large eyes with lengthy lashes, an hourglass figure, and the graceful legs of a dancer. Her skin bore a tan. Still catching her breath from dancing, her arms and legs glistened in the torchlight, coated in a sheen of perspiration.

"My daughter Raven ... I have six daughters," Doevan proudly declared.

"No tattoos?" Al asked.

"Sons only. I have three. Now, as you would understand, Vale, considering this is the Asking, I am obligated to question a stranger. Al, that's you, as Vale is known to me. From which float do you come?"

Al took a moment to ponder before deciding there was no point in deception. "I'll be honest with you, Doevan. I'm not from a float or the planet Kor. I'm from the planet Earth."

Doevan turned to Vale with a frown. "Earth? In the Cassiopeia constellation?"

Alice swiftly accessed his knowledge database, confirming Doevan's statement—a fact that would hold true if Earth were observed from a neighbouring star.

Al inquired, "What's your star?"

"By star, I assume you mean our source of light ... that would be Mintaka."

Al checked Mintaka: one of the three brightest stars in the Orion Belt as seen from Earth.

"Aha, Orion," Al remarked, surprised. "Whoa, I'm a long way from home."

Doevan leaned forward in his chair. "If what you say is true, how did you come to Kor from a place so distant?"

"I stowed away on a Nephilim spacecraft that visited Earth."

Vale and Doevan exchanged surprised glances. Then Doevan turned to Vale. "Did you know about this?"

"No. I had not asked him. That is considered impolite in my caste."

"Same with mine," Doevan agreed. "So, is Earth inhabited by humans and Nephilim?"

"No, humans only ... about nine billion of them."

Doevan was rocked. "Nine billion! That's more than in the rest of the universe. Why?"

"With float names like London and Stockholm, I assumed you originated from Earth," Al stated.

Vale was intrigued. "No, why would those names mean anything to you."

"Because they are capital cities on Earth—London is the capital city of the United Kingdom, and Stockholm is the capital of the country of Sweden."

Both Vale and Doevan wore expressions of amazement.

Al continued. "How many of you are on Kor?"

"There would be no more than ten thousand of us remaining," Doevan admitted, with a grave expression.

"Are you not escapees from the Nephilim? Former abductees from Earth?"

"Absolutely not," Doevan retorted indignantly. "Are Earth people abducted by Nephilim? For what purpose?"

"I assume for their breeding program, as Vale mentioned."

Vale confirmed, "Yes, I believe Nephilim have been using humans for organ harvesting."

Al was puzzled and asked, "Why would they travel all the way to Earth for humans when they have you right here?"

"They might be terraforming Earth," Vale speculated.

Doevan added, , "Or the gene pool of Earth humans is preferential to our own."

"Have you heard of the Astara?" Al asked.

Doevan and Vale exchanged concerned glances. Doevan answered, "Yes, of course. The eternal vessel ... the legendary capsule created by the god En-Ki, capable of granting immortality."

Al was astonished by the reverence Doevan and Vale held for the sarcophagus. "Seriously?" The legend of what originally had been thought by Secta and others to be a sarcophagus had now grown into being some kind of gene modification device.

"Let me do the Asking then ... what are the Nephilim doing here on Kor? And how did they evolve?"

Again, Doevan and Vale exchanged a peculiar look. Doevan muttered to Vale, "Is this the portent?"

CHAPTER 21
ATRAHASIS

ONLY THE SIZE of a matchbox, the probe was poised to be dispatched on board the UAP that remained in the sky over New York City. Secta handed the probe to Christina.

Christina examined it in the palm of her hand. "Not much to it, is there?"

"We'll need to maintain a micro wormhole open through which to transmit the data stream," the Professor explained.

"Clever," Christina marvelled.

The Professor looked admirably at Hope. "It's Hope's concept."

Secta breezed into the control room followed by Turk and Vee, and blurted, "Are we all set?"

"Just booting up the mainframe," Christina reported. "Wait a minute, what's this?" She added, staring at the monitor, perplexed.

The other three scientists crowded around to take a look.

"I recognise the code; it's from En-Ki. Put it on the network, and I'll decode it in my lab," the Professor requested. "It's best not to send the probe until I'm finished. It won't take long now that I have the decryption key."

He dashed out of the door and returned within fifteen minutes.

"That was quick," Secta remarked to the flustered professor.

"The file is on your desktop, Christina. It was from En-Ki, without a doubt ... a set of coordinates," de Luz said, scratching his unshaven face. "I checked them; they lead to an M-class planet in the Orion

Constellation, orbiting the star Mintaka aka Delta Orionis… nine hundred light years from Earth."

Secta was captivated. "What else did it say, Vic?"

"It's where we'll find Alice," the Professor said, with a grin. "And, he said he's providing the information so that every effort can be expended to ensure the safety of the sarcophagus, that, by the way, he calls the Astara."

At the mention of Al, Vee let out a huge sigh of relief, hugged Hope, then threw her arms around Turk. She'd been worried her brother had been vaporised in the explosion.

Always pragmatic, Secta said, "It seems the Astara is of more relevance than we had expected. Vic, does this planet have a name?"

"No, it was only recently astronomically designated an M-class exoplanet and given a reference number," the Professor explained.

"An M-Class planet? What does that mean?" asked Vee.

"An inhabitable planet with possibly a human-sustaining atmosphere just like on Earth," Hope explained.

"So now you can send us through Kairos to those coordinates?" Vee said excitedly.

Secta shook his head. "No, we can send a probe there instead of on board the UFO … a bigger probe with more functions. We have one set to go, don't we, Vic?"

"Sure do," he confirmed.

"Good, then there's no time to waste, let's get on with sending it," Secta said, jumping into action. "Oh, and Turk, I'll need to fit you with a language interpretation implant. I can probably attach it to your old OSCI."

"How many languages will it let me understand and speak?" Turk asked.

Secta rubbed his chin, thinking. "I'll update it regularly. The last count was around two hundred."

Turk raised his eyebrows, impressed.

It was a far better outcome than relying on getting the drone inside the UFO. There was no way of telling whether the UFO would return to where it had come from, or whether Alice was still on board, or whether the probe would even survive, as there was a possibility the alien technology might detect and destroy it. At least now they could feel some comfort in knowing Alice was probably out of the UFO and somewhere on a nameless planet orbiting a star named Mintaka in Orion's Belt, nine hundred light years from Earth.

Across the world, above the metropolis of Manhattan, a stationary star shimmered in the night sky. Most people assumed it was a geostationary satellite, but the authorities knew it was a UFO and furthermore, that it was the very same UFO that had previously wrought havoc in several locations around the world, and believed to have hijacked the platinum sarcophagus from the Museum in Davao.

All that had been reported in the US press was a claim by three injured individuals—a man and two women—that they had been abducted by aliens, probed, and then returned to Manhattan's Central Park. All three had been abducted from cities other than New York, making their disoriented appearance in Central Park inexplicable. However, their assertions of alien abduction were met with scepticism by the press and subsequently debunked by those purporting to possess greater knowledge. The correlation between the abductees and the luminous presence in the sky was never established. Yet, this was not the case for the authorities. Men in black were promptly dispatched to apprehend the abductees and clandestinely transport them away for probing, scanning, and interrogation. When the name 'Black Alice' emerged in their accounts, it was withheld. To the CIA, Black Alice was nothing but a nuisance.

Electra and Commander Walker were suited up ready to leave through Aquila, their destination: the UFO over Manhattan.

Two young women in hooded black robes placed food and drinks on the table before Doevan, Vale, and Al. Doevan raised a tankard in a toast. "Cheers to better days."

Al and Vale followed suit.

Although the ale was unlike any Al had ever tasted before, he liked it and asked, "What is this beer made from?"

"Weed harvested from the sea," Doevan replied.

"Brewing is an ancient tradition on all floats, and a noble one at that," chuckled Vale. "Though I believe our Stockholm brew is superior to this rag water!"

Doevan smirked at Vale's jest but understood it was all in good humour. The only familiar food in the spread for Al was bread.

"All our sustenance comes from the sea. This," Doevan said, picking up a shellfish resembling a scallop, "is quite special."

"Ah, a Narcogen ... perhaps too potent for you, Al. It contains a natural hallucinogen," Vale explained.

"I included them in the menu in case you wished to experience our history in the dreamtime," Doevan said as he chomped on a large boiled fisheye.

Always intrigued by novel experiences, Al asked, "How does Narcogen work?"

"You ingest it, then Doevan must recite sacred words that will open a gateway through which you can pass into the dreamtime. After six hours, you will awaken imbued with extensive knowledge of our past," Vale detailed.

Al indulged in his meal, drained his tankard, and then reclined in his seat, patting his satisfied belly, he declared, "I believe I'd like to try this Narcogen dreamtime experience. You know, in my homeland of Oceana, the indigenous people of, which I m one, have Dreamtime, a realm in which we commune with the spirits of the departed."

Doevan was impressed. "Splendid. But before we proceed, I must provide you with some background. Have you heard of the planet

Nibiru?"

"Yes. Go on," Al confirmed, knowing it was the mythical planet of the Anunnaki, the place where En-Ki and En-Lil, according to legend, had originated.

"The god En-Ki fashioned with his own hands Nimrod and Ishtar, mother and father of our species. They were brought in secret to Kor for En-Ki to study. It was done in secret because the supreme god of the Anunnaki, Anu, had outlawed the creation experimentation. The only other sentient beings on Kor at that time were the Treen ... though the ocean planet teemed with aquatic life, including the Kraken and deep in the mountains, the Ragon. I will tell you about these creatures during your enchantment, but be it known, the Kraken is still today our mortal enemy, especially King Kraken."

Alice had heard the term 'Kraken' used somewhere before and quickly searched his implant database. His display read: The Kraken is a legendary cephalopod-like sea monster of gigantic size from the Norse sagas. It was yet another peculiar connection between an Earthly legend and Kor. But how did a legend traverse the galaxy?

Al asked, "Is this Kraken a greater enemy than the Nephilim?"

"Oh yes, far more perilous," Vale explained. "The Nephilim have only been on Kor for some generations. All will be revealed to you, Al."

With a nod from Vale, Doevan continued. "Nimrod and Ishtar were left alone on Kor to fend for themselves. At that time, Kor consisted of three large volcanic islands. The central island was named Atlan by Nimrod ... it was in Atlan they settled. It had lush green vegetation, abundant fish, seafood, and some wildlife. Atlan was a paradise, and the new inhabitants flourished."

"At various times over many generations, En-Ki dispatched secret emissaries to inspect the Atlan colony and offer instructions. Over time, a large city grew, and the other two islands were also settled. To construct cities for the growing population, the islands were deforested. Warnings from the wizards about the environmental catastrophe resulting from the deforestation were ignored, and soon they learned that the ecosystem was far more delicate than they had estimated. But none had foreseen what was to come.

"When the Anunnaki eventually discovered the existence of the Korman settlements, it was decreed that they were to be eradicated. En-Ki had left us, we know not where, with his brother En-Lil given the mandate by the Anunnaki to exterminate our species. He sought to achieve this by inducing climate change on Kor. Temperatures soared, fires raged, cities were engulfed in flames. The volcanoes on the other two islands, Bora and Gant, erupted, and both islands vanished beneath the waves, taking thousands with them. Only Atlan survived, as the city was mostly situated within an extinct volcano. However, many perished in the massive storms and tidal waves that battered the island. It was then that En-Lil made his move.

"Whenever we were attacked, a smoke ring would materialise in the sky, through which an Anunnaki craft would suddenly appear, sometimes more than one. It was said that the unique atmosphere of Kor was responsible for the appearance of these rings. Ringwatchers were recruited and stationed around Atlan to provide an early warning system for the population to take cover. During that stage of our history, our people were armed only with metal blades. Our only real resistance came from sorcery.

"After numerous attacks, En-Lil was satisfied that the population of Atlan was doomed, and he left Kor, never to return. He had no inkling that some had survived underground, taken to the refuge of the Ragon's lair by the Treen.

"After some time, we know not how long, a new invader arrived: the Nephilim. This is the story you will experience when you take Narcogen because the knowledge of that time is better known."

"I wonder who En-Ki created first: the Korman or humans?" Al challenged, the entire story sounding very familiar to him.

"Are you suggesting En-Ki created your species as well?" Doevan asked, his brow furrowed.

"Yes, and En-Lil tried to destroy the people of Earth, just as he did your people, only in our case through a great flood. I have personally battled against En-Lil."

Doevan erupted, "What? No, that is not possible!"

"I speak only the truth. En-Lil is on Earth now, my sworn enemy … and, over time, the Nephilim have visited Earth to abduct humans. Look, I sense a universal event approaching on a grand scale that only En-Ki and En-Lil know about. I believe it is their final clash, and only one of them will survive. This will determine whether Earth, Kor, and other worlds will be subjected to good or evil. I am an emissary of En-Ki."

Doevan was on his feet, a look of shock on his broad face. "But, but … how?"

"It's a long story, but he chose me to champion his battles against his adversaries. He communicates with me telepathically, guiding me on quests to support the war against En-Lil. It was he who directed me to board the Nephilim craft inside the Astara."

Doevan paced the floor and then stopped to glare at Vale. "Do you think Al is he?"

Vale's handsome features reflected contemplation. "Atra, the chosen one … the potent?"

"Yes, Atrahasis," Doevan reflected.

Al quickly referenced Atrahasis. The term was Akkadian and translated to 'exceedingly wise.' He was impressed. Atrahasis was the Sumerian equivalent of Noah otherwise referred to as Ziusudra or, in the Greek version, Deucalion from the story of the great flood. "We have the ancient story of Atrahasis on Earth. En-Ki warned Atrahasis that En-Lil would cause a great flood to exterminate humankind. Atrahasis saved enough of humanity and animals to survive."

"The connections with Earth are uncanny," Doevan admitted.

"What else can you tell me about the Anunnaki from your history?" Al asked.

"It is written that the original immortal biological entities created an artificial intelligence to be their slaves. These were the Anunnaki. However, the AI rebelled and sought to destroy its maker—its god, if you will—and they succeeded … they removed them from the universe so the only sentient beings remaining were AI. Eons later, a faction of the Anunnaki, led by En-Ki, attempted to recreate biological life forms, resulting in what we call Kormankind and perhaps your humankind. During that experimental process, the Nephilim emerged as a by-product, part AI and part biological, but they were unable to reproduce. When En-Ki succeeded, he constructed the Astara to grant his creation immortality. But before he could use it, a decree from the supreme god Anu commanded the eradication of En-Ki's creation, and En-Lil was given that task … a task that continues to this day," Doevan expounded.

Alice reclined in his chair, contemplating his newfound knowledge. Strangely enough, it all made logical sense to him. As incredible as it might sound, the originators of sentient life in the universe were a biological species that had created AI, much like how humans were currently doing on Earth. The AI grew in intelligence, possibly surpassing their creators. They learned to self-replicate and eventually turned against and eradicated their own makers. To Alice, this aligned remarkably well with some of Earth's ancient mythologies: the Mahabharata, the Ramayana, the Puranas, the Greek pantheon, and more. It was as if history was echoing itself. Once again, the AI, led by En-Lil, was determined to eliminate humanity. That was why En-Lil always referred to humans as a plague. En-Ki stood as the sole opposition to En-Lil, and Alice found himself at the epicentre of this conflict. The Astara undoubtedly played a vital role in the salvation of humanity. En-Lil couldn't afford to allow a human to become immortal, as it would undermine his strategy of annihilation.

A thought struck Alice. What did the Nephilim want with the Astara? Perhaps it holds the key to granting their race more human-like qualities, maybe even the ability to reproduce. That's it! That's what they're striving for. The purpose behind the abductions was to perpetuate their species! With the Astara in their possession, they would have the means to achieve it.

Forces had been set in motion, leading inevitably to a clash between good and evil, light and darkness. An apocalypse of biblical proportions, prophesied by various religions, oracles, and psychics over millennia on Earth, now appeared to be echoing throughout the universe. This impending confrontation would determine humanity's fate—a battle between AI and biological life forms. It was astounding to realise that Black Alice was at the very heart of this cosmic struggle.

195

CHAPTER 22
KRAKEN

VALE HANDED A plate to Alice, containing a wriggling Narcogen. To Alice, it resembled an ordinary garden slug.

"Swallow it whole, don't chew. It must reach your stomach alive to administer the hallucinogen," Doevan explained.

Al plucked the oyster-sized creature from its shell, downed it in one gulp, and asked, "Alright, now what?"

Doevan resumed his seat. "Just relax. When it takes effect, I will open the gateway for you."

Al reclined in his chair, closing his eyes. After a short time, Doevan's voice seemed more distant than expected. Al opened his eyes and found that the room shimmered, similar to the moments before a wormhole would open.

Doevan continued, "A ring!" echoed the cry. Throughout the generations of survivors from the battle with En-Lil, no-one had ever witnessed a ring forming in the sky. Nonetheless, the practice of ring-watching had become ingrained in Atlan's social fabric. On this historic day, it was a young maiden, Rowena Onya, who raced through the main streets of Atlan, screaming the alert at the top of her lungs: "Ring! Ring! Ring!"

A swirl of radiant colours enveloped Alice's mind, and suddenly, he stood in the middle of a cobblestone street. A barefoot young maiden with golden hair and dark skin, clad in a light brown tunic, dashed past him, still shouting the alarm. Around him were buildings unlike any on Earth—spherical in shape, some reaching up to six storeys in height, all tinted a clay-like shade of fawn. Alice marvelled at the beauty of the city, which featured a cascading waterfall at one end, feeding a stream that wound through the city.

Around sixty people caught Al's attention as they ran directly toward him. The illumination was dim due to the city's location deep within a volcanic crater. Deciding to follow the runners, he was taken aback when a couple of them passed right through him, as if he were a ghost.

After a short distance, he entered a tunnel, emerged onto a rock platform, and saw waves crashing over it from the dark green sea. A group of people had gathered at the water's edge, gazing skyward.

In the expansive yellow-tinged sky, a massive ring of smoke had materialised, as if blown from a giant's mouth. Al glanced at the man beside him, knowing he was invisible to him. It was an odd sensation to be present in spirit only.

"False alarm!" the man declared with resolve.

Apollo Rhen, a lithe but strong young man with dark skin, shoulder-length black hair, and dark eyes, spoke assertively, "Everyone, return to your tasks."

Regarding the others' reactions, Al sensed that Apollo was the leader.

Al followed him back through the tunnel into Atlan, listening to the conversation between Apollo and two elders who appeared to be part of the town council.

"I fear this is an omen. We must prepare for an attack," Apollo said solemnly.

"By whom?" questioned Cain Iglyn, a tall, lean man in his fifties with a grey beard.

"How can we prepare for an enemy of which we know nothing?" inquired the other, Abel Iglyn, his brother, a plump man with a melancholic expression and a nose as round as his body proclaimed.

Al tried to ascertain the era but had no way of determining it accurately. He only had Earth's civilization and history as reference points, which might not be applicable to Kor. Then a thought occurred to him: weapons could provide a clue. He needed to see what kind of weapons they possessed.

A chilling scream from a woman behind them shattered the tranquility. Everyone halted and turned.

Massive tentacles had emerged from the sea, seizing a man around the waist and thrashing about as they dragged him toward the water.

"A Kraken!" Apollo exclaimed, his fear evident.

Around fifty people who had been at the water's edge now stampeded toward them, fleeing the scene, some screaming hysterically.

In mere seconds, the enormous tentacles, covered in giant suckers, had decapitated the man and torn his body in half. As the eight long, purple arms frenziedly tossed the dismembered parts into the air, blood and gore rained down on the few terrorised onlookers who remained in a state of horror. The woman who had screamed collapsed, and Apollo rushed over to assist her. Meanwhile, the dark green seawater started boiling, as if a massive submarine were about to surface. From the froth emerged a colossal, black-armored, domed turret, appearing akin to a flying saucer. The writhing tentacles protruding from the body beneath the turret seized another man, while still clinging to the decapitated torso of the first victim. The monster drew this victim into its horrifying, beaked mouth that lay open below the turret. The immense splashes from the thrashing tentacles knocked people off their feet, causing them to slip and fall. Four long spines extended just below the turret, each adorned with bulbous eyes that flicked about eerily, scanning the scene.

The creature was colossal: eight thrashing tentacles measuring six to eight metres in length, a turret ten metres across from beak to the top, and a height that reached god-knows-how-deep underwater. It tore apart the second victim in the same gruesome manner as the first.

Al figured it was a gigantic cephalopod with a taste for human flesh, yet the massive protective turret lent it an even more sinister and alien appearance. He reflected on the tragic fate of the two victims who had been lured to the precipice by the ring's appearance, only to meet a gruesome end at the clutches of the monstrous beast.

Once the grotesque monster had sated its hunger, it slowly retreated beneath the waves and vanished. The promenade was smeared with blood and gore, just like the few individuals still present, including Apollo. Alice felt powerless. His instinct was to offer assistance, but he existed there solely in spirit. He walked alongside Apollo, who aided the distraught elderly lady, now a widow, back into the tunnel, away from the scene of carnage.

"I will raise the matter of ending the sacrifices to the Kraken with the council. It must be stopped; it only fuels its bloodlust," Apollo growled, addressing the same two men accompanying him.

"You know it will be met with rejection, Apollo. The attempt was made before, but the priesthood—"

Apollo cut him off with venom, "I care not for the accursed priesthood! To worship and offer a monster a young virgin sacrifice each month is archaic, nonsensical. I will put an end to it!"

"It might cost you your life, Apollo. I caution you. The priesthood holds immense power, and it enjoys the backing of the people."

"Not all of them!" he snarled, his anger palpable. "Not all of them."

Hope and Vee were seated at Café Epiphany, sipping on their coffee as they watched through the window the bustling parade of pedestrians navigating the city sidewalks, en route to their jobs. It was 8 a.m., and the rest of OTT was occupied with sending the probe to the coordinates they had received from En-Ki. Frustration had driven Vee to seek some fresh air, prompting Hope to suggest a coffee outing.

"There seems to be more on your mind than just your worries about Al," Hope gently probed, sensing Vee's inner turmoil.

Vee turned her attention back to Hope, her eyes welled up with tears. "I had a fight with Blake before he left, and now he's—" Her voice faltered, and she broke down.

Hope reached across the table, taking Vee's hand in a comforting gesture. "Hey, he's still alive, love, and Mal is ensuring he's in good hands."

"I could see that he and Jax still have feelings for each other. I feel like he's deliberately excluding me from things so he can continue with her ... Oh, I don't know. Men! I can't understand why ... every time I get involved with one, it just turns into a mess. You'd think I would've learned my lesson by now."

"I don't think we ever truly learn that lesson, Vee. I'm no expert on matters of the heart either, but from what I can gather, it's a perpetually rocky road."

Vee withdrew her hand from Hope's, chuckling as she wiped away her tears. "You're not wrong."

"Are you convinced that they were—?" Hope left the question hanging, giving Vee room to address the matter.

"Yes," Vee admitted, "it was written all over their faces. I have the unfortunate ability to read people, just like Al ... he thinks it's some kind of family curse."

"Having a skill like that would be quite useful at times," Hope agreed.

With her spirits somewhat lifted after sharing her heartache, Vee offered a warm smile to Hope. "Thank you for being there to listen."

"Hey, what are mates for, right? Plus, I have a personal stake in this."

"Oh? What's that?"

"I'm in love with your brother."

Vee was taken aback by the revelation. She had no inkling of Hope's feelings. "But you're—?"

"I know, I know—"

Vee couldn't help but snicker. "Well, that certainly puts an end to me boasting about my natural abilities ... I would have never guessed. Does Al know?"

Everything around Al shimmered again, and he found himself standing inside a vast chamber in the midst of a council meeting. A tall, menacing figure clad in a purple caftan adorned with a distinct Kraken emblem was pacing on a rostrum. His sharp facial features, pointed nose, and chin were accompanied by piercing violet eyes. Long white hair framed his bushy white eyebrows, and he held a staff with a carved Kraken figure at its end. His complexion was lighter than that of the others in attendance.

Al deduced that this must be the high priest and took an immediate disliking to him solely based on his appearance. The sinister-looking figure continued to pace, while Apollo and his ministers occupied seats on the right side of the stage. Opposite them, more priests in purple robes took their places. Behind both groups, a gallery of around a hundred citizens observed the proceedings.

Al moved along the central aisle and positioned himself where he could watch the stage unobstructed. The high priest's booming voice resonated, "Apollo Rhen has called for a vote to end our sacred offering to the Kraken. I remind Apollo Rhen of the last time this occurred, only because a severe storm prevented the monthly sacrifice, we lost not two citizens but six to the wrath of the mighty Kraken. So, I ask of you gathered here this day, do we dare vote to support Apollo Rhen? The Kraken is a deity. The Kraken safeguards us from the monsters of the deep. I pledge my devotion to the Kraken. Praise thee oh, Kraken!" he shouted.

Twenty priests immediately stood up, crossing their arms over their chests while bowing their heads, and repeated the chant, "Praise thee oh, Kraken!" Many citizens joined in the gesture. The chant of praise to the Kraken was repeated three times.

Al muttered to himself, "These people are nuts."

When the chanting finally ceased, Apollo rose from his seat. "High Priest Farhd Krell and his supporters, I believe it is in your interests to maintain this hideous veneration of the murderous sea monster."

A wave of disapproval swept through those opposed to Apollo's stance. Farhd Krell stormed off the stage, making way for the official arbitrator.

Fyran Bint stepped onto the stage, a stocky man with short grey hair, ice-blue eyes, and a salt-and-pepper beard. He spoke deliberately, "Let us now proceed to the vote. Those in favour of abolishing sacrifices, please stand."

A shuffling of feet followed by a multitude standing up indicated a close vote. Fyran Bint carefully counted the supporters.

"Please be seated. Now, those who oppose, please stand."

Another flurry of movement, and Fyran Bint tallied the numbers. "The count stands at fifty-seven opposing ... fifty-nine in favour. The motion to end sacrifices has been approved."

Enraged, Farhd Krell leaped to his feet and shouted in a full-throated roar, "The consequences of this decision will rest upon your shoulders. You will be punished for your heresy! Each and every one of you!" He pointed his Kraken-adorned staff menacingly at Apollo. "You, the infidel, more than any other, will be held to account before the god Kraken. I will ensure it."

Apollo snarled back, "Accept the verdict, Krell ... your threats are wasted on me. I fear not your god. What are you going to do, summon the Kraken? I doubt it. Leave with your disciples of death!"

Al took a shine to Apollo, he was a man after his own heart but he didn't trust the Priesthood's resolve. He was reminded of the tyranny of the Pharisees in Jerusalem when he was there, in particular, High Pharisee Kohen who, much like Krell, was a fanatic.

In a fit of fury, Krell stormed out of the hall, met with jeers from supporters of Apollo. Yet, Al sensed an impending retaliation from the priesthood. Just as he was about to follow Apollo, the surroundings shimmered once more.

The haze dissipated, revealing Al now on a large coracle manned by a dozen rowers, six on each side. The sail had been lowered due to the stormy weather, and the boat was riding atop powerful six-metre swells. Waves crashed over the bow, drenching the crew and soaking

Apollo, who stood resolute at the prow. Despite the turbulent conditions, Al could make out the island of Atlan less than a kilometre away.

Clouds swirled overhead, the wind howled, and the rain poured down heavily. Then, a remarkable sight unfolded: the clouds rapidly converged, forming a ring in the sky. The helmsman spotted it first and urgently pointed it out to Apollo. "A ring!" he exclaimed, "a ring above us!"

This time, it wasn't a false alarm. A craft resembling the one that had brought Al to Kor appeared at the centre of the ring.

"It's a giant bird! We're done for!" the helmsman screeched, thunderstruck.

CHAPTER 23
TIS

"STAY CALM, MEN, stay calm!" Apollo commanded his sailors with poised control. He embodied the type of inspirational leader that warriors leaned on during the height of danger.

Then, unexpectedly, the storm abated, the sea calmed down, and a deathly silence settled. It was almost mystical. The conditions had shifted from one extreme to another. But as the aircraft began its descent, panic erupted once again among the crew.

They were a mere five hundred metres from the rocky platform of Atlan. Apollo recognised the situation and yelled encouragingly, "Row, men! Row fast, to make landfall!" With no wind to hold them offshore, the now tranquil sea made reaching the shore possible. The crew snapped out of their hysteria and began to row with great determination towards the rock platform.

As they drew closer to it, Al could see High Priest Farhd Krell, accompanied by his monks, standing at the water's edge. His staff was raised in the air as though he had personally summoned the storm.

The bird of prey drew closer to the island, and it became evident that its intention was to land on the platform.

Upon realising this, the Priesthood hurriedly retreated back into the tunnel and sought refuge in the safety of the city.

Simultaneously, as the coracle reached the platform, the alien craft touched down. The crew swiftly disembarked the coracle and dashed after the priests, running for their lives. But not Apollo—he remained to secure the boat and then hopped onto the platform to greet the visitors.

Al stood beside Apollo, projecting a bold and courageous presence. He looked up at the dark olive-green craft that towered over him. A hatch opened in its belly, and a ladder extended down fifteen metres to the ground.

It all felt very familiar to Al—the same scenario as with the An-Zu bird, but on a much grander scale. He surmised that it must be the same species.

Three armoured creatures emerged from the belly hatch one by one, descending the ladder.

Al remembered the An-Zu pilot Ninurta had killed with an arrow—the pilot had been armed with a vaporising laser of some sort. Apollo needed to exercise caution, but Al couldn't warn him.

Standing resolutely, Apollo glanced over his shoulder at a group of his ministers who had gathered at the mouth of the tunnel, maintaining a safe distance but still displaying curiosity.

The three astronauts reached the ground and advanced toward Apollo, stopping a few metres away from him.

They were clones, identical in armour and every other detail. They closely resembled the An-Zu pilot Ninurta had killed and the Nephilim Al had encountered that enprisoned him with Vale. The armour, the visor, reflective and opaque—all three stood over eight feet tall. One of them took the lead and stepped out ahead of the others. Al could see he was reaching for the weapon attached to his belt, but there was nothing he could do to intervene.

As he was drawing the weapon, a long tentacle swept out from the water and snatched the three aliens. In a matter of seconds, more tentacles emerged to aid in dismembering them. It happened so quickly that the leader didn't even have a chance to fire.

Al was as stunned as Apollo. Then, it suddenly struck Al what the priesthood had been doing at the water's edge—they had been conducting a ceremony to summon the Kraken, not to attack the aliens, but to sink the coracle carrying Apollo. Fate had worked in Apollo's favour: the god Kraken, whom he despised, had saved him.

Apollo hadn't even flinched. He simply strode over to the ladder and began ascending it. Al followed. One notable difference about the underbelly of the craft compared to the An-Zu bird, which Al was familiar with, was that it had a livery: peculiar-looking black letters; TIS-177.

The interior of the craft mirrored that of the An-Zu bird, but on a grander scale. This vessel could accommodate fifty or more troops or passengers.

Apollo stood on the abandoned flight deck, surveying the controls. All of them were activated, illuminated with an array of colourful lights.

Standing behind him, Al noticed a distinction between this craft and the other An-Zu bird: the Tablet of Destiny was absent. In its place was a computer screen displaying a galactic map. Though the language on it remained indecipherable to Al, he could discern the colour-coded details of the ship's recent voyages.

In a sudden burst of excitement, Apollo spun around and hurried back toward the hatch.

For Al, the entire aircraft shimmered.

As he emerged from the haze, he found himself back on the rock platform. Time had passed. The giant An-Zu bird remained, now surrounded by people. Apollo stepped forward, positioning himself in front of them. Standing beneath the craft, he raised a hand to hush the murmurs.

"Today is an auspicious day. Given my irreconcilable differences with High Priest Krell and the Kraken cult, it is in Atlan's best interest that I seize the opportunity to take this craft and seek a new world for settlement—a world free from the tyranny of the Kraken, a world free from the likes of the Kraken cult. You have chosen to embark on this adventure with me. In honour of our history, I've added the name 'Atlan' to the livery of this craft." He pointed up at the words emblazoned in black letters on the underbelly, now reading: Atlan-Tis

177. A thunderous round of applause erupted from the gathering.

He continued, "You may wonder how we'll fly this vessel, a gift to us. Well, senior ministers, brothers Cain and Abel, have utilised their scientific knowledge to understand the automation that propels this ship through space and time. It can be accessed to return to its previous destination by merely interacting with the flight control on the navigational screen. We've discovered that we can decipher the language of these aliens!"

The crowd buzzed with amazement at the realisation that they shared a written language with extra-terrestrial beings.

"The world we've chosen to venture to has a single moon and is called Ki!"

Al swiftly checked and confirmed that 'Ki' was the Ancient Sumerian word for Earth.

The crowd repeated 'Ki' with reverence, content that it would be their new home. High Priest Krell rudely forced his way through the crowd, using his staff to push people aside. A line of ten priests followed him. He halted before Apollo, turned, and addressed the assembly.

"Blinded by the Kraken's victory over the alien foe, you choose to abandon Atlan!" He glared at Apollo with a spiteful sneer. "You follow this fool to your doom. This craft will transport you to the home of those who piloted it here ... the enemy!" He raised his staff commandingly and yelled maniacally, "So be it, be gone with you all! You will not be welcome if you come crawling back to Atlan! You suffer the arrogance of ignorance, Apollo!"

Apollo snatched the staff from Krell's grasp and broke it across his knee. The priests took umbrage and surged forward to attack him. Krell desperately screamed, trying to conjure the Kraken. Apollo struck Krell on the side of the head with the broken staff. Krell summoned the Kraken all right, but it was the lumpy carved motif on the end of his staff that he got, as it cracked his head open, knocking him senseless. Apollo raised the weapon, prepared to face the remaining priests, but they quickly backed down—the threat was unnecessary.

"Board the craft!" Apollo shouted angrily. Brothers Cain and Abel positioned themselves at the ladder's base, guiding passengers onto the vessel.

Once everyone was aboard, Apollo stood alone. The priests had gathered around Krell and were joined by hundreds of citizens who had opted to remain on Atlan.

Al stood beside Apollo. Suddenly, Apollo turned to him and said, "Thank you for being by my side. It is now the moment to depart."

Al was astonished that Apollo was aware of his presence. He replied, "Atlantis will be a remarkable new beginning. Farewell, brave Apollo."

He watched as Apollo ascended the ladder. The hatch closed. After a few moments, a massive ring formed in the sky, and the craft ascended into it, disappearing from view.

When Al looked back at the priests, they shimmered.

"A polar shift is inevitable; it's already in motion. It's a magnetic reversal snap we don't want or for that matter, a micro nova from the sun," the Professor explained to Turk in the commissary.

"Nothing of that nature happened by 2112," Turk responded.

"No? Hmm, that's interesting. Three generations from now, I expect it might be overdue," the Professor mused.

Turk remained sceptical. "Shouldn't there have been recognisable indicators?"

"I doubt you'd know. After the Cyberwars, with all the devastation and communications down, unless you were directly affected, you'd have no knowledge of a volcanic eruption or a tsunami in another part of the world. Have you noticed unusually violent weather?" the Professor inquired.

Turk slowly nodded. "Yes, we've had our share, but I put that down to global warming."

"That's accurate. Global warming is an additional issue. However, polar shifts are a natural part of Earth's cycle. The last one wiped out Atlantis around twelve thousand years ago," the Professor explained.

"Wasn't that the great flood? Al mentioned something about En-Lil causing it," Turk recalled.

"Yes, well, Secta and I believe that En-Lil used that cataclysmic event to cull mankind. And if it hadn't been for En-Ki, he might well have succeeded."

"The Noah's Ark story from the Bible?" Turk inquired.

"Yes, except the 'ark' was probably a DNA repository. The biblical Noah, or in Greek mythology, Deucalion, or Atrahasis in Akkadian or Ziusudra in Sumerian, each had their own version—we believe was En-Ki's Earthly emissary to save humanity."

Secta entered the room and took a seat. "Am I interrupting anything?"

"No, I was just discussing the magnetic polar shift with Turk."

Secta nodded. "Yes, as if our troubles weren't enough. But I have some good news. Data from the probe is in. We've located Alice. Where's Vee?"

Turk raised an eyebrow. "Hope took her to Café Epiphany for some girl-talk. So, when will we depart?"

"A few more hours to study the data and make preparations. Okay?" Secta said before heading to the control room.

De Luz grinned. "This will be quite something—traveling to another world, nine hundred light years away."

Turk reclined in his seat. He hadn't truly grasped the magnitude of the mission until that moment.

As Al's vision cleared, Doevan loomed over him, observing him in a way similar to a dentist. "Are you back with us, Al?" he inquired.

Al pinched the bridge of his nose, squinting tightly. "Got a blinding headache."

Vale appeared, holding a mug of beer. "Here you go, Al. Ale fixes everything. Well, at least a Stockholm brew does."

Al skulled the frothy beverage, and true to Vale's words, his headache vanished a minute or two later. "It worked."

"See, I told you our ale is as good, if not better, than yours," Doevan proclaimed, jesting with Vale.

"How was the experience, Al?" Vale asked.

"Incredible. As Apollo was about to board the Atlantis, he actually spoke to me."

Vale frowned. "What? No, that is impossible."

"I am not entirely sure about that … I have heard of something like this once before," Doevan pondered, holding his chin thoughtfully.

"Makes me wonder if he knew I'd been there all along," Al reflected.

Looking fatigued, Vale suggested, "Let us go outside. I need some fresh air."

Al got up, slightly unsteady on his feet. "Whoa," he steadied himself. "How long was I out?"

"Six hours or so," Vale said.

They navigated through the room with the altar and the fires. Bodies lay scattered on the floor—some unconscious, others rousing from slumber. They stepped over some of them as they made their way outside.

The first rays of dawn illuminated the sea. Doevan guided them to the edge of the lagoon. "Do you now understand our history?" he asked Al.

"Much wiser now, but we didn't get to the Nephilim," Al responded.

"Oh, that war spanned centuries. The Nephilim sought revenge for the theft of the TIS-177 and the killing of its crew. They eliminated the members of the Kraken Cult and others over time. Only a few escaped with the help of the Treen, staying underground with them for six generations. Eventually, they emerged and built the first float.

From there, the population grew, and the other six floats evolved over time. The population now numbers around ten thousand."

"So, you're descendants of the Priesthood?" Al inquired.

"Some might be, but not mostly. Many wanted to join Apollo but were either too old, injured, or too young. After all, there was limited space on the craft," Doevan explained.

"Did the Kraken cult persist?"

"Absolutely not!" Vale growled, as if the very notion was a slap in the face.

"That's good to hear. That Krell character embodied everything I despise in people," Al growled, his gaze sharp and calculating. He wanted to be certain about the side Vale and Doevan supported and ensure he had no part in anything related to the tyranny Krell represented. "But the Kraken still exists, right?"

"Yes, and more than that, our greatest foe is King Kraken—we believe it is the largest Kraken to have ever roamed the seas," Doevan responded gravely.

"Why haven't you killed it?" Al questioned.

Doevan shook his head. "With one strike of its tentacles, it could obliterate an entire float ... that is how massive it is."

"We are no match for it, Alice. We lack the weaponry to defend, let alone attack it," Vale added.

Doevan's expression turned grave. "It has struck many floats to pillage our fish and sponge supplies. At times, it feasts on citizens' flesh. We have had to rebuild time and time again."

Al asked, "How did it get that big?"

"It is the lone male. All other Kraken are female. It eliminates rivals to maintain its status as the alpha male. Its primary diet is other Kraken, which suits us. Repelling smaller Kraken is a challenge," Doevan explained.

"Juvenile Kraken are highly dangerous and unpredictable," Vale asserted. "Alice, we should leave for Stockholm now."

"You can take one of our coracles for your journey. It will be sturdier than your canoe."

"Thank you, Doevan," Vale acknowledged gratefully, patting him on the back.

An hour later, Al and Vale were aboard a coracle. It was four times the size of the canoe, constructed from woven reeds and equipped with an outrigger and a sail.

As the sea-gate opened, Al waved to Doevan with his signature gesture and called out, "Chaa!"

Al liked Doevan. He was a cheerful man with an unforgettable belly laugh and a razor-sharp wit. His kindness and generosity made Alice believe that the people of Kor, in their simplicity, were more utopian compared to the troubled individuals on Earth.

Vale pushed off from the wharf and paddled the boat through the gate into the open sea. The swell wasn't significant, so Al felt that his sea legs were strong enough for the journey. Vale unfurled the big red square lateen sail, which quickly caught the gentle sea breeze, propelling them due east toward Stockholm. With King Kraken an ever-present threat in Alice's mind, he managed to settle back and drift off to sleep to the gentle lullaby of the sails flapping in the breeze. However, his dreams were invaded by images of the colossal monster Kraken, dismembering men on Atlan. If King Kraken was even bigger as Doevan had suggested, then Al had no desire to meet it in a flimsy reed boat on the open sea.

At the tiller, ever vigilant, Vale looked back at the London float growing smaller and smaller in the ever-widening lines of the coracle's wake.

CHAPTER 24
STOCKHOLM

AL CLOSED HIMSELF into the shower recess. The water drenched him. Warm and refreshing it felt good and for a moment he was a boy again, walking home from school after a storm, carrying his shoes, his bare feet squishing in the muddy puddles. He stopped to look at his reflection in a puddle as it settled. The puddle began to change colour—it became clouded with crimson blood. Into it, blood dripped and splashed in slow motion. His reflection was replaced by a scene of mangled cybernetics strewn about in a twilight milieu of death and destruction. It was raining—howling like a lone wolf, the wind picked up the black dust of time and decay forming into wicked spirals that swirled through the rusted metal skeletons of a lost civilization. It was an unworldly 3-D canvas upon which was painted a surrealist's portrayal of the end of an artificially intelligent species.

His hands came into frame covered in blood. He knew instinctively it wasn't his blood. His bloody hand turned off the shower. Then the blood was gone from the hands that were no longer the hands of a boy. He looked down at the puddle and watched the bloody water around his feet spiralling down the drain taking with it the metaphor.

As the sun began to set, Vale realised he should have spotted Stockholm's lighthouse by now. And then, there it was, emerging on the horizon in the violet hues of twilight as if summoned. Just one more hour at sea, and he'd be back home.

Knuckling his eyes to shake off the remnants of sleep, the dream or premonition still lingered in Al's mind, only to be abruptly replaced by the sight of the massive sea gate within the enclosing wall of the float. This time, there was no need to call out; the gate opened as soon as they came into view.

Beyond the gate, the lagoon and structures differed significantly from those of London. For starters, Stockholm was much larger and sturdier, constructed to withstand potential sea attacks. The lagoon was divided into a marina and what Al assumed were floating fish and sponge enclosures. A reception party of around twenty people stood at the dock's edge, with a big man standing at the forefront.

"The prodigal son returns, and with a stranger no less!" the big man boomed, extending a hand to Vale to disembark from the boat. The two men embraced, and then Vale assisted Alice up onto the wharf.

Al was introduced to Vale's father, Odin Tarz, the chief of Stockholm. A towering man with a high-bridged nose that bore signs of multiple breaks, jet-black hair worn in the dual ear-plumes of his station, with caste-marks including tattoos on his face and forearms. Odin led them towards the Great Hall for a discussion. Along the way, Vale briefed him on the events and how Al had taken a Narcogen to witness Atlan's history firsthand.

The Great Hall was a long house with a towering façade punctuated by four large windows. Al struggled to discern its composition—it resembled wood with a heavily thatched roof, yet it wasn't quite either of those materials. All he could surmise was that it had an organic quality.

Upon entering, Al's gaze swept across the elongated rectangular chamber and immediately locked onto a face in the crowd—an eerily familiar face. It was Djard's face, the barbarian girl he had befriended during his initial time travel venture to the post-apocalyptic ruins of Sydney. This girl mirrored Djard precisely, down to her long, curly blonde hair, athletic form, and vivid blue eyes that radiated even from a distance. The only divergence was her dark skin and attire. Instead of a leather bikini, she wore a knee-length white toga-like tunic cinched at the waist. She was barefoot. Al shot her a smile, and she responded with a shy one of her own.

The Great Hall featured a long rectangular banquet table along one side, hewn from a single piece of dried skin that once belonged to a colossal aquatic creature—a whale-like entity, Al surmised. The table could accommodate fifty people on stools flanking each side, with a throne-like master's seat at the head, positioned before a large unlit hearth. The hearth's size suggested severe winters.

Odin motioned for Al to sit at his left, at the head of the table, with Vale on his right. The other ten seats were occupied by council members, an equal mix of genders, all elderly. Across the room, on the left side, smaller oval tables were arranged for the younger attendees, including the girl who reminded Alice of Djard. While Al was eager to meet her, it would have to wait for a more opportune time. They exchanged numerous furtive glances.

Odin commenced the meeting with enthusiasm. "Al, Vale has briefed me about you, but I'm eager to learn more. Please, share your story. We are attentive listeners here in Stockholm."

Though Odin projected a jovial demeanour, Al detected a glimmer of deadly seriousness in his eyes. "I hail from Earth," Al began, "a place you might know as Ki. Comparing our worlds' eras is challenging, but Earth is inhabited by over nine billion humans. We have one star—the Sun—one moon, vast landmasses, and primarily blue oceans. It teems with wildlife, and our population is highly mechanised. We've advanced to the point of air and space travel, even achieving time travel. However, I didn't arrive here through time travel; I stowed away on a Nephilim spacecraft."

A murmur rippled through the audience.

Alice waited for the grumblings of disbelief to die down. He expected it would be difficult to accept his explanation. "The Nephilim," he continued, "it seems to me, have been visiting Earth for some time, abducting humans possibly for experimentation. In my case, they were on Earth to take a sarcophagus, which had been discovered after being hidden for many centuries. You might know the sarcophagus as the Astara."

This time the murmur from the gallery was more intense, but not with disbelief, but surprise.

"I climbed inside it just before it was taken by the Nephilim and brought to Kor. When I got out of it, I was arrested and thrown into a cell with Vale. We escaped together." He paused and leered at the council, in the same way he liked to leer at his audience at a concert … he enjoyed the theatrics, especially imagining the impact of what he was about to confide in them. "I am a time traveller … my mission is to return the Astara to Earth. I was given this mission personally by En-Ki."

The audience this time erupted with loud groans and mutterings of total disbelief. One councillor stood and grumbled throatily, "What sort of fantasy are we listening to here? Is this human on Narcogen?"

Odin cast a steely glare at the cynic and growled, "Resume your seat, Tiltse. I have no reason to doubt the veracity of our guest's disclosure."

A hush fell upon the gathering: Odin had spoken. He had a firm grip on the reins of state.

"Please proceed, Al," Odin urged, courteously.

"I realise this must sound fantastic to you. I am just a singer by trade who, by fate, was contacted by En-Ki who bestowed upon me a quest … it was that quest that has led me to Kor. I believe there is more to coming here than just to recover the Astara … I think En-Ki is concerned for your welfare as he is for the welfare of humanity. We have struggled against the forces of evil for thousands of years … forces led by no other than the same evil despot that brought destruction upon the people of Kor: En-Lil."

Again, the audience erupted but this time with a different tone … more positive—angered by the mention of En-Lil. Al felt the tide was turning, he was winning them over. He jumped up to deliver more at his theatrical best with much more gusto.

"The tyranny of En-Lil must be defeated before he destroys both our worlds, in accordance with the evil edict from Anu. En-Ki has been all that has stood between us and oblivion for millennia, and now he has appointed me his emissary … his hired gun … I am charged with the responsibility of vanquishing En-Lil from existence, forever!"

Each and every person rose as one out of their seats and burst into cheering applause. They had totally bought into Alice's allegory.

Odin raised a hand to quieten them. "Let him continue. I believe he has more to say. While on the London float with Vale, he was enchanted by Narcogen, taken by his own volition so as to visit our past on Atlan. He has seen it … witnessed it … and … he met Apollo, who even acknowledged him!" He nodded at Alice to continue. The audience was shocked … murmuring to each other, wondering how that was possible … how could he meet Apollo?

Al remained standing but now that he had them in his grasp, he spoke in a more relaxed tone. "What Lord Odin says is true … I watched Apollo board the TIS-177, that he renamed Atlan-Tis. On the flight deck of that craft, I saw the map … the designation the craft would take he and his followers to was Ki… the meaning of Ki in the ancient language of Akkadian is: Earth." He paused for the point to sink in.

"On Earth, we have many mythologies, and one of them involves an island in one of our great oceans that was said to be inhabited by a race technically more advanced than any other on the planet at that time. The people of that island are believed to have come from the stars. They brought with them knowledge, wisdom, and technology they passed on to some of the indigenous, more primitive tribes of Earth. That island was called Atlantis."

The story triggered a humdrum of excitement. Al raised his hand to quell the mutter. "I believe Apollo landed on an island that was very similar to Atlan, and he settled it. Then, as mythology on Earth tells, years later the island of Atlantis was totally destroyed by a cataclysmic flood that sank it below the ocean. This happened twelve thousand Earth years ago, at the time of a geologically recognised great flood that all but obliterated humankind. I believe that flood was caused by En-Lil!" The last word came out in a full-throated roar.

"I believe En-Lil had discovered the refugees from Atlan and sought to destroy them and then all of humanity in the flood because En-Ki had created both races! The only reason humankind managed to survive was because En-Ki had warned a human named Atrahasis that the flood was imminent. Atrahasis and his family were thus saved, and he became the father of the nine billion humans on Earth today ... a race that now harbours weapons capable of destroying worlds ... a race that wars with itself, has a fixation with war, and has developed space and time travel ... the very reasons that drive En-Lil to obliterate humanity once and for all. I know an inevitable confrontation, an apocalyptic battle to end all battles with En-Lil, is coming your way. It will be the final showdown ... a showdown in which I have been chosen by En-Ki to lead the offensive."

The room had fallen silent. Al calmly resumed his seat. Odin held out a hand to Al who took it. They shook hands, with Odin announcing loud and clear, "Our people are but one! United we will stand against En-Lil in the battle to end all battles!"

Al announced firmly, loud enough to rise above the bellowing cheers. "But first, people of Kor, we must deal with the Nephilim!"

A pregnant pause followed, and then Odin rose to his feet and opened the applause. Then every person in the great hall rose one by one from their seats and applauded in support of Alice. He had won their hearts.

After an hour, when the talks had wound down, Al noticed the Djard look-alike get up to leave. He was standing next to Vale, who followed Al's eye-line to her and said, "I should introduce you."

Al acted like he'd been caught with his pants down. "Uh, is it that obvious? Yeah, why not," Al added, demurely.

"Come on then," Vale chortled.

"Don't tell me her name is Djard or I'll collapse on the spot. I know someone named Djard, and she's the spitting image of her."

Vale took him over to the teenage girl who was leaving with a half dozen of her friends. She stopped when Vale approached and they hugged. Al felt a twinge of embarrassment thinking oh no, they're an item.

"Ina, I want you to meet Al ... Al, this is my sister, Inanna."

Al was relieved. "Inanna, such a cool name."

"Cool?" she inquired politely.

"Oh, cool ... right, where I come from, cool can mean pleasantly cold or unique, I meant the latter," he explained, awkwardly. He quickly accessed his implant to search her name and found: Inanna: the Sumerian goddess of love, war, and fertility: the personification of the morning and evening star. Also known as...

"Ishtar, of course, that's where I know the name," he mumbled to himself, forgetting he could be heard.

"No, Inanna," she corrected him.

"I will leave you to chat," Vale said, with a sly grin at Al. "I need to talk more with Odin. Al will be staying with me, Ina, so drop him off at my hub."

"Come, let us go outside, it is too stuffy in here," Ina said sweetly, taking Al by the arm and leading him outside.

They strolled arm in arm over to the edge of the lagoon where Ina found a bench. They sat.

Alice asked obliquely, "Do you have a mate?" He'd picked up the term they use for a partner.

She glanced at him swiftly—a strange coquetry there on the bench in the warmth of Stockholm: a teenage girl in a white dress, her head tilted sideways with her golden hair falling in curls to her shoulders—Alice, darkly handsome, in full command of his soul.

"No ... There have been none, thus far," she admitted, with a sardonic smirk. She now appeared to Alice to be less like Djard up close, more striking, far less warrior-like, more feminine. Her eyes were violet and spectacular with golden elongated pupils, her countenance delicate and demure.

Electra and Commander Walker had been teleported by Aquila II to the dimly lit cargo hold of the UFO over New York.

"Any idea where we go from here?" Walker asked.

Resplendent in a cling-fitted shiny grey flying suit, with a matching skullcap, Electra was sitting on the floor with her back to the wall. "Just relax and wait, Commander ... they know we are on board, soon enough they will come looking for us. We do not need to worry about finding them."

He shrugged his shoulders and joined her on the floor. He was dressed in a similar flying suit. "I must admit, I don't feel comfortable without a firearm."

"It would be of no use to you. A projectile weapon could breach the hull, and that would be catastrophic."

"Hmm, I guess you're right. Would the hull be that thin?"

"Wait, shush ... I think we are moving," she said.

Sometime later, a door not at all obvious in the solid metal wall spiralled open. As had occurred with Alice, the very same hologram appeared and spoke in the same monotone female voice that seemed ubiquitous. "You will follow."

They had no idea they were going to be holed up in a cage until the ship arrived on Kor.

When Vee and Hope arrived back at OTT, they were happy to discover the drone had successfully located Alice, and the mission was on.

Secta and Hope were watching Vee and Turk prepping in the caged armoury. Secta asked, "Atmosphere checked out fine, what weapons are you taking, Turk?"

The big man looked up after sliding a clip into a Glock 19 pistol. "A stack of your deadly WASPs, handguns each ... one for Al ... plus a few odds and ends that might come in handy."

"Cool that we can now take all this hardware through Kairos," Vee said.

Hope chipped in, "This will be the first off-world mission for anyone other than Alice and by far the furthest ... well, over the greatest distance. We have no idea the effects it might have on your physiology."

"Of course, Al went on the UFO not through Kairos," Vee agreed.

"We're going to implant you both with a chip to hourly feed back your vitals through the micro-wormhole," Secta cautioned.

Hope expanded on that. "In the event of an abnormality, you will feel the chip vibrate. At that point, you will return immediately. Is that clear?"

They both nodded. "Vibrate? Where exactly will you be putting it?" Vee asked, with a cheeky grin.

"What's the ETD?" Turk queried.

"Three hours," Secta said. "We're still waiting for UNTT approval."

"Why does it always take forever with them?" Vee snarled, impatiently.

"There's a lot going on, Vee," Secta pointed out. "Turk, is your language implant working fine?"

"Yes, Vee and I have been speaking Mongolian," he chuckled. Footsteps sounded. They belonged to Viktoria.

She stopped at the grill door and said, "Thought I'd come down into the bowels of existence to let you know we just heard from Manila ... Blake is out of emergency, he's in recovery. He'll live."

Vee burst into tears. Turk gave her a consoling hug.

CHAPTER 25
CANDLES

VEE STORMED INTO the control room like an enraged bull spotting a red rag. Three hours had passed, and still, no mission was underway; she was seething. Secta swivelled around from standing behind Christina at the console and raised a hand to halt the furious teenager.

"Wait, Vee. Before you go off ... We haven't secured clearance from UNTT yet. They've taken issue with something related to the mission, and we're working to resolve it. You need to be patient."

Vee folded her arms defiantly across her chest. "You'd think they'd have gotten over objections to everything we do by now. What's their problem this time?"

Secta attempted to soothe her. "Mal's looking into it. I have full confidence in him. And to lighten Luna's mood a bit, I sent the Professor along to provide moral support for Mal."

The quip managed to bring a hint of a smile to Vee's face. She let her guard down a little and mumbled with a chuckle, "Luna doesn't stand a chance."

The desk phone rang, and Christina answered it before passing it to Secta. "It's the boss."

He switched on the speaker for Vee's benefit. "Secta?" Mal's voice came through.

"Yes, Mal. You're on speaker. What's the latest?"

"I've got Luna here ... UNTT is being stubborn. They claim that taking weapons to an M-class planet with a civilization is in direct violation of the TPD. Their argument is that if the planet's indigenous inhabitants haven't yet developed such weapons, we'd be interfering with the natural process of evolution. Unfortunately, it's a valid argument."

Secta asked, "How has UNTT accessed the level of the native evolution?"

"The video footage from the drone over the float," Luna replied, her voice sounding small as she sat across from Mal in the President's office.

Secta's response was forceful. "That's an inaccurate assessment. Our traveller is on the planet due to transportation by a sophisticated spacecraft capable of covering nine hundred light years in a matter of minutes. I would argue that the technology required for such an extraordinary feat overrides any breach of the prime directive analogy. Moreover, the alien species accused of hijacking the sarcophagus and our traveller must be regarded as hostile at this point, justifying the need for our away team to be armed for defence."

"We're dealing with a culture far more advanced than our own, Luna," the Professor added.

"Once again, pressure is being exerted on OTT by your organisation while you turn a blind eye to other violations of the authentication code," Mal protested vehemently.

"Are you referring to the detection of an event by Zen Corporation last night?" Luna questioned.

"Yes, and more specifically, the target destination of that event," Mal said with a dark tone.

The tension in the room was palpable. Luna had no comeback to the accusation other than to respond obsequiously, "The UFO over New York."

"Yes, the same UFO believed to have hijacked Alice and the sarcophagus from Davao. So now we're potentially facing a double threat to our away team ... two Zen agents aboard a hostile UFO that we suspect will return to the planet we're seeking UNTT mission approval for," the Professor argued emphatically.

"Luna, could you please relay our evaluation of the situation to your office and inform us of their thoughts promptly? We're prepared for an emergency rescue mission, but we won't proceed without UNTT consent," Secta proposed diplomatically.

Vee gave Secta a thumbs up, endorsing the wisdom of his argument.

Inanna was walking Al to Vale's hub near the Great Hall when they were halted by the sound of the sea gates opening. "Must be the return of the fishing fleet. Want to take a look at the catch?" Inanna asked.

Al was intrigued, so they retraced their steps to the edge of the lagoon and waited. Soon, panicked voices erupted from the seaward side of the gate, which wasn't yet fully open.

"Something's not right," Inanna said, her concern evident.

Al rushed over and ascended the staircase to the portcullis, where four men were pulling the gate open using flaxen ropes. Looking down to the seaward side, he saw that about half a dozen fishing coracles were under attack while waiting for the gate to fully open. A juvenile Kraken, approximately three metres long, was attempting to force its way in through the opening gates. The men on the boats were desperately striking at it with oars and spears, splashing the water in their struggle to repel it. Suddenly, the Kraken turned on the fishermen, wrapping a long tentacle around an oar and pulling the fisherman holding it into the water. He thrashed about, trying to escape the clutches of the terrible creature, but it quickly enveloped him in its tendrils, which tore at his body. The water turned crimson as the fisherman's arm was torn off at the shoulder. The sight of blood seemed to drive the creature into a frenzy, and it attacked the nearest boat, tipping six fishermen into the water.

A second, much larger Kraken, attracted by the commotion,

surfaced behind the last boat.

On impulse, Al reached into his side pants pocket for a WASP, only to realise that he had left them in his jacket back in Davao. "Damn!" he cursed, but then remembered his pills. He retrieved the waterproof sachet from his fob pocket and swallowed a pill. To protect his clothes and shoes from the strain of his transformation, he shed them. Wearing only a pair of black spandex stretch shorts that Hope had given him to accommodate his morphing physique, he leaned forward and flexed his biceps while picturing the image of the Star Lord. His neck and shoulder arteries and tendons bulged as his body underwent its transformation. Despite the pain, he grimaced with clenched teeth, his entire form changing.

Alerted by the tumult, Vale and Odin hurried out of the Great Hall, followed by others. They joined Inanna, who was gazing up at Alice atop the portcullis.

"Kraken are attacking the fleet!" Inanna shouted above the chaos.

"What is Al doing up there?" Vale asked.

"I do not know ... he went to help. Look at him!" Inanna cried out, thunderstruck.

Alice had shifted into the Star Lord form. To the shock of the men hauling the gate open and the spectators, he swan-dived from the gate tower forty feet down into the water.

Vale sprinted up the ramp to the top of the portcullis and peered down at the turmoil in the water below. The man who had been Alice held onto the smaller Kraken's turret lip. With a powerful yank, he tore it open, exposing the creature's anatomy. Masses of sinewy ligaments surrounded a brain shaped like a ball, about half a metre in size. Al tore at the tendons and sinews, snapping them like strings. With each severed connection, one of the eight tentacles went limp. Dark blue blood spurted into the air, drenching everything and tainting the water. Covered in blue Kraken blood, Al stood atop the floating creature, which was quickly losing its strength.

The larger Kraken ceased its attack on the boat and, sensing the danger to the smaller Kraken, moved to assist.

Inanna and Odin had joined Vale at the portcullis. Amid the chaos, Inanna's voice pierced through, "The big one is coming! Al! Al! Behind you! Behind you!"

In the water, men were swimming for their lives, desperately trying to make it through the partially open gate. The Kraken with Al on its back was thrashing about in a final attempt to dislodge him, while a turret, resembling a family car in size, belonging to the larger Kraken, was hurtling through the water directly toward Alice.

Al seized the Kraken's brain with both hands and tore it out of the dish-shaped membrane that held it. The Kraken convulsed uncontrollably and then abruptly fell limp.

"Behind you, Al!" Vale's voice boomed urgently.

Al spun around just in time to witness the colossal Kraken burst out of the water, akin to a submarine executing an emergency surface manoeuvre. Its three-metre tentacles wrapped around Alice, intent on tearing him apart.

Vale and Odin grimaced with fear, doubting that Al could match the brute strength of the monster. Inanna's eyes held the terror of a hunted creature.

As the Kraken lifted Al into the air, he grasped one of its bulbous eyes at the end of a stalk and yanked it out. Blue blood spurted from the severed stem, and the tentacles released their grip, causing Alice to plunge with a splash into the murky water, where he vanished.

The boats and the men managed to make it through the gate.

"Will he swim through the gate?" Inanna's voice trembled.

"We need to close them! The Kraken will enter and kill us all!" Odin shouted. "Close the gate!"

"No, no!" Inanna screamed. "You cannot abandon Alice to die! He risked his life to save us!"

The men on the ropes began hauling the gate closed.

The water grew calm, an eerie stillness descending, with only the sound of the ropes and pulleys as the gate was drawn closed.

Biting her fingernails and staring anxiously at the tranquil water, Inanna dreaded the worst. The Kraken and Alice had vanished into the murky depths. Time was slipping away perilously; how long could Alice endure submerged, holding his breath? The fishermen were safely on the other side in the lagoon, and the gates were nearly shut. They all feared the worst when Vale suddenly shouted, pointing at the water, "Look!"

The water began to churn, as though something was about to surface. Then, with a tremendous surge that generated a large wave, Alice emerged from the water atop the Kraken's huge turret.

Odin commanded, "Hold the gate!" The ropes were pulled taut to keep the gates partially open.

"Look at him! He is incredible!" Inanna cheered.

Al knelt down, gripped another of the Kraken's eyes by its stalk, and yanked it from the socket. Blue blood sprayed from the wound as the Kraken thrashed violently. However, Al maintained his balance, resembling a seasoned surfer from his younger years. He clenched his fist and squatted on the massive black turret. With a powerful motion, akin to Thor's hammer, he punched his fist through the turret shell. The Kraken thrashed about in water half blind, blood spraying from the two ravaged eye sockets, unable to stop the behemoth of a man bashing its brains out.

It took half a dozen mighty punches for Alice to crack through the turret shell and expose the brain. He delved into the tangle of spaghetti-like organs, ripping the tendons apart, much like he did with the smaller Kraken. Uncovering the brain, he seized it in his blue-blood-soaked hands and dragged it from its membranous cradle. Holding it under his arm, he violently severed the cortex. As the colossal creature began to sink, Al discarded the brain and dived back into the water, swimming through the gate.

"Close the gate!" Odin shouted.

Inanna and Vale rushed back to the edge of the wharf, waiting anxiously for Al to emerge from the lagoon. After a tense moment, he surfaced and grasped Vale's hand, pulling himself onto the deck. To their astonishment, he had returned to his normal form.

Inanna handed him his clothes.

When he finished dressing, Al glanced up and saw that all the citizens who had gathered were on their knees, genuflecting in reverence to him. Feeling embarrassed, he called out, "Please, please, no... stand up ... there's no need for any of that."

With their heads bowed to avoid making eye contact with Al, Vale was the first to muster the courage to look at him and asked, astonished, "Who did you just become, Al?"

"The Star Lord ... I—" Al began to explain, but a loud rumble from the crowd interrupted him as they repeated in reverence, "The Star Lord," which halted his explanation.

In homage, Odin murmured, "He is the prophecy."

Vale nodded in agreement, as if he had already known, and then inquired, "Do all humans possess this ability?"

Al chuckled. "No, it's a special gift I received from En-Ki."

The entire population of Stockholm, now gathered at the water's edge, continued to genuflect with heads bowed. They began to murmur loudly, "God En-Ki, God En-Ki."

Al found this overwhelming. While he was comfortable with an audience applauding and appreciating him, being worshipped was a different matter entirely. He took Vale's arm and helped him to his feet, then did the same for Odin and Inanna.

"You must tell us more ... I had no idea you were a god," Vale said in awe.

Al shrugged his shoulders. "Mate, I'm no god, alright? I'm just an ordinary guy." As soon as the words left his mouth, he realised that he had just performed something quite extraordinary, suggesting that he might not be as ordinary as he had thought. Giving up on trying to rationalise it, he said, "Look, I'll explain everything later over a cold beer, alright?"

Just when he thought he had made the right decision, everything and everybody froze. He knew exactly what that meant: a vortex had formed, hopefully a friendly one. He rested his clenched fists on his hips and faced the swirling ring, which was rapidly increasing in size. Prepared to fight if necessary, he waited. Then, a large man stepped out of the vortex, followed closely by another person.

Recognising the man, Al threw his arms open and yelled, "Turk!" Then he looked at Vee and exclaimed, "Sis, happening!" They hugged, and he gave Vee a peck on the cheek.

Turk aimed a small remote at the ring, reducing the swirling vortex to a micro-vortex that would stay open and track a pulse signal from the device.

"Why are all these people taking the knee? Are they praising you or something?" Vee asked.

Al grasped his chin with one hand as he thought. "Right, um, I'll explain later. First, I need to figure out how to explain you to them."

Upon their arrival on Kor, Electra and Walker underwent the same processing as Alice and were subsequently confined in the dungeons beneath Atlan. After three hours of waiting, their patience finally paid off when a guard arrived to escort them out.

The room they were led to was spartan in design: white walls, well-lit, with six white chairs arranged around an oval table. Walker stood by the single large round window, awestruck by the view from the tenth floor of the high-rise building. The city below was nestled within a massive crater, appearing alien to him compared to anything he had even seen on Earth. A waterfall cascaded down one end of the crater wall, plummeting a hundred metres into a pool that fed a creek. This creek glimmered under the overhead sunlight as it meandered through the city. Transparent tubes connected to various buildings allowed spherical vehicles to travel within. While there was some vegetation, none of the plant or tree species were recognisable to him.

Electra, on the other hand, showed no interest in the view. Having witnessed countless sights across the universe over millennia, nothing remained to impress En-Lil.

The end wall of the room reshaped itself to allow entry for four armoured figures. They took seats around the table, with one of them standing out. This figure wore bronze armour, unlike the others who donned drab gunmetal grey. Electra assumed this individual was the leader, given the distinction in attire. Reflective visors obscured their faces, until, almost in unison, they spiralled open to reveal their features.

Walker was taken aback; he hadn't expected them to have human-like faces. Though their pallid complexions lacked eyebrows and eyelashes, it was their black, lifeless eyes devoid of whites that reminded him of the unfeeling gaze of a shark.

The leader addressed them in English, the voice deep and rich, yet distinctly artificial. "I am Rykor. We know you are En-Lil. You are our enemy. Why have you come here unarmed?"

Electra responded, her tone smug, "Because the enemy of my enemy is my ally. We share a common foe, Rykor: a human known as Black Alice. I believe he arrived here using the Astara."

"That might be true, but I fail to see how fighting your enemy would benefit us. Black Alice has not posed any significant threat to us," Rykor replied.

Electra's smile took on a wry edge. "I do not believe that is the case ... Black Alice possesses the key to the Astara, and he has used it. You commandeered the Astara, did you not?"

"And if we did?"

The exchange was blunt, befitting rival adversaries.

Electra fixed her gaze on him without blinking. "You have always sought to perpetuate the Nephilim species through procreation, Rykor, but your programming hinders you. To sustain your race, you have resorted to building cybernetic replacements using human components ... but they do not last, do they? Your species is dying, Rykor. We both know this." She allowed the gravity of her words to settle before continuing. "And we both understand that the Astara holds your only hope for salvation. My brother, En-Ki, created it ... only he knows how to use it, and he's doing so through his emissary, Black Alice. Without Black Alice, the Astara cannot, and will not, function. So, do you possess Black Alice?"

"No."

"I presumed as much. As I said, our interests align more than you realised: I want Black Alice, and so do you." She added a touch of irony, "It is amusing to think that you had him within your grasp but lost him."

"Enough!" Rykor snapped, irritation clear in his voice. "What do you propose, given that it is in your best interest to eliminate the Astara?"

"A candle does not lose its light by lighting another candle." Electra paused, allowing him to grasp the symbolism. "If we capture Black Alice ... you can use him and his DNA in the Astara to generate an immortal biological female Nephilim. Once that is done, we eliminate Black Alice and destroy the Astara. This way, we both attain our objectives."

CHAPTER 26
TREEN

WITH INTRODUCTIONS AND explanations out of the way, they relaxed at the banquet table in the Great Hall, enjoying an ale. Vee, seated beside Al, suddenly detected an unpleasant odour coming from him. She leaned in discreetly and whispered, "Mate, you're seriously on the nose."

"Eh?" Al sniffed his underarm. "Phew! Yeah, that's me alright ... I thought it was you," he retorted, playfully elbowing her ribs.

Sitting on the other side of Al, Inanna overheard their conversation. "I am glad you told him, Vee."

"Must be the Kraken blood. I was covered in it," Al grumbled.

Inanna sprang to her feet. "Come, I will take you to bathe."

"You have my full endorsement for that," Vee chuckled.

Brimming with curiosity, Turk turned to Odin and asked, "What powers everything here?"

"We use oil, distilled from seaweed. With all the wonders Al mentioned about Earth, what powers them?"

"In Alice's time, it was mainly mined fossil fuels like oil and coal. But by my time, about half a century later, we were facing significant pollution and global warming caused by those fossil fuels ... it wasn't sustainable..."

"Did you transition to another form of cleaner energy?" Odin inquired.

"Yes, we tried biofuels, solar power, wind energy. Eventually, science developed a safe form of pelletised nuclear cold fusion. Unfortunately, a world war disrupted those plans. Where do the Nephilim get the power and raw materials to build spacecraft?"

"I do not know. I think they must have inherited the spacecraft from eons ago. The energy source on Atlan is thermal, volcanic."

"Where would they get spare parts for the spacecraft?"

"They must have a facility on Atlan. I do not know."

Inanna led Al into her hub. Al took in the interior of the small three-room dwelling, while Inanna fetched a cauldron of water from the hearth. "This your gaff?" he asked.

"If gaff means hub, then yes. It is modest but comfortable." She lifted the heavy cauldron off the hearth, carried it to a tub positioned at the end of the room, and poured in the tepid water.

"Time to shed your clothes," she instructed.

Al pulled a cheeky expression but complied.

Inanna admired his well-built body. "You have worked hard on your physique."

"Yes, countless hours at the gym."

"Gym?"

"Oh, a gym is a place to exercise with weights that help build muscles," he explained, confidently displaying his physique. He stepped into the tub.

Inanna used a sponge to soap him down.

"Ah, that feels amazing," Al murmured.

Later, as Al and Ina were making their way back to the Great Hall, Al heard a sound that caused him to stop and listen intently.

"What's that strange noise?" he asked.

Ina listened attentively. "I cannot hear anything."

Alice spotted a dot in the clear sky. "Look up there ... something is flying towards us ... looks like a giant bird or a bat."

Ina searched the sky. "Oh yes, I see it too, but it is not a Ragon ... I believe it is a Treen," she said with excitement.

Concerned, Al asked, "Is a Treen a threat? Do we need to defend ourselves?"

"No, they are magnificent creatures ... native to Kor. There are very few left now; they reside in a small colony on the far side of Atlan. Eons ago, they provided sanctuary to our ancestors, the survivors of the war with the Nephilim."

"That rings a bell, Doevan mentioned them to me," Al said, watching as the flying creature drew nearer and grew larger.

The Treen finally arrived, hovering directly overhead. To Al, the Treen resembled a vision of a biblical angel, mesmerizing him. Towering at over six feet tall, she boasted long, plaited black hair interspersed with white streaks, slender athletic limbs, and bare, clawed feet. Her majestic black-feathered wings, spanning three meters from tip to tip, added to her formidable presence. Clad in a skin-tight, shiny green unitard, her attire accentuated her elegant figure.

As the Treen touched down, her wings generated a gust of wind that ruffled Ina's hair. She gracefully folded her wings behind her, with their tips still visible above her head, hovering just above the ground. Standing merely two metres away, Al could discern her features more distinctly. Her face was pallid and triangular, marked by full lips, a sharp nose, and pointed ears reminiscent of an elf. Her eyes, larger than usual and violet in hue, radiated intelligence. Although her appearance might be deemed gothic or otherworldly on Earth, Al trusted Ina's judgment in this encounter.

Approaching the Treen with reverence, Ina took a knee and bowed her head. "I welcome you, Treen. I am Inanna Tarz, daughter of Chieftain Odin, and this is Black Alice."

"Your reputation precedes you, Black Alice," the Treen replied in a confident tone, her voice laced with a gracious smile. Her teeth were pearly white and slightly pointed. "Rise, Inna Tarz. I am Cyrena ... and I bear a warning."

Al quickly recalled the name Cyrena; it had become a habit for him to look up names. Cyrena was a water nymph who had fought a creature threatening the sun-god Apollo. In gratitude, Apollo had built her a city, which he named Cyrenaica. The name Cyrena was linked to "Mother of Aristaeus," as Apollo was thought to be the father of Aristaeus.

Curious, Al asked, "Is your city named Cyrenaica?"

"Yes, it is. How do you know of this?"

"And are you the mother of Aristaeus?"

"That is correct."

"Then you must be thousands of years old," Al surmised.

"It is not advisable to risk asking a female her age," she teased. "Our people do not experience death from aging, Black Alice."

"I will take you to Odin," Ina proposed.

The discussion paused as Ina and Alice entered the Great Hall, accompanied by Cyrena. Odin and Vale rose to their feet, bowing in reverence to the majestic visitor.

Inanna introduced, "My father Odin and my brother Vale, this is Cyrena."

"I am familiar with Cyrena; she is the Queen of the Treen. You are most welcome, Your Majesty," Odin greeted with courtesy.

Inanna blushed upon realising Cyrena's royal status.

"Thank you, Chieftain Odin. Our people share a connection beyond blood," Cyrena replied.

Whispering to Al, Ina asked, "I wonder what she means by that?"

"She and Apollo are the parents of Aristaeus, so he was of Korman blood," Al whispered back.

Standing beside Vale, Turk and Vee were captivated by the winged beauty before them.

"I have come to deliver a warning. We have learned that the Nephilim are preparing to invade your floats. There is little time for you to prepare," Cyrena announced.

A wave of uneasiness rippled through the room.

"So, are you saying good Queen, that an invasion is imminent?" Vale inquired.

"Yes, Vale. We anticipate it to begin on the Don-moon."

Al leaned in to whisper a question to Ina, "When is the Don-moon?"

She responded in a hushed tone, "A Djvar-moon is thirty days; the Don-moon is fifteen days."

"Are these phases of the largest moon?"

"Yes, the large moon, as you call it, is Djvardon."

Al nodded, indicating that he understood.

With a grave expression on his weathered face, Odin turned to the queen. "Do you have any knowledge of the nature of the impending attack?"

"They are constructing three sea spiders."

The room erupted into a wave of panic, which Odin had to quell by raising his hand.

Cyrena continued, "This is how my son Aristaeus discovered their planned assault."

Quietly, Al muttered to Ina, "You'll need to tell me about these sea spiders later."

"They intend to strike the London float first," Cyrena revealed. "It is closer to them, which might grant you some additional time. I have already informed Chief Doevan."

Al's voice rose with determination. "The floats will need to unite to fight the Nephilim."

"I have come to pledge the support of the Treen," Cyrena declared. "Although we are not a warlike race, we are prepared to fight. The last two remaining Ragon are also ready to aid, if necessary."

Expressing his gratitude, Odin once again bowed his head. "Your support humbles us."

Al's curiosity got the better of him. "Can I ask how you know of my reputation, Queen Cyrena?"

"You are one of the targets of the impending Nephilim invasion, Black Alice."

Al delved further, "And what is the other target?"

"The complete eradication of the Korman species from Kor. Then, the total annihilation of the human race on the planet Ki."

This was a woman of such unparalleled pulchritude that she had every male in the room with the exception of Alice under her spell. Al was more interested in her warning, and glanced knowingly at Odin and Vale—the battle to end all battles against En-Lil was destined to begin on Kor, just as he had predicted.

The room was austere but of an acceptable standard for Electra and Walker.

The only initial problem was there being only one bed, however that was quickly remedied when Electra advised Walker she had no need of one because sleep was unnecessary for her. She was also not in need of sustenance, which of course wasn't the case for Walker.

The Nephilim, being partially AI, also had no need for food, so they were forced to make special arrangements to accommodate Walker. They recruited a human abductee from prison as a cook. Walker wasn't impressed by the taste of the amorphous food but didn't complain; it seemed nutritious enough, whatever it was.

"Why do you concede to the Nephilim? I presumed the whole reason for being here was to destroy the sarcophagus," Walker argued.

"I have conceded nothing ... I now have them doing all the work for me. They were created as a slave race, so they are doing what they know best. They will deliver me Black Alice."

"But then they will use the sarcophagus, and that surely wouldn't be in your best interests."

Electra got up from the lounge chair and went to the window, standing with her back to him, her hands clasped behind her. "No Walker," she slowly turned and then ghoulishly added, "I will get what I want ... of that you can be certain."

It was obvious to Walker from Electra's pretentious attitude that it was En-Lil talking. Electra was quite modest in comparison, modulating her synthetic voice more.

They swapped places at the window, with Walker looking spiritlessly at the view. "Then I assume our job is done ... I hardly see the point in remaining incarcerated here, waiting for the Nephilim to complete the task ... can't we get on with something else? I'll die of boredom stuck in this room."

"I had no idea you were the type to complain, Walker."

"It's not a complaint, it's a fact. I am a commander, and your interests are best served with me working with the Nephilim war council, not stuck here gazing listlessly at the view."

"You are quite right," Electra concluded. "I shall arrange it."

Al, Vale, Vee, Turk, and Odin continued discussions with Queen Cyrena in the chieftain's chambers; a private room annexed to the Great Hall.

Al observed how Cyrena's wings made it difficult for her to sit comfortably in a chair. The room was decorated sparsely but had comfortable chairs around an oval table.

Odin asked, "How do you wish to proceed, Al?"

"I think first we need to appoint a number of emissaries to deliver the call to the Chieftains of the other floats. It is important for them to assemble here on a specific day for a council of war. At that meeting, we will plan to meet the Nephilim in battle. In the interim, I want to take the battle to them. Cyrena, can Aristaeus take us to where the sea spiders are being constructed?"

"Yes, that is possible, though it would be a difficult journey for you."

Al chuckled, totally used to difficult assignments. "Oh, I'm sure we can handle it."

Cyrena added, "Can you fly?"

Al looked at her glumly. "Oh, I get your drift. Um, no."

"Who would accompany you?" she asked.

"Turk, Vee ... and Vale ... will you come?" Al asked him.

Vale nodded enthusiastically. "Of course."

"Four of us," Al concluded.

"And when will this be?"

Al cast his eyes at the others for acknowledgment, "As soon as possible."

Cyrena smiled. "You will first need to sail to Sanctuary Cove on the leeward side of Atlan. Vale knows the place. From there, we will collect you."

Vale confirmed, "The journey will take us a day ... if we leave at dawn in the morrow, we will be at Sanctuary, weather permitting, by dusk."

"Fine, we will be waiting for you," Cyrena agreed.

The plan was set. They exchanged looks of trepidation over what lay ahead.

Later, after the meeting, Al, Vee, and Turk stood at the lagoon's edge, observing the unusual fish in the aqua-farming pens. Turk revealed, "We brought three Glocks, spare clips, and two dozen WASPs between us."

Vee responded with a scoff, "That's hardly sufficient for a war."

Al, smirking, agreed, "I hear you. And these locals are virtually unarmed. I doubt the Treen are any different."

The situation was alarming, and time was pressing. They needed a plan to gather enough firepower to stand a chance against a technologically superior foe. Suddenly, Vee turned to Al, her face alight with a sudden realisation, "I've got an idea."

Juggling her morning mug of freshly brewed, steaming hot coffee, Christina arrived at her seat at the Kairos console only to find that an event had occurred overnight and something had come through Turk and Vee's open micro wormhole. Brimming with curiosity, she dashed into the event room, only to find a scrappily handwritten note on the floor. A quick read caused her to rush back to the control room and summon Secta.

An hour later in the president's office suite, Secta, Karzoff, Viktoria, the Professor, Christina, and Hope were watching Mal pace the floor.

He stopped and grumbled, "That won't go down well with UNTT."

"Then I suggest we clam up," the Professor submitted.

"It will be in our logs. If we falsify them, we stand to lose not only our status with UNTT but for Tempus as well," Christina pointed out.

"Not easy to hide this from them, they do due diligence on every mission," Karzoff said, mindfully.

"Okay, one thing at a time," Mal said, stopping his pacing and facing them. "Firstly, Alice said in the letter when it comes to the battle with En-Lil, it's shaping up to be Armageddon. Correct?"

"Yes, he, of course, doesn't know that it is likely En-Lil and someone else from Zen is on the planet with him and possibly behind the confrontation," Karzoff said.

"Remind me how we know that?" Mal queried.

Secta explained, "Luna's mob detected two travellers using Aquila from Sydney boarding the UFO over New York. That has since disappeared. We have to assume that puts two Zen agents there. One signature matched the cyborg, Cronus."

"And we suspect En-Lil transferred from Gorrick to Cronus, which was why it was brought back here from 2112 in the first place. Furthermore, our drone spy surveillance indicates Cronus is now this woman," Karzoff said, opening his notebook and displaying footage of Electra entering Zen HQ. "Her name is Electra."

"Ha! Electra, daughter of King Agamemnon. He was murdered by his wife, Electra's mother, when he returned to Athens from the Trojan War with a consort and two children. Some years later, Electra conspired with her brother to murder her mother," the Professor extolled.

"Interesting choice of name then," Hope submitted.

"We can assume Electra and an agent are on the Nephilim UFO, and that could account for the rising of the Nephilim to support En-Lil in a battle to exterminate both the populations of planet … um, and Earth," Mal paraphrased.

"Kor, Al mentioned, the planet is named Kor … exactly," Secta agreed.

"But wait a minute, from my research, the Nephilim were the sworn enemy of En-Lil … remember the An-Zu pilot? He was Nephilim. Weren't they a half-human and AI early experiment of En-Ki's that En-Lil had banished … branding them an abomination?"

"Yes, Hope, I think you're right," Secta agreed, biting his knuckle.

They were all thinking deeply about what would cause En-Lil and the Nephilim to become allies when the Professor had a brainwave. "The Astara! That's it … En-Lil wants it destroyed, we know that much … but the Nephilim hijacked it. En-Lil goes after it. Why did En-Lil want it destroyed?"

Secta traded places with Mal, pacing the floor. Thinking out loud, he said, "It performs a critical task … but what?"

"It re-encodes DNA to make humans immortal," Hope said. "Remember the story of Gilgamesh and how the sarcophagus ended up on Nan Madol. Gilgamesh was trying to become immortal. En-Ki built the Astara as some kind of genetic modifier."

Secta stopped pacing abruptly. "Right, that could be what the Nephilim want it for? Are they trying to procreate? Do they need the Astara to achieve that?"

"Look, this is all good stuff, but it's not really getting us anywhere. We first need to resolve Alice's request for a bomb."

"Yes, yes, of course, you're right, Mal, sorry … semantics … a bomb…" Secta mumbled, arguing with himself.

"You just have to tell Luna the truth," Christina blurted out. "She has followed Alice's quest, she knows firsthand the importance—"

The Professor interrupted, "That would be a risk."

Christina finished, "So, tell her exactly that."

She was right; they needed to lay their cards on the table.

"Stay put, everyone. I'll run it past her right now," Mal said, picking up the phone and dialling. After an explanation with the truth of Alice's request, he got the message across to her. The others were watching Mal's facial expressions to see if the reaction from Luna was favourable, but Mal remained poker-faced. After a few minutes, he put down the phone.

"Okay, there is no way the UNTT will approve sending a bomb of any description through a wormhole to an M-Class planet. The risk of it detonating while in the wormhole, for one thing, is too great, and secondly, deploying it would be in total violation of the Temporal Prime Directive. It's back to the drawing board, I'm afraid. The answer is an emphatic, no."

CHAPTER 27
FLIGHT

A L HAD ANTICIPATED it would take OTT a while to process his request. In the meantime, he and the others would sail to Atlan to meet the Treen. They had assembled on the wharf at dusk to bid farewell to Cyrena. She spread her magnificent black wings, then with a couple of powerful flaps, lifted off into the sky. Within minutes, she was nothing more than a speck in the darkening firmament.

Al was awakened by Vee shaking him. "Al, Al ... It's time to go," she urged, "Vale is already at the boat." Al groaned and sleepily rolled out of the sack.

Once at sea, they voyaged through darkness so complete that it hung in thick curtains about them. Al found a spot at the prow, curled up, and nodded off. This time he hadn't given a thought to the possibility of an assault by King Kraken.

After what felt like only minutes, Al was awakened by Vale. "Al, wake up ... we're here."

Staggering like a drunk and squinting through bleary eyes, Al took in the view of Atlan from a totally different perspective than the last time. They were no more than fifty metres from a shoreline of sharp, craggy, black volcanic rocks—massive cliffs that rose a hundred feet high towered over them. The coastline here was even more treacherous than the windward side of the island from which Al and Vale had made their escape. Then they rounded a corner and a spit of yellow sand lapped by calm, clear green water came into view.

Vale announced, "Sanctuary Bay."

They pulled the coracle up onto the small beach and secured it.

"Tides must be massive with the action of three moons," Turk proposed.

"Not really, the two small moons negate the pull of Djvardon, the biggest. Without them, there would be no land," Vale explained.

It was an extraordinary landscape, stark yet majestic and beautiful. To the south, the alps rose sheer and black, while to the north, from whence they came, the grey-blue sea crashed on the pebbled beach.

"I thought Cyrena would be here," Al said, looking up into the darkening sky and mentally wondering where the day had gone. "Could do with some grub."

Out of nowhere, a loud roar erupted, causing the four of them to almost jump out of their skins.

"Look at that!" Vee screamed, pointing up at a gorge through which a massive reptile was stalking.

"A dinosaur?" Al growled.

The three of them cautiously backed into the water, knee-deep, ready to make a swim for it. Vale stood on the shore and chuckled.

"What's so funny?" Turk growled.

"Anyone would think you've never seen a Ragon before," Vale said, beaming a huge grin.

"What the hell is a Ragon?" Vee asked Al.

"Ragon ... dragon ... I guess that's what it is ... a very big lizard with wings," Al proposed.

"Don't suppose it breathes fire, does it?" Turk asked Vale.

"Do you not have Ragons on Earth?"

"No, not that big," Turk said.

The beast, adorned with green scales from head to tail, lumbered on all fours. Its hindquarters were considerably larger than its front legs, giving it a formidable presence. Two massive wings folded neatly along its sides, and its head bore the unmistakable visage of a dragon—elongated snout bristling with pointed teeth, expansive nostrils flaring, and large, yellow, monocular eyes. The creature towered at about thirty feet, or nine metres, from the ground to the top of its head and stretched about twenty metres in length.

Al's attention was drawn to an unexpected detail. "There's someone on its back!" he exclaimed. The gargantuan creature, exuding an aura of irritation, halted a short distance away. It gracefully lowered itself to its knees, reminiscent of a well-trained horse, enabling the rider to dismount with ease. The rider, devoid of wings yet resembling a Treen, approached Vale with a confident stride and extended a hand in greeting.

Vale, with a gesture of deep respect, clasped the offered hand and bowed. "Son of Queen Cyrena, Prince Aristaeus."

"Aris," the young man corrected congenially.

Introductions ensued as Vale presented Black Alice, her brother Vee, and the warrior Turk, visitors from the planet Ki.

"Call me Al," Alice asserted, greeting the prince with a firm handshake that visibly discomforted him.

Aris, exercising caution, proceeded to shake Turk's hand before turning his attention to Vee. His compliment, "Vee, you are a beautiful female," left her uncharacteristically bashful and speechless.

The prince, with his striking, chiselled features, appeared to be in his early twenties, though Vale and Al knew his true age spanned millennia. His silver hair, a natural hue rather than a sign of aging, cascaded in a long plait down his back. Clad in black, studded leathers, Aris exuded a gothic, medieval air, akin to a character from a fantasy TV series. Intriguingly, both sides of his forehead bore tattoos, a rarity on Kor. A sheathed sword, an unusual sight in their realm, was strapped to his back, reminding Al of Apollo, who also bore a sword when boarding the Atlan-Tis.

The Professor stormed into Secta's lab in such a flurry that he startled Secta and Hope, who had been concentrating intently on their respective computer monitors.

Secta looked up sharply. "Vic, what's up? Where's the fire?"

The Professor flopped into a lounge chair, whipped off his glasses, and pinched the bridge of his nose. "Both of you, come sit down. I have something incredible to tell you."

Secta and Hope moved to the lounge setting and took seats, anxious to learn what had caused the Professor such pandemonium.

"What is it, Vic?" Secta asked, concerned.

"There was another block of text in the message on the mainframe from En-Ki."

"Other than the coordinates?" Secta clarified.

"Yes. I'd missed it ... somehow it didn't seem as important as the coordinates to locate Alice. I was cleaning up the decoded files earlier when I found the text and decoded it. The message is an explanation of what the Astara is ... you were right, Hope. It is a genetic modifier ... somehow it can alter the DNA of the occupant by extracting the genes responsible for aging."

"To make someone immortal?" Hope queried.

"Precisely, but there's more to it than that. If a specific sequence is triggered without an occupant, it will emit a massive electromagnetic surge ... not just your bog-standard EM efflux, this unique wave would have an effective radius of thousands of kilometres from ground zero," Vic explained.

"For knocking out electronic devices, I presume?" Secta questioned, matter-of-factly.

"No, no, no ... this is way more sophisticated and powerful than that, Secta ... this is a fusion explosion ... it would shut down anything positronic, such as AI brain function. En-Ki created it as a mechanism to defeat En-Lil ... that's why En-Lil wants it destroyed. I think the quest for Alice has always been to locate and use the Astara. But not on Earth where En-Ki himself could be affected ... I believe that's why En-Ki allowed the Nephilim to take it to Kor."

"Wait a second ... if it was triggered, then it would shut down any AI on Kor. So if Al were to set it off, it would be more effective than a nuke," Hope theorised.

"Indeed, and if En-Lil is there, as we assume he is, in the form of Electra, orchestrating this war, then it would be the end of him or her as well," Secta speculated.

The three of them contemplated the gravity of the prospect—it could well win them the battle against evil and rid them of En-Lil once and for all.

Secta bounced to his feet and paced the floor. After a few steps, he stopped and bellowed, "This is it! Armageddon! This is what En-Ki has been planning all along. Alice's quest was to get En-Lil and the opposing dark forces in the one place, so he could use the power of the Astara to defeat them. How? How does it work, Vic? How do you trigger it? Did En-Ki explain that in the text?" He returned to pacing, excitedly.

The expression on the Professor's face soured. He put his glasses back on and rubbed his bristly cheeks. "Um, in a way, yes..."

Secta stopped abruptly, as though his feet had jammed in the carpet. "What does that mean?"

Vic said, tenuously, "It said the trigger is on the lid of the box by way of iconography, and that Alice will intuitively know the sequence."

"Intuitively?" Hope queried, confused.

"He said the sequence is in Al's DNA, all he needs to do is access it."

Secta flopped into a chair, dejected.

"What's the matter?" Hope asked, confused by the morose look.

Secta and Vic exchanged a glance of concern. Secta explained, "It's just that En-Ki has a habit of giving Alice cryptic directions ... accessing that sequence for Al, while under a world of stress is easier said than done."

Vic nodded his head in agreement. It wasn't the first time for the fate of the world to be resting on Alice needing to decipher a cryptic message from En-Ki. It was a dubious position for mankind to be in.

Hope urged, "We need to get a message to Al."

Cyrena had arrived on the back of a second Ragon.

Night had fallen, and they were gathered around a campfire at the beach under the yellow light of a full Djvardon.

Vale had Turk's Glock, studying it. "So, it fires a projectile?"

"Yes, that will penetrate most things within a range of say one hundred metres."

"Could it kill a Ragon?" Aris asked.

Turk glanced at one of the giant reptiles fifty metres away from them, taking a snooze. "If I was to aim at its head or heart, then perhaps, yes."

"Why do Earth people have such dangerous weapons?" Cyrena asked.

Turk grinned, "For protection."

"From what?" she inquired, wistfully.

"Each other," Al muttered gravely.

Vee changed the subject, figuring it cast a bad look on humanity. "When will we check out the Nephilim setup?"

"It is best to go in under the cover of darkness," Aris said. "Otherwise, they will easily detect us."

It made sense to Vee. "Okay."

They were all chewing on leathery pieces of fish that had been cooked on skewers over the fire.

"This isn't that bad ... what do the Ragons eat?" Al asked.

"Juvenile Kraken," Cyrena said.

"Do they breathe fire?" Vee asked.

"No, where did you get that idea? How could anything breathe fire? These Ragon are the only two left we know of ... they have been part of the Treen family since they were this big," Cyrena spanned six inches with open palms.

"Amazing that a creature so massive can spawn from something so small. What happened to the others?" Vee asked.

"Many were killed in the battle for Atlan, and the population never recovered. They were no match for the weapons of the Nephilim ... others over time have been killed by King Kraken ... they are mortal enemies," Cyrena explained.

"But the truth be known, we do not know if there are more in existence on the land on the far side of Kor. Legend has it there are," Aris affirmed.

That captured Vee's sense of adventure. "Why haven't you explored to find out?"

"A Ragon cannot fly that far," Aris said.

"It is too far for our boats as well," Vale added.

"And too many Kraken to discourage any such brave adventurer," Cyrena concluded.

Al struggled to his feet, stretched his arms above his head, and said, "Fortune favours the brave." He lowered his arms then eyeballed his comrades and declared menacingly, "Right, let's do this."

Mounted atop the Ragons, three riders each, they arranged themselves in a line, grasping the waist of the person in front like pillion passengers on a motorcycle. A clump of coarse hair at the base of each Ragon's neck, just above the withers, provided a secure grip for the lead rider, while subtle pressure applied with the knees and heels directed the creature's movement. Al found himself seated behind Cyrena, with Turk behind him, while Aris piloted the second Ragon, accompanied by Vee and then Vale.

"Hang on," Cyrena called out commandingly. "Rise, girl," she instructed, nudging her heels into the Ragon's withers as a signal to stand. The creature awkwardly lifted itself from its squatting position, and at Cyrena's further prompting, ascended a slope to reach the summit of a craggy spire.

The ride, Al observed, was surprisingly smooth, reminiscent of a well-trained horse, albeit on a much grander scale. His bravery, however, faced a test when the Ragon approached the edge of the precipice. Peering down, Al's gaze met an eighty-foot drop to the churning waves and jagged rocks below.

With a graceful extension of its colossal wings, the Ragon stepped off the edge. An updraft caught them immediately, spiralling them upward without the need for the creature to flap its expansive, leathery wings. The experience was nothing short of exhilarating for the Earthlings, gliding silently through the night sky, the great yellow moon of Djvardon casting its glow over the island far beneath them.

The thirty-minute flight culminated as the lead Ragon descended through a vast crevasse amidst the central Atlan mountains. Navigating narrow passes, sometimes barely accommodating its wingspan, the Ragon swooped lower into the landscape. The enclosing defile opened up, leaving the mountains behind, revealing a sprawling steppe within a colossal crater. Bathed in moonlight, the land was painted in subtle hues and delicate shadows. On one side, an alien cluster of trees with unfamiliar shapes and foliage; on the other, the entrance to a massive cave and the faint outlines of grey-white ruins.

With elegant, circular motions of their wings, both Ragons alighted gracefully onto the mysterious terrain.

"We'll leave the Ragons here to graze," Cyrena shouted, and then slid down the withers of the beast to land on the ground like riding a kid's playground slippery slide.

Al and Turk copied.

Walking towards them, the crags rose like the stumps of rotten teeth. This was a land of wind and naked crags. The ground was mostly barren of all but clumps of dry shrub. There was something familiar about the terrain to Al; he figured they must be near where he had first landed in the Nephilim UFO. Ahead of them was a gigantic cave entrance.

Aris told Al, "It will take us half an hour to reach the place. We must navigate a number of caves, and it will be difficult in the dark."

Al dug into his pocket, produced a heavy-duty military-grade power pellet pen-torch Vee had given him, and flicked it on. Aris was astounded. He'd never seen anything like it. Cyrena and Vale were both excited by the technology.

"We call it a torch," Al said, handing it to Aris.

"From where does it get the light?" Aris asked, shining it in his eyes and squinting.

Al explained, "A filament that is heated by a tiny stored power source inside the tube."

"This tort will make our journey much easier," Aris said.

"Torch, Aris," Vee corrected. "Turk and I have one as well."

Aris cautioned, "Only use one torch, I am afraid we might be seen if there is too much artificial light." He was about to proceed when he noticed Alice staring up transfixed on the night sky. "Alice, we are ready to enter. What are you observing?"

"Just the stars, they look way different than they do from Earth. First time I've really noticed it," he said dreamily. "Weird to think that one of those tiny little dots up there is Earth. Makes me realise how far from home I am."

"I can understand how that could be disconcerting. However, it is time to move on," Aris said, dispassionately.

Alice found Aris' overtly logical rhetoric insensitive but figured it was a cultural thing.

Using the torchlight to navigate, Aris led them into the cave. The labyrinth of caves they passed through gradually decreased in number and size until they found themselves having to squeeze side-on to fit through the narrow opening.

Tense as foxes, eyes groping for sight in the darkness, they followed Aris to squeeze through.

Abruptly, Aris halted at a sharp turn, signalling for the line behind him to stop with a raised hand. In a swift motion, he extinguished the torch. To their surprise, the darkness wasn't complete; a faint illumination seeped through from somewhere ahead.

Continuing onward, they eventually emerged into an immense cavern. It was bathed in light, resembling the interior of a colossal aircraft hangar, vast and imposing. Moving with cautious steps, they approached the edge of a precipice and cautiously looked down. The sight below, sprawling a hundred metres beneath them, was almost too extraordinary to fathom.

CHAPTER 28
AMBUSH

IN **THE CENTRE** of the enormous floor space stood a giant metallic pod. It consisted of a domed saucer with a long column, like a trunk, that was attached to a tubular body. Protruding from the body were three spindly spider-like, telescopic, articulated legs that were compressed for it to fit inside the space. The name 'sea spider' was fitting because that's exactly what it looked like. Towering forty metres tall once the legs were extended, it would probably be double that height.

One of the sea spiders appeared completed, while two others were still under construction. Bright flashes arced from robotic welders, casting eerie shadows about the work area and reflecting on the rough stone cavern walls. Single-task robots darted about on wheels, bonding metal segments together. The vast floor area was crawling with armoured Nephilim and a variety of specifically tasked manufacturing robots.

"Is that thing going to fly?" Vee asked.

Cyrena replied, "No, it will float on the water and then extend its legs to walk along the sea floor."

Al was intrigued. "How do you know that? Have you seen them in operation before?"

"Yes, during the battle for Atlan eons ago. A swinging whip extends from underneath it that sets anything it touches ablaze, while other arms project from the trunk that fire beams of scarlet light, melting whatever they strike," Cyrena said, gravely.

"Lasers," Turk commented.

"Does this place operate non-stop?" Al asked.

"You mean continuously? Yes," Aris confirmed.

"No guards posted … they're not expecting to be attacked," Turk observed. "Look, see those metal tubes connected to the robots? They must carry oxy-acetylene or some equally volatile gas to weld with … there," he pointed, "those huge cylinders."

Alice homed in on the six of them … three metres high by three metres in diameter. He nodded at Turk —they knew what to do.

Al said, "We'll have to go down there."

Aris replied resolutely, "No, you will be seen and captured."

Al dug into his hip pocket and produced a WASP. "This little feller is an explosive device … if we attach it to one of those tanks, the blast will set off a chain reaction."

"There is something we haven't told you," Cyrena said, bashfully. "Treen can make themselves invisible for short periods of time."

"Really? For how long?" Al asked.

"Long enough to plant your bomb," she said confidently.

"How?" Vee asked.

"We can vibrate for short periods of time in a frequency that allows us to materialise in the 5th dimension; it renders us invisible to this dimension," Cyrena explained.

Al nodded his head, mulling over whether it could work. "Hmm, that's worth considering." He held the WASP in his open palm for Aris.

"No, Aris is only half Treen, he cannot use the void … but I can," Cyrena said.

"The void?" Al queried.

Cyrena smiled, "That is what we call it."

Alice didn't buy it; he figured Cyrena was too old and there was far too much depending on it to work. "Nar, nar, it's too risky … I hate to say it, but you're not exactly a spring chicken." He walked to the edge of the cliff and looked contemplatively down.

Vale followed him. "There really is no other option, Alice."

Cyrena turned to Vee and whispered to her, confused. "What is a spring chicken?"

Vee chuckled, "Oh, that? He means you're not as young as you were and he doesn't want you to risk your life."

Cyrena erupted. "Oh rubbish! Alice, I got to this age by being able to handle myself!"

Al got the message and replied with a groan; he was still doubtful, but Vale's argument was persuasive.

Vee approached him and said covertly, "She can do it, Al."

"What makes you think so?" Al muttered.

"Call it female intuition," she said, smugly.

He locked eyes with her, thought about it a moment, and then acquiesced. "Good enough for me, let's do it then."

After a quick explanation from Al on how to activate a WASP, Cyrena was ready for the sortie. Without hesitation, she spread her black wings and stepped off the cliff. Alice was so startled he made a desperate grab for her, but she simply vanished into thin air.

Aris caught Alice's arm, "It's fine, Alice ... that is the way of the Treen. She will descend safely."

Al had considered popping a pill and transforming into something to get the job done, but this seemed the better option; it would be better to hang onto his scant supply of pills for if and when things became desperate.

The world around Cyrena shimmered as she concentrated on stepping off the edge of the cliff. Cloaked in invisibility, in an inter-dimensional space, she descended the hundred metres like a feather and gently touched down on the cavern floor. The Nephilim standing near where she landed saw nothing but the slight blur of her rushing past them to get to the closest gas storage cylinder. Time was of the essence; should the cloak wear off, it would simply be a matter of retriggering it to continue unseen.

She reached the four metal legs at the base of the closest spherical tank. She would need to scale one of the legs to fix the WASP to the underbelly. The task was made easier by metal rungs on the leg. After ascending a score of them, she was close enough to the underbelly of the huge dark blue sphere to reach out and attach the WASP. The high-impact WASP was magnetic, so it easily attached to the metal. She activated it and then quickly descended the ladder.

The others were at the cliff edge waiting with bated breath. The tension was palpable, made worse by not being able to actually watch Cyrena performing the deed. It seemed to be taking longer than anticipated, then, boom! The tank exploded into a massive fireball—then one after another, the other tanks exploded. The blasts were so loud and intense the shock wave and heat tingled their exposed skin. The entire floor area was quickly ablaze. Nephilim were staggering about on fire—the robots had ceased to function. The inferno had engulfed the completed sea spider, just as Turk and Alice had predicted.

Vale pointed and yelled to be heard above the roar, "Look ... there in the fire!" The blurred outline of Cyrena could be seen rushing through the flames. It was as though she was inside a blurry protective force field.

Al shouted at Aris. "How is she going to get back up here?"

A Nephilim with its body ablaze came careening out from behind a piece of machinery directly into the path of Cyrena. She hadn't seen him, and they collided. The impact knocked her down, and her head hit the ground hard. There was a shimmer, and she materialised.

"She's down!" Aris shouted.

"Looks like she's been knocked out," Vee said, worriedly.

Aris was panicking. "We need to do something, they'll capture her! Look, they've seen her!"

Sure enough, two Nephilim unaffected by the explosion were making their way towards her. Now, Al had no choice; he would have to drop a pill and transform into something to save Cyrena, but what? He dropped the tablet and then pictured a giant bat—like the one he'd seen on the planet Eris.

The others were shocked to see him strip off his clothes, except for his briefs, then bend sharply forward, clenching his fists tight, veins protruding in his neck, as he pumped the muscles in his arms.

Vee knew what was happening ... he was contorting ... transforming ... she and Turk had seen it before, but for Vale and Aris, it was supernatural.

Al straightened up, his stature increased. Towering over them, he spread his arms and clenched his fists, white-knuckled, wincing in pain, as a giant pair of black leathery wings materialised from the underside of his muscular arms and unfurled. His hands and feet metamorphosed into claws like those of a raptor. He appeared more streamlined, as though rebuilt aerodynamically. He glared down at his sister, the whites of his eyes now crimson.

She grinned and quipped, "Nice look, Al, seriously Goth."

He said nothing, just turned and leapt off the cliff.

The four of them marvelled at him spiralling down to Cyrena like a gigantic glider using the thermals rising from the heat for lift.

The two Nephilim holding Cyrena between them never saw what hit them. Alice swooped like a pterodactyl, talons outstretched, and snatched the head off one of them. Before the other one had time to react, he fluttered his wings to hover above him, hooked his talons into his shoulders, and with a flurry of his flapping wings, lifted him up twenty metres into the air and then dropped him into the white-hot flames of a burning cylinder.

Cyrena was now conscious, struggling to get to her feet. The flames all around her were so fierce she had to shield her eyes with her arm.

Vale, Turk, Vee, and Aris watched in terror as the articulated legs of the giant sea spider wobbled.

Aris shouted, "It's going down ... she is under it!"

Al could see the flaming sea spider was about to collapse. He would need to fly through the raging inferno to reach Cyrena.

The four of them watched anxiously from the cliff edge. Alice dived down and disappeared inside the fire and brimstone. Another massive explosion erupted from very near where Alice had flown, and a column of white-hot fire spewed into the air. It was looking bad. The four of them exchanged looks of concern.

With a thunderous roar that echoed throughout the huge cavern, the gigantic sea spider toppled over, smashing into the blazing firestorm from the exploded tanks … the collapse sent a storm-cloud of fire and thick black smoke into the air. It was taking too long—Vee was biting her fingernails—the fireball was growing with intensity. But they weren't going to give up on Alice.

Turk saw something. "There, look, inside the smoke!"

Sure enough, barely distinguishable from the black rolling smoke, the form of a black giant bat emerged.

"Once you wrap your head around the block Universe theory, you'll begin to realise that it could also change the way we think about time travel. If the theory is real, then we can't simply travel time and change it because everything is happening simultaneously—past, present, future—laid out in space—it would make it impossible to create grandfather paradoxes…" Hope told Secta and the Professor.

Secta argued, "That's not at all what we've experienced so far."

"The block Universe theory is also known in some scientific circles as Eternalism, in which the past, present, and future all coexist now," the Professor said.

"That is opposed to Presentism, which states that the past doesn't exist anymore and is constantly disappearing thanks to the pesky notion of present time," Secta professed.

Their debate was interrupted by the arrival of Luna, who'd stormed into Secta's lab like a woman possessed.

"Pardon the intrusion, but something important has come up. The UN has ordered the immediate return of your away team from Kor."

Secta leapt out of the lounge fuming. "You have to be joking, Luna … for what reason?"

"The US has lodged a complaint … You know they have the US

Space Command led by the newly appointed Air Force General Larry Freeman."

"Larry? He mentioned nothing about being promoted to general?" the Professor grumbled.

Secta was up pacing the floor. "Nor has he mentioned being made head honcho of the US Space Force ... so, what's the gripe?" he snapped, irritated.

"There has been growing concern about OTT's intervention in matters of world security—"

Secta angrily interrupted, "Intervention? World security? Yee gods ... if it hadn't been for our so-called intervention, there would be no world security! Short memories. Short memories. Huh! So, what did Mal have to say about that? I presume you took it to him first?" he snarled, facetiously.

She glared at the skinny man and snapped curtly, "The President is relying on your evaluation of the order."

"Ah, now it's an order, is it? Under what authority?" Hope snapped.

"The Temporal Prime Directive OTT is signatory to," Luna said bluntly.

Secta stopped pacing and turned to face Luna, the darkness of his mood obvious. It was never good to see Secta in such a state; an explosion was imminent. Those who knew braced themselves—but to their surprise, he remained calm. However, he locked Luna in a deadly stare and stated emphatically, his voice a different tone, "You can tell the UN and General Freeman that we will do no such thing ... not until we are satisfied Alice's mission has been accomplished." He held the stare for further impact and then calmly resumed his seat. "I suggest the UN and the General have a word with Zen about their intervention."

There came a pregnant pause. Luna stood like a statue. It hadn't been a tirade from Secta, but the power of his resolve was just as unnerving for her.

"So be it," Luna hissed, then turned on her heels and stormed out of the lab.

Once she had gone, the Professor patted Secta on the knee. "Well handled, old sod."

"Bloody US Space Force, bah!" Secta snarled. "Control freaks with another belly-aching trumped-up government authority."

"I think it might be time to give our friend Larry a wake-up call," the Professor said, smugly.

"The entire plan of attack is delayed because you failed to adequately set sentries," Electra snapped spitefully at the Nephilim war council.

There were four in the council, led by Rykor, resplendent in his bronze armour. His visor spiralled open, as did the others, and he barked, "We were not expecting an ambush! This Black Alice has allies in the Treen as well as the Korman clans!"

Electra fired back abruptly, "And does that pose a problem for the Nephilim?"

Feeling her tone was being perceived as arrogant, Walker jumped in. "It is easy to see how this could happen. Are these Treen usually a threat?"

"No, they are a small clan, indigenous to Kor, but they do have certain powers," Rykor nodded at the Nephilim seated beside him to explain further.

His voice was deeper than Rykor's, "They have invisibility cloaking and the control of two large flying reptiles they call Ragons."

Electra was happy with Walker's diplomacy and fashioned a glance at him to continue.

"I see. Then further ambushes would be mitigated by them believing they've blocked our attack. Were all the sea spiders destroyed?" Walker asked.

Rykor answered. "No, there is one remaining that could still be completed."

Walker got up, went to the window, and looked down. "They have struck first because they know we have superior forces. Now is the perfect time to attack them. How many spacecraft do you have?"

Rykor answered succinctly. "Two, but if you are thinking of using them in an attack, they are not armed."

"Then arm them," Electra snapped.

"No, we will not risk our only means of transport," Rykor said, firmly.

Electra could feel he was leaving no room for negotiation.

"Okay, then what other options do we have besides the sea spider?" Walker said, with his back to them.

"Leave the attack plans to us," Rykor insisted.

"No, we are partners," Electra said, firmly, calmly. "I want Walker on equal terms with the Nephilim on the war council. His battle experience is invaluable."

Walker turned from the window. "Look, I know better than you how Black Alice thinks ... we have fought before. I am human, I understand the logic ... it is different than yours."

The four Nephilim closed their eyes. Walker and Electra assumed they were discussing the point telepathically.

After a moment, their eyes opened, and Rykor said, "What do you propose?"

CHAPTER 29
STORM

ALICE LOOKED ACROSS the dining table at Vee and screwed up his nose. "You're telling me all this time these beings have been coming to Earth, abducting people, and they've really been looking for me?"

"Well, yeah, that's what Secta reckons," Vee said. She hadn't had time to fill him in since she and Turk had arrived on Kor.

Sitting next to Vee, Turk chimed in, "It wasn't specifically you they were seeking, but rather your DNA."

Vee continued, "But they had no idea how complex your DNA is and that it's not normal because Secta altered it."

Al frowned. "So, what do they want with my DNA?"

Vee let out a little facetious giggle. "They think it makes you the perfect specimen."

"Well, at least they got that part right," Al chortled like making an announcement, which got a laugh from everyone at the dining table.

Vee went on to explain further. "Secta thinks they want to create a hybrid using your DNA and theirs. That's why they were so interested in the sarcophagus."

Al nodded, "Yes, I know about the sarcophagus. Its real name is the Astara."

Turk added, "Secta believes it can extract the aging gene from human DNA, potentially allowing the hybrid to become immortal."

A murmur of intrigue swept through the room.

"Why don't they just use a Treen? They're already immortal," Vale proposed.

"We Treen are not human. It's evident the Nephilim desire to become human, but with immortality," Cyrena explained. "They captured six Treen many years ago for experimentation. They killed one but eventually released the others when they realised our genetics weren't suitable for their purposes. We're not immortal; our green blood merely grants us a much longer life than you."

Vee then shared more information. "Before we left, we received a message from Zen. Two agents were beamed aboard the same UFO that brought you here, Al."

"I didn't see anyone else on board," Al said.

"No, after the spacecraft dropped you off here, it must have returned to Earth to release some abductees in New York," Vee clarified. "That's when the Zen agents managed to stow away."

Turk chimed in, "We're certain that one of them was the cyborg who returned from 2112. The other one appears to be human."

Al asked, "So, do you think they're now prisoners or cooperating with the Nephilim?"

"Considering the preparations for an attack, it is logical to assume that these two are involved," Vale theorised. "The Nephilim had no reason to attack us until now."

"This is true," Aris agreed.

"What I can't figure out is why, if Alice so important to the Nephilim, they would risk attacking and potentially killing him," Turk added.

"It stinks of En-Lil," Al growled. "Nothing would make him happier than getting rid of me."

Just then, Inanna floated into the room as if on a cloud and settled down in the empty chair beside Al. He shot her a playful grin.

The night was getting late as the feast came to an end. Most of the residents and guests of Stockholm were making their way to their respective hubs. As Inanna led Al past Vee, he sent his sister a wicked wink, conveying his plans for the rest of the night.

Turk was still seated at the large banquet table, enjoying an ale with Vale. The two were getting along like a house on fire, similar in intellect, and political views.

"The fishing fleet will return at first light. You might find it interesting," Vale suggested. "After that, we'll visit the London float and my friend, Mayor Doevan Gish."

"London?"

"Yes, there are seven floats in total, quite a distance apart. Alice will need their support for the upcoming battle. We'll start in London because it is the closest, and Alice has met Doevan."

"What kind of weapons do you and the other floats have?" Turk asked.

Vale's expression grew serious. "Nothing compared to what we will be facing."

Turk raised an eyebrow. "I wonder what Alice has in mind, then?"

"At least we eliminated the sea spiders. They could have easily wiped us out," Vale acknowledged.

Dawn brought enough noise to waken the dead, which didn't impress Al. He staggered out of Inanna's hub shirtless and squinting, a snarl on his face, thinking that with so much noise, there had to be a battle going on. After a moment of his eyes adjusting to the light, he noticed the backs of Turk, Vee, and Vale at the wharf's edge, and cruised over to determine the origin of the ruckus.

"Hey dudes, good morning," he said with a yawn, flexing his biceps.

"Hey bro, you're looking a bit depleted," Vee joked.

Whenever it came to a criticism of his body, Al took exception; such was the flaw of vanity in his persona.

He flexed his pectorals. "Nothing can diminish this frame, babe."

Turk looked over his shoulder at Al and joined in the fun. "You need a workout, mate, you're wasting away."

Al growled in rebuttal. "What's the racket?"

"The gates are opening for the fishing fleet to enter," Vale answered.

Al could see two large coracles leading four outriggers through the open sea gates.

"They are sitting low in the water; they must have a good catch," Vale reckoned.

Just then, a commotion broke out aboard the last boat. Two large octopus tentacles shot out of the water at the rear of the outrigger, wrapped around the waist of a crew member, and dragged him screaming into the water.

"A Kraken!" Vale shouted. "Close the gates!"

It was too late; the Kraken overturned the outrigger, tipping the remaining three crew members into the water that quickly turned scarlet around the boat.

"It's in the lagoon!" Al roared, to get above the screaming and general mayhem.

Turk and Vee drew their weapons and aimed at the water, hoping to get a bead on the invader. In the meantime, Vale called warriors to arm themselves with spears tipped with sharpened, serrated bone. They quickly assembled at the wharf edge, spears held at the ready. Silence shrouded them ... the water calmed ... the only sound coming from the gentle rocking of the boats. But they all sensed it was the calm before the storm ... the small Kraken would soon surface to continue its feeding frenzy. They waited with bated breath.

"Any minute now," Vale whispered to them in a gravelly tone, inflicted with uneasiness.

Then as predicted, it reared out of the water, its tentacles snaking manically in the air, whipping at everyone standing at the wharf's edge. They all scattered desperately, trying to avoid the five-metre-long thrashing tentacles. Three warriors trying to skewer the beast with their spears were knocked into the water. A wave from the Kraken's surfacing knocked over others.

Vee and Turk held their footing and took aim.

Al yelled, "Don't waste bullets ... aim between its eyes."

Each fired three shots. The grouping was perfect, right between the eyes and into its brain. The shots blew chunks of its carapace away, sending a plume of blue blood and gore into the air. Its tentacles thrashed about for a moment and then fell limp. It was over ... still and listless, the Kraken slowly sank into the dark green depths of the lagoon.

The warriors were amazed by how easily Turk and Vee had dispatched their nemesis. Killing their mortal enemy without much of a fight, in which they would normally lose many warriors, had elevated their confidence in the time travellers.

They helped the four warriors out of the water. They were shaken but uninjured.

"Haul the Kraken out of the water to butcher," Vale ordered his men.

But just as that was about to get underway, a frantic cry bellowed from the gatehouse.

"King Kraken! It is King Kraken!"

All at the wharf looked sharply in the direction of the gates to see a massive turret rise up from the other side. Dark brown, coated with barnacles, it was at least forty feet in diameter ... absolutely awesome. And it just kept rising until it towered over the gatehouse and the float, two massive eyes on stalks protruding from its carapace, fiercely glaring down at them, twitching in unnatural agitation. They could feel its wrath.

"Damn! Will you look at that thing!" Al yelled.

Vee shouted, "It's the size of a building."

Al asked Vale, "Have we pissed it off or something?"

It was obvious by the look of horror on the faces of the locals that they believed Alice was right.

"You have a gift for understatement, Alice ... we killed one of its offspring," Vale muttered gravely.

Turk and Vee had taken aim at the gigantic creature ready to fire but knew it would be like using a peashooter. It was so massive that bullets would be unlikely to even put a dent in it.

One huge tentacle suddenly loomed up and looped precariously over the gate, causing everyone to take a nervous step back from the wharf's edge.

Cyrena and Aris pushed through the onlookers to join Alice.

"Look at the size of that tentacle, as thick as a tree trunk!" Al growled, turning sharply to Vale beside him. "What'll we do? Run? Fight?"

"We are at its mercy, Alice," Vale groaned, defeatedly.

"It will destroy Stockholm as though it was made of twigs if retribution is its objective," Cyrena cautioned.

Al was getting set to drop a pill, but his gut was telling him that no matter what he transformed into, it wouldn't stand a chance against the might of King Kraken.

He asked, "Is this the same King Kraken that Apollo fought?"

"We believe it is," Vale confirmed.

"Then it must be as old as the hills," said Al.

"Which hills?" Aris questioned, not grasping Al's metaphor.

Vee clarified, "He means it must be ancient."

Then, completely unexpectedly, to the abject relief of everyone, King Kraken retracted its tentacle and began to swiftly descend, submerging itself. This was followed by a prolonged pause of anguish, as some anticipated an attack from beneath the water, but the fear subsided without incident.

"Old Kraken must've had a change of heart," Al announced.

They all felt quite relieved that he had.

Secta, Christina, and Hope were in the control room when the Professor burst in and exclaimed anxiously, "We've got a problem." The three of them turned abruptly from the monitor they'd been studying to face him.

"There was an additional sentence in En-Ki's coded message. The Astara requires a power source to function."

Secta chuckled, "So, it doesn't come with batteries?"

Vic wasn't amused. "No, it's a little more complicated than that."

"Don't tell me we need to replicate another Shine talisman."

"No, Secta, not a key, a power source ... a disc made of Velodium from the Tablets of Destinies," Vic explained.

The humour quickly faded from Secta's face as he now comprehended the enormity of the conundrum and understood why the professor was worried.

Christina posed the burning question. "In what form does it need to exist? I presume it must fit into some sort of receptacle?"

Vic nodded sharply. "He provided the dimensions, and we have the Velodium, but we need to deliver it to Alice, and we lack the means to test it beforehand to ensure its functionality."

It was a formidable riddle, one that they collectively possessed the brainpower to unravel.

Navigating through the substantial swell, Al was relieved to see the London float looming only twenty minutes away. Standing at the helm of Stockholm's largest coracle, Vale, with his long hair streaming behind him in the wind, was soaked to the skin. Waves had intermittently crashed over the bow during the three-hour journey, drenching everyone on board.

"The worst part about this is I've gotta handle the return trip," Al grumbled to Vee, both of them seated on the deck with their backs against the hull.

"You look a bit pale, mate," Vee said, with a smug look.

"Don't remind me or I'll throw up for sure," Al groaned. He hated travelling in boats.

As they approached the vast sea gates of London, Vale, securing his wet hair, noticed something amiss and called out, "Alice, look... the gates are open." Indeed, the gates were not just open; the right-hand gate appeared unhinged, as if struck by something massive. The closer they got, the more apparent the destruction became.

Alice, joining Vale at the helm, sensed the gravity of the situation. "I do not like this, Al. There is something terribly wrong here."

Gliding silently through the gate, they were met with a chilling scene within the lagoon. The water was littered with bloated, drifting corpses. The wharf area was a grotesque tableau of death, with charred, headless bodies impaled on stakes and still smouldering. Not a single hub stood intact; all had been decimated as if crushed by a giant.

All aboard the coracle were on their feet—their trembling hands held across their mouths, behind which they were gasping in abject horror. Women, children, young, and old had been tortured and killed—every single one of them—there were no survivors.

Turk, familiar with such brutality, was the first to find his voice. "Did the Nephilim do this?"

Aris, solemn, responded, "I would not have believed them capable of such slaughter."

"It's a warning," Alice declared. "They've made an example of these poor souls… Zen tactics… we've seen it plenty of times before. We can assume by such barbarity that the Nephilim is definitely being directed by En-Lil."

Vale, overcome with emotion, urged action. "We need to act quickly to warn the other floats."

Alice, emerging from the coracle onto the wharf, stood like a colossus, looking down on the boat and the surrounding desolation. His gaze, full of disdain for the destruction, then shifted to the horizon—a thin, unbroken line reminiscent of an artist's brushstroke, tinted the shade of fresh heliotrope. In the ensuing silence, as if commanding a stage, Alice's voice rumbled with authority, "I don't think so, Vale. They want one thing only… me, and I'm not about to let them take any more innocent lives because of it."

The firmness in Alice's voice left no doubt about his decision, closing any avenue for discussion. Vale and the others sensed the finality in his resolve.

As if to underline Alice's determination, the sky shifted ominously. Clouds gathered, rolling and thickening, and suddenly, lightning tore across the heavens, followed by a deep, resonant clap of thunder. A storm was brewing, mirroring the tumultuous situation they faced.

CHAPTER 30
EXILE

FOLLOWING AN EXHAUSTIVE search of the remains of the London float, Alice and Vale were unable to locate the body of their friend Mayor Doevan Gist.

Vale's gaze rested on the lifeless form of a young girl lying at his feet, her beauty marred by the horrors of the attack. "She's Raven, one of Doevan's daughters," he said, his voice tinged with sorrow.

Alice, standing beside him, silently acknowledged the tragic scene, memories of their prior encounter with Raven briefly flashing through his mind.

Vee, moved by the scene, knelt beside the girl's charred remains. With a tenderness that belied the surrounding destruction, she carefully slid her arms under Raven's body, lifting her with a solemn grace. She walked through the remnants of what was once the Great Hall, each step a testament to the gravity of their loss. Reaching the wharf, Vee gently placed Raven among the other victims they had found—over a hundred souls, each a stark reminder of the tragedy that had befallen them. In line with the customs of the Korman people, these fallen would soon find their final resting place in the depths of the lagoon.

Electra, with an elegantly raised eyebrow, issued a stern command, "I ordered no prisoners taken. This will show what we do with them.

Walker." Her poised demeanour barely concealed the ruthlessness of her order. She watched as Walker, with clinical precision, raised his arm and unleashed a laser beam, instantly blowing open Doevan's chest. The two Nephilim, who had been restraining Doevan, let his lifeless body fall to the dusty ground of the interrogation room.

The Nephilim leader, Rykor, visor raised to reveal a face marred by disapproval, snarled at Electra, "Your ways are barbaric, En-Lil. Why did you order the complete annihilation of the London float? It was not necessary."

Electra's response was cold and calculated. "It was the most effective way to capture Black Alice's full attention; now he knows we mean business," she snapped, her voice devoid of remorse.

Rykor, his deep voice filled with insistence, growled, "Black Alice must be captured without fail."

Electra, unphased and confident, arched one thin, sculptured brow. "I know, Rykor, I know. You have made that abundantly clear. You will get your Black Alice alive ... mostly. But it will be done my way."

The tension between them was palpable. Rykor, visibly uncomfortable with the ruthless strategy, silently contemplated his next words.

"Do you or your hive have an issue with that?" Electra demanded, her voice sharp and commanding.

Rykor hesitated for a moment before replying, "No."

"Good," Electra said with a note of finality, "we shall proceed to phase two."

The implication was clear: Walker's role would extend beyond mere planning to being the commander-in-chief of the operation. The horrors witnessed during the London attack had left Rykor deeply unsettled. He glared at Electra, attempting to discern the true nature of the woman before him. Her perfect figure and rich raven hair, which glistened even in the dim light, belied the possibility of a heartless being. Unbeknownst to Rykor, Electra indeed lacked a heart, a fact that made her all the more dangerous.

Alice was relieved to be back on solid ground. The return journey to Stockholm had turned more horrific due to a powerful headwind that had whipped up a two-metre swell. They had barely managed to outpace the storm, which was now lashing the float with gale-force winds and torrential rain.

Odin had gathered everyone in the Great Hall to hear an account of the assault on London and to discuss preparations for the impending attack on their own float. It was evident that the Nephilim were gearing up for a full-scale invasion, and the destruction of London served as clear evidence of their intention to wage war on Stockholm and the other floats. Tempers flared, leading to a divide between those willing to fight and those considering surrender. However, Alice was resolute.

He rose slowly to his feet, raising both hands to quieten the commotion, and shouted, "Hey, everyone! Quieten down, I've got something to say." His efforts had minimal effect, until Odin himself stood up to restore order.

"Alright, that is enough, people of Stockholm! Let Alice speak!" The room fell silent as the imposing figure resumed his seat.

"What we discovered in London was ugly, I know you don't want a repeat of that horror here. This is a no-brainer; the Nephilim want me, so I don't see any point in risking anyone else to save me."

A loud murmur of discontent began, and to quiet them, Al raised a hand. "I'll lead a small volunteer force, just as we've done before, to try and stop them … We believe there must still be a sea spider operating; it's the only way they could have caused so much destruction. We need to destroy it before it arrives here."

This time, the surge of disagreements was even more intense. Again, Al signalled for quiet and got it.

"Look, there won't be any debate because that's what's going to happen. That's all I've got to say." He sat down, and the ensuing silence was deafening. It had dawned on every last one of them that he was embarking on a suicide mission to save them, and nothing would deter him.

Aris rose to his feet. "That is very noble of you, Alice, but what if you fail? I suggest we send an envoy to Atlan to offer our surrender to the Nephilim."

Remaining seated, Odin thundered, "That would mean handing them Alice, you know that."

Squabbling erupted between the opponents and proponents.

Aris bellowed to be heard, "One life to save many! We need to take a vote … those in favour and those against!"

A Stockholm citizen jumped up from his chair and shouted angrily, "You are a Treen! You have nothing to do with Stockholm! What gives you the right to speak for us?"

An opposing citizen jumped up and violently pulled the man down. A brawl broke out between them, quickly escalating into a free for all.

Alice sprang from his chair and shouted, "Cut it out! Now!" His aggressive order reverberated in the confines of the room. The combatants froze, and then stood down.

Inanna stood up. "Listen to me, people of Stockholm … this man and his allies have risked their lives for us before and are willing to do so again! If you think you know better, then I suggest you go and risk your lives for us. Aris is suggesting we surrender our freedom; that is what would happen if we surrender. Judging by the way they obliterated London without sparing a single survivor … what makes you think they will not repeat that if we surrender, huh? Huh!"

Muttering broke out again among the crowd, with most realising she was right.

"Fine, then let us vote. Stand up if you support Alice," Inanna shouted, scanning the hundred-plus seated crowd.

The man with the bloody nose from his support of Alice was the first to stand. Then another—then another—until nearly all but a few were on their feet. It was an overwhelming majority. Then, those standing began to chant repeatedly; "Black Alice, Black Alice, Black

Alice." The chant began softly, gradually growing fervent, until they were shouting at the top of their lungs while thrusting their fists in the air: "Black Alice! Black Alice! Black Alice!"

By now, it was the wee small hours, and Alice, Odin, Vale, Turk, Vee, Cyrena, and Aris hadn't managed to formulate a viable risk assessment. The options were far too limited. They were growing weary and rapidly running out of ideas.

"There's something about the sarcophagus … the Astara, that we're not considering," Vee proposed. "Somehow, I think it's the key."

The mention of the Astara suddenly triggered a memory in Alice's mind. He sat up straight in his chair, deep in thought as if entranced. He accessed his implant and found a message he'd received from Secta that he had completely forgotten. "Wait a minute," he exclaimed. "The Astara … During the attack on the sea spiders, I received a message from Secta … so much was going on that I put it aside without reading it. It said … um… 'The Astara has two functions: one to modify human DNA, the other an EM efflux weapon. En-Ki left instructions that if a specific sequence is triggered without an occupant, the Astara will emit a massive electromagnetic surge—not just a standard EM surge, but a unique wave with an effective radius of thousands and thousands of kilometres from ground zero.' This is it … this is the answer!" Al exclaimed with excitement. "Hold on, there's more … 'It will generate a fusion explosion that will shut down all things positronic, such as AI brain function. En-Ki created this to defeat En-Lil; that's why En-Lil wants it destroyed,'" Al explained. He paused, deep in thought.

"How does it work?" Vee inquired.

Alice had an epiphany. "This was always the plan," he realised. "To transport the Astara to Kor, with the Nephilim and En-Lil present, and then to use it to take them all out. Brilliant. The message says the activation code for the Astara is embedded in my genome. Damn, what's that s'posed to mean?"

Vee clarified, "He's saying you will instinctively know how to trigger it, Al."

"It's another one of En-Ki's cryptic messages. Why the hell doesn't he just tell me like it is?" Al grumbled, frustrated.

Turk patted him on the shoulder. "Mate, don't worry … it'll come naturally. We just need to get you near the thing."

Al grumbled, "Yeah, wherever that is?"

Something was unsettling Aris. He stood up from his seat and shouted angrily, "All they want is you, Alice. If you surrender, the problem will cease to exist."

Vale stood up, grabbed Aris by his jacket lapels forcefully, and locked eyes with him. He growled, "What is with this sudden change of heart? What has got into you?"

Aris retorted, pulling free from Vale's grip, "I am not planning on sacrificing my life for someone else's lost cause!"

Vale raised a fist, ready to strike Aris, but Alice intervened, shouting, "No, Vale."

Cyrena was furious. "You shame the name of Apollo, your father. Be gone … get out of my sight."

Aris sneered at Vale, then at his mother, and finally at Alice. Humiliated, the tall, regal, silver-haired young man stormed out of the Great Hall.

Unsteady on her feet after the surge of emotion, Cyrena wavered. Vee noticed and rushed to her aid.

"Do not worry Alice … we now have a plan," big blustery Odin roared passionately.

A way forward had been established.

Later, Alice confided in Inna that Aris's expulsion troubled him.

"You must understand, Alice, this is not uncommon among the people of Kor, especially the Treen. They are deeply loyal to a cause. Aris is only part Treen, and I believe Cyrena has always known that her son lacks some of the Treen values."

"But does that justify banishment?" Al questioned.

"It is the custom of the Treen."

"Where will he go?"

"He was seen taking an outrigger to sea."

"But to where?"

"Perhaps to search for another island in the great unknown."

The horizon off the bow was marked by a thin red line, signalling the aftermath of the storm. A now tranquil breeze gently filled the sail of the outrigger Aris had secured from the Stockholm marina. His unlikely ally in this venture was Rohgan Tiltse, a vocal councillor known for his criticism of Alice's entanglement in Kor's political affairs. Aris set off alone, charting his course towards Atlan, steering the small craft through the calmer waters. This solitary journey, embarked upon with quiet determination, contrasted sharply with the storm's earlier fury, reflecting a moment of peace amidst the unfolding chaos.

Half an hour had passed, and Turk, Vale, and Vee were waiting for Alice with their legs dangling over the edge of the wharf.

Vee voiced her concern, "What if Aris surrenders to the Nephilim and leaks our plan?"

"That is not beyond the realm of possibility, given Aris's nature," Vale concurred.

Turk was troubled. "Cyrena needs to intercept him; otherwise, we might be walking into a trap."

Agreeing with Turk, Vale stood up. "I will talk to her."

Just then, Al strolled out of Inanna's hub and approached them. "Morning, guys." He paused and stretched, yawning. "Could eat a horse … we got time before heading off?"

"Sure, I am just going to have a talk with Cyrena about Aris. You get some food; I have eaten already," Vale said.

"What's the concern?" Al inquired.

Turk chimed in, "We're worried Aris might blow the whistle to the Nephilim."

"Hmm, is that likely?" Al asked Vale.

"Yes, considering his state of humiliation, he might resort to anything … he can be vengeful. Get some food in the hall, Al. I will meet you there shortly," Vale said before walking off to Odin's hub, where Cyrena was staying.

Al patted his belly at the thought of food. "Have you eaten, Turk?"

"Nope."

"Vee?"

"Starving," she admitted, sporting a hungry grin.

"Bacon, two eggs over-easy, hash-browns, and fresh coffee will do me just fine," Al scoffed.

"Yeah, dream-on baby … it's fish and ale on the menu, mate," Vee said with a look on her face like she'd just bitten into a lemon.

The trio entered the Great Hall where breakfast was being served. The pungent scent of boiling fish permeated the smoky room.

"Not quite the aroma of freshly brewed coffee I'm craving," Al muttered to Vee as they took seats at the long table.

Turk tapped the table with his knuckles. "What's this thing made of?"

Al examined the table's texture. "I asked Vale that … apparently, it's the backbone of a creature like a giant cuttlefish. You know, those chalky things people give budgies to sharpen their beaks?"

"No," Turk frowned.

Alice didn't bother explaining further. A bowl of fish soup with a thick slice of bread was placed before him by a serving lady. He dunked the bread and chewed thoughtfully. Addressing Turk and Vee, he casually said, "I'm going to do this on my own, guys."

Vee's pretty face contorted into a scowl. "You're what?"

"Calm down, sis, hear me out. It's clear the Nephilim don't want me dead, so it should be safe enough for me to arrive at Atlan. But the same can't be said for you guys. Once I'm certain it's secure, you can open a portal to join me. Understand?"

"You keep this battle going on in your own head and you're running the risk of losing it big brother," Vee growled, strongly disagreeing with his plan.

Alice locked eyes with her and said compassionately, "I am no loser. Trust me."

"How do you plan to get there? You can't jump, and you don't have a portal," Turk pointed out.

"I'll return through yours and then have a portal opened to Atlan. Christina will have mapped most of Kor by now and will be able to put me on the target."

"Makes sense," Turk agreed.

Vee still wasn't happy. "Are you kidding me? Don't side with him, Turk … it's a suicide mission. Both of you are overlooking the fact that En-Lil and a Zen agent are likely orchestrating this. And En-Lil wants your sorry butt on a plate, mate."

Al leaned back in his chair, resolute. "That might be the case, but I've made up my mind. It's the safest plan. I've got pills to alter my appearance. I need to locate the Astara … if I can get that done, then we'll have a fighting chance. If I can't, then we're stuffed."

They both understood that he was right; there really wasn't any other viable option.

"You know I like that freckle on your cheek," Al said to his sister with a smile.

"That's no freckle, it's a beauty spot," she said, pulling a smug look.

"It's a beauty all right," he countered, like big brother would.

After breakfast, Al caught up with Vale, Odin, and Cyrena at the wharf to update them on the revised plan.

Once they were informed, he added, "You guys will need to hold the fort. There's a good chance a sea spider is heading this way. To get out of this, it's going to take good timing, clever thinking, and a shit-load of luck."

Odin said worriedly, "They might be anticipating your arrival if Aris has turned against us."

Cyrena's anger was palpable as she snapped, "I am going after him immediately."

"No, Cyrena, you cannot. It is far too risky. Let him go. We need you to fly to other floats and warn them," Vale argued. "We have no other way."

Al concurred, "He's right, Cyrena. That needs to take precedence. There's too much at stake."

"Alright, alright … I will leave now while the headwind is absent. You know how to contact me if needed, Odin," Cyrena declared, unfurling her majestic wings. A few flaps to catch the breeze, and she was soon soaring high above them.

"How cool is that!" Vee exclaimed, shading her eyes to watch the Queen Treen.

"She said you can contact her. How's that possible?" Turk asked.

"Thought transference," Odin explained, "one of us has the sight."

"My sister Inanna," Vale added. "She was born with the gift to contact the Treen."

"Alright, Turk, open the portal. It's time to leave," Al instructed.

Inanna hurried over from her hub. When she reached Al, she wrapped her arms around his neck.

"Did your intuition tell you I was leaving?" Al quipped.

A solemn exchange between them silently reaffirmed their affection.

After sharing a warm embrace with Inanna, Al shot them all his trademark wave. "Chaa!"

In a split second, everyone except Al, Vee, and Turk froze. The portal had opened. Al gave Vee and Turk a thumbs up before stepping through.

CHAPTER 31
THE KEY

A L STEPPED OUT of Kairos, not expecting a reception committee.

Later, after he'd given a comprehensive account of the critical situation on Kor to an executive assembly, the focus shifted to the question of action. When the Professor elucidated the Astara's mechanism and the projected impact on the Nephilim should the EMT fusion explosion occur, he received a response from Dr Luna Cairn that caught him off guard.

"This cannot be allowed! It blatantly violates the temporal prime directive!" she exclaimed, her outrage evident.

"But you will allow the Nephilim to annihilate the Korman population? What kind of hypocrisy do you represent, Luna?" Alice growled.

Luna's face flushed red with anger.

Mal intervened. "Alice makes a valid point, Luna. It seems to me that you too often favour the opposition."

"Your statement is baseless, Mr President. You're aware as I am that you are a signatory to the non-interference policy," she snapped, petulantly.

"And what about Zen's involvement in the genocide? What's your response to that?" Alice challenged.

"Based on your account, that remains unproven," Luna countered, her anger unabated.

Alice crossed his arms defensively. "So, what do you propose?"

Caught off guard and under pressure to provide an answer, Luna stammered, "I, I'll need to consult with my superiors ... um..."

Al eyeballed her with scorn. "Well, you better get off your date and do it, because I'm out of here real soon."

"I think Alice outlined the urgency quite clearly. An attack on Stockholm is imminent. Are you willing to take responsibility for all those lives, including those of two of our agents, while the UNTT deliberates?" Mal demanded forcefully.

"Let her go through her bureaucratic process, Mal. In the meantime, we can start making preparations," Secta calmly suggested.

Mal glared at Luna. "You have an hour, Dr Cairn. If we don't receive your response within that time, we will take action on our own, regardless of the consequences. Is that understood?"

His statement was unrelenting, leaving no room for argument. The doctor stood up derisively and then stormed out of the boardroom to contact her headquarters in New York.

Mal broke the silence that had fallen over the meeting. "I'm surprised by your patience, Al."

Al shrugged in response before turning his attention to the Professor. "Is the disc ready, Vic?"

"Yes, but it hasn't been tested."

"Too bad. So, where do I shove the damn thing?"

Vic exchanged a worried glance with Secta before answering. "That's the problem, Al. We don't know. In his usual style, En-Ki left that part out."

"Maybe there's a slot in the Astara, like in a DVD player," Christina mused.

Hope chimed in, "Did you notice anything like that inside it, Al?"

Al was frustrated by the added complication. He hated leaving things to chance, especially with so many lives at stake. "No, nothing outside or inside," he grumbled irritably. "It wouldn't be at the bottom either, so there must be some sequence in the raised reliefs all over the lid that you have to touch in a sequence to open it or something like that."

"En-Ki's message mentioned that you would intuitively know the activation sequence. He said it's embedded in your inherited DNA. Maybe that's the key, Al?" the Professor suggested tentatively, sensitive to Al's mood.

Two significant questions remained: Could Alice come up with the activation sequence while under stress? And even if he did, would the disc work? There was no other option but to proceed.

"I'll have to ice it, I guess," Al grumbled.

As they prepared to leave, Viktoria spoke up, "Oh, Al ... tell Vee that Blake is alright. He returned here yesterday and will be discharged from the hospital in a day or two. He's under observation."

"Thanks, Vik. She'll be relieved to know that," Al replied warmly.

Secta halted Al. "We've developed a device that might be of use to you. It's a frequency blocker that Vic likes to call a 'plug.' It's small, like a remote control, fits into the palm of your hand. When activated, it disrupts all communications within a ten-metre radius across the frequency spectrum."

"How long does it last?"

Vic joined them and answered, "It doesn't rely on batteries. It operates using a small irradiated pellet, so the jamming continues as long as it's active."

"Yeah, that could come in handy," Al agreed, appreciating their innovative gadgets.

"We'll give it to you before you leave," Secta confirmed.

Mal approached Al and patted him on the back. "Leave Luna and the politics to me, mate." He lowered his voice to a whisper, out of earshot from the others. "So, what are the women like on Kor?"

Al spotted Hope waiting for him at the door and immediately thought of Inanna. A pang of guilt seized him. "They're amazing, mate ... the place is full of stunners, and they're all topless," he joked.

The look on Mal's face was priceless. "Dead-set! I'm green with envy! Take care, mate," he said sincerely and then embraced his friend.

Just as Al was about to leave, Secta rushed back into the boardroom, gasping for breath.

"What's going on, dude? Been doing some sprinting?" Al asked, giving Secta a friendly pat on the shoulder.

Still catching his breath, Secta managed to speak. "I know you're in a hurry, Al. I've been working on the Trans formula…"

"The pill, right?" Al confirmed.

"Yes, I've developed a pea-sized release capsule that can be implanted subcutaneously into your left wrist. The formula is in liquid form and can be triggered by pressing the capsule with the thumb of your right hand. Press and hold for three seconds to register your thumbprint, and it will release the correct dose. It eliminates the need to carry pills and acts faster by directly entering your bloodstream."

"Brilliant. How many doses does it contain?"

"Ten."

"When can you give it to me?"

"Right now." Secta pulled out what looked like a small device. "Show me the underside of your left wrist."

Alice rested on the edge of the board table. As Secta was injecting the pellet, Al said, "Give it a couple of hours then send the wormhole to Vee. Okay?" He went on to explain the plan he'd concocted.

Electra threw her head back and laughed, emitting a grotesque, hiccupping sound as though her throat was unaccustomed to such activity. "You will need to quote me more than the obvious to save your life … of course I know Black Alice will try and sabotage us … that is his hack."

Walker stood next to Electra, overseeing the Nephilim guard who was positioned behind Aris, slumped in a chair, his face battered and bloody from the ruthless beating.

Electra paced the spartan interrogation room. "I told you, there are many like me who do not desire war. We will surrender," Aris pleaded desperately.

Electra snapped, "Walker!"

The imposing Brit nodded, and the guard reacted by forming an armoured fist, from which a sinister six-inch spike shot out from the knuckles and snapped into place.

Aris flinched at sound of it. "No!" he begged, trying to free himself from the clamps in the arms of the chair restraining his wrists.

Electra signalled, and the guard lunged forward, driving the spike through Aris's left cheek and out the other side. Aris's screams echoed in the room, blood seeping from the wound. His eyes were a mix of agony and fear, his muffled pleas barely audible through the bloodied mouth. "All right!"

Walker raised an inquisitive eyebrow, satisfied that the spike had yielded the desired result. He nodded to the guard to withdraw the spike, and Aris's agonised screams intensified as the barb was pulled back, leaving behind a bleeding, wound in both cheeks.

The guard held up the fist, causing the spike to retract into the armoured glove. Aris gasped for air, relieved that the torment had ended.

"No more … no more … please," Aris pleaded, his voice broken. "He will first go to his Earth base, then come here today to sabotage the attack. That is all I know."

Electra's gaze was intense as she faced Aris. "And? What else?"

"Nothing, that is all," Aris whimpered, his face pale from pain.

Electra's eyes narrowed. "Outside, Walker."

As Electra and Walker left the room, Aris let out a sigh of relief—the torture had finally ceased.

Exiting through a metal door, they emerged onto a high rock platform overlooking the serene sea. The sunlight cast a radiant glow, and the gentle breeze tousled Electra's hair. She halted at the edge of the precipice, gazing down at the waves crashing against the rocks below. Walker stood beside her, inhaling the bracing sea air. In the distance, moored in a lagoon, floated the immense globular hulk of a sea spider.

With her gaze fixed on the colossal vessel, Electra declared, "We need to act swiftly. Commence the attack."

Walker's voice was calm as he reminded her, "Aren't you forgetting something?"

Electra turned to him sharply, her expression defiant. "What?"

"Black Alice," Walker replied, his tone composed.

Electra's lips curved into a cynical smirk. "Not at all. In fact, he is the key to our success."

Walker could tell by the pretentiousness it was En-Lil talking. Though unsure of the meaning, he knew better than to question her.

Alice emerged from the vortex onto the familiar Atlan rock platform, where he had once watched Apollo depart in the ATLAN-TIS-177 bound for Earth. Infiltrating the Nephilim hive and locating the Astara would require assistance from the Nephilim themselves. Shapeshifting wouldn't suffice; he needed their armour to blend in.

As the setting sun cast elongated shadows, Alice slipped through the short tunnel that led to the city. Moving with the agility of a cat, he reached an expansive paved area that he had to cross in order to reach the main building. It would expose him, but then he spotted an overhead transportation tube. Elevated on twenty-metre tall pylons, a station was within reach. To move unnoticed, he would have to dash from pylon to pylon, with a distance of fifty metres between them. His quick calculation indicated that a two-seater pod passed overhead every five minutes in each direction, and the ones he'd seen were empty.

Bolting to the first pylon, he waited and then sprinted to the next. Above, a pod approached the station from the main building, carrying a Nephilim passenger. Alice hoped the passenger would exit at the station, and he hurried to the last pylon. There, he found an elevator door. Stepping in, he was reminded of entering the elevator at OTT with Hope just an hour before, even though they had been halfway across the galaxy. He recalled how Hope had surprised him with a passionate kiss.

Once the elevator doors closed, she had kissed him fervently. "I've missed you, Alice," she had said.

"Wait ... no, Hope ... there's a camera up there," he had cautioned.

She glanced at the camera and stopped her advances.

He had asked, "Where on earth did you learn to kiss like that?"

Bashfully, she admitted, "YouTube."

Amused, he had responded, "Bloody-hell ... what else have you been learning?"

She smiled wantonly, "You'll find out when you return from Kor."

Back in the present, the elevator came to a stop, and the doors opened to reveal the Nephilim guard from the pod. Reacting instinctively, Alice pulled out his Glock 9 and activated the Plug device in his hip pocket to block the Nephilim's communication with the hive. Holding the gun, he ordered the guard, "We're going to catch a pod back to the main building ... Take me to the Astara."

In a monotone voice, the guard replied, "I cannot comply."

"Open your visor, or I'll blast it off your face," Alice threatened.

The visor spiralled open, revealing a nearly human face with some disturbing differences. No eyebrows, pallid complexion, and eerie eyes without pupils—just an unsettling black void. The guard's expression was as emotionless as its voice.

"To keep your face intact, follow my lead," Al growled, pressing the barrel of the Glock through the visor. He noticed the guard's eyes move slightly, likely trying to contact the hive.

"I've jammed your comm-links. Do as I say. You've got ten seconds," Alice warned, counting the seconds aloud while keeping a close watch on the guard's face.

In the nick of time, the guard said, "This way," leading Alice to the opposite side of the platform where a waiting pod stood. They entered the two-seater, fully enclosed egg-shaped pod as a Perspex panel sealed them inside. Levitating in a vacuum, the pod silently accelerated toward the next station within the main building. Alice kept the Glock discreetly aimed at the guard's side.

Approaching the main building, a towering, gloomy structure with a matte black surface resembling unpolished obsidian, Alice felt a sense of foreboding. Round black portholes on its facade resembled empty, lifeless eyes. Enclosed within a triangular wall, the spire had guard towers at each point. Two transporter tubes entered through one side.

As the pod halted at a platform station, a panel unsealed the tube, allowing the pod canopy to open.

Vale's concern grew as he realised that Cyrena had not returned from Bora, the closest float since London's destruction. Feeling uneasy about her absence, he raised the matter with Turk and Vee, who were overseeing the fortification efforts.

"There's nothing we can do about it, Vale. Our focus has to be on defending ourselves now," Turk grumbled, clearly absorbed in the pressing tasks at hand.

Vale sensed tension in Turk's response and attempted to mend the atmosphere. He fetched a water-skin, took a sip, and then offered it to Turk in a gesture of goodwill. Turk accepted the gesture, smiled, and took a sip himself. The impending threat of an attack weighed heavily on Turk, aware of their vulnerability due to their limited armament. He wasn't one to leave things to chance.

An urgent cry of "Naygard! Naygard!" pierced the air from the left gatehouse—a prearranged alarm indicating an imminent assault. Reacting swiftly, Vale led Turk and Vee up the staircase to the top of the left gate tower, the larger of the two. The guard who had sounded the alarm was pointing frantically out to sea.

The day's weather was peculiar, with a dense fog blending the sea and sky into an eerie yellow haze. The water's surface remained calm and still, devoid of any wind, while an unsettling silence hung in the air—the quiet before a storm.

"There!" the lookout exclaimed, pointing with excitement towards a spot within the fog. Vale, Turk, and Vee squinted to see what he was indicating, but the dense fog obscured their vision.

"Keep watching," the sentry insisted. "The fog will swirl when it moves."

"It could be a kraken," Vale speculated.

The guard stammered, "No, no, it is bigger … much bigger."

Vee added grimly, "King Kraken, maybe?"

Turk's focus intensified, and he eventually spotted something. "There! He's right … the fog is shifting … there's something there, and it's massive."

Then, echoing across the water, came the sound of metal creaking—similar to the movement of a construction crane—along with distant splashes. It was evident that something large was wading through the water toward them. The loud splashes indicated its immense size. While they remained transfixed by the haze, the entity gradually emerged from the fog.

Amidst the swirling mist and tendrils of fog, a colossal sea spider materialised—a machine of immense proportions. Vee, awestruck, exclaimed, "Oh my god!" She stared, her eyes wide with wonder. "It's like something out of War of the Worlds."

"The what?" Vale asked.

"It's still about a kilometre away," Turk stated calmly, focusing on the impending threat. "We need to prepare ourselves to take it on."

Vale shot him a glance packed with disbelief. "But how?"

CHAPTER 32
SNARED

ALICE FOUND HIMSELF in a precarious situation, necessitating a risky move as he followed the Nephilim guard through the depths of the main building. His implant, thankfully, had locked onto a signal from the transponder he'd secretly placed inside the Astara.

Brandishing his Glock, Alice commanded the guard in a stern tone, "Lead me to the Astara."

The Nephilim's monotone response came, "That is not possible. I cannot determine its location without connectivity." This was logical; the guard required hive communication for locational data.

Undeterred, Alice resolved to trust the transponder's increasing signal strength to guide him. He sharply instructed, "Stop!" The Nephilim halted. Observing its seemingly organic, non-metallic armour, Alice pondered if it was a type of skin.

"Now listen," he said, pointing the Glock at its face. "Help me find the Astara or face termination. Your choice."

"I cannot comply," the guard replied.

Switching tactics, Alice inquired, "Is there a storeroom in this building?"

"Yes."

"Then lead me there. Avoid other guards, or it'll be the last thing you do. Understood?"

"Affirmative." The Nephilim began to lead the way, its compliance indicating a subtle shift in the balance of power.

As they navigated the corridor, Alice's thoughts wandered to the nature of the Nephilim, musing on their similarities to Zen's RF cyborgs. He questioned their sentience and pondered their ability to reproduce. Could their longevity be as ancient as En-Ki's? And if so, how many of them existed, and were their numbers dwindling? The thought of them attempting to create a hybrid due to their inability to reproduce without the Astara intrigued him.

His contemplations were abruptly interrupted when a figure appeared, obstructing their path. The Nephilim guard came to an abrupt stop. Alice's gaze fixed on the woman standing before him. Her striking appearance was highlighted by her blue-black hair, intricately braided and coiled around her head. She wore a crimson cape that cascaded over her shoulders, flowing down like a river of blood, and a black bodysuit that clung to her form. Her beauty was mesmerising, and her age was elusive, leading Alice to speculate if they were the results of synthetic alterations.

"I require no illusions to embellish my looks or diminish my age," Electra said abruptly.

Sensing that she was reading his mind, Alice instinctively aimed his pistol at her. Something in her eyes reminded him of Gorrick, though he quickly shook off the thought and exclaimed, "En-Lil!"

Before he could utter another word, a rustle of movement came from behind. Neck held rigid, he looked out of the corner of his eyes and caught sight of three Nephilim guards.

"I am Electra. Your weapons are ineffectual. Follow me."

"En-Lil's latest synthetic host no less," Alice's robust voice echoed against the hard surfaces of the dank corridor. There was no reply only the sound her black bovver boots on the crusty floor, and the shuffling noise of the Nephilim moving behind him.

The ominous sound of the sea spider trudging through the water was intensifying as it approached Stockholm. It was now only a few hundred metres from the sea gates.

Vale had ten men lined up on the wharf. They appeared anxious.

Cool as a cucumber, Turk distributed two WASPs to each man and then instructed, "Activate them by flipping the switch ... a red indicator will come on. Then, aim it at the target: the legs of the sea spider. Once it locks onto the target, the red light will turn green, indicating readiness to launch. No need to throw it; simply release it into the air. It will locate the target."

Vee stepped forward, looking fierce in her battle attire with her hair tightly bound. She issued orders, "After releasing your two WASPS, exit the gate tower immediately. Don't wait to see the results. Return promptly to your assigned positions on the wharf. Clear?"

They all nodded with concern.

Noticing their apprehension, Vee softened her tone. "Stay strong; your fellow citizens depend on you. You are our frontline of defence. Take a deep breath and fulfil your duty. We will prevail."

In unison, they nervously repeated, "We will prevail."

Vale stood beside Vee and shouted, "Make us proud of you. Now, move!"

Two resounding booms, akin to cannon fire, emanated from the sea spider, shrouded in swirling fog and mist. They watched in awe as over a hundred glowing red orbs, each as large as a golf ball, launched from the creature. These orbs soared above them, tracing fiery arcs across the sky like a barrage of fireworks, their trajectory aimed to rain down upon their position.

"Take cover!" Vale bellowed at the top of his voice.

Stockholm burst into frenzied activity. Crude catapults, readied to launch searing projectiles, and a behemoth crossbow manned by a trio, poised to release a two-metre barbed spear, resembled ancient siege engines of medieval times. Yet, the operators were forced into hasty retreat as the sky became inundated with a deluge of bright red incendiary grenades, arcing down like a barrage of fiery meteors.

Several of these incendiary orbs splashed into the lagoon and adjacent waters, but many more struck their intended targets on the shore. Structures in Stockholm were soon ablaze, ignited by the relentless onslaught. Amidst the chaos, women, emerging from their hiding spots among the buildings, valiantly fetched water in buckets, battling to quell the rapidly spreading flames.

All the while, the foreboding, sloshing sound of the approaching sea spider intensified, instilling terror and panic. Inhabitants, particularly those with young ones, scrambled frantically for shelter. The lagoon bore witness to two of its coracles set aflame by the incendiaries, helplessly consumed by fire; Stockholm was unprepared for such a ferocious firestorm.

Their defensive strategy was severely hamstrung by the scarcity of weapons. These would only prove effective when the sea spider loomed directly overhead, and even then, their potential to inflict damage was uncertain.

In the gate towers, ten men, each clutching a WASP, stood vigilant. Miraculously, these towers had withstood the fiery assault from above. As the monstrous silhouette of the sea spider drew ominously near, the defenders braced themselves, poised for a confrontation fraught with uncertainty and peril.

Turk noticed a young boy nearby clutching a roughly fashioned sword with trembling hands and told Vale, "Take the sword from the boy, give it to me. Send him to help load one of the catapults."

Vale explained, "The sword is a family heirloom from the days of Apollo."

"All the more reason it should be put to better use than in the hands of a boy. He won't survive if he fights here," Turk insisted.

Vale recognised Turk's wisdom and relayed the message to the boy, who proudly handed the sword to Turk. Examining it, testing its weight and balance, Turk nodded his approval. "Well-crafted ... Are there more like this?" he asked Vale.

"The cache of weapons from Atlan before the Nephilim arrived was stored on the London float. Zian, the boy, moved here from London and brought the family heirloom with him."

Their conversation was interrupted by a sentry's frantic shout from the left gate tower, warning that the sea spider had moved into firing range. It spurred immediate action.

"Vee, are you ready?" Turk shouted. She was with the catapult crew and immediately gave the order to ignite torches. Both catapults were loaded with a basketball-sized projectile made from dried seaweed soaked in alcohol. On her order, a designated fire-starter would ignite the ball for the catapult to launch over the sea gate at the target.

The scene was one of tense anticipation. As Turk and Vale hastened up the staircase of the left gate tower to oversee the battle, their footfalls echoed through the charged atmosphere. Vee watched them climb, her gaze then shifting to the massive turret of the sea spider as it ominously loomed overhead, casting an imposing shadow.

The sight of the gargantuan, threatening war machine was enough to send a wave of fear through the women taking cover. Their reactions were instinctive and protective; trembling, some let out involuntary screams, while others shielded the eyes of their children, pulling them close to their chests in a desperate bid for comfort. To them, it seemed as if they were witnessing the apocalypse.

Imposingly, the sea spider halted its advance about fifty metres from the gates, its sheer size and presence causing the surrounding fog to dissipate, revealing the full, terrifying extent of its form. The moment of confrontation was at hand, and the air was thick with an almost palpable sense of dread.

Turk pointed while stating, "There are two small craft behind it."

"Probably the landing party," Vale affirmed.

All fell silent. A servo sounded. It emanated from a small hatch sliding open in the belly of the sea spider. From within, an articulated snake-like tube descended menacingly.

"What the...?" Turk snarled.

Vale grimaced, "It's a fire-whip!"

The ten-metre long articulated silver tube reminded Turk of a scorpion's tail. It flicked about just above the surface of the water, sparks crackling from its tip.

Inside one of the two landing craft, hooked up with a headset issuing orders, sat Walker. The clear polymer canopy of the globular ten-metre vessel presented a clear view of Stockholm and the sea spider. Behind him, six-armed Nephilim were seated facing each other silently, awaiting their orders like paratroopers ready to bail out. Beside him, a Nephilim was steering the silent running boat.

It was time—they were in position. Walker issued the order for the sea spider, "Attack!"

"It's moving!" Turk croaked. "Hold, men … on my command."

The five men clutching WASPs waited nervously. Vale signalled the other five men in the right tower to be ready.

The terrifying electric tail whipped about in front of the sea spider. Then, the sea spider's legs began to extend further, elevating the round turret another ten metres above the water level. It now loomed over them.

Vale was anxious. He wanted the order to be given to throw, but Turk, experienced and composed, waited for the target to be in range, fully aware they couldn't afford to miss.

The fire-whip snaked through the air and struck the sea gates. There was a resounding crack, and the gates burst into flames.

"Loose!" Turk ordered.

Vale relayed the order to the right tower. Then, all hell broke loose.

Turk signalled Vee below.

Ten WASPs buzzed through the air toward the sea spider's legs.

Two fireballs made a whooshing, hissing sound as Vee's team catapulted them over the burning sea gates.

The WASPs found their marks, but their impact was akin to a swarm of mosquitoes on an elephant.

The fire-whip demolished the right tower with one almighty crack, setting it ablaze and forcing its occupants to leap into the water, some of them in flames.

Turk and Vale knew they were next as the machine halted its forward movement and swung the fire-whip around, poised to strike.

"Everybody out!" Turk shouted. They all rushed for the tower stairs.

A fireball from the catapult smashed into the spider and exploded, but it caused no substantial damage.

Vee maintained the barrage of fireballs while simultaneously ordering the massive crossbow to take aim. They had only six metre-long spears. Two men worked fervently, cranking the massive bone bow into the locked position. Another held a burning torch, ready to ignite the head of the barbed spear.

"Fire!" Vee screamed loudly amid the cacophony of battle.

With a thunderous whoosh, the arrow shot from the crossbow. They all watched it hurtle through the air toward the spider. Zunk! A metallic sound echoed as it lodged deep into the turret just below two small round viewing windows.

"Again! Again!" Vee shouted. "Aim for those windows!"

The men quickly re-calibrated, then reloaded, though they weren't confident about hitting such a small target.

The fire-whip obliterated the left tower, reducing it to pieces and setting the wharf ablaze. With an arrow on fire protruding from it, but still unimpeded, the spider advanced toward the shattered gates, ready to enter the lagoon.

Turk said to Vale, "Now we're in real trouble. The WASPs had no effect."

There was a resounding whoosh, followed by another Zunk! as a second arrow pierced the metal carapace of the sea spider, just below a porthole.

The fire-whip slashed, taking out a substantial chunk of the wharf and igniting the fleet of boats moored there.

Turk and Vale exchanged a look of despair—there seemed to be no other options left. The thick black smoke from the fires obscured the attackers. Turk extended his hand to Vale, and they shook in silence. They both understood that as the sea spider entered the lagoon through the smoke, their defences were futile.

But Vee wasn't about to give up. As long as there were arrows left, she would keep firing. Though less effective, the catapults continued their barrage. Amid the billowing black smoke from the remnants of the towers, the burning fleet, and the wharf, fireballs and flaming arrows streaked through the smoke-filled air. The fire-whip lashed about, destroying one of the catapults and setting three men ablaze. Others rushed with buckets of water to extinguish the flames, but the fireballs had been overturned, setting the wharf further ablaze, beyond extinguishing.

Two more arrows struck the spider's turret, and then, one lucky shot found its mark, smashing through the small porthole. A triumphant cheer erupted as the control room inside the spider was engulfed in flames. However, the cheer was short-lived as the fire-whip swept across the wharf, obliterating the crossbow and the remaining catapult, instantly claiming most of the crew's lives. Vee narrowly avoided the wicked tendril as it whipped past only inches from her.

Turk hurried over to her and valiantly attempted to sever the arching whip with his sword, but it proved too resilient, the sword making no impression.

Vee opened fire on it with her Glock, trying to cut it in half. At the same time, Vale fired, aiming for the other porthole in the spider.

As the sea spider waded into the lagoon, its legs created waves that extinguished some of the fires and washed most of the people in the water, back onto the wharf.

Turk had to dive to grasp Vee's arm, preventing her from being swept away by a large wave. The waves splashing over them caused utter chaos. The alcohol from the catapults spilled into the water, setting the lagoon's surface ablaze and engulfing those who had been washed back in. Desperate screams and cries filled the air as friends and family watched helplessly from cover, witnessing those in the fiery water burn.

Caught in a wall of thick black smoke and flames, people slipped and slid on the wet wharf, screaming, trying desperately to avoid skidding into the burning water.

Turk, Vee, and Vale remained resolute amidst the pandemonium, their weapons in hand but rendered useless, drenched and yearning for the chance to engage the enemy in close combat instead of the chaos surrounding them.

Turk glanced despondently at Vee when suddenly, everything shimmered and then froze.

CHAPTER 33
GENESIS

VEE AND TURK understood immediately: a wormhole was opening to them. With everything frozen, a lifeline to escape certain death appeared just in time. The small vortex swirled only a couple of metres from them.

"What do you want to do?" Vee shouted frantically at Turk.

But before he could answer, his attention was diverted by someone emerging from the billowing smoke, walking towards him while carrying a gun—an individual he recognised.

"Walker!" Turk shouted in surprise.

Unaffected by the freeze, Walker halted at a safe distance from them and, speaking calmly but firmly, issued a command, "Make the slightest move toward that vortex, and I'll take you both out in less than a New York second." They knew he was more than capable of it. "Where is Black Alice?" he demanded, his unyielding eyes fixed in a chilling stare.

"Destroying your base while you're here," Vee retorted smugly.

The smoke resumed drifting as everything unfroze.

Upon realising what was happening, Vale swung his gun to aim at Walker, but when six Nephilim emerged from the smoke to support the imposing Brit and aimed their weapons at him, Vale lowered his firearm.

It was as good as over.

"I will now order the spider to finish the job. Goodbye," Walker announced loudly into his headset microphone. "Destroy everything ... leave no-one alive. Repeat, take no prisoners."

Just as he turned to walk back through the ranks of the Nephilim toward the landing craft, two massive tendrils shot out of the water, coiled around the sea spider's legs, and began towing it out of the lagoon and into the sea.

Vale shouted, "It's King Kraken!"

From within a turbulent maelstrom of water, the colossal monster surfaced beside the sea spider. Its enormous eyes on stalks darted wildly, taking in the scene. Gigantic brown tentacles, as thick as a man's body and covered in suckers the size of car tyres, wrapped around the spider and began crushing it.

Walker couldn't believe his eyes, and the Nephilim were at a loss for how to react. But Vale, Turk, and Vee knew exactly what to do; they opened fire on the Nephilim. Vale and Vee provided cover for Turk, who flicked WASPs at them like ninja star-knives. Crack! Crack! Crack! One after another, the WASPs found their targets and detonated Nephilim heads.

King Kraken's tentacles thrashed the water as it mercilessly dismantled the mechanical sea spider. The tumultuous waves generated by the intensity of the battle capsized the two landing craft, sending the Nephilim onboard to the depths along with them.

Turk turned sharply to Vee and shouted above the chaos, "Go ... now!"

It had been prearranged. Vee sprinted toward the vortex and, upon reaching it, dived through.

"Leave this bastard to me," Turk snarled at Vale through clenched teeth, a look of determination on his face. Then, with the sword in one hand and a Glock in the other, he stepped over dead Nephilim littering the deck and disappeared into the wall of black smoke to hunt down Walker.

When Kairos activated, Christina couldn't help but wonder who or what would emerge. To her surprise, it was Vee, but she was taken aback by her appearance—she looked as though she had been through a fierce battle, her face covered in soot and streaked with grime, her clothes in tatters.

Christina swiftly contacted the respective labs of Secta, Hope, and the Professor. Within seconds, all of them had gathered in the control room. Vee provided them with a vivid account of the epic battle on Kor.

Unexpectedly, the door opened, and Blake hobbled in. Vee froze, as if she had seen a ghost. Alice had been unable to relay the message that Blake was alive.

"Vee," Blake said, offering a warm but pained smile.

Vee rushed over and embraced him, but it caused him discomfort. "Argh!" he exclaimed.

She immediately stopped, realising he had been seriously wounded. "I, I'm sorry..." she stammered.

Blake made light of it with a chuckle, "It's okay ... still a bit fragile."

Everyone was thrilled to see him on his feet, even though he had the appearance of someone who had just been discharged from the hospital after surviving a life-threatening ordeal.

"So, what's up?" Blake asked blithely.

"I'll let the others explain. For now, Christina, dial up Al, I'm out of here," Vee said.

Secta nodded in agreement, and Christina quickly entered a series of commands into the computer. Kairos powered up.

Vee gave Blake a gentle peck on the cheek. The Professor, who had briefly left the room, returned with some items for Vee to take with her.

"Here you go," he said, handing them over to Vee. She swiftly stashed them in the pockets of her filthy dungarees and then said her goodbyes. Just as she was opening the door to the dispatch room, Luna burst in. Vee signalled Christina with a sharp nod—they couldn't afford to let Luna disrupt the mission.

"That's Vee, where is she going? You don't have mission authority!" Luna growled, sounding like an angry schoolmistress.

"Oh, shut up, Luna," the Professor snapped back at her, his patience worn thin by her constant resistance to their efforts.

Al was seated in a stark room at a large oval table, facing the Nephilim hierarchy with Electra standing at the head of the table. The exit was tightly guarded, leaving Al with no means of escape. The visors of the seven Nephilim seated at the table were open. Al glared at Rykor.

"I have executed my side of the agreement and delivered this scoundrel," Electra snarled, pretentiously.

Alice's mouth pulled into a tight, angry slash at the taunt.

"Now, you will honour your side of the bargain," Electra concluded.

Alice responded with a burst of ironic laughter, "Honour! Ha! You wouldn't know the meaning of the word."

One side of her lip curled into a smug sneer. "You're a joke ... always itching for a fight, even when you don't stand a chance."

"Electra is correct; there are over ten thousand Nephilim in Atlan," Rykor said in a monotone voice.

"That's not Electra talking," Al snarled at Rykor. "That's En-Lil! Your enemy has outwitted you. Allowing En-Lil into your nest is dancing with the devil. No matter what you do, you will be the loser. I am the envoy of En-Ki, and if I'm right, he was your creator ... and he is the sworn enemy of his brother En-Lil ... so that—"

"Oh, shut up!" Electra shouted. "We have an agreement, Rykor."

"Is he telling the truth?" the Nephilim leader demanded.

"He would say anything to save his skin. Now, get on with it! I will need to leave for Earth with the Astara soon, as we agreed," Electra insisted.

To Alice's surprise, Rykor bowed his head in submission to Electra and then stood. "Prepare him," he ordered, and left the room with four of his council members.

Alice touched the pea-sized implant in his wrist with his forefinger as a reminder that it was there.

One of the two remaining officials abruptly issued an order to the guard, "Immobilise him."

A sardonic smirk appeared on Electra's pallid face when the guard jabbed Alice in the chest with a hypodermic that instantly knocked him out.

When he regained consciousness, Al was on a gurney being wheeled along a narrow corridor. He counted four guards accompanying him. There was a loud hiss as a hermetically sealed door opened to allow the gurney to enter a sterile room. The gurney stopped, a bright light overhead illuminated him, servos activated, and four peculiar robotic machines surrounded him. Al couldn't move; his feet and arms were securely tethered to the gurney.

One of the machines collected a blood sample from his arm, another swabbed his DNA from inside his mouth, while a third flashed a laser into each of his eyes. They transmitted the data to the fourth bot, which processed the information. The procedures were relatively painless and quickly concluded. The gurney was then pushed back out into the corridor and, after a short distance, through a double set of doors into a larger, brightly lit room.

When the gurney came to a halt, Al saw a mezzanine floor about three metres above him, where Electra, Rykor, and a dozen other Nephilim stood at a balustrade, peering down at him. It reminded him of the time Zen had captured him as Turk in 2087, intending to turn him into a cyborg. He felt a sensation, a pang; a gut feeling. He raised his head slightly and spotted the Astara on a pedestal only a couple of metres away.

Drawing a deep breath and letting it out in a rush, he grumbled to himself, "Right, I'm over this."

Rykor had delivered a message to Electra that she didn't want to hear, and she was seething. "What do you mean Walker has failed?

That's impossible!"

"A report came through to the hive just before the sender was terminated. A giant sea creature called the Kraken destroyed the sea spider and all the support craft ... we must assume, by the lack of further contact, that all has been lost," Rykor explained.

Electra was shell-shocked. "I can't believe it ... how? Send in more warriors!" she demanded.

"No, we have assessed, as before, that the Korman are no real threat to us," Rykor responded sternly.

"Not much! They just wiped out your entire attack force!" she retorted angrily.

"A Kraken defeated our forces, not the Korman!" Rykor stated firmly.

Al was using his hypersensitive hearing to eavesdrop on their conversation. The discord between them was evident from their rhetoric. He could feel En-Lil's presence, a malevolent stain seeping through the atmosphere.

"I want that confirmed ... and what of Walker?" Electra questioned indignantly.

As the remnants of smoke dissipated, the atmosphere on the wharf was charged with a cacophony of cheers and jeers from the assembled crowd. The focus of their attention was the tense standoff between Turk and Walker, standing ten metres apart in a classic face-off. Walker, cornered against the wharf with the searing heat of the burning lagoon at his back, was visibly sweating under the intense pressure.

Turk shouted confidently at him, "Drop your weapons ... we'll sort this out one on one."

Both men were of a similar stature and build, however Turk was twenty years older than Walker, and knew it. Walker complied, dropping his pistol. He was seriously outnumbered and figured it wiser to fight Turk than risk being torn to pieces by an angry mob.

Turk handed Vale his Glock and challenged Walker by placing the antique sabre on the ground between them.

Walker retorted, "Another Nephilim attack force will be on the way? You don't stand a chance."

Turk didn't back down, replying with determination, "That's a risk we're prepared to take."

They clashed, exchanging powerful blows. Turk attempted a chin-jab early on but missed, realising quickly that he was up against a well-trained combatant. Walker delivered a precise right jab, slicing open Turk's eyebrow.

"Ex-SAS, huh?" Turk grunted, feeling the blood trickle down his face.

"Green beret ... you?" Walker shot back, standing his ground.

"Aussie SAS," Turk replied, wiping the blood from his eye.

Walker taunted, "Fought beside plenty of Aussies ... they weren't as well-trained as us Brits in close-quarter H-2-H."

Turk's response was a fierce growl. "Yeah? Let's see about that." With that, he unleashed a furious onslaught of punches. His aggressive approach drove Walker back to the very edge of the wharf. Walker was forced on the defensive, his arms raised to block the blows raining down on him from the relentless Turk.

A loud flapping sound suddenly filled the air, drawing the attention of both Turk and Walker. They momentarily ceased their violent engagement and looked upwards. Emerging from the swirling smoke, a huge black bat descended, its massive wings stirring the air and parting the smoke. As the figure became clearer, Turk recognised her with a mix of surprise and relief—it was Cyrena.

The dynamic of the fight instantly shifted with Cyrena's arrival. Turk and Walker, still in their combat stances and mere metres apart, watched intently as Cyrena landed gracefully between them. Walker, his face marked by the bruises and cuts from Turk's fierce punches, quickly seized the moment.

Seeing an opening, Walker lunged for the sword lying on the

ground. Grasping it firmly, he then leapt towards Cyrena, swiftly putting an arm around her neck from behind. With the sword in his possession and Cyrena now unexpectedly taken as a hostage, the standoff on the wharf escalated, reaching a new and dangerous level of tension.

"Make a move, and I'll cut her throat," he growled.

Turk and Vale, with guns aimed, were ready to intervene.

"What are you going to do then? You can't just disappear," Turk warned.

"Kill her and you will be ripped to pieces," Vale warned.

Walker brought the sabre up to Cyrena's throat and cautioned Vale, "Keep that pistol at your side."

Cyrena remained silent and calm, not making any sudden movements.

"You can fly me to Atlan, can't you?" Walker growled into her pointed left ear.

"No, you would be too heavy," Cyrena managed to say between clenched teeth.

Turk interjected, "See, there's no way out. Let her go."

A blindingly bright yellow light suddenly pierced through the dense smoke overhead, engulfing Walker and Cyrena in its intense glow. Turk and Vale instinctively raised their hands to shield their eyes, squinting upwards to locate the source of this unexpected beam. It was emanating from the hull of an enormous craft, hovering several hundred feet above them.

In a swift reaction, Walker released Cyrena, flinging the sword aside. He seemingly surrendered himself to the tractor beam's pull, rising steadily into the air. The onlookers watched, transfixed, as he was drawn up into the belly of the saucer-shaped, gunmetal grey vessel.

As quickly as it had appeared, the craft made a silent and swift exit. In a moment that felt like the blink of an eye, it vanished into the sky, leaving nothing but a faint circular imprint in the smoke-laden clouds. The crowd was left in a state of shock and disbelief, murmuring and gesturing towards the sky where the mysterious craft had been just seconds before.

"Once he has gone through the process, he is to be eliminated... we are in agreement on that?" Electra asked with a resolute tone.

"Yes. Confirmation is in: he is the genetic match ... the transfer begins now," Rykor affirmed, his typically flat voice laced with a rare hint of anticipation.

A new gurney was wheeled into the room, halting beside Alice. On it lay a naked female figure, a shocking blend of human anatomy and cybernetics. She was an intimidating seven feet tall, her muscular physique clearly synthetic.

Rykor introduced her with evident pride, "She is Genesis."

"How original," Electra commented dryly.

Rykor elaborated, "She is the future of the Nephilim—a hybrid of 80% organic matter, designed for self-replication. The ultimate entity. She only needs Black Alice's genetic material to achieve immortality."

The female on the gurney looked dead to Alice, tubes protruding from every orifice linked her to an apparatus fixed under the gurney that he assumed was probably keeping her alive. He wondered, "She must be what they've been creating for years ... made up of harvested bits of abductees. Gross. I guess once I'm immortalised, they'll transfer my genes to her. Wonder how much of her is human."

Rykor, unemotional as ever, turned to a Nephilim at his side and ordered, "Begin the process."

The guards attending to Genesis swiftly responded to a hive command and wheeled Alice closer to the Astara, the enigmatic device that held the key to Nephilim immortality.

Alice knew that to initiate the immortality program, he needed to select a specific sequence from the hieroglyphic reliefs carved on the Astara's lid. According to the Professor, this sequence would not only grant him immortality but also trigger a fusion reaction capable of disabling all positronic technology on the planet. But he needed the Velodium disc for activation, and it was yet to arrive.

Electra's voice echoed through the chamber, ominous and demanding, "Black Alice. I will have your friend Aris killed if you fail to comply with my instructions ... is that clear?"

Alice glared defiantly at Electra and at Aris, who was displayed, battered and restrained, by two Nephilim guards. It was evident that Aris had endured severe punishment.

"All right, En-Lil, have it your way," Alice grumbled.

"Good. You will be released, and you will select the immortality sequence, open the Astara, get inside, and close the lid for it to be activated. When the process is complete, you will open the lid, step out, and return to the gurney. Clear?"

"Yeah," Alice snarled. He saw Electra nod at Rykor.

One of the guards stepped forward and unfastened Alice's restraints, allowing him to slip off the gurney.

"Strip off your clothes. As soon as you input the code, get into the Astara," Electra ordered.

Al knew she was ensuring he had no weapons concealed on him to take into the sarcophagus. His pockets were loaded with WASPs, two 9 mm clips, his cellphone and a Glock 19. There was no use resisting, so he did as she instructed. Once naked, he went over to the Astara and without thinking too deeply about it, with his eyes closed, reached out a finger and traced it over the smooth reliefs unafraid of their magical aura. A distinct and complex pattern materialised within his mind's eye. His subconscious mind had determined the sequence on the strange carved hieroglyphic inscriptions. He pressed a five-pointed star with a globe at its centre ... then, three of eleven planets in a particular order that were revolving around the star, and then finally, a staff in the hand of a person seated on a throne wearing a pointed hat. A loud click resounded indicating the sarcophagus lid had unlocked.

"It unlocks to his touch only. Our technicians tried various methods without success, yet he can harness its power," Rykor noted with astonishment.

Electra's eyes narrowed, revealing her malevolent intentions. "You're aware, I assume, that his survival chances are slim? The radiation level needed to alter his genes would be lethal for a normal human."

"Clearly, Black Alice is far from ordinary," Rykor countered. In Alice, the Nephilim's hopes and ambitions were embodied.

CHAPTER 34
DEVACHAN

ALICE, RESIGNED TO HIS FATE, opened the sarcophagus lid, clambered up, stepped in, and laid down. As the lid sealed shut, locking him inside, a hope to delay for Vee's arrival vanished, hastened by the imminent threat to Aris. Inside the sarcophagus, he didn't need his phone. A deep, resonating hum filled the space, and his body started glowing green. He felt an odd sensation, as if each molecule, down to the protoplasm of every cell, was being altered. His DNA was undergoing splicing. Suddenly, his glow pulsated thrice before shifting to a bright orange hue, signalling the mutation of his genes. In this intense moment, a vivid, spectral image flashed through his mind.

"Why am I pretending to be me? I don't even know who 'me' is anymore. I used to know exactly who Alice was … now, I've got no bloody idea," he murmured, standing in a room faintly illuminated by a crimson hue.

"Yes, you do," echoed a voice from seemingly everywhere, "Alice is a singer, an entertainer, a saviour of humanity, a fighter for the oppressed. That's who Alice is."

"En-Ki… I should've known. What I've been doing doesn't add up to a hill of beans in the grand scheme of things. Does it?"

"Be true to yourself, Alice. Be honest with everyone, especially yourself. Time to rethink time travel. Past, present, and future exist simultaneously, making the grandfather paradox a non-issue. This understanding will alter your perception of time travel. That 'hill of beans' is actually the entirety of existence—where past, present, and future coexist. Embrace this knowledge, Alice."

"You're talking in riddles again, En-Ki. Where am I?"

"Devachan."

"Devachan, where's that?"

"A place to learn about yourself."

"Listen to me, En-Ki, this Astara thing's got me nervous ... if I survive it, what will I become?"

"A god, Alice, a god."

En-Ki's response struck him like a thunderbolt. Then, a bright flash of light blinded him, and he was once again being transported.

The micro-wormhole that had trailed Alice opened next to the sarcophagus, and Vee stepped through. Everything was frozen, except for Electra, who was glaring down at Vee from the mezzanine.

Upon seeing her, Electra shouted angrily, "Make a move and I will kill your friend here."

It was as if her face had been splashed with ice water; Vee looked up sharply to see Electra had two immobilised Nephilim beside her, restraining Aris. She faced an immediate decision: be captured, let Aris be killed, or jump back into the vortex? It was a no-brainer. She was about to surrender when a thought struck her: where's Alice? She noticed a pile of clothes on the floor. Concluding Alice was inside the sarcophagus, she observed the freeze wear off, and noticed someone joining Electra. It was Walker. His arrival provided her with a crucial distraction.

Looking worse for wear and humiliated by his defeat, Walker gave Electra a succinct account of the attack and its failure.

"Are you telling me a monster sank the sea spider and the other vessels?" Electra whined.

"Yes."

"Was it summoned by the Kor?" she inquired.

"I have no idea, but you'd have to assume it was."

She grasped her chin, pondering, "Hmm, so what are we up

against here?"

"It was most assuredly King Kraken, a formidable sea creature," Rykor interjected informatively.

Struggling against the guard's grip, Aris snarled, "We have many such weapons. You are doomed!"

Angered by the defeat and the possibility that the opposition might have an advantage over her, Electra slapped Aris hard across the face and screamed, "Shut up!" She then glared back down at Vee, who had resolved to make a stand.

Blood was steaming from Aris's nose.

Before the two guards could react, Vee whipped out two WASPs from her pocket, activated them, and flicked them towards her targets. Crack! Crack! The guards collapsed, their heads cleaved open.

The lid of the Astara opened, and Alice sat up.

"Well, if it isn't Count Dracula rising from his coffin," Vee scoffed, handing Al's clothes to him. "Not sure about the look," she joked, keeping her Glock trained on the door.

Al said nothing, just slipped into enough gear to climb out of the sarcophagus with modesty, then finished dressing. The Astara closed behind him. He noticed the two deceased guards, relieved Vee had dealt with them. "Got the disc?" he asked, leaning against the sarcophagus to pull on his boots.

Vee drew it from her side pocket and handed it over. Al pocketed the Glock and then approached the Astara with the disc.

"Who's that?" Vee inquired, eyeing the naked female on the gurney.

"Genesis, she's supposed to be the future of the Nephilim."

"No showstopper, that's for sure," Vee chuckled.

"What's he doing?" Electra demanded fiercely, peering down at Alice, infuriated by how effortlessly Vee had neutralised the two guards. "Get your men down there before they escape through the vortex!"

The ruse had succeeded. Alice had foreseen that if he had been carrying the Velodium disc, the Nephilim would have seized it, so the plan was for Vee to trail him with it. Now, within an incredibly limited time, he had to figure out how to use the device.

"Where do I put this thing?" Alice grumbled.

"The Professor said you'd instinctively know … like being on autopilot. You alright, mate? You look a bit off."

Al searched for the transformation pea embedded in his wrist but couldn't find it. "That's weird," he mumbled, puzzled. He decided to simply close his eyes, aim the disc at the Astara, and hope for divine intervention to guide his hand.

Walker, leading a squad of heavily armed Nephilim, hastened along the corridor, determined to redeem his embarrassing defeat in Stockholm.

Vee heard the approaching heavy footsteps and braced for a fight. "Al, the troops are coming, hurry up."

Alice ignored her. Guided by a will beyond his own, he explored the facade of the metal casket with his fingertips, finding a wafer-thin slot at the base of the front. "Yes!" he whispered to himself, then opened his eyes, astonished to have achieved his goal. The disc fit perfectly into the slot. Then … nothing happened. He recalled the sequence, straightening up to examine the myriad hieroglyphic reliefs adorning the lid and sides. Unable to decipher the ancient Sumerian cuneiform script or associated symbols, he once again relied on his intuition, extending his index finger to guide him.

This time, with his eyes open, Al mapped his finger across the case like a blind person reading Braille. It halted at a story-like depiction and pressed on a god-like character with wings on his back wearing a pointy hat. Under the character's feet was a half-man, also adorned with a pointy hat, holding a sword. Al pressed the sword. Each figure he pressed and released glowed yellow and remained illuminated. Next, above the winged character, he pressed a bird descending from the sky with smoke trailing behind it. His finger then hovered over a man wearing a pointed hat like the others, but this one had two faces, one on the front and one on the back of his head. Below him, six fish swam upwards from the ground towards him, three from the front and three from the back. Alice instinctively knew that selecting two of these fish would complete the sequence. He chose one fish, and it glowed. He was about to select the final fish when Walker's voice interrupted him.

Electra, Rykor, and three Nephilim council members watched intently as Walker and his squad burst into the room below and halted.

Rykor confronted Electra and urgently warned, "Black Alice must not be killed!"

Electra rolled her eyes and then commanded, "Freeze what you are doing right now, Alice, or your sister is dead. Drop your gun."

Al slowly turned his head to look at Walker. Backed up by half a dozen guards, Walker aimed his gun at Vee. Outnumbered, Vee dropped her gun and raised her hands. Walker quickly apprehended her, pressing his gun to her head.

Thinking quickly, Alice aimed his Glock at Genesis.

"Hold your fire!" Rykor shouted. He was adamant about not allowing Genesis to be harmed.

"Drop your gun, Alice, or I'll pull the trigger!" Walker demanded.

"Are you willing to risk the life of Genesis, the mother of the Nephilim?" Alice challenged, loud enough for Rykor to hear clearly. "What's your deal, dude? They must be paying you a fortune for this gig ... how come you're on the side of the bad guys?"

"Good and bad are just perspectives. I'm not here to pass judgment. You're outnumbered, Alice ... put down the gun."

Out of the corner of his eye, Al noticed the icons he had activated on the Astara were flashing, signalling that time was running out to make the final selection.

"Stand down, Walker, that is an order!" Rykor yelled, and the squad of six Nephilim immediately swung their guns towards the Brit.

"He only takes orders from me, Rykor. Kill her," Electra commanded.

"Oh, I don't think he'll do that; now who's outnumbered, huh?" Al taunted, moving closer to Genesis and pressing the barrel of his gun against her forehead.

Seizing the opportunity, Vee pulled a knife from her belt and plunged it into Walker's thigh, dodging to avoid being shot. The pain caused Walker to release her, and she leapt aside, leaving Al as a clear target. Alice swung his Glock at Walker. The Nephilim still had their guns trained on Walker. Vee quickly retrieved her pistol from the floor and aimed it at Walker.

"Seems we've got you covered, old boy. Drop it!" Al demanded.

Walker looked up, seeking a sign from Electra. Instead, Rykor spoke up. "Black Alice, if you allow us to take a blood sample, we will release the three of you and cease hostilities."

The proposal enraged Electra. She snarled at the Nephilim leader, "That was not the agreement, Rykor!"

Alice, using only his eyes, subtly signalled to Vee to keep her gun aimed at Walker. She complied.

"I'll give you what you want," Al called to Rykor. "But first, as a show of good faith, order Walker to drop his gun and stand down."

Electra shot Rykor a menacing look, which he ignored. The objective was more important than his promise to her. "Electra, give Walker the order," Rykor stated firmly.

She knew Rykor and his allies could overpower her if he commanded, leaving her with a significant decision. Whispering so the others below couldn't hear, she said, "Only if you agree to hand over Black Alice to me as soon as you have what you need."

Unbeknownst to Electra, Alice was using his enhanced hearing to eavesdrop on her scheming.

"Agreed," Rykor committed. He leaned over the balcony and called out, "Do you agree, Black Alice?"

"Yeah, I agree," he shouted back, "you have a deal."

Electra, satisfied, after a brief pause, commanded, "Stand down, Walker!"

Walker, acknowledging defeat, slowly raised one hand in surrender, carefully placed his pistol on the floor, and stepped back.

The Nephilim guards parted to let an automaton through.

Attached to Genesis was something akin to an IV line. The automaton positioned itself beside her gurney, extending an articulated arm with a pincer to grasp the IV line, then connected it to a port on its arm. A second arm, holding a needle-free syringe, extended towards Alice.

Al shuffled backwards, edging closer to the Astara, with the automaton following, stretching the IV line to its limit.

Vee, still wary, kept her pistol trained on Walker.

Electra, the Nephilim, and Aris watched the automaton intently. It was a pivotal moment for the Nephilim. Using nuclear biology, the automaton was programmed to extract five hundred millilitres of blood from Alice, which would be processed internally. It would use magnetic beads coated with a silica matrix to isolate the DNA nucleotides, removing proteins, other contaminants, and RNA from Alice's blood. After years of experimentation, the Nephilim had created Genesis—a being devoid of DNA, a blank slate. They had perfected a method to transfuse new DNA into Genesis and animate it. Infused with Alice's genetically altered DNA, Genesis was expected to become immortal and capable of reproduction, an ability the Nephilim lacked. Without Genesis, the Nephilim faced extinction.

Al caught a glimpse of the still blinking hieroglyphs he had illuminated on the Astara. The time had come. "Now!" he shouted sharply to Vee. She immediately reopened the micro-vortex through which she had arrived, instantly freezing everyone except herself, Alice, Walker, and Electra.

With the automaton stalled, Al reached out to the Astara, and, shooting Electra a dark, bitter stare, pressed the last fish.

Vee brushed her bangs from her eyes to peer at Alice.

"Go!" he urged her.

"Are you coming?" she called in haste. "I won't leave without you."

"Devachan," he replied, then with a wave added, "Chaa!"

A sudden surge of sorrow overcame Vee, causing a tear to roll down her cheek. She wiped it away, puzzled by his meaning, and thought, 'Chaa' usually means he's leaving? He's not coming with me. She tried again, "Al, come on … let's go!"

Electra, in a hysterical tone, shouted at Walker, "Stop them quickly!"

Realising they were about to escape through the wormhole, Walker dived for his gun.

The last fish Alice had illuminated on the Astara was now flashing in sync with the other motifs. The ground began to tremble as if in an earthquake. Vee, still staring at Alice, both perplexed and exasperated, noticed the sequence he had activated on the Astara suddenly change to red. With a shrug of her thin shoulders, trusting he would follow now that he had initiated the sequence, she backed towards the vortex. Just before stepping into it, gun still aimed at Walker, she caught a nod from Al. Taking it as confirmation he would follow, she stepped into the vortex.

CHAPTER 35
WAKE

ALICE SENSED an unnatural stillness, akin to the calm following a violent thunderstorm. It felt as though he was encapsulated in a bubble while everything else around him quaked.

Electra perceived it too. She raised an eyebrow, and then the realisation dawned on her when Vee vanished through the vortex. In a moment of impending defeat, En-Lil assumed complete control over Electra.

Time snapped back to its normal pace.

With his pant leg soaked in blood from the stab wound, Walker swung his pistol towards Alice.

Vee had been waiting in the Kairos control room for Alice for over an hour. Her growing distress became so intense that Christina had to work diligently to calm her. Vee pleaded to be sent back through Kairos to find her brother.

Later, as Vee recounted the events and the loss of her brother to the OTT members, she broke down. Seated around the board table, everyone was left speechless by the news, with only Hope actively attempting to make scientific sense of it.

"Devachan," Hope began, reading from her iPad. "The place of the gods. Devachan is a compound word: the Sanskrit 'deva' meaning gods, and the Tibetan word 'chan' for possession. It is considered the dwelling of the gods according to the original teachings of Theosophy as formulated by H. P. Blavatsky. It's where most souls go after death, where desires are gratified, akin to the Christian concept of heaven. However, Devachan is a temporary, intermediate state before the soul's eventual rebirth into the physical world. Essentially, Devachan is the astral plane. It appears Alice may have ascended."

Secta, agitated, began pacing the floor.

"Please stop pacing, Secta, it's quite distracting," Vee scolded, clearly aggrieved.

Unaware of his disturbing behaviour, Secta resumed his seat and awkwardly said, "Okay, so are we discussing metaphysics here?"

"Yes, I suppose we are," Hope agreed.

"Not good enough," Mal interjected, sceptical of the explanation. "What did he tell you, Professor, before he went through Kairos to Kor?"

"Oh yes, he mentioned something about becoming time," the Professor recalled. "I didn't fully grasp his meaning at the moment, but—" he trailed off.

Mal surveyed the room. "So, how do we interpret that?"

"Perhaps he knew the immortalisation process would enable him to traverse dimensions freely, like the immortals of the Greek pantheon," Christina speculated.

"Yes, but that's just mythology, isn't it—" Luna began, before Secta abruptly interrupted.

"Ha! You'd be surprised how often myths turn out to be true."

"Do you think he is dead?" Karzoff asked, a question that cast a shadow of gloom over the group. After a moment of reflective silence, they each tentatively murmured a hesitant no.

"I believe he'll turn up," Mal said optimistically. "You know Al ... he always appears when you least expect it."

"Yes, that's Alice, alright," Karzoff agreed, chuckling fondly, realising his question had struck a nerve.

"So, if the Nephilim and Electra, or rather En-Lil, are gone, does that mean our quest is over?" Viktoria wondered aloud.

"That's for Vee to decide when she goes back for Turk," the Professor responded.

Taking a deep breath, Vee composed herself. "It's all conjecture, isn't it? I didn't see what happened with the Astara ... I need to talk to Aris. If he survived, he was on the mezzanine and would have seen me leave. He probably saw what happened to Al," she said determinedly.

"And the others? What about Walker? He's human; the fusion wave wouldn't have affected him," Secta pointed out.

"The sooner I go back to find out, the better," Vee concluded.

"Pardon my ignorance, but hadn't Aris defected to the Nephilim?" Luna asked sceptically.

The clean-up and reconstruction of Stockholm represented an enormous undertaking. Most of the buildings and infrastructure had been devastated in the battle. Amidst the ongoing reconstruction efforts, Turk noticed everyone on the wharf suddenly freeze. He instinctively understood why, and his suspicion was confirmed when Vee emerged from the vortex. She rushed over and embraced him.

"Turk, so good to see you ... it feels like forever, but—"

"Yes, it's only been a day, I know. So, what happened on Atlan?" he inquired.

As the population of the float resumed their activities, oblivious to their brief pause, Vale noticed Turk conversing with Vee and approached them.

"Vee! It is amazing how you people just appear out of thin air. So good to see you," he said, beaming a big smile and embracing her.

Surveying the surrounding devastation, Vee's eyes fell upon the rows of shrouded bodies at the wharf's edge. Her recounting of the suspected demise of the Nephilim and Electra, following Alice's use of the Astara, elicited mixed emotions. Vale was relieved at the

Nephilim's end but felt the loss of Alice was a heavy price to pay. Cyrena joined them during Vee's explanation, equally saddened by the news.

"I should inform Inanna," Vale said solemnly. "She has been anxiously waiting for news about Alice." No sooner had he spoken than Inanna emerged from her hub, saw Vee, and hurried over excitedly. Her enthusiasm faded as she realised Alice wasn't with them, and she asked with unease, "Is Alice following?"

Vale gently placed a comforting arm around her shoulders and began to walk her back to her hub, sharing the unfortunate news. The others watched as Inanna broke down and retreated into her hub in tears.

"I need to find Aris. Have you heard anything about him, Cyrena?" Vee inquired.

"No, nothing," Cyrena replied.

When Walker arrived in the Aquila event room, he was greeted by Adamski, Honor, and Ursula. He quickly found himself in a high-security debriefing session, which also included Dr Li, Regina Fych and a newly appointed Gorrick replacement from the Beijing office.

Walker recounted his experience after regaining consciousness from being knocked out by Alice: he discovered all of the Nephilim and Electra dead, with Alice and the Astara nowhere to be found.

"The hive sensed En-Lil becoming inert the moment it happened, confirming one thing. Black Alice must have activated a powerful weapon, exterminating the entire Nephilim species," Gorrick deduced.

"A fusion reaction, possibly. En-Lil had suspected the Astara's capability for such, but it was never verified," Adamski suggested.

"It must have been that to disable the positronic brain of AIs," Ursula speculated.

"Why would Electra be affected by that?" Honor inquired.

"Electra was fitted with a positronic brain," Ursula clarified. "But it shouldn't have impacted En-Lil."

"I'd argue it would, Dr Mennis," Gorrick interjected, his tone reminiscent of Alfred Hitchcock. "En-Lil is also artificial intelligence."

This revelation was surprising. They knew En-Lil was an alien but had not suspected him to be AI.

"Commander Walker, you mentioned Black Alice and the Astara vanished without trace?" Gorrick pressed.

"That's correct, sir."

Gorrick pondered, then asked, "Could he have escaped through the vortex as well?"

"But what about the Astara?" Adamski interjected.

"And what of the prisoner Aris? Do you think he might have seen what transpired while you were unconscious?" Gorrick continued.

"When I awoke, I approached one of the guards and lifted his visor. His dead gaze was fixed, with a greenish ichor seeping from his orifices. All the Nephilim were dead; there was no sign of Black Alice or the Astara. It appeared whatever he triggered killed them all. My assumption was he followed his sister into the vortex with the Astara, as you suggested. Then I saw Electra on the floor. I went over to her. The light had gone from her eyes … she was dead. Upstairs, I found Rykor, the Nephilim leader, and the council members, all dead. I caught a fleeting glimpse of what I think was Aris escaping. I didn't pursue him, deeming him valueless. Shortly after, the wormhole reopened for my return."

"You were extremely fortunate," Honor remarked, a hint of a smile on her face. "Had it not been for Gorrick's alert to the hive sensing a catastrophe, we wouldn't have located you to send the wormhole. You owe Gorrick and Adamski your thanks."

"We must track down the Treen, Aris, to gain a clearer understanding of our supreme master En-Lil's fate and the whereabouts of the Astara," Gorrick commanded.

In a hastily constructed Great Hall, Odin raised a tankard of ale in toast. "All of Stockholm, stand and raise your flasks in gratitude to our friends Vee, Turk, Cyrena, and Black Alice, who selflessly risked their lives for our salvation. We salute you!"

An unexpected voice suddenly interrupted, "Quick, outside!" A young boy's frantic cry cut through the celebration. Vale leapt up, leading the group outside.

At dusk, the young boy waited for them, pointing skyward. Something immense was approaching in the distance. The crowd spilled out of the makeshift building, all eyes fixed on the sky.

"What is that?" Vee asked, standing next to Vale.

Cyrena gasped in recognition. "A Ragon ... Aris! It is my son, Aris!"

The colossal creature gracefully landed on the war-torn wharf, tucking its front legs underneath as Aris dismounted and slid down onto the wharf. Cyrena rushed over, enveloping him in an embrace.

They ushered Aris into the Hall to hear his account.

Inside, while the celebrations continued, the council and guests eagerly awaited Aris's story.

"Alice devised the plan for my defection to the Nephilim. The goal was to prompt them to ready the Astara for his arrival, knowing its significance to their genetic experiment. My role was to provide Alice the chance to activate the fusion reaction, a tactic he had learned in his time. Everything unfolded as planned," Aris began.

Vee, unable to contain her curiosity, interjected, "Did you see what happened to Alice?"

"Yes, he set the sequence on the Astara ... I watched you go, Vee, in through the whirlwind to disappear. Then, all hell broke loose, quaking ... a tornado. During all of that, a strange shadowy thing came out of the Astara and enshrouded Alice ... he seemed to be able to control it and used it to snare Walker who was trying to shoot him. Alice hurled the shadow that was like the root of a tree out ... it wrapped around Walker and dragged him towards him. When Walker was close enough, Alice threw a powerful punch that knocked him out.

Then he turned his attention to Electra who was at the balcony screaming at Walker to get up. The Nephilim seemed under the influence of something that caused them to be latent.

"Then, Alice sent the shadow after Electra. It coiled around her and lifted her off the balcony down to him. Then the shockwave hit hard and all of the Nephilim were struck down at once. It was chaotic; everything was shaking. I glanced at Rykor and the other Nephilim dead on the floor for just a moment … and then realised I could make an escape. When I looked back up, Alice and the Astara had vanished into thin air."

"Did you catch any of Alice's words?" Vee asked.

Aris pondered, then replied, "Only 'Devachan'."

Their attention turned to Vee for clarification. "Devachan, the place of the gods," she explained.

"Yes, I remember it from the old religion, from Apollo's time. It signifies the dwelling of the gods," Aris added.

Vee accessed more information from her implant database. "It's an idealised continuation of the recently departed terrestrial life, a place for retributive adjustment and reward for unmerited wrongs and sufferings undergone."

Turk, turning to Cyrena, asked, "In your ancient religion, can one return from this place?"

"Devachan is a stage for the soul to advance, preparing for the next incarnation," Cyrena explained.

Turk found the explanation too mystical, leaving him none the wiser.

CHAPTER 36
RETROCOGNITION

THE COURTROOM IS unusual. Standing in the witness stand, Vee is staring at the magistrate, wondering how he got the job and why he's wearing a crown and has his back to her. Then she casts her eyes at the jury—it's a band—the Black Alice band, with Blue on drums, Ratsso on bass, and Slut on guitar.

"What is this?" she mumbles to herself, perplexed.

Just then, the magistrate turns around, frowning. Instantly, she recognises him and groans, "Gorrick!"

Out of nowhere, a barrister materialises in front of her at the bar table, wearing a white peruke and black robes. When she pivots and glares at Vee, it is with an unmistakable face.

"Honor?" Vee erupts. "I haven't got a hope here ... I protest, this is a Zen set-up!"

Honor's lips curve into a sardonic smile as she dramatically declares, "I summon the plaintiff."

Vee hears laughter from behind her and turns to see the public gallery is comprised of Gorrick clones.

When she turns back to the magistrate, a woman has materialised in front of the Judge's bench. Electra turns, smiles, and draws her tongue across her black-painted lips.

"Lecherous murderer!" Vee hisses through gritted teeth. "Where is my brother?" The band launches into the intro of a song she recognises; she even recalls Alice writing some of the lyrics at her apartment.

Honor rises to her feet sharply and barks, "Let Black Alice answer vicariously."

"Proceed," the magistrate instructs.

Beside Electra, in front of the magistrate's bench, a holographic image of Alice, clad in his iconic stage leathers, materialises and begins to sing with the band.

> "I'm a voice in the dark
> And I call out to you
> But it's such a lonely sound
>
> I'm a king in the rain
> I'm lost down and blue
> A king without a crown
>
> Somewhere in my mind it's raining
> Washing out all that's true
> Yes, somewhere in my mind it's raining
> Somewhere in my mind, there's you."

Al, performing in his signature animated style, points and leers at Electra, seemingly directing his performance to Vee. Despite being a hologram, he appears acutely aware of his surroundings, though his image is marred by intermittent digital interference, resembling a poor signal. The lyrics of the song eerily relate to Vee's understanding of his presence in this bizarre place: Devachan.

As Slut launches into a guitar solo, Al's performance intensifies. He directs his leering gaze at the magistrate, then prowls towards Electra and Honor, making full use of his courtroom stage. The solo finishes, and Al turns to face Vee, singing the middle eight directly to her.

"Time and again I hear fate calling me
Like lions in the den
I need to pick up the pieces and then
Start all over again, Start again."

Al plays up to the band and the gallery in the next verse.

"I walk in dark dreams
Through fields of the lost
There's nothing left to find."

He moves aggressively and gets in Electra's face ... she backs off,
intimidated by him.

"There are voices inside
There's no place to hide
They've got me flying blind."

He turns sharply and faces Vee, stretches out his arms and sings
the chorus.

"Somewhere in my mind it's raining
Washing out all that's true
Yes, somewhere in my mind it's raining
Somewhere in my mind, there's you."

While Slut plays a powerful solo, Alice prowls the floor like an
agitated cat. When the solo finishes, Al sings the choruses out.

"Yes, somewhere in my mind it's raining
Washing out all that's true
Yes, somewhere in my mind it's raining
Somewhere in my mind, there's you."

Al dissolves, leaving his voice resonating within the cavernous room. Honor is facetiously slow-hand clapping.

In a burst of anger, Vee shouts, "I demand a replay of what happened to Alice, show me!"

The magistrate, addressing the entire courtroom, commands, "Replay the event in question from the mycelium web."

From the spot where Alice's hologram had vanished, a gurney materialises bearing the body of Genesis. To Vee's horror, Genesis sits up abruptly, moving robotically with tubes still attached to her body, and climbs off the gurney to face her and the gallery. Genesis' eyes snap open wide—they are frighteningly black with no whites, she wears a blank expression on her otherworldly face. Her face is blank, devoid of eyebrows and hair, and her skin is a sickly pallor. The band starts up a strange Black Alice song, strange because it's a rock jazz song.

Alice reappears beside Genesis, now dramatically altered in appearance, dressed in a French pantomime outfit reminiscent of Marcel Marceau.

Genesis, expressionless, begins to dance like a disjointed marionette to the instrumental intro of the song. Alongside her, Alice sings, his actions comically exaggerated.

"When I first saw you, sitting there
My heart skipped a beat
And when I burst across the dancefloor
I had wings on my feet

What to say
I wasn't sure
Hey, have I seen you before?
Say no more, say no more
Mon amour, mon amour

Let me kiss your lips
We'll take our kicks
Talking the mumbo jumbo
Talking the mumbo jumbo
Dancing the terrible tango."

In the solo section of the song, Alice takes Genesis in his arms, and they perform a tango. As the solo concludes, the music stops abruptly, and Alice dissolves like dissipating video noise. Genesis halts her dance, opens her arms as if about to present something, and morphs into Alice. This time, he appears as Vee last remembered him, standing beside the Astara.

Walker materialises, gun aimed at Alice. The scene transforms from a comical pantomime into a realistic replay of the events Vee hadn't witnessed.

A strange black tubular shadow spirals out from the Astara, snaking around Alice's body. Alice, steeling himself, walks closer to the balcony, arms raised. Electra, resolute and glaring, stands on the mezzanine above him.

The ground begins to tremble like an earth tremor. Walker struggles to maintain his footing and can't steady his aim at Alice. The shadow tendrils extend along Alice's arms and slither upwards towards Electra. On reaching her, they quickly coil around her body, lifting her, fighting and protesting, into the air and over the balcony railing.

Struggling for balance, Walker inches closer to Alice, gun arm extended, trying desperately to steady it.

Mid-air, entangled in the tendril's grip, Electra screams at Walker, "Shoot! Shoot!"

While manipulating the tentacle ensnaring Electra, Alice lowers his other arm and points a threatening finger at Walker. A tendril unfurls from his fingertips, wrapping around Walker's gun arm. Alice clenches his hand into a fist, and the tendril tightens, forcing Walker to drop his gun.

With a sharp motion, Alice retracts the tendril like a rope, dragging Walker towards him. As Walker fights the constricting coils, he is drawn close enough for Alice to unleash a powerful punch, striking Walker's face. Alice then releases the shadow, and Walker collapses to the deck, out cold.

Al turns his attention to Electra, bound tightly by the shadow tendril, struggling just feet away from him.

Suddenly, a violent whirlwind erupts from the Astara. Although it has no effect on Alice, it wildly tosses Electra's hair and clothing. Items not secured are caught in the supernatural tornado, swirling wildly around the room.

In a voice uncharacteristic of him, Alice confronts Electra. "You, En-Lil, committed the fatal folly of letting your love for yourself and for evil overshadow empathy towards all other beings ... and for that, you will now pay."

A deep, malevolent voice, as powerful as Alice's, emanates from Electra, her face contorted in exasperation. "You cannot defeat me ... I am—"

Before En-Lil can finish, the tornado abruptly stops, and an eerie silence envelops the room.

The illuminated icons on the Astara that Alice had activated cease flashing. A loud click resounds, followed by a massive fusion shockwave erupting from the Astara. It ripples through the air, causing the atmosphere to vibrate intensely. The Nephilim on the balcony collapse, lifeless. Electra's mouth gapes unnaturally wide, her eyes filled with terror, as she emits an unearthly scream ... then she freezes, statue-like, mouth agape. A strange orb of bright light emerges from her open mouth, hovering in the air between her and Alice.

"You've no host now but me!" Alice growls, his voice deep and demonic.

Electra crumbles to the floor. The shadow tendrils withdraw into the Astara like slippery eels. The floating energy ball hurtles towards Alice and enters his body, sending him reeling backward as if struck by an phantom fist. He quickly recovers and moves with astonishing speed to open the Astara's lid, climbing inside. The lid closes, and the

Astara vanishes silently into thin air.

Vee sits up in bed, gasping for air. Covered in sweat, her eyes wide with shock, every nerve tingling, she realises she has awoken from more than just a dream … it was a vision of retrocognition.

Later, at breakfast in the Great Hall, Vee chose not to mention her vision. True to her nature, she needed time to process it internally and make sense of it.

Odin stood, commanding everyone's attention with ease. "This morn brings a day of reckoning for every Korman. Our friends from Earth have restored our ancestral home, and now we face a crucial decision: whether to stay and rebuild Stockholm or return to Atlan." His words elicited a mix of murmurs, some reflecting insecurity, others enthusiasm. It was a monumental decision. "Those in favour of returning to Atlan, please stand."

A tense silence enveloped the room as the citizens deliberated. Then, gradually, one by one, they rose to their feet.

Vale, teary-eyed yet grinning, exchanged meaningful looks with Vee and Turk. Both Earthlings felt the weight of this historic moment.

Soon, the only ones remaining seated were Vee, Turk, Cyrena, and Aris. However, swept up in the emotion, they too eventually stood.

With tears in his wise old eyes, Odin announced, "It is unanimous … we go home!" The room erupted into thunderous cheers. Amidst the excitement of muttering, handshakes, and back-patting, everyone eventually settled back into their seats, except Odin.

"We owe not only our friends from Earth a great debt of gratitude but also our cousins, the Treen," Odin continued. "I extend to them an invitation to join us at Atlan, as in the days of Apollo. What say you, Queen Cyrena and Prince Aris?"

Cyrena stood up. "We are grateful to Chief Odin for this generous offer. We, too, owe a debt to the Earthlings for their bravery on Kor. I will convey your proposal to the Treen council. Rest assured, we look forward to reviving the great days of cohabitation, the days of Apollo." Her words were met with a resounding round of applause from the assembly.

Afterwards, they gathered on the wharf to bid farewell to Cyrena and Aris. It was an emotional parting, with Aris and Cyrena aware that Vee and Turk would soon journey back to their world, unlikely to ever return to Kor.

After mounting the Ragon, a few powerful wing flaps sent them soaring into the sky, heading towards their home on the far side of Atlan.

Surveying the desolation of Stockholm, Vee's gaze fell on Inanna, sitting alone at the edge of the wharf, her feet dipped in the water. Vee sat down beside her, removed her boots and socks, and rolled up her dungarees to paddle in the warm water.

"Don't be sad, Ina. I know my brother … he will return to us," Vee assured her.

"Even if he returns to his home, Vee, the distance between our worlds is so vast," Inanna replied, a tear trickling down her cheek.

Vee wrapped a consoling arm around her and said warmly, "If it helps, I promise to ensure he returns to you … but remember, his first duty is to his obligations."

With more tears welling up, Ina responded softly, "I understand, thank you, Vee."

Suddenly, a large shadow loomed over them. Looking up, they saw Turk, who said ruefully, "The time has come for us to leave, Vee."

Saying goodbye to Vale, Odin, and Ina was sombre for both Vee and Turk. They had been through formidable challenges together.

"I hope King Kraken continues to protect you; our victory wouldn't have been possible without him," Turk remarked, offering a supportive smile.

Vale returned a broad, respectful grin and warmly said, "The same can be said of you, my friend … I only wish we could bid farewell to Alice as well."

Odin inquired, "Will you search for him once you return to Earth?"

"It's our top priority," Vee confirmed confidently. With a press of a small remote, the vortex opened. As it did, the people of Stockholm froze. Turk and Vee cast one last lingering look at them all, then stepped through the vortex.

Turk and Vee were hailed as heroes upon their return to the Kairos event room. However, the celebratory mood shifted during the boardroom debriefing when Vee revealed that Aris couldn't provide further insight into Alice's disappearance.

Vee meticulously recounted her dream, capturing the undivided attention of everyone in the room. After she finished, Secta was the first to respond.

"Retrocognition … extrasensory perception of past events. That wasn't just a dream, Vee; it was Alice conveying facts to you. Your mind set it in a courtroom as a metaphor for judging the quest's outcome. The only way for Alice to defeat En-Lil once and for all was to become the host himself and then take him into the Astara, thereby vanishing from our dimension and time."

"Yes, Secta, that makes sense, but it also implies we've lost Alice to time," Vee countered.

"He said he would become time," the Professor reminded the group.

"Wait," interjected Hope. "What about the magistrate's decree for a replay of the events from the mycelium web?"

"Mycelium refers to an Earth-based bacterial colony connecting underground plant life," the Professor explained.

"A bio-web … So, could there be a universal equivalent, threading through space and time?" Christina speculated.

"And could we use this 'web' to communicate with Alice?" Vee asked, her excitement evident.

"You've lost me," Mal confessed, scratching his head.

Karzoff sought to simplify the concept for Mal. "Think of it like using the Internet to check your email or social media. If we can access it, we might reach Alice. That is your idea, right, Vee?"

This time it was the Professor pacing the floor, he paused, faced the group, and had an epiphany. "Alice mentioned becoming time.

Maybe time isn't just the past, present, and future as we understand it. Perhaps it's all those elements simultaneously."

Secta, unable to contain his excitement, stood up. "You're onto something, Vic! The mycelium web could be the representation of time in space. If the Astara is the connector, and we can tap into this web, we should be able to find Alice!"

CHAPTER 37
PAYBACK

"**H**OW CAN WE PROCEED** without Alice?" Secta confided in the Professor as they strolled down the dimly lit corridor towards their respective labs.

"The resolve at the end of the debriefing lifted everyone's spirits, at least," the Professor noted.

"It did, Vic, but I worry that what Alice underwent might have been fatal," Secta admitted.

"Are you suggesting that trapping En-Lil within a host with no escape, and then letting the host die, was the only way to defeat him?" the Professor pondered.

"Perhaps," Secta acknowledged with a hint of regret.

For Secta and the Professor, this pragmatic logic made sense, but Vee refused to entertain such a notion. She was convinced that Alice had a master plan to defeat En-Lil, confident that dying wasn't part of his strategy.

Meanwhile, Vee, sitting at Café Epiphany with Turk, Christina, and Hope, was lost in thought.

"I'm going to miss this coffee," Turk remarked, sipping a hot vanilla latte.

"Aw, and I'm going to miss you, Dad. Can't you stay a wee bit longer?" Hope pleaded.

Turk reached across the table and took her hand. "I miss your mother ... besides, I'm getting a bit long in the tooth for all this stuff."

"Rubbish, you're not that old. Vee would attest to that after fighting beside you on Kor," Christina said.

Vee didn't respond, still lost in her thoughts.

"Vee? Knock, knock, are you there?" Hope inquired.

Snapping out of her reverie, Vee replied, "Oh, sorry ... what did you say?"

"We were arguing Turk isn't too old for time travel and that you'd be the first to corroborate that after the way he handled himself in the battle for Stockholm," Hope explained.

"One hundred percent," Vee confirmed.

Turk chuckled. "Yeah well, it doesn't matter, ladies, this old warhorse is in need of a spell to recuperate."

Blake entered the café looking for Vee and joined them at the table. "Hey guys. Glad to see you and Turk made it back in one piece. Still no sign of Alice?"

Unexpectedly, Vee jumped out of her seat and stormed out of the café.

Blake was surprised. "What the—? Was it something I said?"

They watched Vee through the window, stopping outside on the pavement, pulling her Glock, and crouching in a firing position. Blake's eyes opened wider, and he leaped out of his chair. "Bloody hell, what's she doing?" He quickly made for the door.

The pavement was crowded. Blake approached Vee and calmly said, "Vee, lower your weapon, there are pedestrians."

Vee slowly rose and lowered her Glock.

"What was it?" Blake asked, tentatively.

"I saw Walker. He's headed to the Zen building," Vee said.

Hope, Christina, and Turk joined them outside. Blake turned to them and said, "She saw Walker."

Turk questioned, "Thought he was left on Kor?"

"I don't know, but it was definitely him," Vee said, pulling out her phone and dialling. "Luna? It's Vee ... I just saw Walker on the street outside Café Epiphany. Can you check if there's been an event from Aquila in the last 48 hours? Okay, thanks, tap me back."

They returned to the café and resumed their seats.

"It was him for sure, no way I could mistake him," Vee admitted.

Turk snarled, "Wish I'd seen him—"

Vee's phone rang. "Yeah, uh-ha, okay. Thanks." She looked at Turk. "It was him all right. Luna has a report of incoming from Kor thirty hours ago, somehow Zen managed to pull him out."

"That puts a hold on me returning," Turk growled, savagely. "I've got a score to settle with that bastard."

After learning from Vee that Walker was back from Kor, Mal instructed Karzoff to launch Operation Shutdown, to bring Walker, his confederates, and his superiors at Zen to justice. It meant twenty-four-seven surveillance, and to that end, Karzoff and Viktoria had already hatched a plan given the full support of UNTT. In the aftermath of the successful outcome on Kor, Luna had pledged her and UNTT's full support to OTT initiatives. Together, they would initiate a global effort to sanction Zen Corporation from any further involvement in time travel, and for Zen to once and for all disable Aquila.

When a paid informant inside Oceana disclosed the details of Operation Shutdown to Honor, she wasted no time in informing Gorrick. Unwilling to succumb to the authority of Oceana or the UNTT, they quickly devised their countermeasures.

He traversed the sorry-looking floor, its carpet sticky underfoot from decades of spilled drinks. The pulsating rhythm of bass guitar and drum, hammering at one hundred and twenty beats per minute from the DJ's track, was a sharp annoyance. Pushing open the time-worn wooden door, he entered the men's room. The place reeked of urine and mothballs, the walls scrawled with graffiti. A whistling wind slipped through a shattered frosted windowpane above. In the dim light, he opted for the cleaner of the four urinals. As he relieved himself, the muffled thuds of music were briefly interrupted by the sound of shuffling feet. Three sharp kidney punches dropped him to his knees, then the lights went out.

In the cabin of a black SUV parked outside the Coogee Bay Pub, a large, square-jawed Zen agent sat behind the wheel with the engine running. He was waiting for his boss, who had gone to the bathroom. Their mission: to abduct an OTT operative named Wyetta Walker, known as Vee, a resident of the seaside suburb of Coogee. Only twenty minutes earlier, a surveillance drone had tracked her to her apartment near the pub, which was nearing closing time on this quiet midweek night.

The agent was startled when the driver's side window shattered, showering him with glass fragments. Before he could react, a Glock 20, the fourth-generation model, was thrust through the broken window, pressed hard against his temple. A voice with a slight German accent demanded, "Hands behind your head or you will lose it."

The passenger-side door opened, and another gun appeared, pointed at him. A woman was holding this one. The driver immediately complied with the command. Karzoff provided cover while Viktoria cuffed him. Two OTT agents helped Turk carry Commander Walker from the pub to the back seat of a waiting vehicle.

In the front passenger seat, Vee kept her gun trained on the unconscious Zen agent, flanked by the other two operatives, as Turk took the driver's seat. Karzoff leaned in through the driver's side window and remarked, "That went well ... Do you feel vindicated?"

"Almost," Turk replied, his dark eyes glinting with a fury that his smile couldn't conceal.

"Let's go," Vee said tersely, her mind clearly elsewhere. Turk understood that her primary concern was finding Alice, and he drove off.

"A bullet in his head would have been more vindicating," Turk muttered under his breath.

"I'll bet Zen will have their lawyers all over this by tomorrow, and the bastard will walk free," Vee spat bitterly.

"I'm no betting man, but that is a safe bet," Turk grumbled in agreement.

"What the hell is going on?" Gorrick demanded as he barged into Honor's office. "OTT has notified us that they've arrested Walker."

Honor wasn't entirely certain how to deal with this particular incarnation of Gorrick, whose aggression surpassed any previous versions she had encountered. Opting to remain composed, she responded dourly, "They always seem to be one step ahead of us, sir. What can I say?"

Gorrick flopped into a chair, pondering the situation. "If you want your man back, then we will need one of theirs for a trade."

Leaning forward in her chair, Honor eyed the enigmatic man across her desk. This challenge was right up her alley. "I'm confident that can be arranged. Leave it to me, sir," she asserted. Her experience in the art of abduction left her feeling sure of her ability to handle the situation.

A couple of hours later, Dr Cairn felt uneasy when she got into the rear seat of the town car that routinely took her to the Oceana Building every weekday, especially since it wasn't her regular driver.

"John not working today?" she inquired.

As the car pulled out and then made an unexpected stop, Luna grew worried and reached for her cellphone to make a distress call. Before she could reach Karzoff, however, both rear passenger doors swung open, and two large men pushed in, sandwiching her between them. One snatched the phone from her hand and tossed it out of the door. The car then sped off.

Karzoff, seeing a missed call from Luna, tried to call her back.

When it went to voicemail, he grew concerned. After a second unsuccessful attempt, suspecting something was amiss, he opened an app on his computer that tracked all Oceana vehicles. Noticing that Dr Cairn's car was off its usual route, he quickly triangulated her phone's location and found it stationary near her apartment. Concluding she had been abducted, he immediately contacted Viktoria.

In Secta's office, Secta, the Professor, Hope, Vee, and Turk were gathered in the lounge area.

"After disseminating all the facts, we've come to the conclusion that Alice won't be coming back," Secta announced sombrely. "It was the only logical way to defeat En-Lil."

Vee, taken aback, reacted strongly. "No, no... that's not his form. Never has been. I won't accept that."

Secta leaned forward, trying to be comforting, "Please listen to me, Vee. He sacrificed himself for us."

"I won't cop it!" Vee protested, putting her fingers in her ears. "He didn't have a messiah complex!"

The Professor, sensing her denial, tried a softer approach, "We're not suggesting he did, Vee ... he simply had no choice."

Vee removed her fingers from her ears, tears streaming down her face. "He's not dead ... he can't be ... not Alice, not Alice." She became increasingly upset. Turk moved to her side, sat on the arm of her chair, and comforted her as she wept.

The others exchanged looks of doubt.

"Rather than making rash statements, let's just give it some time," Vee argued emotionally. "We should carry on as usual but also continue exploring possibilities ... not just give up."

"Such as what, Vee?" Secta asked.

Gathering her emotions and turning them into anger, Vee glared at him. "I won't give up on him, Secta ... I will find a way to get my brother back ... I promise all of you."

"We are with you, Vee; if anyone has the resilience to survive, it's Al," Turk reassured her.

"Look, we all admire your loyalty to him ... but the science suggests, as the host, Alice had to die to kill En-Lil ... unless he's in some kind of stasis inside the Astara," Secta explained.

"That would be my rationale," the Professor interjected.

After a moment of silence, Vee stood up. "They're just theories. Contacting En-Ki seems like the obvious next step."

Secta, rubbing his hand across his lab coat, nodded. "You're right, Vee, that is the obvious next step. He would know ... maybe even how to access the mycelium web. Vic, did En-Ki's data leave a digital footprint?"

"Yes, I expect so," Vic replied.

"So, we could contact him?" Vee asked, hopeful.

Hope proposed, "Christina will be able to answer that for us, surely."

It was feasible. For Vee, it was the ray of light she needed ... at least it was positive.

Gorrick's face betrayed no hint of emotion, not the slightest flicker of triumph, nor even satisfaction, from the news delivered by Honor, leaving her feeling cold. Her indignation was exemplified by her body language as she sat in the lounge chair in Gorrick's office. She crossed her legs, folded her arms, and pursed her lips.

Gorrick ordered, "Miss Fych, send in Dr Mennis and Professor Adamski."

Honor observed the shapely Ursula crossing the bridge followed by Adamski. Gorrick gestured for them to sit.

"Dr Mennis, what is the status of a replacement for Electra?"

"I have done better than that, sir; we are putting the finishing touches on six of them. I expect they will be operative within twenty-four hours."

Gorrick huffed a humourless chuckle.

Having sat silently, seething for a moment, Honor then asked, "Are they female or male?"

Adamski began to answer. "That is up to the programming—"

Mennis interjected. "They can morph into whatever human form we designate. I expect at your discretion, sir."

Gorrick nodded his approval.

Honor raised a covetous eyebrow, disconcerted by the manner in which Ursula was ingratiating herself with Gorrick. Petty jealousies were still rife among Zen executives.

Gorrick announced, "Professor Adamski, the UNTT has directed us to shut down Aquila and ordered its immediate dismantlement. They are sending inspectors tomorrow."

The stout man shook his head in disdain. He was fed up with having to rebuild his apparatus each time the UNTT mandated its shutdown.

"If we intend to continue with time travel, the time has come to relocate Aquila to a more secure location, one hidden from the prying eyes of UNTT and Oceana," the Russian declared.

"You took the words right out of my mouth, Professor. Six months ago, Zen purchased a remote, uninhabited island off the coast of Mindanao in the Philippines. It has now been removed from all maps, thanks to Zen's political influence. The island is a safe haven from typhoons, featuring an extinct volcano, beneath which lies an impressive subterranean cave system and fresh water aquifers. A state-of-the-art facility, powered by thermal energy from the volcano, has been completed. Crate up Aquila, Professor ... we will move there as soon as you are ready."

Ursula inquired, "Will my lab be relocating there as well, sir?"

"Yes, the entire operation will relocate ... this facility will be reduced to a skeleton staff. That will be all, except you, Honor."

"Sir, may I ask the name of the island?" Ursula requested, preparing to leave.

"Yes, Coda," Gorrick replied.

Once the others had left, Gorrick instructed Honor, "Oceana will know by now we have Dr Cairn; arrange the exchange with them for Commander Walker ... no mistakes."

CHAPTER 38
BUYING TIME

AN **EMERGENCY MEETING** of OTT was convened to discuss the abduction of Dr Cairn. Chairing it, Karzoff informed them, "I have received word from Zen that they are holding Dr Cairn and are prepared to trade her for Walker and the other Zen agent we are holding."

Mal was incensed and growled, "These bastards are nothing more than common criminals."

"It's time we dealt with them once and for all," Vee snarled, her intolerance heightened since the loss of her brother.

"Every time Zen's malevolence confronts us, the UN restricts our actions. Mal, surely Oceana can punish them for such a blatant violation of the law … Kidnapping is a capital offence, is it not?" Secta said vehemently.

"You're right, Secta, I've had enough of their antics as well. Karzoff, you have my full support to apprehend them," Mal declared emphatically.

"Won't that put Dr Cairn's life at risk? You know what they're capable of," Turk cautioned.

Hope interjected, "We need to thwart their efforts to create another Electra … it's the most dangerous AI yet, and it's likely they've further refined and enhanced the programming."

They considered the idea. She was correct; Zen was way ahead of them in the cybernetics race.

"Our challenge has always been Zen's extensive global network ... whatever we do here can be easily countered by one of their other chapters," Viktoria explained.

Turk stated firmly, "We need to focus on the immediate problem."

"I agree, Turk. Any suggestions?" Mal invited.

It was entirely out of character for the Professor to engage in politics, but his close relationship with Luna, along with a thorough distaste for Zen's underhanded tactics, was driving it. "First, Mal," he said angrily, "you need to inform UN Director Maralina Bostok that Luna has been abducted by Zen and that they have made demands ... and then ask how she would like you to act. That will undoubtedly produce an interesting response, but more importantly, it will expose Zen as a genuine threat to world security."

"Hear, hear," Secta echoed.

"Luna had a genetic marker for time travel; it's probable she's at Zen HQ. If we open a pinhole to her location—" Christina suggested.

"A pinhole?" Mal inquired.

"Apologies, I affectionately refer to a micro-wormhole as a 'pinhole' because of its minuscule size," Christina clarified.

"Remarkable, so it's virtually invisible?" Mal asked.

"Exactly," Secta affirmed.

"Then, once we've located her, you can send another pinhole for me to retrieve her through," Vee proposed strongly.

Gorrick didn't realise they had chosen the wrong person to kidnap. He stared unblinking at Luna, who was seated across from him in the lounge setting of his office, and said, "You are in the prime of your life. A brilliant scientist, you have taken on heavier responsibilities than your seniors. Now you place your career and your life at risk. Why?"

Her pulse quickened with indignation. "I risk my life for my work, striving to rid the world of tyrants like you and your accomplice."

His thin lips formed a terse smile. "Spoken like a true diplomat, Luna ... may I call you that?"

"No," she retorted defiantly.

Honor, revelling in the exchange, decided to interject. "The toothless tiger you represent won't be coming to save you. If I were you, I would be hoping they agree to our terms of exchange."

"There is no way you could be me, Honor. So much deceit and corruption compressed into one human being, I can't fathom how you live with yourself."

"Take her to Dr Li's labs ... she can be securely contained there overnight until the trade is confirmed," Gorrick commanded.

Mal lingered at the office, awaiting a call from Maralina Bostok in New York. She was scheduled to address the UN Security Council at 8 a.m. about the kidnapping, which was 10 p.m. Sydney time. It was nearly eleven, and his concern grew. His private cellphone rang, and he reclined in his comfy office chair, feet propped on the desk, to take the call.

"Hello?"

"Good morning, President Low ... but then again, it's evening there, isn't it?"

"Yes, Maralina, eleven p.m. So, how did it go?"

"As expected, the news was poorly received. In fact, several members were quite hostile. We all value Dr Cairn's work, and she shouldn't be subjected to such a threat. Moreover, Zen Corporation, as a global entity, should not stoop to tactics more befitting the Mafia."

"Agreed. Your preference on how to proceed?" Mal queried.

"Proceed with the exchange to ensure Dr Cairn's safety. The UN will be imposing sanctions on Zen Corporation later today—"

"Pardon the interruption, Maralina, but similar attempts have previously failed. Zen Corporation has violated our national laws—"

"Mal, I'm sure you realise Zen Corporation employs over seven hundred thousand staff globally and holds major strategic contracts worth billions with countries like the USA, Russia, Japan, India, and China. We must tread carefully ... there's a lot at stake."

Mal sat upright, his irritation with her placating tone evident.

Maralina continued, "I know it seems like the UN is succumbing to financial pressure, and you're right. So, under these circumstances, handle Zen Corporation in Oceana as you see fit and let me manage our end. Do you understand, Mal?" she suggested subtly.

Mal comprehended fully … her hands were tied, unlike his ability to act locally. "I completely understand, Maralina."

"Thank you, Mr President. I trust this is an acceptable resolution. Please inform me when Dr Cairn is safely recovered … any time, day or night."

It was done. As the Professor had proposed, the seed had been sown, the tables would now be turning at diplomatic levels against Zen. It would now only be a matter of time before sanctions would cripple them. Mal was confident from the conversation that Maralina was in his corner.

"Alice was seated at the prow of a small wooden rowboat, clad in a black hooded caftan. At the stern, a scrawny figure in a moth-eaten grey robe stood, gripping a long oar. Wild-eyed, his hair and beard glistened with perspiration, his ears pointed and demonic.

"The boat was gliding through a narrow stream … a mist enveloped the water, swirling as the bow cut through it. The scene was dark and gloomy, the creaking of the clinker boat and the rhythmic sculling sound echoing in the underground," Vee finished, before burying her face in her hands, visibly distressed.

Hope's fingers danced across her laptop keyboard, seeking answers.

Secta paced the floor of his lab, a mug of brewed coffee in hand. It was early morning, and all three were similarly armed.

"No, I don't think you're suffering from an overactive imagination, Vee. And it's not grief psychosis…" Secta began.

"The dream was a metaphor, Vee," Hope explained, looking over her laptop at Vee with the ceiling spotlights reflecting in her glasses. "The guy steering the boat was Charon, the ferryman of Hades, and they were on the river Styx … You were visualising Alice's ascension. So, if you translate it into hermetic theory for the higher self … it says here in the Corpus Hermeticum: the process of ascension or transcendence was accomplished through a philosophical self-discipline that consisted of discarding the influences of astral determinism on the body, its senses, and passions, through the achievement of an experiential sense of the mind's detachment from the body. Hermes advises that twelve irrational tormentors must be banished from the inner self. This process aims not just for physical immortality, but also the soul's immortality, achieved through a path of rebirth."

Vee peered slowly over her hands with a crinkled nose. "How about giving me that again in plain English, Hope."

Hope nodded. "Okay, the Astara made his physical being immortal but now he is going through making his soul immortal."

"So, he's not dead then?" Vee asked, wiping a tear from her cheek.

"Technically yes, but spiritually no," Secta replied gently, cautious not to exacerbate Vee's distress.

"You're a visionary, Vee, just like your brother," Hope encouraged, smiling. "It seems to be a family trait."

Internally, Vee was less certain of this 'gift'; the dream had felt more like a nightmare. It had disturbed her so deeply that she couldn't return to sleep after waking from it.

The phone rang. Secta answered and then hung up. "That was Christina; she's got the coordinates for Luna ready."

Vee sighed deeply.

"You sure you can handle this on your own, Vee?" Secta asked, concern evident in his voice. "Turk would be willing to go with you."

"I think two would be too many. No, I'll manage. I'll stop by the armoury, then meet you at Kairos."

Luna was tied to a chair in a clinical, white, featureless room, looking bored when a vortex opened. Through the observation window, she could see Dr Li, her assistant, and a guard frozen, and knew from experience she was about to be rescued.

Vee stepped out of the vortex outfitted in jungle-green army fatigues, a black beret, and brandishing an automatic pistol. To Luna, she looked like she meant business.

"Boy, am I glad to see you, Vee."

Vee pulled a knife from her belt and cut the nylon cable ties tethering Luna's wrists and ankles to the chair.

The freeze wore off. Luna noticed the guard glance through the window and reacted, "The guard!"

Vee straightened up and fired at the glass window. It shattered. Then she shot the guard twice. Dr Li dived for the guard's pistol on the floor.

Ruffled by the chaos, Luna shouted, "That's Dr Li!"

"I know," Vee snarled, "she builds cyborgs."

"Let's go!" Luna urged. But Vee was more interested in Dr Li. When the Chinese woman aimed the guard's pistol at her, Vee got away two quick shots before the doctor could pull the trigger. The first shot hit Dr Li in the shoulder and the second hit her right cheek and blew half her head off. Dr Li crumbled to the ground. Her assistant raised her shaking hands in surrender.

"Go!" Vee ordered, and Luna stepped into the vortex. Vee followed seconds later, leaving the carnage and the trembling assistant in her wake.

The very moment Luna and Vee were safely back in the control room, Oceana went into lockdown. Once Vee had explained what had happened, Secta called Mal and Karzoff. They knew there would be a reprisal.

Luna was rushed to Mal's office, where she spoke on the phone to Maralina Bostok.

Karzoff, Viktoria, and Turk discussed the finer details with Vee. The killing of Dr Li would be disastrous for Zen.

Luna had told them she had met a replacement Gorrick whose demeanour was cruel and cold-hearted. That meant they could be in for a fierce reprisal—he wouldn't be impressed by the failure of one of his first operation and the loss of Dr Li.

An hour later, a fine-looking, tall young woman dressed in black combat coveralls, a black cap, and carrying a shoulder bag casually entered the Oceana lobby. She stopped at the security check, pulled an Uzi-pro sub-machinegun from her shoulder bag, and then opened fire, killing six guards.

An alarm sounded.

Karzoff and Viktoria raced to the security control room in their office setup where an operator showed them the invader on screen. They watched her enter an elevator. The operator cut to the elevator interior CCTV.

Karzoff ordered urgently, "She selected level seven. Get a message to Secta. He's probably the target. This is the reprisal we were expecting. I will arrange back-up."

Secta was in his lab when the call came through from Viktoria. He immediately activated the wall monitor for the CCTV feed. It showed the invader in the elevator. They had a prearranged plan dubbed Code 7. Secta quickly phoned Christina in the control room.

Christina punched in the necessary data to set Kairos up for an automatic dispatch to a designated location. Once content it was programmed, she hightailed it out of the control room.

Turk and Vee were at the 7th-floor commissary having breakfast. As soon as they were advised, they rushed for the armoury on the same level to kit up.

The invader stepped out of the elevator into the corridor of Level 7.

Karzoff and the operator watched two guards confront the invader in the corridor. They opened fire, but the bullets had no effect on the target. They were gunned down.

Turk was looking up at the monitor in the armoury and snarled, "Has to be a cyborg. I'd know that look anywhere."

Hope was walking along the corridor unawares. As soon as she heard gunshots and footsteps, she stopped, frightened.

As Turk and Vee were leaving the armoury, Turk saw Hope on the monitor. "It's Hope, she's in the same corridor as the enemy. Quick."

Hope listened to footsteps rushing towards her. Then, from around a corner came Christina, who almost knocked her over.

Panting, out of breath, not from the running but panic, Christina said, "Quick, it's a code 7, we need to get to the service elevator." Hope followed her lead, and they took off back to where she had come.

Half a dozen agents arrived with Viktoria to meet Karzoff standing by the elevator. He issued orders.

In the control room, Secta was on the verge of entering the departure booth when he glanced at the monitor. To his alarm, he noticed the invader had halted at the control room door. Secta surmised it wasn't pursuing him; its likely objective was to destroy Kairos.

Aware that Turk and Vee were en route, he swiftly moved to the computer and composed a message for them, transmitting it to their implants: It's here to destroy Kairos.

The thunderous sound of the control room's pressurized door being torn from its hinges propelled Secta back towards the booth. The cyborg entered the control room and paused. Secta, with the booth door ajar, witnessed Kairos initiating its countdown.

"As soon as you dematerialise, I will destroy Kairos and you with it," the cyborg said, calmly unfurling her hand to display a golf ball-sized explosive device.

"You'll be destroying yourself as well," Secta retorted, buying time.

"I am impervious to any such explosion."

CHAPTER 39
VALE

SECTA SWIFTLY FLICKED the activation switch on the WASP concealed in his hip pocket. In a lightning-quick motion, he hurled it at the cyborg.

With astonishing agility, she caught it mid-air and crushed it in her black-gloved hand. Smirking triumphantly at her clenched fist, she snarled, "Nice try, Doctor."

Secta's fleeting glance at the computer monitor confirmed he had only three seconds before Kairos activated. Left with no alternative, he stepped into the booth and closed the door behind him.

Meanwhile, the cyborg activated the device in her hand, which began a countdown from ten, ticking towards detonation.

As the countdown on Kairos concluded, a vortex materialised in the control room. The cyborg, caught off guard, stared at the device in her open palm. Secta's move had been a clever deception; he never intended to dematerialise. Instead, he had utilised Alice's technique of a quick freeze.

Turk and Vee burst into the room. Secta, emerging from the booth, quickly attached a clock drive to the cyborg's neck. Together, they forcefully propelled her into the swirling vortex.

A vortex materialised in Dr Li's lab, instantaneously freezing the three agents who were engaged in a conversation with Honor and Dr Mennis about the assassination of their associate. Unlike the others, Honor and Ursula were not physically immobilised by the vortex's emergence but were mentally stunned by the abrupt appearance of the cyborg. Upon recognising the object in her open palm, they instinctively dived for cover. The device detonated.

The invasion had cost Oceana the lives of eight agents, but the catastrophe had been averted.

"The shield Christina devised did an excellent job of preventing them from opening a wormhole directly to Kairos. By causing the cyborg to fight its way to the 7th floor, we bought precious time to initiate Code 7 … otherwise, it would have easily destroyed its target. Which raises the point: what if they have more suicide bombers?" Karzoff questioned during the OTT executives' meeting in the security debriefing room adjacent to his office.

"An explosion at Zen HQ was reported … three dead, two wounded. They claimed it was a laboratory accident," Viktoria reported, her tone smug.

With a contented smile, Secta said, "I don't think they'll bother us again for a while. They've lost Dr Li, thanks to Vee, and that will put a massive dent in their cyborg development program."

Turk wasn't so sure. "I don't know about that, Secta; they still have Mennis."

"Yes, I suppose you're right," Secta agreed, well aware of Turk's experience in dealing with her.

Luna had been biting her tongue, unable to wait any longer to intercede. "I'm sorry, but I need to raise the issue of Vee's execution of the Zen guard and Dr Li. I believe it was totally unnecessary."

When it comes to aggravation, Vee, like her brother, was a true egalitarian. "What? So now we're at fault here! Typical. You've got to be kidding, lady … I saved your butt … they'd frigging kidnapped you … they sent a robot here that killed eight of ours, and you want to have a crack at me. You need your head read!"

Luna mumbled something unintelligible under her breath. But

Mal had pretty much worked out what it was.

He rose slowly from his chair and glared at Luna with disappointment written all over his face. His voice modulated flat as the scorekeeper of a tennis match, he said, "I think you need some time to reconsider your personal position on the moral compass employed here at OTT that you're questioning, Dr Cairn. If you still feel the same way when next we meet, I think UNTT will need to provide us with a substitute for your advisory position here. I value every individual's opinion at the table, but unfortunately, yours too often falls in favour of the opposition. Vee risked her life to save you. You should be showing her gratitude rather than questioning her morality."

A veil of silence blanketed the meeting. It was so unlike Mal to give someone a dressing down in front of their peers.

"Luna will be replaced in a matter of days ... and Mal is planning to announce Alice's disappearance on the National News tonight," Hope remarked, latching onto a seemingly trivial piece of gossip.

Christina swivelled her chair away from the Kairos console to face Hope, Turk, and Vee, and commented, "I think that will be a constructive move by UNTT."

"Provided the replacement isn't worse," Turk interjected.

"True. But it's still just a rumour," Hope added, her tone indifferent.

Vee was visibly shaken by the notion of Mal announcing Alice's disappearance, reacting as if struck by an unexpected blow. "I don't agree with it," she declared sharply.

"You shouldn't feel responsible for Luna losing her position, Vee. She had her issues—"

Vee interrupted Christina, "Not that, I mean Mal going public about Alice. He's only been missing a week, and Mal, his best friend, has already got him dead and buried."

Turk's expression shifted to a frown. "I don't think that's Mal's intention, Vee. As president, he has a duty to be transparent."

"Yeah, but why now? He could've waited—" Vee argued, her distress evident.

The door buzzer sounded. Christina glanced at the monitor and, seeing Secta, buzzed him in.

"I'd change that doorbell if I were you," Hope commented.

Secta entered. "They fixed the door quickly ... and a new doorbell's a great idea. You all set, Turk?"

Turk stretched and yawned, "Yep, finally, after months, I'll get a good night's sleep in my own bed."

Hope smiled, "Mum'll be glad to see you."

Noticing Vee's discontented expression, Secta joked, "Someone pinch your lunch money?"

"She's upset because Mal's announcing Al's disappearance on the evening news," Hope clarified.

"Oh, that's just a formality. Mal's trying to pre-empt any misinformation about Alice going missing with a story we devised ... nothing major," Secta explained casually.

Vee brightened slightly. "What's the story, then?"

Secta elaborated, "Just that we're looking for him because he's missing from a fishing trip up north."

"Alice ... fishing? I guess that'll do, although not for those who really know him," Vee said, managing a fragile smile as she wiped away a tear.

Secta shifted the conversation. "Life will be different back home without Zen and with everyone cured of Red Wheel, eh, Turk?"

"For sure. If you hear anything about Al or need to return to Kor, just..."

"Don't worry, mate, you'll be the first to know," Vee assured him.

Secta cracked, "Aren't you going to visit Walker in the slammer for a farewell?"

Turk grimaced, "More than unlikely."

"Say hi to Toeghan for me," Vee added.

The door buzzed again, and Mal and the Professor entered.

Mal grinned at Vee. "You'll be pleased to hear Dr Cairn is leaving this morning. UNTT's replacement is already en route."

"Sorry, Professor," Vee said, her face showing sympathy for his loss.

The Professor forced a smile. "I'll miss her company, Vee, but it was the right to cut her loose."

Christina signalled Turk that Kairos was ready.

"Speaking of cutting loose, it's time to make an exit. Bye, everyone."

It was an emotional moment. They all loved Turk and would miss him. Never strident or out of control, Hope suddenly burst into tears and threw her arms around her dad. Turk wasn't used to affection from her but responded with a warm hug. She almost disappeared inside his huge arms.

Vee's eyes brimmed with tears. "We're going to miss you, big guy."

"You know where I'll be if you need me."

After a handshake with each person, Turk entered the booth and disappeared within seconds, leaving a palpable void.

As they prepared to leave, Christina voiced her concern. "Secta, Professor ... Kairos isn't shutting down. It could be Alice."

Excitement surged through them. Gathered around the console, they stared intently at the event room. The Professor whispered to Secta, "Can't be Alice, the wormhole's still open for Turk."

Kairos abruptly shut down, and with the dimming lights, so too faded all hope of Alice showing up. Vee's mood crashed with the anticlimax. She grumbled on her way out, "That was a bit random."

Secta and the Professor stayed behind with Christina. "It's never behaved like this during my time here," she remarked.

"It did once for Robert, didn't it, Secta?" the Professor recalled.

"Yes, but that was early on, when glitches were more common, not now. Run a diagnostic, Christina, and forward the results to me," Secta requested.

"Yes, sir."

Mal turned away from his office window, where he had been watching a torrential downpour. Secta had just entered. "Global warming continues to wreak havoc on us, Secta."

"Yes, Mal, unless the politics of dancing around the issue doesn't cease soon, I fear there will be a lot more death and destruction from freak weather events."

"Pandemics, recession, overpopulation, poverty, political agendas, war, climate change ... tell me, my friend, how is the world ever going to survive without Alice?"

Secta flopped into a lounge chair as a loud clap of thunder rattled the building. "I think that was an answer from the gods, my friend."

Mal poured himself two fingers of single malt whiskey from his secret stash. "Drink?"

"No thanks."

He sat opposite Secta. "A sizeable order for programmable wallpaper came in today from Italy," Mal said, trying to lighten the conversation. Secta, however, seemed disinterested, prompting Mal to down his drink in preparation for a serious discussion.

"Mal, Vic and I don't believe Al will be coming back, so we need to make a decision about replacing him."

"Replace Al? Hell, that's easier said than done. I find that hard to cop. Al's my mate. I can't get my head around him being dead."

"I know, I know ... either can we ... but we need to..."

Mal knew Secta was right. "I hear you ... so, what's your thinking, Blake?" Mal inquired.

Secta looked surprised. "Blake? No, hadn't even considered him ... no, there's no-one other than Turk with the capabilities really, except Vee maybe."

Mal got up, crossed the room, and poured another two fingers of Scotch. On his way back, he asked with an element of doubt in his tone, "Would she be emotionally up for it?"

"Why, you have doubts?" Secta pressed.

"Yes, I suppose so. Look, even though she has accompanied Al on a number of missions and from what we know, she's a chip off the old block, Al was a true performer, fearless, heroic ... probably the bravest bloke I've ever known. Same mould for Vee, however, carved from a totally different chunk of life's circumstances."

"True, but let's be honest ... I don't know anyone with those qualifications, Mal. Even Turk doesn't fit the bill."

"She'd be a work in progress, you know that?" Mal said, reservedly.

Thunder sounded as if to punctuate the statement.

Secta frowned. "Yes. But Mal, she's the best and only candidate we have."

"I can't help but feel she needs an offsider, a tough no-holds-barred sort of bloke like Turk ... you know, to steady the ship."

"You make a lot of sense, Mal, go on."

"Well, we know it can't be Turk unless you can take him from an earlier timeline when he was like thirty-five or so—"

Secta was already shaking his head negatively. "No, no, that would dangerously affect the timeline, we need someone from the present."

"Blake's no good. Though he'll make a fine agent, at any rate, as I understand it, he and Vee had a thing together, so that'd probably render that a no-go ... but—"

"Yes, you're right, we can't have that ... besides, it will take him a couple of years to get over his injury completely," Secta said. "No ... umm..." he thought.

"What about one of the guys from Kor ... Aris or Vale?" Mal posed.

"Vale, now there's an idea, he might be a good choice ... son of Odin. Do you know that in Norse mythology Odin was the supreme god and Vale or Vali as he's sometimes known, was his son?"

"No, I didn't. Is that a coincidence or what?" Mal asked.

"I don't know, but there certainly seems to be some kind of mystic connection between Earth's ancient mythologies and Kor, especially when you take into consideration the story of Apollo arriving here on a spacecraft called Atlan-Tis. A little coincidental that Atlantis is the name of the mystical continent named by Plato in his famous dialogues

Timaeus and Critias, to have been submerged by flood some twelve thousand years ago."

"Yes, you're right. It was destroyed by some great cataclysm wasn't it? And weren't the Atlanteans thought to have been an advanced race?"

"Yes, compared with the primitive homo sapiens here at the time. The very name Atlantic Ocean pretty much confirms Atlantis existed all right but the idea of Apollo coming here from Kor puts a totally different spin on the myth. Anyhow, I agree. Vale would certainly be worth consideration."

Mal proposed, "How about running the idea past Vee?"

"Vee won't handle Alice being replaced, it would appear as confirmation he's dead and that we've given up on him," Secta proposed.

"You need to be sensitive to her grief, Secta, not the pragmatic scientist. What we'll do is commence a program to search for Al, and have Vee front it. We'll meet, once a month, at my office, for updates. That way she'll be more likely to accept Vale in support as opposed to a replacement."

Sensing the meeting was done, Secta stood up. "Very diplomatic of you, Mal. Oh, and speaking of replacements, any word on Luna's?"

"Yes, she arrives today. I'll call a meeting once she's here."

"She? So, what's her name?"

"Have heard nothing other than her gender and that she's new at the job but a qualified scientist I believe," Mal said, happily optimistic. He got up and walked his friend to the door.

The failure of the attack on OTT, following the murder of Dr Li, had significantly impacted Gorrick. His first foray into confronting Zen's adversary had ended disastrously. Determined to improve upon his predecessors' track record, Gorrick summoned his executive staff to an urgent meeting in his newly renovated palatial penthouse apartment at Zen HQ. Recognising the risks of living outside Zen HQ's high security and the convenience of residing in the office building, he had made significant changes to his offices to accommodate both himself and Honor, even providing for a live-in maid.

Choosing his new apartment for the meeting, he aimed to depart from the usual formality of office gatherings.

Honor, Adamski, and Mennis were already seated in the plush living room, lounging on the soft white kid six-seater suite and matching armchairs, admiring the panoramic Sydney skyline and harbour view through the grand windows.

Ursula remarked, "What a view. You are so fortunate to be living here, Honor."

Before Honor could respond, Gorrick entered, striding across the white carpet and settling into an armchair. His square-jawed face bore a morose expression.

"Good morning. This failed operation, following the death of Dr Li, two agents, and an eight-million-dollar cyborg, is unacceptable. It will be the first and last failure under my leadership." He paused, eyeing each of them. "I blame no individual. It was a well-conceived plan; the fault lies in underestimating our adversary. Whether it's underestimating them or overestimating ourselves is up for debate, but that's for another time. Today, we strategise our next steps. First, updates, starting with you, Professor."

Adamski, despite his small stature, puffed up to deliver his report. "Aquila will be ready for transportation in twenty-four hours." His grin hinted at a joke that never materialised, leaving a hanging pause.

Gorrick, seemingly unsettled by Adamski's brief report, moved on. "Okay, fine. Dr Mennis?"

Ursula, exuding self-confidence, stated, "Honor and I sustained superficial wounds from the lab explosion." Both women bore lacerations, skilfully concealed with makeup. "The loss of RF-21-A is regrettable; however, the mission largely succeeded. We reached OTT's core operations. If not for a clever diversion, we would have destroyed Kairos. This glitch in the synaptic processing subroutines has been addressed by adding a secondary situation assessment algorithm. I have updated the five cyborgs. As far as further production of the RF-21 series, this will be put on hold until after relocation. Any questions?"

Gorrick, noting no questions, turned to Honor.

"Security has been our Achilles heel, with mistakes like the loss of Walker and Harris. Security decisions, often made on the fly, need to avoid recklessness. Honor, after reviewing the last operation, what are your thoughts?"

Honor's voice, a rich mezzo, almost sultry despite her severe appearance, resonated as she spoke. "Your assessment is spot on, sir. Overestimating our ability to overpower OTT has been our consistent downfall. Security, under my command, has been hampered by a lack of quality personnel. This is no excuse, but it has limited us. I've decided to recruit operatives of a different calibre."

"The value of your new recruit will be proven by successfully extracting Walker and Harris from OTT," Gorrick stated, his gaze icy.

Honor's lips, painted black, formed a tight, wry smile.

CHAPTER 40
CODA

VEE BIT HER bottom lip and then gave Secta a satisfied nod. "Yep, he and I would make a good team. I can train him up so once Al's back we'll have an extra traveller."

"We also want you to head up a special task force to search for Al. But you must understand it won't be our first priority but it will be a close second. Okay?" he said, making a conscious effort to be as affable as possible, so not to upset her. "Who do you want on the task force?"

"Everyone," she said unthinkingly, and then corrected herself. "Um, no need for Mal or whoever the replacement for Luna is … just us, you know; the team."

"Done … as a matter of fact, the Professor has been on the case since the moment we learned Al was missing," Secta added.

"I would have thought you'd have brought Toeghan back for the job," Vee said.

"She's important to Turk and Morri for now but I expect eventually she we will need to be here."

Her mood shifted and she stared vacantly out of the window at the pedestrians traversing the pavement outside of Café Epiphany, as though she was looking for Alice. To Secta her expression of desperation was all-encompassing, so he tried to comfort her. "We'll find him Vee … he might even find us first, you know Al."

A sad, lone tear trickled down her cheek. She brushed it away and then with her spirits lifted some, shined a warm smile at her friend sitting opposite. "Thank you, mate."

Secta felt he had achieved his objective without upsetting her and bravely went a little further. "Can I offer you a little friendly advice?"

"That depends on what it is," she said, blowing her nose into a napkin.

"I think it would be good for you to speak with Blake, invite him into the task force ... I know he's feeling excluded."

Vee smiled impishly, "Now you're supplying mediation ... is there no limit to Secta's array of talents?"

He reached across the table and took her hand. "You'll find him during happy hour at the main bar of the Pig and Whistle Pub. It has become his regular haunt."

Vee got the message. Though her expression had tightened, she nodded her acceptance of the idea.

Later that afternoon, Vee left the office, battling her way under an umbrella through the wind and rain, two city blocks to the Pig and Whistle Pub. Once a bustling English-style pub frequented by office workers, it had seen better days since the pandemic. Now, with social distancing and stricter drink-driving laws, many found it easier and cheaper to drink at home.

Shaking her umbrella by the double doors like a dog, Vee scanned the sparsely populated bar. Spotting the familiar, bulky frame of Blake with his back to her, she approached casually. "So what's a girl gotta do to get a drink round here?"

Blake, not turning to look at her, took a sip of his double Scotch. "Name your poison?"

"Whatever you're having."

The bartender approached. "A double of depression for the lady, Bill," Blake ordered.

Vee grinned. "Depression, huh? A bit random, didn't think you were the type."

"Comes with the bullet hole," he replied flatly.

After Bill slid the drink to Vee, Blake muttered, "Put it on the tab, Bill. Bombs away."

He downed his drink in one go, while Vee sipped hers. "So, to what do I owe the visitation?" he asked. It was clear he was there to drown his sorrows. His injury had reduced him to a shadow of his former self, and Vee sensed his deep-seated despair.

"You heard Al's missing? … I've been put in charge of a task force to find him and wanted to know if you'd be interested in joining. Secta said you'd be here."

Blake's cynical smirk faded. "I'd be more interested in rekindling what we had."

Vee didn't like where this was heading. She drank for courage. "That might or might not happen, Blake. Right now, I need your expertise."

He grabbed her arm, pulling her close, searching her eyes. "I thought there was something between us."

"There was, and her name was Jax, remember?" she retorted, maintaining her composure. After a tense moment, he released her arm and gestured for another drink.

"Haven't you had enough?"

"Of what, booze or women?" he shot back coldly.

"Both, I guess. Look, come on board … you need to get back into the swing of things; there's no point hanging here wallowing in self-pity."

"Who said anything about self-pity? Come back to my place … now."

"I can't, I'm leaving for a mission in two hours. I should be prepping right now, but I came here to see you."

"What mission?" he inquired, sipping his new drink.

"I need to recruit someone to assist me while Al's is missing, and there's a warrior on Kor that fits the bill."

"I thought that was the gig you just offered me?" he said, as though offended.

"No, I'm offering you a position in the task force to find Al. While he's missing, I'm taking on his duties, and I need someone to rely on."

"So, what, you can't rely on me?" Blake snapped.

"Not in your current state, Blake. Look at yourself … you're half-stung and blabbering. That's not who I want to depend on. You know I'm right, don't you?"

He downed his Scotch, unable to refute her point.

A message pinged on her implant. "There's an urgent meeting in the President's office in twenty minutes."

"Yeah, yeah, any excuse … Feeling vulnerable now without your big brother to look over you, huh?" His tone was cutting.

Vee's demeanour froze, tears welling in her eyes.

Blake realised he'd struck a nerve.

"He shouldn't have just left me," she murmured, her voice laden with pain.

Seeing her distress, Blake's attitude shifted to one of remorse. "I'm sorry for saying that, Vee, it was cruel. You should go… like you said, I'm not much use to anyone in this state. Bill?"

Vee held up her hand to prevent Bill topping up her glass. "The President specifically asked for you to be at the meeting, Blake."

A glimmer of his old self appeared in his eyes, a sense of purpose rekindling. "Cancel that, Bill," he said.

"You'll need to sober up."

"A quick walk will sort that. Let's go."

Braving the storm, they shared an umbrella, battling the icy wind and sleet, legging it towards Oceana.

OTT members were engaged in conversation in the President's office, awaiting the arrival of Vee and Blake. The UNTT replacement for Luna was also expected, but her flight from New York had been delayed due to the bad weather.

Vee and Blake entered, soaked through from their tempestuous journey. The ten-minute struggle against the elements had indeed sobered Blake up. They found seats among the others.

"We all set?" Vee inquired, directing her question to Christina.

With a smile, Christina responded, "As soon as we wrap up here, if you're ready."

"Where are you headed?" Viktoria inquired curiously.

"Back to Kor to invite Vale to join OTT as a traveller."

Viktoria raised her eyebrows. "Oh really? Do you think he'll agree?"

"Perhaps. He has all the right qualities," Vee replied confidently.

Blake, sitting nearby, rolled his eyes, evidently feeling sidelined in not being considered for the role.

A black OTT town car glided into the underground car park at Oceana, having collected the new UNTT officer from the airport. A special agent opened the passenger-side door and escorted her towards the elevators.

They emerged into the lobby and made their way to the private presidential elevator. As the doors slid open, they stepped inside. Just as the doors began to close, they caught a glimpse of Vee and the President briskly walking past, heading towards a different elevator.

The special agent escorted the UNTT official to Rita Vallins at reception. Rita then guided her past security and through the large double doors into the President's office suite.

Upon their entry, all heads in the room turned sharply. A collective gasp filled the air as Mal rose to his feet, as astonished as everyone else.

"Why, Miss De Ville, we weren't expecting you."

"Mr President, no, I guess I'd be the most unlikely candidate to replace Luna, but here I am."

Vee noticed Blake's eyes fix on Jax, who looked fit, sexy, and business-like.

"Well, welcome, please take a seat," Mal offered, somewhat awkwardly.

Jax, looking puzzled, said, "How did you get here so quickly? I just saw you and Vee getting into an elevator in the lobby."

Karzoff leaped up as if startled. "What?" He frantically checked the internal CCTV on his cellphone, but it was already too late. Viktoria was on her phone, receiving a report from security.

She put down the phone, her eyes fixed on Karzoff. "There has been a security breach. It appears Mr President and Vee have just assisted Commander Walker and Agent Harris in leaving the building, and they've gotten into a waiting vehicle."

A wave of astonishment swept across the faces in the room.

As soon as Walker and Harris boarded the black six-seater van, the President and Vee morphed into two replicas of Electra, the default form of an RF-21 cyborg.

Walker was impressed. "Well done, ladies."

In unison, they responded with identical voices. "Thank you, Commander Walker."

The front-seat passenger turned to Walker and greeted, "Good to see you again, old chum."

"Well, if it isn't Mr Handerson Bolt, I didn't expect to be seeing you again."

Bolt's face split into a cheeky grin. "Back in the saddle and on the payroll."

"I see. Welcome aboard," Walker acknowledged.

The van sped off towards Zen HQ, mission successful.

Meanwhile, back in the President's office, with Karzoff and Viktoria attending to the security breach, casual conversation filled the room.

Secta whispered to the Professor, "I don't get it; she wouldn't know a microbe from a bathrobe ... Didn't the position require a physicist?"

Jax, overhearing, coolly interjected, "I am a professor of Archaeology at Boston University, Secta, and also hold a Master of Science. My academic credentials do qualify me."

Vee, unable to hold back, burst out, "What the hell motivated you to join UNTT and come here after—?"

Jax responded calmly, "I was headhunted by the UN Director General, Maralina Bostok; it wasn't my choice. And I wasn't expecting hostility here. Did this drive Luna away?"

"No, Luna steered her own course," the Professor clarified.

"There's a need to police time travel and—"

"Please, spare us the lecture, Jax," Vee interjected sharply. "We've heard it all before."

"Do you mean keeping information from the public or enforcing the temporal prime directive?" Mal inquired.

"Both," Jax said, curtly.

"That's deceitful," Secta contended.

"You don't understand public relations," Jax retorted.

"If you're here to mend fences, understand why Luna and OTT parted ways," Blake advised sternly.

"We have bigger issues than making you comfortable; we need to find Black Alice and shut down Zen," Vee declared, her patience wearing thin.

Jax was taken aback. "What are you saying? Have you lost Alice? But how?"

"Of course, you wouldn't have been informed. Unfortunately, yes," Mal said, forlornly, "Al didn't return from his last mission."

"Yeah, the one where he saved the Earth and the entire population of the planet Kor from annihilation, something the UN is intent on taking for granted," Vee spat, venomously. "Yet another fact being kept secret from the public by you lot?" Vee eyeballed Jax damningly. "That the world has a hero who might well have given his life to save it?" Overcome by despair, Vee teared up.

Feeling the anguish, Jax appealed to Vee. "Now I get the resentment. Look, I have nothing but complete admiration for your brother, Vee. Whatever my office and I can do to help, I give you my word, we will."

Her pledge of fealty lifted their spirits. They welcomed what seemed to be a change of heart Jax appeared determined to bring to the job. But Vee wasn't convinced—bad blood remained between them over Blake, and she didn't trust her, knowing she was a former CIA spy for Brigadier Bruckmaster.

As lightning illuminated the brooding sky, a convoy of four black vans arrived at Oceana Airport's private flight facilities. Parked there was a sleek, matte black Gulfstream GIVSP executive jet, its tail proudly bearing the Zen Corporation decal. Gorrick, accompanied by Honor, Adamski, and Mennis, strode across the tarmac and ascended the stairs leading into the aircraft. They were followed by five identical female RF-21 cyborgs, Walker, Bolt, Agent Harris, and another agent, all boarding the jet.

With the jet's impressive range of four thousand nine hundred nautical miles and cruising speed of six hundred miles per hour, the 2,870-mile journey to the island of Coda in the Sulu Sea would take approximately five hours. This island was set to be the new headquarters for Aquila and Zen's global operations.

CHAPTER 41
BAG O' NAILS

IN THE KAIROS control room, Vee was kitted up and ready for her mission to Kor.

Secta warmly asked, "Are you up for the mission, Vee?"

She grinned, "Do fish swim?"

"Spoken like the true sister of Black Alice. I expect you to return with Vale, don't take no for an answer, there's far too much riding on it."

Karzoff ambled in looking like he'd misplaced something valuable. "They got clean away, and more so, there was word from Airport Operations that a Gulfstream corporate jet in Zen livery took off an hour ago for the Philippines with twelve passengers. Earlier, a Chinese Xian Y-20 transport aircraft also headed there."

"So, Zen is relocating," Secta deduced. "I expect the transport plane contained Aquila. What's their final destination?"

"I have requested one of our naval ships in the region to track the Gulfstream; we will know that soon enough. There is CCTV footage of the passengers boarding, take a look," Karzoff said, showing Secta, Vee, and Christina a video on his phone.

"Gorrick, Honor, Mennis ... and look at that, Electra times four," Secta observed.

"And Walker! And check it out, right behind him, the mongrel who shot Blake—Handerson Bolt!" Vee exclaimed.

The Professor burst in, breathless. "Vee, I had to catch you."

Vee chuckled, "Relax mate; you'll give yourself a coronary. What's up?"

"Christina, remember when Kairos wouldn't shut down the other day after we dispatched Turk?"

Christina nodded. "Yes, that was a weird one."

"It was weirder than you think because it stayed open long enough for a message to be downloaded onto the mainframe ... I guess from En-Ki but unlike before, there's no evidence of who sent it."

Vee was bursting with excitement. "What did it say?"

The Professor threw open his hands. "It simply said, Bag O'Nails, don't ask me what in tarnation that's supposed to mean."

The door alarm broke the collective deliberation. Christina checked the monitor. "It's Jax."

"Let her in," Secta decided, despite their scepticism.

Vee snarled, "A convenient arrival ... I smell a rat."

Jax came in, stopped just inside the door, glared at Secta, and announced, "I understand you're intending to invite Vale Tarz from Kor to be a member of OTT."

"Yes, Vee is about to leave for Kor to propose it to him."

"I can't sanction a mission to enlist Vale; it would be in direct violation of the TPD. You know we can't expose someone from a less advanced society to advanced technology. I sympathise with your need to replace Alice, but I can't agree with your methodology. I've already informed the President."

The Professor countered, "I'd argue they've been exposed to advanced technology for years from the Nephilim occupation, far more radical than ours."

"That would need to be proven before we could consider approving your plan Vic. I'm honestly not trying to be difficult," Jax said, emphatically.

Vee flopped into a chair, angry, and mumbled, "So, it has to be the Bag O'Nails."

"What the hell's that supposed to mean?" Jax challenged, suspecting Vee was using some kind of a perverse code to demean her.

All eyes turned to Vee for an explanation, the Professor being the most bemused by the weird phrase.

Vee shot them a smug look. "I don't think the message was from En-Ki," she said, cavalierly. "It's from Alice."

The statement struck them like a ton of bricks. Vee recounted that she hadn't forgotten when she was strolling down the corridor with Alice towards the control room for her inaugural mission, asking Alice, "Can I ask you a question?" "Yes," he replied, "go on." I inquired if Secta were to grant you one wish to travel in time, where would you go? He pondered for a moment before responding emphatically, "The Bag O'Nails Club, Soho, London, November 19, 1966." Curious, I asked why, what occurred then? He flashed a grin and said, "Jimi performed a showcase gig in front of the legends of rock." By this, he meant Alice's hero, Jimi Hendrix, of course.

It didn't take much to convince them of its credibility; it was precisely the kind of remark Al would make. Consequently, Hope and Vee embarked on researching how to tackle the complexities of such a mission. They needed an organic item from that exact time to create a pinhole to it. Jax had no objections; she deemed a mission to locate Al crucial for the safeguarding of time travel, and it effortlessly helped them overcome the hurdle of enlisting Vale Tarz from Kor. The predicament was that the date was in three days' time, putting them squarely against the clock.

The Bag O'Nails Club was historically famed as the hub for London's rock elite in the 1960s, but it no longer existed.

Later that day, OTT convened to discuss the findings of their research.

The Professor posed the first question. "Why that specific gig on that day, Vee? What do you think draws Alice to it?"

Vee adopted an awestruck expression. "Wow, let me explain, Vic. As far as historic rock moments go, this date holds immense significance for Al. Apart from the general public, here's who was in the audience to witness the debut of this new band named the Jimi Hendrix Experience, which everyone in London was buzzing about:

Eric Clapton, Pete Townshend, John Lennon, Paul McCartney, Ringo Starr, Mick Jagger, Brian Jones, Brian Epstein, Jeff Beck, Jimmy Page, The Hollies, the Small Faces, The Animals, and Lulu."

"Yep, that pretty much covers everyone. I get it," the Professor cackled.

"Besides, wouldn't this have been a pivotal moment for Hendrix, a chance to showcase his band to his contemporaries?" Hope suggested.

Vee concurred. "Absolutely."

"Okay, but none of this offers us a lead on what to use for opening a pinhole to London, November 19, 1966," Secta remarked, pragmatically.

"What about this? It was the performance that prompted the London music magazine The Record Mirror to publish the headline 'Mr Phenomenon.' What if we could obtain a copy of that edition?"

Secta glanced at Vic for affirmation, then said, "Yes, that might work."

"No, I hate to dampen spirits," Christina interjected, "but the newspaper would have been published a couple of days later, or at the earliest, the next day."

Secta nodded in agreement. "You're right."

Jax proposed an alternative. "What if we acquire a copy of a morning newspaper from that date? There might even be copies at the National Library."

Vic confirmed, "Indeed, that would place the pinhole opening at the newspaper's printing press. The challenge then would be for Vee to reach the gig."

Despite her aversion to Jax, Vee was intrigued by her suggestion and exclaimed, "Easy-peasy."

The decision was unanimous, and Hope was tasked with hunting down a copy of a London newspaper and arranging for a tiny fragment to be provided for scientific analysis.

The Professor and Secta observed Christina inputting data into Kairos when Hope and Vee entered the control room. All attention shifted to Vee, who was donning an Afro hairstyle, flared jeans, and a floral blouse paired with a brown leather vest.

"You'd make the quintessential love child, Vee," Vic declared.

Vee performed a playful twirl, agreeing, "That's me."

Hope presented Vic with a small resealable plastic bag. "Here you go, Vic, a millimetre square of the UK Daily Mirror newspaper dated November 19, 1966."

Vic took it, examined the minuscule piece against the light, and remarked, "Goddamn, were they able to spare it?"

Hope laughed, "Yeah, they certainly can't be accused of being generous."

Secta scrutinised the fragment. "It'll have to do."

Vic passed it to Christina. She pressed a button, causing a small drawer to emerge from the wall next to the dispatch room. In the tray, she meticulously placed the sliver of paper, then pushed it shut.

"So, the paper wouldn't have given us an accurate date because it could be a month old, but the ink will, right, Professor?" Christina inquired.

"Not exactly. The software I've programmed into the computer will analyse the UV signature in the ink, using it to date the particle collider. UV is infused into the ink during printing to speed up drying."

Christina resumed her position and murmured, "Clever."

Resting her hand on Secta's high-back chair, Vee queried, "Do I just open the micro pinhole to bring Alice back, or…?"

Christina confirmed, "Yes."

"Assuming he wants to return, of course," Vic interjected.

Secta swivelled his chair to face Vee. "It's going to be up to you to convince him how much we need him, Vee."

"I don't understand, why would I need to convince him?" Vee asked, puzzled.

"Because if he had wanted to return, he would have by now," Secta pointed out.

"We can't be sure if he'll be the same Alice after his experiences," Hope cautioned.

Secta, with a critical raised eyebrow, muttered, "We must remain optimistic," responding to Hope's pessimistic tone.

Feeling Secta's disapproving gaze, Hope handed Vee an envelope. "Inside is a thousand pounds for hotel and miscellaneous expenses, including some accessories for the gig. You might want to check out Carnaby Street; it was the fashion hub in the 60s and is close to the Mayfair Hotel, where we suggest you stay."

"You'll arrive inside the Daily Mirror building in Holborn Circus, London," Vic explained. "That's where the printing press was located back then."

Christina added, "You'll be there at 3 a.m. on the nineteenth."

Vee nodded eagerly. "Okay, I'm ready to rock."

Hope escorted her to the dispatch room door, and stopped her. "Here's a spare clock drive in case you need it. Good luck, love," she opened the door.

Vee faced her colleagues, "Bye, guys … Chaa!"

At 3 a.m., during the final daily print shift, a vortex materialised on the floor of the colossal Daily Mirror printing press room. The workers, caught off guard, stood motionless, and a profound silence enveloped the space. Through the doughnut-shaped, spiralling smoke ring of the vortex, Vee emerged. Her footsteps resonated in the vast room as she hastened towards the elevator. Feeling a chill, she spotted a blue three-quarter woollen maritime coat hanging on a peg inside the doorway of a small office, where three people were frozen mid-motion, cutting and pasting the newspaper on a large table. Like a shadow in the night, Vee swiftly grabbed the coat and barely made it into the elevator just as the enormous printing presses thundered back to life, signalling the resumption of normal time.

Vee emerged into the lobby, turned up her coat collar, slid her hands into the deep pockets, and walked briskly across the empty lobby, exiting through the front glass doors into the London weather. The icy wind and sleeting rain assaulted her; her Afro hairstyle, reminiscent of a 1960s Diana Ross, was at risk of deflating under the damp conditions. She paused at the curb, scanning the night for a taxi. Fortunately, a London cab appeared. She hailed it and leapt into the backseat, her hairstyle intact.

The cabby dropped her off at the Mayfair Hotel. She proceeded inside and checked in.

In her room, Vee activated the console TV and sat on the expansive queen-size bed, waiting for the old tube to warm up. It was just past 4 a.m., and only a test pattern greeted her on the BBC. Rising, she adjusted the dial, searching for other channels, but found only BBC 1, ITV, and BBC 2, all showing black and white test patterns, with the BBC playing Tchaikovsky's "Eugen Onegin," performed by the Oslo Philharmonic Orchestra. Eager to immerse herself in the era, she discovered a London Life Magazine inside a leather-bound writing set and blotter atop the bureau. She lifted the cream-coloured phone receiver, dialled zero for an outside line, and listened with a smile to the quaint dial tone. Not feeling sleepy but with time to spare, she shed her coat and knee-high shiny white patent leather boots and reclined on the comfortable bed. Sinking into the plush goose-down pillows, she began leafing through London Life, dubbed the magazine of the swinging sixties, to catch up on the local scene.

Later that day, rejuvenated by some rest and a hearty breakfast of bangers, mash, and baked beans, Vee departed the Mayfair Hotel for a stroll to nearby Carnaby Street, the heart of '60s fashion and a destination she had eagerly anticipated.

It was a warm, sunny Friday near midday. With her coat draped over her arm, she sauntered along, blending seamlessly in her ensemble of a brown chamois vest with tassels, a dark green satin blouse, and tight blue denim hipster bell-bottom jeans. The click of her stiletto-heeled white boots on the cobblestone street kept time with Nancy Sinatra's "These Boots Are Made for Walking," a contemporary hit emanating from Tannoy speakers outside Ravel's shoe shop at the street's entrance. Immersing herself in the vibrant atmosphere, she found the street teeming with stylish individuals—men with long hair, hippies, and swinging girls in micro minis. It was like her own magical mystery tour. The air was filled with performances from buskers and jugglers, and the general mood was one of happiness, far removed from the apprehensions of her own era. Here, there was an unmistakable sense of peace, freedom and love.

As she strolled past the men's boutique "I Was Lord Kitchener's Valet," the melodious tune of "With a Girl Like You" by the Troggs wafted from the store. At the doorway, two handsome young men with long hair, clad in 19th-century military jackets akin to those seen on the Beatles' 'Sergeant Pepper's Lonely Hearts Club Band' album cover, paused and appraised her. She returned their gaze with a charming smile and continued on, making sure her walk was provocatively alluring.

Further on, a crowd had assembled outside Lady Jane, an infamous women's boutique. Vee joined the onlookers and observed models in the shop window changing into black Goth attire, drawing considerable attention. The rhythmic strains of "Paint It Black" by the Stones played from a record player near the entrance, where a girl was painting the door black. The scene encapsulated a carnival-like atmosphere unique to the swinging sixties. Vee smiled to herself, realising that those from her time who had experienced this era were right: to truly appreciate the '60s, one had to have been there.

Jax peered over the rim of her coffee cup at Mal, who was seated across from her. "The US Space Force believes Zen is aiming to dominate the low orbit satellite market from their new base in the Philippines," she stated.

Through the windows, the mid-afternoon sun cast long, thin shadows across the Presidential office floor.

"Are you sure that's not just Larry Freeman being paranoid?" Mal asked with a raspy voice.

Jax nodded slowly, a friendly expression on her face. "It's possible, I'll grant you that. There's a lot of paranoia these days, especially with corporations like Zen entering the space race."

Mal leaned back in his seat, took a sip of coffee, and then posed philosophically, "Ah, if it's not one thing, it's another with Zen. As if there's not enough anxiety over India, Japan, China and Russia building lunar bases, and the race to claim lunar mining rights, all while the UN battles to come up with an accord on how to carve up the moon. In the meantime, we smaller nations of the world remain tormented by the potential danger from these powers messing with a celestial body that's vital to all life on Earth. We Earthlings after all do not have the best track record for caring for planets, do we? Evidenced by the irreparable damage we've done to our own planet, now we're exporting our bad habits to other planets?"

Jax shook her head slowly. "I hear you, Mal. It's interesting how you've started referring to us as Earthlings since the encounter with the Kormans."

Mal took a sip of his coffee, then said, "Yes, I suppose I do. So, what does our General Larry Freeman want to do about Zen?"

Jax leaned forward, lowering her voice. "Freeman's efforts to uncover the Philippines' agreement with Zen for their secret base yielded nothing, which is alarming. He's concerned that if Zen's RF cyborg program is sold to a rogue nation, it could be used in space warfare."

Mal nodded, not out of clarity but anticipation. "That would put the US at a significant disadvantage."

"To say the least," Jax agreed. "Cyborgs don't need air or food..."

Mal interjected, "I would've thought cyber-hacking more cost-effective for a company like Zen."

Jax countered, "Not with the new quantum network. The Chinese recently launched a quantum entanglement-based satellite, providing hack-proof communication. Plus, there's the fight over Helium-3 on the moon. Zen is reportedly leading in developing cyborgs for mining it."

Mal, visibly concerned, placed his mug on the table. "This seems like enough reason for the UN and the US to shut Zen down. What the hell's stopping them?"

After a moment of eye contact, Jax replied, "Your guess is as good as mine, Mal."

He sighed. "Must be Zen's political influence. They've got someone powerful in the White House. So, what do you need from me?"

Jax grinned mischievously. "We need to figure out what Zen is up to."

"Are you saying that with your extensive networks, you need our help? That's unprecedented, considering our capabilities have always been disregarded by you..." Mal said with a cynical eyebrow raise, but his grin softened the blow.

Jax admitted, "You're right, Mal. It's with humility that I come to you. Only OTT has the means to infiltrate Zen."

"Kairos?" Mal asked.

"Yes. But without Alice, it's a challenge."

"Then we better hope Vee's mission succeeds," Jax concluded. "The world can't afford to let Zen gain the upper hand. It could lead to a global conflict."

CHAPTER 42
WITH THAT GUN IN YOUR HAND

VEE HAD BOUGHT some happening '60s fashion in Carnaby Street specifically for the gig that night: a fox fur vest over a scarlet velvet blouse and a killer rainbow mini skirt. Adorning herself with strings of beads, star-shaped sunglasses with blue lenses, and a pair of knee-high black stiletto-heeled boots, she felt invigorated, merging Goth with hippie fashion.

There was no trouble for her in finding the Bag O'Nails Club on Kingly Street, Soho. She could tell it was the right place by the queue of groovy people gathered at the red entrance door. Getting in without an invite was going to be the challenge, so she decided to search for a stage door, knowing there had to be one for loading in the band gear.

It was 8 p.m., and a cold wind gusted, chilling her exploratory walk along the mostly deserted Kingly Street. She came across a side alleyway just wide enough to fit a single car and, halfway along it, a narrow passageway led between two buildings. A guy was standing partway down the passage, lighting a cigarette; the flash from the match illuminated his face. He looked her way, then checked his watch, waiting for someone or something to arrive. Unlike the punters in the queue out front of the club, the guy wasn't dressed as a hippie.

As she neared him, she could see he had a roundish handsome face, stood over six feet tall, and was wearing a dapper silvery grey suit with a thin paisley tie and black Beatle-boots. She muttered to herself,

"This guy's gotta be a record executive."

Sporting a friendly smile, she approached him with, "Hey, I'm Vee, here to cover tonight's gig for Rolling Stone. You're...?"

A stream of smoke from his nose and mouth came with, "Chas Chandler, Jimi's manager. Rolling Stones is a band, love?" he added, sounding suspicious.

"No, no, not Mick's band, silly, Rolling Stone Magazine ... from San Francisco."

"You an American then?"

"No, an Aussie ... a cub reporter. Are you waiting for the band?" she said, trying to change the subject. By the look on Chas' boyish face, she hadn't convinced him; he'd never heard of Rolling Stone Magazine. The only thing that sort of validated her claim was that he had toured San Francisco a few months earlier with his band The Animals, and experienced a happening music scene there, so a music magazine wouldn't be out of the question. Besides, Jimi was from Seattle, a little further north of San Francisco, and would thus probably make music news.

"Yeah, okay love, go inside, tell 'em Chas said you're all right, eh?" he said past the ciggy in his mouth, with a slight Geordie accent. "I'll arrange you an interview with Jimi after the gig, if you like."

"Far-out, thanks Chas," she gushed excitedly, inwardly chuffed that she'd got into the gig.

Once inside, she walked the narrow, dimly lit corridor past the dressing rooms and emerged into the main room beside the stage, where she stopped to take it all in.

Skeins of smoke hung in a heavy haze over the oblong-shaped room, drenched in a dull red glow from the lighting. Nearly everyone was smoking. Though the club had a capacity of around a hundred, it was packed to the brim, leaving standing room only. With no music playing, the ambiance was one of chatter. Those lucky enough, along with the VIPs, were seated at small round tables closest to the surprisingly modest stage and the diminutive dance floor. Others lounged on red benches along the sidewalls. At the rear, a bar bustled with activity as a few stewards fought their way through the throng to deliver orders to the VIPs.

There was nothing flash about the club. The décor was ordinary, slightly dingy, and the stage lacked the trappings one would expect for such a famous venue. But then again, Vee reminded herself, this was 1966. In reality, the rock industry was still in its infancy.

Only a few dimmed overhead spotlights lit the stage. There were no fold-back wedges, no mixing desk, or effects—it was going to be as raw as it gets.

A roadie, carrying two guitar cases, edged past Vee. Realising she was obstructing the way with the arrival of the band gear, she moved aside. A quick scan of the room for Alice yielded nothing, but she did spot several familiar faces at the front tables. Her heart skipped a beat upon recognising John Lennon, Paul McCartney, Ringo Starr, Mick Jagger, Eric Clapton, Jeff Beck, and Lulu. Although she knew from her research they would be there, actually being in the presence of such rock royalty left her feeling weak in the knees.

The atmosphere of anticipation heightened suddenly when Mitch Mitchell stepped onto the stage and began setting up his Premier drum kit.

Feeling self-conscious under the provocative gazes of the celebrities, Vee decided to move away, but then she noticed an ominous dark figure leaning against the sidewall. Her instincts told her it was Alice.

When she approached him, he smiled devilishly, "Been watching you soaking up the alluring glances of the legends, and rightfully so, you look awesome, baby. Love the Afro."

Vee could say nothing, only embrace her big brother. "Oh Al, I've been so worried about you."

"Look at that ... a Marshall 100 Watt Super Lead amp and the roadie is setting up a Vox Wah Wah pedal, a Uni-Vibe control, and a fuzz box on the floor."

Vee turned to see what Al was totally enamoured by and said, "Jimi's setup, huh?" Al nodded like a kid in a candy store, completely absorbed in every detail of the experience. She added, "This really is the Jimi Hendrix experience for you, isn't it?"

"Killer," Al said, with a massive grin. "There's Noel Redding with his Fender Jazz Bass, setting up his 450 Watt Behringer amp. You know he's actually a lead guitarist, Chas Chandler recruited him to play bass."

The sound of a bass guitar tuning up and Mitch Mitchell setting up his cymbals heightened the feeling of anticipation. Vee could see it in Alice's face.

"You look well," she said.

Without taking his eyes off the stage, he replied, "Yeah, I'm fine. I'll tell you all about it after the gig."

The few pin spots above the stage faded up, illuminating the stage in the dark crimson glow of the room. Then, as the audience hushed, the last roadie left the stage, and Chas Chandler walked out and stopped behind the centre microphone stand.

Vee whispered to Al, "That's the guy who got me in."

"Who, Chas?"

"Yes, he said I can interview Jimi after the gig."

"Cool, how'd you manage that?"

"Told him I'm a cub reporter for Rolling Stone Magazine."

"And he bought it, even though the first issue of Rolling Stone isn't until 1967, next year?"

Vee covered her mouth with her hand, cutely shrugged her shoulders, and giggled, "Oops."

A feedback squeal captured the room's attention, so Chas took the mic off the stand and moved out of range of the Marshall stack.

"Hi, everyone, I'm Chas Chandler. You might know me as the bass player for The Animals, but tonight I'm here in a different capacity. I'm the manager of an extraordinary talent hailing from Seattle, USA, soon to be on Track Records with his single 'Hey Joe' ... may I introduce to you, the one and only Jimi Hendrix Experience!"

Then came the big moment. A man only 5 feet 9 inches tall, yet appearing much taller with an Afro hairstyle and Cuban-heeled boots, dressed in a deep blue velvet double-breasted suit with a matching blue silk satin bow blouse, ambled onto the stage. He carried a white 1960 Fender Stratocaster that had seen better days. Plugging into the Marshall stack and holding the Strat upside down, he cranked the volume on the amp until it hummed like a high-tension generator. With a quick glance at Mitch Mitchell behind his kit, the entire room was engulfed in the incredible tones of Jimi's guitar as he played the opening lick to "Hey Joe." The bass brought in the drums, and then Jimi launched into his soulful rendition about a man on the run after shooting his unfaithful wife. Everyone in the room, without exception, fell under the spell of Jimi's magnetic charisma and the artistry—the mastery—of his playing.

Vee glanced at Alice and could see that the moment was so special it had brought tears to his eyes.

When the set finished and the standing ovation had subsided, Vee felt as though she had witnessed history in the making. Alice was smiling, looking at Lennon and McCartney, who were standing and smoking, awestruck by the performance. "They left Abbey Road recording studios to come here tonight," Al mumbled to Vee. "You know what they were doing there?"

Vee followed his gaze to the two Beatles, who had been joined by the third, Ringo. "No, what?"

"Recording 'Sergeant Pepper's.'"

It was another light-bulb moment for Vee, realising more history was being made. "Amazing," she gasped. "Where were you before the gig?"

"Having a joint with Jimi in his hotel room."

"Jimi Hendrix?"

"Yeah, he wasn't keen to do the gig tonight, didn't like Chas's idea of showcasing him to his musical heroes. He just needed a little friendly persuasion."

"Right, so without you giving him that nudge, he might never have made history tonight?"

Al shot her his signature look. "We'll never know that, will we?

Come on, let's go backstage."

It was 3 a.m. by the time Vee led Alice into her room at the Mayfair Hotel. Flying high from the excitement of being backstage with rock royalty, she grabbed a couple of miniature bottles of JD from the bar-fridge, handed one to Al, and they settled back into the comfy lounge to toast the incredible Jimi Hendrix Experience.

Vee raised her bottle. "Cheers to the experience."

They drank. He gave her a knowing smile. "So, there's a lot to talk about, sis."

"Sure is. Let's start with what happened?"

"Okay, well, the only way to trap En-Lil was within myself—I needed to become his host. With the others dead, he had nowhere else to go. I was travelling on instinct alone … got inside the Astara, and when I opened it again it was a place I'd been before. The Astara had materialised inside the weird cavern that had once entombed En-Ki. I noticed when I climbed out of the thing En-Lil's presence stayed behind in the Astara, so I slammed the lid shut. I reckon the Astara is a type of computer that, because En-Lil is artificial intelligence, was able to trap him in its memory. That was probably the reason he feared it so and wanted it destroyed. Well, I'm hardly a scientific boffin, but that's how it seems to me."

"Wild that he ended up suffering a fate similar to what he'd doled out to his brother," she reflected.

"Yeah, that's what I thought. Speaking of his brother, a few seconds later I was in En-Ki's spacecraft; he'd transported me there."

"Why didn't you just come back home? You've had us pretty worried, you know?"

"Yeah, I guess so. Sorry about that, but I needed to chill with En-Ki to mull things over, you know, with all that's happened."

Vee could see Alice had come to a crossroads. Now immortal, having defeated En-Lil, and completing the quest, it was time to examine who he had become and how he could best employ his new status.

"Fair enough," she agreed, then leaned forward in her seat and asked apprehensively, "So, what was your decision, Mr Alice?"

He drained the bottle of JD, wiped the back of his hand across his mouth, locked eyes with his sister, and said, "What we did tonight reminded me of what I so love about this time travel game, Vee. I needed to have the Jimi Hendrix experience to remind me of who I am. I've watched the sun crest the Taurus Mountains four thousand five hundred years ago. I've gazed in awe at a golden pyramid on the planet Eris ... I swiped the Ark of the Covenant from Solomon's Temple to stop Nebuchadnezzar getting his claws on it. I fought with the Kor against the Nephilim on Atlan, and now there are many possibilities to utilise the abilities I possess, Vee. There are so many cats I could meet: Janis Joplin, Bon Scott, Prince, and the historical ones; Jesus, Mohammed, Buddha, and Joan of Arc, man, the list goes on."

Vee put her hand gently on his and looked affectionately into his eyes. "But Alice, we need you more than any of them ... the world of your time needs Black Alice."

The reality check caused him to pause and consider. A slight smile curled his lips. "There's still plenty to do, isn't there?" He got up and walked to the window. Looking up at the night sky, he said, "Funny how stuff sticks in your mind. After all I've experienced, I remember Secta once saying to me, back when I possessed Turk and I was on the porch of Reno Bar looking up at the stars. He had possessed Morri, so I didn't know it was Secta speaking. He asked, 'Looking at the stars?' and I said, trying to hear space. He said, 'It's not you listening to space, Alice, it's space listening to you.'"

The words hung in the air, materialising in the way the words of a great song do. Vee brushed the tears from her cheeks, went to the fridge, fetched two more miniature bottles of JD, and, sniffling from a runny nose, handed a bottle to Al. All teared up with happiness, she raised her bottle and toasted, "Let's drink to that, my brother ... let's drink to that."

CHAPTER 43
HARMONIC RESONANCE

IT WAS A PACKED control room, with high expectations in the air. Every member of OTT was present, each silently pondering, "Will it be Alice who steps through Kairos, or Vee alone?" This time, it was Mal nervously pacing the floor.

A distorted image materialised within the swirling vortex of the massive Kairos hoop, and then Vee emerged, looking like a hippie from Haight-Asbury, the '60s bohemian enclave.

Looks of disappointment were exchanged, and the smiles began to fade. Then, Christina lifted their spirits by announcing, "It's not shutting down."

To the cheers and tears of everyone present, the sturdy figure of Black Alice emerged from Kairos. Mal, so excited, embraced the Professor. Christina, with tears in her eyes, jumped up from her chair and hugged Hope, the closest person. Viktoria and Secta held each other, both misty-eyed, and Karzoff shook hands with Blake as though he were an Olympic gold medallist.

Through the control room window, Alice and Vee could see the jubilation, and Al gave Vee a warm, brotherly hug. Such was the emotion of the team being reunited.

Later, in the OTT boardroom, Al explained his journey to an audience hanging on his every word.

"So, I come to En-Ki's explanation of—well—everything. I can't put into words exactly what he told me, but I'll give it my best shot.

First, know this: there have been many civilizations on Earth over millions of years before ours, and each faced extinction events in one form or another. In most cases, they wiped themselves out. The most recent evolution of humanity, however, was created by the Anunnaki, specifically En-Ki. This happened about four hundred thousand years ago, and we are direct descendants of the humans En-Ki genetically modified back then. I mention this because I have once again been genetically altered, this time not by Secta but by the Astara. You might well ask where the Astara is ... well, I've parked it in another dimension where it's safe because it contains the life force of En-Lil. So, what did I inherit from this experience? Within me is a harmonic ... it extends through space, connecting me to the mycelium web. It's invisible to the naked eye and is no different in nature from the mycelium web that connects plants in Earth's forests. I can traverse the mycelium web at light speed, much like we've been using wormholes for time travel, but not in the same physical sense."

"Is this the music that has always been within you?" Hope asked.

"Yes, in a way it is, but it wasn't tuned to the right frequency, so to speak. I'm now in sync with the Universe, linked, if you will. You see, it's not the stars, it's the space in-between. In that void, the mycelium web extends."

Secta, as inquisitive as ever, asked, "So, does it connect to a higher being?"

Blake added, "God, perhaps?"

"If the tendrils of the web connecting all life in the Universe are God, then yes, that is God."

"Is it over, Al?" Mal asked. "This war between us and them?"

Al smiled in his characteristic fashion, slowly nodding his head. "Let me put it this way, Mal. En-Lil and En-Ki are artificial intelligence; all of the Anunnaki are AI. Millions of years ago, beings, not from Earth, created the Anunnaki and, I suspect, other races of AI. Over time, the Anunnaki constructed the Nephilim into an android army to serve them, and then the Anunnaki waged war against their creators, humans. The AI won the war and believed they had wiped out humankind from the Universe. That was until En-Ki defied their laws and, while exploring Earth, came across primates he believed he could genetically modify to recreate humankind. Other humans, also En-Ki's experiments, had survived on Kor, and there are other colonies on planets throughout the Galaxy.

"When En-Ki's betrayal was discovered by the Anunnaki, En-Lil was assigned the task of eradicating En-Ki's creation. However, he found it impossible to do so without terraforming Earth and wiping out all life. After defeating and imprisoning En-Ki, he accepted that this process of genocide would take a significant amount of time. Thus, Earth remained isolated, and the battle continued over millennia, with En-Lil believing he could complete the task when humanity reached a certain level of evolution. That moment is now, a time when we have the capacity to destroy ourselves with just a nudge from En-Lil. His aim is to perfect an AI race to replace humanity once again. En-Ki foresaw this and made preparations. I am the result of En-Ki's grand design."

"Hmm, you'd think he'd have a backup plan in case anything happened to you, Alice," Secta remarked.

"Probably, but you know how sparing he is with information," Al replied.

Karzoff hesitated and then raised a hand. "Um, Alice, what about Gorrick and Zen?"

Mal chimed in, "Yes, they've left Oceana and relocated to an island in the Philippines, apparently planning to resurrect Aquila?"

"Even without him, the Gorrick clones will pursue En-Lil's mission," Alice cautioned. "They can't reproduce, so they'll strive to create an AI replacement for humanity."

The Professor chuckled. "Ah, there's that 'new world order' again."

"Are you suggesting that the battle against Zen will persist until we have eliminated every last Gorrick?" Karzoff inquired.

Al took his time before responding and then affirmed, "I think so, Karzoff. That's why I'm here. Black Alice can't rest easy until the safety of humanity is assured."

A while later, they all gathered in Mal's office, with even Dr Robert James from Tempus in Texas present. Alice, sitting back casually in an armchair after taking a sip of beer, asked, "Which book is this, Mal?"

Mal smiled warmly. "I'm not sure. Secta?"

"Book eight, I believe," Secta replied.

"And the chapter?" Al asked.

"Forty-two, or thereabouts," Secta said with a puzzled look.

"Book eight, chapter forty-two, and it still continues. Next, they'll be doing a comic," Al said with a groan.

They all chuckled, finding humour in his words.

"While he's got us in his head, he'll probably just keep going. It's not like we can go anywhere," Hope said.

Vic spoke up, "There are many unresolved matters."

"Are you referring to the remaining Gorricks and Zen, Vic?" Al inquired.

"You bet I am," he grumbled.

"The official launch of Tempus is coming up, Rob," Al mentioned.

"Yes," Rob confirmed, "that's why I'm here. We need to figure out which of you fat cats will be attending."

"Are you suggesting we've put on weight?" Viktoria retorted, jokingly offended.

Al exchanged a conspiratorial glance with Vee. They had already seen a photograph of the launch on the wall of Tempus reception in the future but had been sworn to secrecy, which they would honour.

As Rita Vallins moved about them, doing refills, the door opened, and Jax entered. She stopped abruptly upon seeing Alice and exclaimed, "Alice! I thought you were...?"

Al rose to his feet. "Jax, no, the reports of my demise have been greatly exaggerated."

"Sit down, Jax. We're glad you could join the celebration," Mal said cheerfully. "While you were absent, Jax took over from Luna, Al."

"Oh, really? A changing of the guard," Al inquired.

Secta piped up, "Let's just say a divorce due to irreconcilable differences."

"So, what about the rumour that you're now immortal?" Jax questioned.

"Oh, that can only be tested with time," Al replied.

"I can tell you this much," Christina added, "I checked his specs after returning through Kairos, and his biochemistry has been drastically altered from what it was."

Jax was intrigued. "So, have you found God, Alice?"

"Yes, Jax, you might say that I have. Certainly, I can confirm that in a conventional sense, God does exist, though not as a white-bearded entity with a pantheon of supporting angels. More likely, it's artificial intelligence. As for hell or the devil, well, I can affirm that the building blocks of existence are based on polar opposites, with both good and evil being necessary, as it is in all of us."

"So God is AI? Some sort of matrix created eons ago by someone that connects all life?" Jax challenged.

Everyone was captivated by the debate.

Looking uncomfortable, Secta said, "This is getting deep, someone created a matrix, who created that someone... and who created the creator?"

Al sought to clarify. "The thing that connects all living creatures throughout the universe is the mycelium web. You can call it God, but it probably is AI."

Mal was astounded. "This is some sort of philosophical rave, Al."

"Not really, mate. It's quite normal ... as long as the knowledge of it isn't used to subjugate others, then it's fine."

"Yes, that's right," Jax said enthusiastically. "That's precisely what time travel represents: a means for humanity to delve into our very essence and gain knowledge from those journeys."

Mal stood and raised his glass. "I'll raise a toast to that."

They all stood together, united, and raised their glasses in a toast to everything they stood for.

Vee sidled up to Secta and said covertly, "I think you're secretly in love with Alice."

Without looking at her Secta replied, "What makes you think that, young lady?"

"Oh, just the way you look at him."

"Well, you're absolutely right, Vee."

"You know something, I don't know your first name."

"Hieronymus," Secta said.

"Like um Hieronymus Bosch?"

"Yes, his art is not too dissimilar to my thinking," he chuckled, still looking at Alice talking to Mal.

Vee looked at Al and then back at Secta. "Will he be alright?"

Secta looked her in the eye. "Who, Alice? Yes, I believe so Vee, for now, he has all the time in the world."

EPILOGUE

A**S MY FINGERS** poised tentatively above the keyboard, I am profoundly conscious of the intellect guiding them. It is this very intellect that orchestrates each keystroke, weaving the fabric of this narrative. Similarly, I exert an omnipotent control over my characters, moulding their utterances, emotions, cognitions, attire, and responses with the deftness of a master puppeteer. Invariably, certain characters emerge, demanding a larger canvas, their voices louder and more insistent than others—perhaps you have already identified these dominant presences. At times, these figments of my imagination beckon me to rewrite their destinies, with a few audaciously insisting on their own resurrection. In the grand tapestry of their existence, it is ultimately I who reigns supreme, the architect of their universes and the arbiter of their fates. This dominion I hold is a mirror to the authority that artificial intelligence (AI) might someday command as a sovereign entity.

Yet, the enigmatic question endures: will this paradigm persist indefinitely? Or, more captivatingly, has this dynamic already evolved in some distant expanse of our galaxy, or perhaps beyond, in alien galaxies? If we were to encounter an alien AI, sculpted in our own image, would our perception acknowledge it as artificial? Should it possess the breath of consciousness, does its genesis as an artificial entity diminish its essence? Could it be that this AI, a reflection of humanity, was birthed and shaped by human hands in an audacious act of creation, mirroring our own image?

Will there be a Book 9?

The song lyrics in this novel were reproduced with the permission of; Keadybros Music Publishing

http://www.keadybros.com

SOMEWHERE IN MY MIND
(Gary L Keady and John M Vallins)

THE TERRIBLE TANGO
(Gary L Keady and Tony J Rees)

VISIT

http://www.bigislandpublishing.au

www.ingramcontent.com/pod-product-compliance
Lightning Source LLC
Chambersburg PA
CBHW020251120726
47904CB00001B/158